RIPPED LACE

A MAFIA ROMANCE

NICOLE FOX

Copyright © 2021 by Nicole Fox

All rights reserved.

No part of this book may be reproduced in any form or by any electronic or mechanical means, including information storage and retrieval systems, without written permission from the author, except for the use of brief quotations in a book review.

❦ Created with Vellum

MAILING LIST

Sign up to my mailing list!
New subscribers receive a FREE steamy bad boy romance novel.

Click the link below to join.
https://sendfox.com/nicolefox

ALSO BY NICOLE FOX

Romanoff Bratva

Immaculate Deception

Immaculate Corruption

Kovalyov Bratva

Gilded Cage

Gilded Tears

Jaded Soul

Jaded Devil

Mazzeo Mafia Duet

Liar's Lullaby (Book 1)

Sinner's Lullaby (Book 2)

Bratva Crime Syndicate

Can be read in any order!

Lies He Told Me

Scars He Gave Me

Sins He Taught Me

Belluci Mafia Trilogy

Corrupted Angel (Book 1)

Corrupted Queen (Book 2)

Corrupted Empire (Book 3)

De Maggio Mafia Duet

Devil in a Suit (Book 1)

Devil at the Altar (Book 2)

Kornilov Bratva Duet

Married to the Don (Book 1)

Til Death Do Us Part (Book 2)

Heirs to the Bratva Empire

Can be read in any order!

Kostya

Maksim

Andrei

Princes of Ravenlake Academy (Bully Romance)

Can be read as standalones!

Cruel Prep

Cruel Academy

Cruel Elite

Tsezar Bratva

Nightfall (Book 1)

Daybreak (Book 2)

Russian Crime Brotherhood

Can be read in any order!

Owned by the Mob Boss

Unprotected with the Mob Boss

Knocked Up by the Mob Boss

Sold to the Mob Boss

Stolen by the Mob Boss

Trapped with the Mob Boss

Volkov Bratva

Broken Vows (Book 1)

Broken Hope (Book 2)

Broken Sins *(standalone)*

Other Standalones

Vin: A Mafia Romance

Box Sets

Bratva Mob Bosses (Russian Crime Brotherhood Books 1-6)

Tsezar Bratva (Tsezar Bratva Duet Books 1-2)

Heirs to the Bratva Empire

The Mafia Dons Collection

The Don's Corruption

RIPPED LACE
BOOK TWO OF THE RIPPED DUET

I fled from the don and retreated into my past.

But I should've known Phoenix would never truly let me go.

On the day of my wedding—the day everything was supposed to be made right again—he shows up with revenge in his heart.

And makes me his again, right on the altar.

But what I don't tell him is this:

I've started to recall things. Things I was better off forgetting.

And by the time I'm done remembering…

Everything he loves might be destroyed.

RIPPED LACE is a secret baby, arranged marriage romantic suspense novel. It is Book Two of the Ripped Duet. Phoenix and Elyssa's story begins in Book One, RIPPED VEIL (so make sure you've read that before starting this one)!

1

PHOENIX

PHOENIX'S OFFICE—THE KOVALYOV MANSION

"It looks like a fucking slaughterhouse in here," Matvei says as he walks into my office.

He takes in Charity's body with a glance and a grimace before turning his attention to the second corpse in the room. His sharp eyes pass over the blood soaking into the Turkish carpet.

When they land on Anna's twisted face, they stay there. Searching for reason where there isn't any.

"I had to see it with my own eyes to believe it," he murmurs. "Even now, I'm not sure I do."

"I've been staring at her for the last ten minutes," I laugh bitterly. "Still hasn't sunk in."

"How long did she live in this house?" Matvei asks.

"Six years," I reply. "No, longer."

"Fuck."

I get to my feet as the cleanup crew swarms in. Half a dozen Bratva men in masks, gloves, and full-body suits, working silently and efficiently. They take Charity's body first.

"You gonna tell me what happened?" Matvei asks, his eyes careening to mine at last.

"Where should I start?" I growl. "I was on my way here to get the truth out of Elyssa. Noticed the door to my office was open. I come in and find Charity's body."

"And Anna?"

"She walked in a few seconds later. With a gun pointed right at me."

"Fuck," Matvei says again. "Six years of watching. Six years of waiting. What a fucking trip."

"It explains everything," I say. "She was always there. Anticipating our attacks, our moves, and reporting back to the fucking 'powers that be.'"

"The 'powers that be'?" he snorts.

"That's what they call themselves. The men who run Astra Tyrannis."

Matvei shakes his head. "Why am I not surprised?"

I suck in a heavy breath as the pain of the last hour's revelations takes its toll on my mind. But I don't want to put the final detail off any longer.

"She was the one who killed Yuri," I say in a low croak. "Aurora, too."

Matvei's expression stills. His eyes flatten with darkness and he looks furious. "What?"

"It was retaliation for Primm. It was her all along."

"Did she say anything about Yuri's body?" Matvei asks immediately.

"She claims he's buried somewhere on the property."

"*This* property?" Matvei balks. "And you believe her?"

"I have no reason not to," I reply. "Why would she lie?"

"She wouldn't have needed a reason," Matvei snaps. "It's clear she was a fucking psychopath from day one. She could have been lying."

"It's possible," I concede.

"What else was a lie? What about her backstory?"

"Fake. No sex trafficking, no getting sold to Gibraltar. She was recruited by Astra Tyrannis when she was a teenager. They snatched her out of an orphanage in France and trained her as an assassin."

"Jesus."

"Once she got too old for heavy action, they made her a spy. She was planted in Gibraltar's home the night we were about to storm it."

Matvei's brows wrinkle as he pieces the puzzle together. "Wait…"

"They wanted us to attack his house that night," I confirm before Matvei can ask the question. "That's why it was so fucking easy to get evidence on his work for Astra Tyrannis."

"They planned everything." He whistles, impressed. "Well, fuck me."

I slump onto the couch. "Do you remember that night? We walked in to see Anna standing over Gibraltar's dead body. She gave me her sob story. And like a fucking idiot, I bought every goddamn word of it."

Matvei clasps a heavy hand on my shoulder. "How were you to know?"

"I should have known," I snap. "I should have been smarter."

"You couldn't have predicted their end game."

"They predicted mine," I respond. "They knew exactly how to get into my house. They knew exactly who to plant and how. They knew how to manipulate me."

"Phoenix—"

"Don't," I snap before he can finish his thought. I know he's trying to absolve me of the blame. But I'm sick of it.

I *need* the guilt now. I thrive off it. It's what is going to light the fire that will eventually burn down that whole fucking machine, along with every last motherfucker who works in it, who revels in it, who profits off of it.

The cleanup crew returns and starts to flock around Anna's corpse. I watch them move her around and wonder how I never noticed. Were there signs? If so, I can't recall a single one. In six years, she'd never let the façade slip. Not one fucking time.

"The limp was a lie, too," I say, mostly to myself.

"You know what this means," Matvei says. "How old is she? Fifties? Sixties? Tyrannis probably has hundreds just like her in important places."

I nod. "I know."

"Assassins and spies you never suspect, never see coming." Matvei shakes his head in amazement. "It's fucking genius."

I agree. Which is what stings even more.

"So… Charity?" Matvei asks, turning to me. "Was she—"

"I don't know," I admit. "She was dead when I got here. I don't know what went down before I arrived. I don't know if they were working together and something went south, if it was personal and unrelated, or if Charity found out something about Anna she was not supposed to know. That's what Elyssa claims, anyway."

Matvei's eyes hit the ceiling. "Elyssa is here?" he exclaims, looking around as though expecting to see her hiding in the corner somewhere. "Where is she?"

"No," I say curtly. "Gone."

"Gone?"

"She's responsible for the bullet in Anna's arm," I explain. "The old bitch had me at gunpoint. She was about to pull the trigger when Elyssa walked in and shot her. Which allowed me to get the upper hand and finish her off."

"Elyssa saved you?" Matvei asks, sounding stunned.

"Yes."

"I don't understand," Matvei says. "Why isn't she here then?"

"Because I told her to get out."

He hesitates for a second. "She could still be an agent for Astra Tyrannis."

"We'll find out soon enough."

Matvei cocks his head to the side. "Wait… did you do something?"

"I had Ilya plant a tracker on her car," I say. "I'm going to be tracking her movements."

Matvei nods approvingly. "And if she is involved with Astra Tyrannis?"

"Then I'll take her out."

"And if she has nothing to do with them?"

It's an equally important question and Matvei knows it. He waits for my answer while I mull it over.

"Then I'll turn my back on her forever," I say icily in the end. "Either way, our paths diverge soon."

"She has your son, Phoenix."

My head throbs. I'm itching for a drink. Desperate for it, in fact. I'm usually good at abstaining. But today, it's hard to distract myself from the raw, aching need that's building in my chest.

"The boy may not be mine."

"Excuse me? Say that one more time."

I run a hand through my hair. "She told me what happened the night she arrived in Vegas. The night the two of us met at Wild Night Blossom."

I can see Matvei bracing himself. Again, I'm not keen on telling the story, but I also want to get it over with. I don't want it to have any power over me.

"The Sanctuary, the commune, whatever the fuck she calls it—it's a fucking cult. She was going to be married off to the leader. The fucker had her get all dressed up and delivered to his doorstep. Then he raped her. So she hit him over the head with a cast-iron paperweight in the shape of a black swan. Which is, incidentally, what she was sent this morning."

"They sent her the murder weapon?" he says in amazement.

"Blood and all."

"Christ. That's some next-level mind fuckery. What does it mean? Is it a threat?"

"Possibly. I don't know at this point. It was enough to get her to go back there."

"But she came back?"

I nod. "She claims she came back because Charity left a note hinting that Anna was dangerous. Said she came back to warn me."

Matvei looks skeptical. But I can see that he's considering this might actually be the true version of events.

"Given that she was raped only hours before I fucked her…" I trail off, leaving the rest unsaid.

"She doesn't know who the father is, either," Matvei finishes. He whistles again. *"Blyat'.* That's a lot of information to unpack in one night. So the leader of this cult, the one she hit with the swan paperweight... she killed him?"

I sigh and slump back against my seat. "She thought she did. But when she went back, apparently, he was there. Alive and well."

"So he's the one who sent her the paperweight?"

"Why does it matter?" I ask.

"Because he could be important. A player."

"A player?" I repeat. "What makes you think that?"

"If not a player, then at the very least, he's a tool. And I think that because of how little there is regarding this 'Sanctuary.'"

I frown. "I'm not following."

"I did more research after you left. It's not just that there isn't much information out there. There isn't *anything.* It feels like everything about these crazy assholes has been buried deep enough to never see the light of day. Whoever the fuck they are, they're keeping stuff close to the chest."

Close to the chest. The phrase sticks in my head for some reason. It's like there's a word on the tip of my tongue, trying to get out, but I just can't place it.

I glance back at Anna's body through the mess of limbs as the cleanup crew prepare her to be moved. Her throat is a jagged slice of drying blood. Her clothes are ripped and bedraggled from our fight and from Elyssa's shot. The collar of her blouse is pulled away, too, revealing a slice of wrinkled collarbone...

The cleanup crew gets ready to hoist her onto the waiting trolley.

"Wait!" I raise my hand.

Everyone stops short. They look up at me, masked and goggled, listening for further instructions.

"Leave her. I'll call you in when I'm ready."

The men nod in deference and back out of the room at once, leaving Matvei and me alone with Anna's body.

Moving in a daze, I step forward to examine her. A weaker man might've retched at all the blood. The human body is such a disgustingly fragile thing.

But I've been immune to the gore since the day I found Aurora.

I grab a cloth left behind by the crew and dab at the spot on her collarbone I noticed. *They're keeping stuff close to the chest…*

Dried blood comes away, little by little by little…

Until I see a tattoo.

It's blurred. Old ink—doing the math, I'd guess that it's been fifty-plus years since Astra Tyrannis marked this on her.

But the shape is unmistakable.

"Fucking hell," I growl. I recoil in shock.

"What?" Matvei asks, leaping over to look along with me.

"See that?" I ask, pointing to the gracefully arched neck.

"Is it a bird?"

"Yes," I rasp. "It's a swan."

Matvei looks at me with confusion. "You're looking at me like I should know what you're talking about."

"Don't you get it? Don't you fucking see?" I ask. My heart is racing and my skin is prickling with cold sweat. I feel like everything is finally resolving itself into shape. Like when you stare at an optical illusion for too long, trying to figure it out, and then all at once you see it.

Your worldview shifts forever. Dots get connected. The big picture emerges.

In this case, it's horrifying.

"It's a swan! It's a fucking black swan."

"Fuck," Matvei repeats, his eyes going wide. "*A black swan paperweight.* That's what you said."

"Exactly."

"So I was right. They are players. But what would an organization like Astra Tyrannis want with a cult in the middle of the desert?"

"That's what I plan to find out," I snarl. "I'm done being careful. It's time to declare fucking war. I'm going to rain hell down on them. Every. Last. One."

Matvei's expression sinks into acceptance. "Guess I better strap in."

I give him a dark smile.

And then we gear up for war.

I'm coming for you, Elyssa, I muse to myself. *You'd better have answers when I find you.*

2

ELYSSA

ONE MONTH LATER—THE SANCTUARY

I stare at my reflection in the mirror. I wore this exact same outfit for a long, long time. The shapeless white linen dress that seems to glow in the desert sun. So why do I feel so uncomfortable in it now?

The jeans and t-shirt I had on when I ran from Phoenix's mansion have been shoved into the darkest corner of my wardrobe. If I had to guess, I'd bet that Anna's blood is still dried into the fabric.

Anna. Phoenix. Astra Tyrannis.

The names swirl around in my head, but they seem vague and unreal now. I'm back on the Sanctuary, where I belong. Those things? They're just a bad dream that won't go away.

I have a future here. Those things are the past.

The problem with the past, though, is that it's never quite as done with you as you are with it.

Josiah can see it in my eyes sometimes, when I'm not doing a good job of hiding my thoughts. He knows that I'm thinking about everything I left behind.

About Charity, lying dead and cold on that miserable office floor.

About Phoenix. How dark and violent his eyes were when he told me to run.

It's been one month since I last set eyes on him. I think about him daily. Every hour, in fact. It's a betrayal to the man I've agreed to marry, but I can't control where my mind goes.

Or my desires.

Maybe it's a good thing I'm back in the commune. The difference in lifestyles is stark, and it makes me realize just how much discipline I've lost in the last year. I used to be able to keep my head down, do my work, and get on with life.

Now, I'm mired down in everything I've lost.

"Miss Elyssa?"

I jerk my head to the side as Zipporah steps into the room.

I'm supposed to be getting my dress fitted for the upcoming ceremony. One more chore in a month that's been chock full of them. Day and night, I'm surrounded by a flock of women who poke and prod and congratulate me on my bright, shining future.

My mother is the proudest of the bunch. She's hoping that my marriage will erase everything that happened before.

But I know better.

People have good memories. Especially when it comes to the shocking, the salacious. And no one holds on to scandal better than a community of zealots.

They think I don't see how they look at me. They think I don't hear what they whisper. I see it, though. I hear it.

And I hate it.

But what choice do I have? I'm not fit for the outside world. It took barely a year out in the wilds of Las Vegas for it to devastate me completely—mind, body, and soul.

No, I have to be here. *The Sanctuary is my home. Josiah is my husband.*

I've repeated those words to myself more times than I can count since I returned. Maybe one day, I'll even start to believe them.

"Hello, Zipporah," I say, giving her a smile.

She's technically my cousin. Second cousin on my mother's side. She's all of fifteen years old, and she's the only one who looks at me with curiosity instead of judgement.

"I've told you before," I add, "just Elyssa is fine."

She looks shocked. "No, I have to call you 'Miss Elyssa.' It's only right."

"I'll keep trying to convince you otherwise. Where's Theo?" I ask, missing my son.

"With the nanny," Zipporah explains. "He's being passed around. Everyone loves him."

I smile faintly. The irony is, as much as everyone seems to hate me, they flock to Theo like moths to a flame. He's been thriving since we got here.

He has his own room, his own nannies, his own routine and playthings. It's almost enough to make my presence in his life moot. It worries me sometimes. I wake up in the middle of the night again and again from horrifying dreams that he's slipping away from me, bit by bit.

"Will they be bringing him in soon?"

"I'm not sure," Zipporah says with a shrug. "Are you ready to try on the dress?"

Resigned, I nod and get to my feet. Deep down in my soul, I'm so sick of this. I'm sick of dress fittings. I'm sick of going to sleep with the weight of fear on my chest and waking up to the sinking feeling that my days are numbered.

But again—what choice do I have?

Zipporah helps me step into the dress and wriggles it up over my hips. She fastens the clasps at my back as I survey my reflection in the full-length mirror.

It's a shimmering mirage of lace. The minimalist lines are clean and sleek. Every stretch of fabric fits me perfectly.

I hate it with a passion.

But no one has stopped to ask me what I think. I don't feel like they've intentionally excluded me or want me to feel left out. It just hasn't occurred even once that I might have a voice.

Maybe they're right. Maybe I don't. Maybe it's best if I swallow my thoughts down forever.

"You have such a gorgeous figure," Zipporah says, admiring my body without apology.

I almost laugh. I can't bear to eat anything anymore. Food just sits in my stomach like a rock. I've lost weight rapidly since coming here.

I turn to look at her. Zipporah's a pretty girl, though her curly dark hair refuses to be tamed. Her face is covered in freckles and her body still has the bony edges of adolescence.

"So thin…" she murmurs, mostly to herself. "No wonder Father Josiah waited for you."

"What do you do when you aren't here, Zipporah?" I ask, eager to change the subject. "You're still in school, aren't you?"

Her eyes flash with excitement. "Only for a month longer. Then I can go to The Garden and begin my life's work there. I've been waiting for this for years."

The Garden. A strange spark of recognition shoots up my body when she says the words, but the familiarity is hidden behind murky, shadowy confusion that I can't quite uproot.

My memory has been unreliable lately—not that that's a shocker. And everything it seems to pull up only reveals another unpleasant truth about myself, about my life here.

So much so that I try to avoid digging too deep.

It's the coward's way out. But I can't deny my true nature anymore: I am a coward. The worst kind. The kind that knows exactly the mistakes they're making, but continues on anyway.

My only justification is my son. I've sacrificed everything I ever loved to give him the security I can't give him on my own.

It stings. But I can't escape the harsh reality anymore—I was not made for the real world. I am only suited for the world within these walls. The confines of the Sanctuary, the rules it follows, the lifestyle it leads… that is what I know. That is what I'm made for.

I was a fool to think I could survive out there for long.

The only reason I lasted as long as I did was because I had Charity.

It takes me a moment to register that Zipporah is still talking. Her voice is bright with enthusiasm as she fluffs the bottom of my dress and talks about The Garden.

"…I love babies," she's saying. "So this is perfect for me. And not everyone gets chosen, you know. I was hand-picked by Father Josiah."

Everything she's saying sounds so hauntingly familiar. Like a past life that I can't quite remember. But the truth, the memory, the understanding—it's all lingering on the horizon, just out of reach.

I hope to God it stays there. I have no interest in uncovering everything my mind has chosen to bury.

"How long does this responsibility last?" I ask.

Zipporah gets to her feet and looks at me with genuine surprise. "I don't quite know," she replies, as if it's a bizarre question. "As long as the powers that be require your work, I suppose. But you'd know more than I would, wouldn't you?"

"Why is that?"

Her eyebrows rise a foot. "Well, you did your service there, didn't you?" she asks. "Least, that's what I heard. And I've heard a lot about you lately. Forgive me; I don't mean to gossip. I know that's a sin."

I cringe. "To be honest, I don't remember much of the past few years."

"Really?" Zipporah remarks, giving me a strange look. "That's weird."

"Tell me about it."

She looks conspiratorial for a moment. Then she lowers her voice. "I was told I wasn't supposed to ask, but... did you really—"

I wince and wait for it. But before she can finish the question, the door opens.

I say a silent prayer and turn to my savior—though my heart shudders a little when I see who's in the doorway.

"Father Josiah!" Zipporah crows. "Hello."

His smile is calm and polite. "Dearest Zipporah," he says, a fatherly twinge to his tone. "How lovely to see you here. Helping my bride, are you?"

"Yes, but... you've seen her dress?" she says uncertainly, glancing back at me as though she's trying to decide if she should jump in front of me to hide the dress from my betrothed's view.

"That's okay," he laughs. "I picked the dress out. So I've seen it before."

"Oh."

"Zipporah, would you mind giving us a moment, please?"

"Yes, of course, Father Josiah."

"May grace guide your steps," he croons after her.

"And yours." She gives me a glance over her shoulder and leaves the room without a word. Just before she shuts the door, I see the curious gleam in her eyes.

Sighing, I move back to the bed and sit down. "You look tired," Josiah says.

"I am."

"And yet utterly beautiful all the same," he says, moving closer.

I stiffen as he comes within arm's reach, but I don't pull away. I keep telling myself it's going to get easier to stomach him touching me, but that hasn't quite happened yet. Soon, though, I'm sure. "Thank you."

His fingers run along my jaw before he pulls my chin up so that I'm looking at him. "Are you ready, my dear?"

There's an iota of concern in his tone. Concern for who, though? For me—or himself?

"I… I think so," I say with as much confidence as I can muster.

"You're understandably nervous," he says. "That's okay."

He sits down beside me. The intimacy of sitting next to each other feels so wrong. I want to move away from him, but I'm worried it'll be too obvious. It also hasn't escaped my notice that this scene is eerily close to the last time we were days from our first wedding.

Standing in a room together. Me in a wedding dress. Him expecting things I can't possibly give him.

But this time is different. I'm prepared. I know what I've signed up for. And I have my son to think of.

So whatever happens next, I'm ready.

"Are you nervous?" I ask, mostly just because I feel like he's waiting for me to reciprocate.

"Not at all," he smiles. "I knew you'd come back."

I stare at him. "You did?"

"Of course."

"How?"

"I told you before, Elyssa: this is where you're meant to be. And I'm the man you're meant to be with."

Of course, the second he says that, the only face I see is Phoenix's.

I can almost feel him in the room with me, glowering at the man next to me, judging me for being here at all. A bubble of anger erupts past the sadness. What's the point of thinking of him? He cast me out. Abandoned me. He doesn't deserve the fantasies and daydreams I waste on him.

I just wish I knew how to stop.

"I can't wait to call you my wife," Josiah is murmuring. "To walk with you through the desert and kiss you freely and often."

I have to suppress the shudder running up and down my spine. Josiah reaches out and takes my hand. He brings it to his lips and my stomach twists.

"We will be happy, Elyssa. Incredibly so. But you must remember…"

I know what he wants from me. I know what I'm expected to say. The words no longer hold the same comfort they used to, but I say them anyway. Hoping that one day, if I repeat them often enough, they'll start to mean more to me than they do right now.

"To serve is to find peace," I recite. *"To obey is to find happiness. To listen is to find truth."*

He nods with approval. "Exactly. You are a beautiful desert rose, my Elyssa."

His words are gentle. His tone is caring. But I sense the threat underneath those honeyed words.

Serve.

Obey.

Listen.

"You understand me, don't you, my dove?"

I nod slowly, swallowing my tears. *Just be patient*, I tell myself. *Wait for tonight.*

"Yes," I say out loud. "I understand."

You can cry about it then.

3

ELYSSA
THE NEXT DAY

Mama's hands are deft as she snaps my veil in place and folds it down over my face. Instantly, I feel both claustrophobic and terrified.

I've been here before, haven't I? Trapped like this. Hooded like this, like a prisoner being led to the guillotine. It took a miracle to get me out. So how have I managed to find myself in the same position again—with the same exact man, no less?

Breathe, Lys.

It's Charity's voice in my head, of course. I've heard her ever since I set foot back on the Sanctuary. Calming me, comforting me, telling me I'm doing the right thing.

Remember when you're here, she says. *Remember why you chose this.*

I turn around, searching for my reason. Searching for my son. But as usual, he's been whisked away by one of Josiah's many nannies.

"Mama, where's—"

"I never thought I'd see this day," Mama interrupts. She takes a step back so she can cast a critical eye over me. "Hopefully, once you're married, people will stop talking."

I sigh and swallow my question. "You're expecting too much, Mama," I say softly. "They'll never stop talking about me."

"Do you know how your father and I lived the last year?" she asks. "Do you know how people looked at us."

"I'm sorry—"

"Save it. 'Sorry' won't remove the stain we have to carry because of what you did. Words are nothing without the deeds to match. If you had just stayed here where you belonged, then everything would have been…"

"Please stop, Mama," I say, struggling to keep my voice from cracking. "Please just stop."

"You are lucky he took you back at all," she hisses, ignoring my plea. Her eyes flash dangerously. "A lesser man would have made you suffer for the sins you wrought."

"*My* sins? Tell me you're joking."

"Why did you come back?" Mama hisses. "If you hate him so much? If you hate us so much?"

"Because my son needs security," I hiss right back at her. "And I'd do anything to keep my child safe. If only you knew how that felt."

She stiffens and pales. "Then do it without complaint," she says eventually. "Get rid of the fight in you. Swallow your feelings and get on with it. This is not the way I raised you. Now, are you ready or not?"

I feel my entire body shudder as she speaks. *Get rid of the fight; swallow your feelings*—it's a direct contrast to everything Charity used to say to me.

Cry when you're sad.

Laugh when you're happy.

Fuck when you're horny.

I shake those thoughts from my head.

Remember why you came back here in the first place, I tell myself. *You couldn't make it out there in the real world. Not without Charity. Not without Phoenix. This is where you belong.*

"Yes, Mama," I whisper, defeated. "I'm ready."

I feel like I'm at war with the voices in my head as I follow my mother out of the room and downstairs where the lily-white carriage is waiting. A man in a white mask is seated up front, holding the reins of the white horse.

He doesn't say a word to us as we clamber up into the compartment and settle into our seats. As soon as the door shuts, he clucks and the horse begins trotting, whisking us away towards the cathedral where everyone is waiting.

"Where's Theo?" I ask Mama.

"Already at the cathedral," she replies. "Zipporah and Evelyn took him there earlier."

"Why wasn't I consulted?"

"Father Josiah's orders," Mama replies brusquely.

I look at my mother. She looks so much older than she did when I left, even though it hasn't been that long. It was a hard year for her. For my father, too. Both of them are gray and weathered, and when I catch them staring off into the distance, it's like they can't wait for this miserable life to be over.

"Are you even going to look at me, Mama?" I ask quietly.

She exhales loudly but still doesn't turn from the window. "Why are you insisting on making everything difficult?" she ponders out loud. "You didn't used to be like this."

"People change, Mama. I've changed."

"This is why we warned you about leaving the compound," she snaps, whirling to face me. "This is the very reason. The outside world exposes you to unnecessary behaviors. It makes you want dangerous things."

"What I want is for you to care," I say softly. "That's all."

Her eyes go wide for a moment and a ripple of sadness flickers across her aged features. "What makes you think I don't?" she asks, but there's no real feeling in her voice.

"Come on, Mama. You haven't even picked up my son. He's your grandchild. Your only grandchild."

"He is the child of sin," she clips.

Her words strike hot and painful in that moment. Like that innocent little boy is something grotesque, something monstrous. The air between us boils. A tear slips from my eye as I turn away from her.

We stay silent for the rest of the ride.

A few minutes later, we draw to a stop. The horse's clomping hooves cease. The driver hops down and opens Mama's door. He helps her down, but when it's my turn to step out of the compartment, he turns away. I'm left to struggle with my skirts on my own.

It's eerily quiet out here. A few tumbleweeds blow past in the hot, sandy breeze. The cathedral beckons just a few yards away. It's the biggest building on the commune, though that isn't saying much. The white adobe walls glow in the sun.

Mama is waiting on the other side of the carriage. She offers me her elbow without a word. It's a silent order. *Take it.*

Sighing, I do as she expects. We carve our way across the hard-packed sand and up the three short steps. The doors swing open.

And hundreds of blank faces turn to look at me.

No one makes a single noise. Just the rustle of fabric and quiet breathing.

Do they envy me? Do they hate me? Am I a princess or a pariah? It's impossible to tell. Nothing on the Sanctuary is ever what it seems to be.

I scan the crowd for my son, but I still don't see him. I try to swallow down the tide of bile that rises in my throat every time I look for Theo without success. A month here and I still haven't gotten used to the separation.

My father stands from his seat in the rearmost pew. No one else has moved. He stalks over, rips my hand from my mother's elbow, and plops it on his own. Then we start the stride down the aisle.

I watch my feet so I don't trip and fall. Papa's grip on my wrist is ironclad. I've never been surrounded by so many silent people before and my heart is starting to beat so fast from the anxiety that I wonder if all these people can hear it.

If they know what I've done.

If they know why I ran.

I reach the lip of the dais. I step onto the first rough-hewn wooden step and then I'm transferred off unceremoniously. Papa takes my hand and firmly places it in Josiah's.

That's when I finally raise my head.

My husband-to-be is standing opposite me in a white linen tunic. It's shapeless and flowing and utterly spotless. His hair is clean and combed back so that the grotesque scar tissue on the right side of his face gleams in the afternoon light.

I hear a whimper behind me and I turn immediately. At long last, I catch sight of Theo in Zipporah's arms. She's standing off to the side, rocking him on her hip, trying to pacify him. He's clearly upset.

"Elyssa." Josiah's voice is gentle but firm.

I force my eyes back to his and he gives me a nod. A reminder. *There will be no escape for me after this.*

Brother Rajnesh steps forward, placing himself between us.

"Elyssa Redmond, you have been honored today. You have been chosen to be the wife of the shepherd of our flock, the light in our darkness, Father Josiah."

The crowd finally speaks. One word, spoken in unison, thundering and overwhelming: *"Hail!"*

"Today, you taking on the mantel of wife. Do you vow to be obedient, patient, and true?"

I look at Josiah. His features might as well be carved from desert rock. But I can see the glint of dark, swirling dominance just beneath. His fingers tighten around mine, almost painfully.

"Yes," I whisper.

"Hail!"

"Do you understand the responsibility you are taking on?"

"Yes."

"Hail!"

"From this day forth, you are bound to Josiah Mathews. He will be your husband and your keeper. He will be your lord and master. Do you accept him as such and vow to please him for all the rest of his days?"

I bristle at the words. A shiver of anger runs up my spine.

Then I hear the sharp melancholy warble of Theo's cry and I remember why I'm here. Why I'm doing this.

"I do so swear," I say, repeating the words I'd heard hundreds of women before me pledge before the whole community.

"Hail! Hail! Hail!"

Silence ensues.

Then I hear something. Like a pin dropping a mile away, but one that's meant for me and me alone. One thump. The squeak of hinges.

And then the doors I walked through just a minute ago explode inwards in a storm of burnt wooden splinters. The sound is ear-splitting. The crowd screams and ducks for cover as the deafening noise reverberates around the cathedral.

All eyes find the gaping maw where the doors once stood.

And all eyes take note of the man who strides through it.

My breath catches in my throat. *It can't be…*

"I hope I didn't miss the call for objections," Phoenix Kovalyov snarls, stepping into the cathedral as armed Bratva men pour into the church behind him.

His eyes meet mine.

"Because I most certainly fucking object."

4

ELYSSA

All I can think is, *He's here.*

He looks so wrong in this place. It's an ocean of white, of purity and obedience, of people who do what they're told and suppress their emotions.

Phoenix Kovalyov, on the other hand, is a black vortex. He's rage incarnate. He's a furious hurricane ripping through and setting the place on fire with every single step.

The suit he's wearing gleams like onyx. It's pure black, cut to his body perfectly. His shoulders are broad. His hair effortlessly tousled. And those eyes—they shine brighter than the stained glass windows rimming the walls.

He's absolutely breathtaking.

And absolutely deadly.

In a matter of seconds, his men form a ring around the entirety of the cathedral. They surround the pews, boxing everyone in.

The men of the Sanctuary are standing now, trying to get a handle of the situation. The women and children remain hunched in their seats, looking around in panic and confusion. I can see my mother in the front pew. She's clutching my father's forearm, her knuckles bone-white.

It's the first time I've ever seen her touch him.

But I don't have time to worry about that now. Or the fact that a new contingent of Phoenix's men have begun dragging select members of the crowd out of the cathedral.

I'm too focused on Phoenix striding down the aisle towards me.

He looks like an Adonis. A cold, unfeeling Adonis with diamond eyes that promise all kinds of suffering.

Josiah is still clinging to me. I can feel the cold sweat of fear moistening his fingertips. Phoenix looks at me for one endless moment before he turns his attention to my almost-husband.

"You must be the noble leader I've heard so much about," he drawls, his tone biting.

Josiah looks ashen. Sweat drips down his forehead. Did I think he looked smart when I first saw him? Composed? Regal? Seeing him beside Phoenix, the thought seems almost laughable. Josiah might as well be a toad squatting next to a prince.

He's almost as tall as Phoenix is, and yet somehow, he seems to shrink more and more the closer Phoenix gets.

Phoenix slows to a halt at the foot of the dais. "Beautiful ceremony," he quips in an unpleasant tone that makes my skin crawl. "So sorry to interrupt."

I want to ask him what he's doing here. But my tongue feels bloated. I can't speak. I can't move. I can only wait and see what he does next.

"Who the fuck are you?" Josiah demands.

I flinch instinctively. I've never heard Josiah speak like that before. Of the people in the crowd who are paying attention to what's happening up here, a few gasp in shock.

Phoenix smiles. It's terrifying.

"Me?" he says innocently. "We'll get to that. But for now, I have a few questions for you."

Josiah is trying to look calm and unaffected by this disruption, but I can see it in the blotchy patches on his skin. In his darting irises. In his sweating brow.

He's just as afraid as the rest of us.

"They call you Father Josiah, yes?"

His Adam's apple jumps as he gulps. "Yes."

"Leader of the Sanctuary and all the dark secrets it holds?"

All the dark secrets it holds? What's that supposed to mean?

I take a look at the terrified people being dragged from their pews at gunpoint. I'd grown up in this place. We're just a small village, cut off from the rest of the world. The people here may be guilty of questionable customs, of antiquated thinking.

But dark secrets?

"I—er, well, you seem to be—"

"Answer the fucking question," Phoenix growls.

"I am the leader of this community," Josiah replies. His tone manages to hold strong. "But I have no idea what you mean about the rest of it."

Phoenix turns and looks as another man joins him at the bottom step. I recognize those broad shoulders. Sure enough, when he tugs down his tactical mask, I see that it's Matvei.

"The man knows how to lie," Phoenix remarks to his colleague. "I'll give him that."

Then he turns back to us. The smirk dies on his face.

"What else are you lying about, Josiah?"

"You know, you're trespassing on private property," Josiah balks, trying to infuse some authority into his tone. The fear in his eyes makes the words fall flat.

"Oh, I'm aware," Phoenix replies. "But I've never been one to play by the rules."

"You don't know who you're dealing with," Josiah hisses suddenly. His face purples with venom.

I frown. Something about the way he says that doesn't sound right.

"Actually," Phoenix chuckles, "I know exactly who I'm dealing with. Which is why I'm here."

Then he turns his gaze to me, piercing me through with his dark, intoxicating eyes. I hate that my heart beats a little faster and my pulse starts racing the moment we make eye contact. After everything that's happened between us, I can't deny that my heart still feels something for him. My body still craves something from him.

"Elyssa, tell me something: is this the man who raped you the night we met?"

Josiah's eyes snap to my face. Even Brother Raj does a little double take. But I stay still, caught in a trap sprung by two men so much more powerful than I am.

"I... I..." I can't seem to get the words out.

Suddenly, Phoenix bounds up the steps, grabs my face in one huge hand, and wrenches my jaw to the side so I have no choice but to look at him.

"Tell me!" he orders. "And don't you dare fucking lie."

The mere touch of his hand—even if it's an angry grasp, a furious grasp—has my brain short-circuiting. The truth slips from my lips despite myself.

"Yes."

He pushes me backwards. I stumble and almost trip over my skirt before I manage to grab hold of the pulpit and keep from falling.

The icy stare is back on his face. He meets me with that cold gaze before he turns it on Josiah.

"Ask me again who I am," he says to Josiah.

Josiah has paled considerably now. The sweat on his brow glows like translucent pearls. "Who are you?" he whispers.

"I'm the man who's coming to take back what's his."

Then he moves, and it all happens so fast that it takes me a second to process what's happening.

His hand finds a sheath on his hip.

Withdraws a dagger.

The silver blade scythes through the air…

And plunges into Josiah's stomach.

I hear a scream from somewhere in the room. I don't have to turn to know it's my mother. Theo starts bawling, too, obviously terrified by the sudden wails. But I can't bring myself to turn to him, either.

I'm rooted in place, staring at the blood burgeoning across Josiah's white outfit.

He sways on his feet for a second and then he stumbles back.

"Matvei," Phoenix says without inflection, "get this fucking pig out of my sight."

Matvei and another of his men come forward and gather Josiah up by his armpits. Then they drag him down the aisle and out the wreckage of the doors.

"Phoenix," I whisper, trying to feel something in my numb limbs. "What are you doing?"

He doesn't answer me as he takes Josiah's place on the raised dais.

"Now," he says, glancing at Brother Raj, "continue."

Raj looks at Phoenix like he's the devil himself. But Phoenix just gives him a mocking smile. "Do I need to stab you, too?" he asks casually, raising the bloody dagger of the knife that's still clutched in his hand.

Raj goes a blotchy red and stutters a few unintelligible words before looking down at the book in his hands. He flips pages and I almost want to laugh. It's like he thinks this turn of events will be covered in the next section.

In the event of a violent assault on the ceremony, skip ahead to page fifty-five...

"Phoenix..." I whisper.

His eyes flicker to mine, but it's as though he doesn't want to look at me longer than he needs to. And even when he does look at me, it's like he's seeing right through me. Like I'm not even there.

He reaches out, snares my wrist in one hand, and tugs me back to my spot across from him. Behind me, I hear Theo and my mother crying in sync.

Raj starts saying something, but I can't hear it or bear to understand it. The only thing I'm able to focus on is the man standing opposite me in his dark suit. My bloody guardian angel. The devil I thought I left behind.

"Do you take this woman to be your lawfully-wedded wife?" Raj asks.

Phoenix clenches his jaw. "I do."

"And do you take this man to be your lawfully-wedded husband?"

Everything is happening so fast. I feel like I'm going to pass out or scream or both. How is he here? Why is he here?

I try and find the answers in his face, but there are none. Just a blank stone wall of secrets and anger and pain.

He's lost a wife. A son. God knows what else.

I can see the weight of those collective losses have twisted him into this darker, angrier version of himself. He's brutal and savage in a way I didn't know a person could ever become.

It makes my heart crack in two.

Phoenix's hand clamps down tight on my wrist. "Answer," he orders.

For all his familiarity, he feels like a stranger to me. I know that face, those eyes, those lips. I've loved them and kissed them. I've given him a son—at least, maybe.

So how can he possibly look at me like *I'm* the monster?

"Elyssa?" Brother Raj tries again. "Do you take this man to be your lawfully wedded husband?"

A single tear falls from my eye as I nod. "Yes," I say in barely a whisper. "I do."

5

PHOENIX

She's lost weight. Her collarbones protrude above the bust of the lacy wedding dress. Her eyes are hazier, more haunted, more distant.

But the blonde hair tumbling over her shoulders looks exactly the same as it always has. And I want to do the same thing to it that I've always wanted: to knot my fists in it, pull her to me, and show her why she can only ever be mine.

I turn to Konstantin, who's standing at the head of the aisle with a rifle nestled in his arms. "Clear the room," I order. "Every last one of them."

I don't let go of Elyssa's hand as my men make quick work of the remaining evacuation. A few hundred crying, frightened cultists are rounded up and herded out, Brother Raj included. My men follow.

In less than two minutes, we're alone in the cathedral. Just the two of us.

I look back at Elyssa once more. The sun slanting through the stained glass lights her dress up with a sickening crimson color. Fitting—the scared girl in the blood-red wedding dress.

Almost exactly the same as the first time we met.

History may not repeat itself, but it often rhymes.

She tries to speak, but her voice breaks. "Theo—"

"Is safe," I assure her coldly. "My men will take care of him."

She nods, gnaws at her lip, and looks around as if there are answers to be found elsewhere. Then she glances back up to me. Maybe because she realizes the truth: the only answers left are inside of each of us.

The question is…

Who will break first?

"Why are you here, Phoenix?" she whispers.

I gaze at her for a while. Even now, knowing everything I know about this place and the people who make it run, it's so goddamn difficult to see anything but innocence in those huge, amber eyes.

She's purity itself—on the outside.

But on the inside, she's as bad as the rest of them.

"I came to make things right."

She shakes her head in dismay. "Well, then, it was a wasted trip. There's nothing to fix. Look around you; this place has nothing to offer. It's just a small little patch of desert with—"

"Dark secrets," I interrupt. "Some very dark fucking secrets."

The crease between her eyebrows gets deeper. "You're mistaken."

"Look around this room," I instruct her. "Is there something here that stands out to you?"

She looks around furtively. I can trace the anxiety running down the lines of her face. She's so fucking beautiful. She'd be even more so if I rid her of all those fucking layers of bloodstained lace.

"I don't know what you want me to notice," she says.

"Look there. And there. And there." I jab my finger at each of the stained glass windows.

"What's your point?" she explodes. "It's just a window!"

"Wrong," I say. "So fucking wrong. Look closer."

She whirls around in place and stares at each of the windows in turn. Then she faces me again, helpless and confused. "I don't know what you want me to see," she whimpers. "I don't know what I'm supposed to say."

"In the corner," I explain impatiently. "The dark pane. What does it look like?"

She follows where I'm pointing. "A hook? No, a bird. Wait. Wait. It's a…" Pirouetting back to me, she looks like she's just seen a ghost. "It's a swan," she finishes. "They're all black swans."

"How many homes are on this commune, Elyssa?" I ask.

"I—I don't know."

"Guess."

"A hundred, maybe? I'm really not—"

"There are one hundred and thirteen homes within the walls. Guess how many of them have a black swan buried beneath the foundation?"

She swallows. I don't have to say the answer—she says it for me. "All of them."

"All of them," I confirm. "Every single fucking one. There are swans in the stained glass. Swans in the foundations. The office of your would-be husband is littered with the motherfuckers. And do you know why?"

She shakes her head. I can see realization dawning in her eyes, but she refuses to accept it. Refuses to see the obvious truth staring her in the face.

"Because the kind of men who traffic in women cannot bear to own something without marking it. Because they cannot sleep at night if their property is not branded."

"What are you saying?" she whispers in the tiniest voice imaginable.

"I think you know."

She shakes her head. "No, you're wrong. That doesn't even make any —it's not like that. It can't be, because…"

"We've been surveilling this place for a month, Elyssa," I cut in. "My men do not make mistakes. You and everyone you've ever known are just property. The playthings of a hundred-year-old organization that trades women like cattle. That deals in blood, in pain, in bodies. The Sanctuary belongs to Astra Tyrannis."

It's like she hasn't heard me at all. She stares off into space, her eyes darting from side to side. Her expression is so sincerely horrified that I find myself taking a step towards her. Now, there's only five feet of space between the two of us. And it's too close. Too fucking close.

Her mouth moves, but no sound comes out. I see her lips starting to turn blue. "I can't… I can't breathe…" She starts clawing at her dress, trying to reach around to the back to undo the zipper. She's gasping and struggling to breathe.

I have to make a choice. Intervene or stand aside?

Touching her was the one thing I swore I wouldn't do. I know what she does to me. The effect she has on me. From the very beginning, she's coaxed me into mistake after mistake.

I can't just stand here and watch her die, though. The panic attack has her in its claws. It'll devour her if I don't do something.

So, growling, I make my decision. I grip her by the shoulders and spin her around. She's so light and fragile in my hands. The back of the dress is a complex patchwork of buttons and hooks.

"We don't have time for this shit," I snarl.

Seizing the fabric in my hands, I tear as hard as I can.

Lace rips. The buttons squeal and pop off one by one, bouncing around on the dais. The dress falls in a ruin around her feet. It's forever destroyed—but when I hear Elyssa suck in a desperate, gasping inhale, I know I did the right thing.

We sink to the ground together. She's a puddle in my arms. Her smooth, cool skin brushes against mine at the wrists, at the neck. Our breath mingles together.

I don't know how long we sit there, slumped on the altar we were just married upon. Long enough for the color to return to her lips. For her eyes to flutter open and look at me again like she's seeing someone new in my skin.

Gradually, the trembling and the gasping eases.

And then I start to realize things.

Like how, beneath her dress, she's wearing porcelain-colored lingerie. The finest, thinnest lace imaginable. She's too frail now, but her curves are crying out for my touch anyway. Demanding that I run my fingertip over the rise of her hip.

"Feel better?" I murmur.

"Not really," she replies. "I don't think I'll ever feel better again." She wraps her hands around her body and hugs herself. "I can't believe this…"

"Which part?"

She raises her troubled eyes to mine. "I brought Theo back here because I thought it was the only way to give him safety and security. I brought him to them, Phoenix."

"Why did you come back here?" I ask, fully aware that I might regret asking at all. "Why here, of all places?"

She looks down. "I had nowhere else to go. I left the duffel bag at the mansion and… well, all the money was in there. It made me realize that without Charity, I was helpless. So I came to the one place I knew would take me. I came home."

Guilt for casting her out of my home claws at my chest. "This is home? Even after what you did?"

She shrugs. "What does it matter? They allowed me back in."

"On the condition that you marry the rapist?"

She sighs. "I had to provide for my son."

"You told him he was the father, didn't you?"

"I'm sorry."

"Fuck *sorry*," I scoff. "I hate that word. No one uses it right."

My eyes flicker down to her breasts. I can see only the tops of them in the cups of her bra. But it's enough to make me hard.

"Phoenix," she says, reaching out as if to cup my face.

I turn away under her hand and she drops it immediately, her expression going slack with disappointment.

"I know you don't trust me," she says. "But I have nothing to do with Astra Tyrannis."

"A number of other sources disagree."

She pauses and seems to reconsider that topic of conversation. "What are you going to do with everyone else here?"

"That's not for you to know."

"If it concerns my parents and me, I think I deserve to know."

"What you think you deserve is immaterial," I snap. "I'm not interested in right or fair or moral. I just want my fucking revenge."

Her eyes go damp with sympathy. "I can't imagine what you must have gone through. Losing you wife, your son—"

"There's no need to speak of him."

"How old was he?"

"I'm not talking about this, Elyssa."

"Phoenix, please," she begs as I stiffen. "I... I care about you—"

"Don't."

"It's the truth. I can't seem to stop. Trust me, I've tried. And I think that deep down, maybe a small part of you cares for me, too."

She twists in my arms to face me properly. I feel my body go hard. Not just my cock—the whole of me. Every cell in me responding to every cell in her, no matter how hard I try to resist it.

"I just want to help, if I can..."

"You've done enough," I say bitingly.

"You're pushing me away because it's easier."

That pisses me off. "I'm pushing you away because you're nothing to me," I growl. "I'm pushing you away because the decision to come here was not about sentiment. It's about fucking war."

"Oh, yeah?" she fires back, some fight seeping into her tone. "Then why marry me?"

My eyes flash dangerously as I lean into her. "Let me be clear, Elyssa: we may be married now, but that doesn't make you my equal."

"Then what does it make me?"

"Whatever I fucking want," I snap. "My whore, my maid, or nothing at all. You will be whatever I need you to be."

Lust and anger compete for dominance. I can see it in her eyes. I wonder if I look the same.

"Then I might as well have married Josiah," she fires back. "At least he would have acknowledged me as his wife."

She's learning how to throw her punches. I'm almost as impressed as I am infuriated.

I stop short, let my stare sit on her for a few long seconds. She can sense the atmosphere change, but she refuses to back down.

"Is that what you want?" I ask. "You want me to acknowledge you as my wife?"

She doesn't say a thing. Like she's suddenly realizing who holds all the cards here.

And it's not her.

"Well, then, let me oblige."

With a flip of my hips, I roll Elyssa onto her back and pin her to the altar floor. I snatch up a wrist in each hand and lock them up over her head.

She's rigid beneath me, her eyes locked onto my face with uncertainty, fear, desire.

"You want to be my wife?" I spit in her face. "Then we'd better start with the consummation."

I notice the burn of her dilated eyes when they flicker down to my groin. Using one hand to keep her wrists pinned, I reach down with the other to free my cock from the zipper. I'm throbbing hard, as hard as I've been in my entire fucking life. My heartbeat is pounding in my temples and throat. My breath comes in hot spurts.

She's writhing below me—but I'm not sure if it's because she wants out... or because she wants me in.

I don't ask or wait to find out. Shoving aside her panties, I plunge into her.

"This is what you wanted, isn't it?" I ask with the first thrust. I have to talk, I have to taunt, I have to be cruel—because if I don't, I'll be forced to feel all the things that lie below that veneer of rage.

She moans in response. I can't hold myself back any longer.

I grind my hips into hers as hard as I can. I want to make it hurt so sweet. I want her to feel the intensity of the things I'm feeling, the things I've always felt for her.

My lips long for hers, but I resist that. I will not cross that line.

This isn't a real marriage. It's a marriage of convenience. A power grab. And even though I'm fucking her, I'm doing it like she's my whore, not my wife.

Something tells me she doesn't mind. She may be purity and innocence itself—but from the very beginning, this is how she's begged to be taken.

I can feel her arms at my back, clawing my skin in an attempt to pull us even closer. Her lips beckon, and I force myself to retain a few inches of space between us even as I continue to ram her.

The motion sends one breast bouncing free of her bra. I drop my head down and clamp it lightly between my teeth. The flicker of my tongue on Elyssa's nipple reduces her to a quivering pile of moans and gasps.

Every clash of our hips draws me closer and closer to coming. I've never wanted to erupt so hard or so fast. Judging by the volume of her screams, Elyssa feels the same.

I do the best I can to ignore it. To ignore her sounds, her smells, her taste, her touch. I just keep fucking her, emptying all my rage and frustration into her with each savage plunge of my hard cock into her wet, greedy pussy.

And she takes it all, with her lips parted and my name lolling off her tongue.

Only when I feel her orgasm envelope my cock do I allow myself to release. I fill her again and again. When it's done, I feel completely and utterly drained. Her arms are still clinging around my neck when I go still.

And that's the only reminder I need.

I push myself off her abruptly and tuck myself away. The whole time, I can feel her eyes on me. Confused and helpless.

"Phoenix," she whispers from the floor. I almost turn to her.

Don't, I roar at myself. *Don't do it, you fucking bastard.*

"Please," she tries again. "Please just look at me."

I start to stalk down the steps of the altar. Elyssa remains where she is.

"All I'm asking for is a little humanity," she says softly. Her tiny, fragile voice carries through the empty cathedral to reach my ears.

"Humanity?" I laugh, looking back over my shoulder. She's a mirage of white up there, lit aglow by the dying sun. "I have none left to give."

6
PHOENIX

Matvei emerges from the shadow of the cathedral as I step outside. "Everything under control?" I ask him.

"There's a lot of people out there, Phoenix," he sighs. He doesn't sound happy. Truth be told, he hasn't sounded happy in a month.

"I'm aware."

"One hundred and thirteen households?" he asks, glaring at me.

"So Ilya showed you the file?"

"The question is, why didn't *you* show me the file?"

"Because I knew you'd disapprove."

"Because this plan involves imprisoning an entire fucking town!" he growls. "There's too many people. Too many variables. Too many wild cards."

"I plan on taming them."

"Where's our evidence, Phoenix? Where's the proof? Who knew what?"

"That's what we're here to sort through."

"And then what?" He's ready to tear his hair out in frustration. "What happens now, Phoenix?"

The compound is teeming with my men. Most of them are clustered around the grand house a few hundred yards away from the central cathedral. It's the brightest and the newest, and I know why: because Elyssa burned the old version to the fucking ground before she left.

It'll serve as our base while I figure out how to answer Matvei's questions.

"I can see the wheels in your head spinning," he butts in accusingly. "Spare me the bullshit."

I take a breath. "Let's find somewhere to talk in private," I suggest.

Growling bitterly, he follows me as we move to a pile of rocks set away from any nearby buildings. I lean against the smooth surface of one boulder. Matvei paces angrily.

"One hundred and thirteen families," he says—as if I've forgotten. "You've got the whole town. Now what?"

"Now, we find out which families are directly involved with Astra Tyrannis. We've already narrowed down a few."

"So not every family is in the know."

"No," I agree, "probably not. Some might be innocent. Or ignorant, at least. But I'm willing to bet no one is unstained."

"It's a whole fucking town, Phoenix!" he says, turning to me. "It may be small, but 'small' still means hundreds of people."

"Your point?"

"My point is, what's the plan?" he asks. "How do you plan on containing this situation? When Astra Tyrannis gets wind of this, they'll come hunting—and you can bet your ass they'll want to make a big, bloody statement."

"We won't be here long enough for that."

Matvei stops his angry pacing and frowns. "You took the town just to abandon it after a few days?"

"I'm not abandoning it. I'm taking it with us."

Matvei stares at me in disbelief.

I'm aware that my plan is bold. In fact, one might even call it insane. But maybe that's exactly the reason why it'll work.

"You're taking them with us?"

"Yes."

"Where?"

"Mexico."

Matvei stares silently at me for a long time. "My ears must be fucked up from the blast. Did you just say *Mexico*?"

I nod. "I have enough space and resources there to keep everyone exactly where we want them. I've spent the last month getting the compound ready for our arrival."

"Fucking hell," Matvei breathes. "You're taking them to the Moreno compound?"

I nod. The estate where my mother was raised is the perfect choice. My father rebuilt it after the fire he set years ago destroyed the original buildings, so now, it's sprawling, easily defended, and complete with cells to interrogate the members of this godforsaken cult to find out who knew what.

"And then what? You can't hope to contain so many prisoners."

"They'll only be prisoners until they answer my questions. If they cooperate, if they're able to prove their innocence, they'll be set free."

"Has it escaped your notice that this is not just a random group of civilians?" Matvei snaps. "It's a fucking cult. If they're not cold-blooded sex traffickers, then they're brainless sheep. If you release them, they'll have nowhere to go. No idea of how to assimilate into the real world."

"I'm not running a fucking rehabilitation clinic, Matvei," I growl harshly. "I don't give two shits about what they do once they've answered my questions."

"More than half your prisoners are women and children," he points. "You do realize that, don't you?"

"They can come back here if they want. Continue their lives."

"Without their men?"

"I'm giving them freedom."

"Freedom can be a curse if it's forced upon you all at once," Matvei says. "They've been brainwashed. That needs to be remedied, not ignored."

"Again, that is not my fucking problem."

"You made it your problem when you stormed this place with a fucking army!"

I glare at him, realizing how badly out of sync the two of us are. What Matvei's asking for is compassion.

And unfortunately for him, I'm fresh out.

"I'm trying to destroy bad men," I remind him coldly. "The men who killed my family. I don't have the patience to hold anyone's hand in the meantime."

"Yeah? What about the hand you just took in marriage?" Matvei drawls. "What about Elyssa, brother?"

"What *about* Elyssa?" I ask.

"She's your wife."

"She's my property," I correct in a ruthless snarl. "I will use her to get what I need from these people. And then I'll cast her aside like the rest of them."

Matvei's eyes flash and he looks at me as though he no longer recognizes me. Then he exhales deeply and looks towards the windows. He's still, but I know his head is a chaos of thoughts. I wish we weren't at odds with one another like this.

But it doesn't matter, ultimately. This is happening, whether he likes it or not.

A trio of figures approach through the evening glare. Ilya, Alexi, and Konstantin join us amongst the huge boulders.

"Reports?" I say.

Ilya starts. "We've got the women and children in the main hall."

I nod. "Good. Make sure they're not uncomfortable."

"They keep asking questions."

"Ignore them for now," I reply. "Next. Konstantin?"

He rubs his beard and sighs. "The men have been confined to warehouses. Or maybe they're barns, I'm not sure. This place is fucking weird. Anyway, we strip-searched each of them. None were armed."

"Good." I turn to Alexi. "Where's the leader?"

"Locked in a room in the big house," he tells me. "I've put two guards on him. But it's unnecessary—he's been bound and gagged. He's also unarmed."

"They're not soldiers, that's for sure," Matvei observes. "Makes you wonder what Astra Tyrannis is using this town for, doesn't it?" His tone is sarcastic, biting. I don't appreciate the disrespect, especially not in front of my other lieutenants. But I'll deal with that later.

"This place holds secrets," I snarl. "We'll find them all before we leave." I turn back to my lieutenants, who are patiently awaiting next steps. "Konstantin, start initial interrogations with the men. See if you can sniff out anything unusual. Ilya, continue searching the properties. Alert me once the first sweeps are complete. Alexi, go prepare the motherfucker I stabbed. He and I are going to have a little chat."

They nod and depart, but Matvei hesitates. I can sense the question in his posture.

"What is it?" I ask, looking at him over my shoulder.

"What role would you have me play?" he asks in a voice so docile that I wonder for a moment if I've lost him completely.

Part of me regrets the harshness of our conversation. But there's no way around it. I needed men to follow orders, not to question me.

And I was steadfast about my plan the moment it took shape in my head.

"I need you to do what you do best," I say. "Try and keep track of any outside movements. When Astra Tyrannis makes their move, I want to know about it."

"You're changing a lot of people's lives here, Phoenix," he says quietly. "I hope you know what you're doing."

I consider answering honestly: *Me fucking too.*

I consider answering harshly: *Don't ever talk to me like that again.*

In the end, I don't answer at all.

Fifteen minutes later, I'm in front of a roughshod wooden door. Two of my men stand guard outside.

"Open it," I instruct. One of them twists the handle and lets me in.

Father Josiah has been chained to a chair in the center of the room. The windows are drawn tight, casting the space in darkness. His head dips low and the loose burlap bag hanging over his head obscures his face. The blood on his stomach is dried into a dark red splatter.

I move forward and rip the hood off. He blinks in pained confusion before raising his eyes to mine. They go wide for a second and I see the fear again.

It's an extremely satisfying reaction.

I drag forward the only other chair in the room and twist it around before straddling it. "Father," I greet pleasantly. "Fancy seeing you here."

"Why are you doing this?" he moans. His words turn into a spluttering cough.

I had one of my doctors examine the knife wound and bandage it as needed. I made sure to aim carefully when I stabbed him. Couldn't have the fucker bleeding out like a stuck pig on me. No, this man knows things. Things that I'd like to know more about myself.

He's going to stay alive for a while longer.

I also wanted to prove a point—I'm the fucking leader now.

"You know why," I answer.

"Is it all for her?"

I freeze. His head is still bobbing forward on his chest, so he doesn't see my reaction. But it takes me a moment to compose myself again.

Focus, Phoenix, I scold myself. *Focus on the fucking mission.*

"How much does she know?" I ask instead of answering his question.

He frowns, spit-flecked lips turning downward. "I don't know what you're talking about."

I sigh. "We're going to play that game?"

I lean back a little and regard him as objectively as I can. He's an older man—late forties, early fifties at most. Good-looking in the generic, trustable sort of way that men like him tend to be. But he's got the crazy eyes that men like him tend to have, too. Eyes that see things that aren't there.

"Why her?" I ask.

"What?"

"She's got to be, what, thirty years younger than you are?" I point out. "Why choose her?"

I can see the debate in his eyes: *Be diplomatic? Or tell the truth?*

He seems to settle on the latter. One of his masks falls away—though there are many more waiting underneath.

"Because I could."

I stay calm, even though I'm seething underneath. "And did you ask her?"

"Ask her what?"

"Ask her if she wanted to marry you, you dumb fuck."

"No more than you did," he snaps back.

I smile. "Touché. But there is one very significant difference."

"And what's that?" he asks, unable to resist taking the bait.

"Her pussy drips with desire every time I get close to her," I whisper. "Whereas she wouldn't even fuck you with a knife to her throat."

He grits his teeth, but doesn't say a word.

"As a matter of fact, I just fucked her on the altar," I remark. "And she moaned for me. Called out my name. Took me deep. Came for me when I told her to."

"You have no right to her!" he roars, writhing in his rickety chair.

I laugh. "I have every right. That woman is mine."

"She doesn't belong to you. She belongs to the Sanctuary."

I shake my head. "She severed ties with this brainwashing fucking cult the moment she bashed that goddamn swan into your head and set fire to your house. She came to Las Vegas and met me the very same night. You wanna know what happened then?"

I can tell he's scared about what I'm about to tell him. He shakes his head imperceptibly. More blood drips from his fat lower lip.

"She asked me for help," I tell him. "And I gave her exactly what she needed. It's poetic, isn't it?"

Josiah's eyes look wild, but he's reining it in, trying to control his reactions.

"Did you really believe her when she told you that baby was yours?" I growl.

I know I'm flipping a coin here, but I do it anyway, chasing the high of this particular kind of torture.

"The child is mine! Mine!"

"Your rape produced nothing but her hatred for you," I hiss. "But *I* gave her a child. *I* tied her to me in ways you never could, you fucking pathetic little bitch." I lean back and rub my hand across my stubbled jaw. "I should thank you, really, for driving her into my arms."

He babbles incoherently and keeps tugging at his bindings, although he doesn't get anywhere with it.

"Forgive me," I say innocently with a wave of my hand, "I'm talking too much about myself. It's rude. Let's talk about you."

I lean forward, elbows on my knees.

"You know, my doctor gave me a full report after he tended to your wound. You were unconscious at that point so you didn't notice. Anyway, point is, you have a tattoo right under your ballsack," I inform him. "A black swan. Odd choice for a tattoo. Odd location, too."

He immediately tenses. "I… it's a personal—"

"I'm going to stop you right there," I say, holding up my hand. "Consider this a friendly warning: don't you ever fucking lie to me."

He disgusts me. He's not even worthy of my pity or my scorn. He's cowardice personified. The kind of sick bastard who can rape a young girl after spending two decades grooming her into his perfect little fuck doll.

Under other circumstances, I'd kill him with my bare hands just so I didn't waste a bullet.

But there are things in that skull of his that matter. So his pathetic life continues—for now.

"Let's try again," I say. "What does the black swan mean?"

Josiah is quiet for so long that I actually believe he's grown a pair and he's planning on keeping his mouth shut. Wrong on that count, though. He speaks after a while.

"It's… a… a symbol."

Bingo.

"A symbol of what?"

"Power."

"But not yours, surely," I scoff. "From where I'm sitting, you're not powerful. And by my assessment, you never really were."

He bristles at that one. The reaction makes me chuckle. Maybe there's a little dignity in the son of a bitch after all. "You don't want to mess with me."

"No? And why is that?"

"Because of the people I work for."

I smile. "Say the name."

"The powers that be!"

I snort. "Fuck you. I don't want to hear that made-up voodoo horseshit. Say the *real* name."

He shakes his head, suddenly cowed. That pushes me over the edge.

With a roar, I leap up, throw my seat aside, and pounce on him. I jam a fist into Josiah's stomach, right where I stabbed him not too long ago. He bellows in pain as stitches rip open.

"Say it, motherfucker!" I bellow in his face. "Say it now!"

He screams, "Astra Tyrannis! Astra Tyrannis! Astra Tyrannis!"

I sigh and release him. "That's what I thought," I murmur. "That's what I fucking thought."

I pick up my chair and set it back in front of Father Josiah. He's panting as the pain finishes surging through his body. Fresh blood trickles onto his thighs.

"Now," I add, "I've got just a few more questions for you, Father."

7
ELYSSA

"Charity?"

I can see her through the thin, gauzy veil that separates us—but just barely. The filmy curtain looks like running water, but every time I try and pass through it, I'm shoved back by a force that's impossible to resist.

Her silhouette crumples in disappointment.

"Charity!" I call again with rising panic as she turns her back on me.

She's standing over there, looking off into the distance like she's searching for someone. Like she might leave any moment.

She can't go. I have so much I want to tell her.

"Charity, please," I beg through the unforgiving veil. "I need you."

She glances back over her shoulder. I realize then that she's crying. "*You* need *me?*" she asks in disbelief. "Where were you when *I* needed *you?*"

A lump forms in my throat and I realize how much I relied on her. She was my constant. My teacher. My friend.

And I failed her.

"I'm sorry…"

"*Sorry*?" she scoffs without really looking at me. "'Sorry' doesn't help me now. 'Sorry' won't bring me back to life."

"I know; I just—"

"I told you, didn't I? I warned you: *Never trust a man.*"

"I thought he was different."

"Does he have a cock between his legs?" she demands. "Huh? Then he's no different. You are nothing more than a place for him to stick it."

I'm not used to seeing Charity angry. Haughty, yes. Proud, yes. Defiant, yes. But angry—at me? Not once in the entire time I knew her.

"I'm sorry," I sob. "I should have listened to you."

She shakes her head and turns her back to me again. She's still staring off into the distance behind the veil, but as far as I can tell, there's nothing there to see. Just a vague gray light.

"I miss you," I whisper softly, not even sure she can hear.

"You have to get on without me now," she replies coldly. She's starting to walk away from me. The further she gets, the lonelier I feel. "You have to let me go. Stand up on your own two feet."

"I'm scared…"

"We all are. I was, too."

"You never showed it."

"What good would that have done?" she laughs. "Showing fear would only have made me more vulnerable. If people know that they can hurt you, they will."

She's drifting off almost out of sight. Fading to a blurred nothingness on the other side of the veil I can't penetrate.

"Wait!" I cry out. "Don't go!"

She doesn't say anything. Just retreats further and further.

"Charity? Charity!" I scream, panic clawing at my throat. "Charity, please come back! I can't do this alone!"

A storm of shadows converges around me, and it's like they have claws. Claws that prick and prod at me, flaying my skin open like needles dragging along my bare limbs.

"Get up. It's time to get up!"

It's Charity's voice speaking—but not really. As I listen in, it's deeper, more commanding. Detached and impatient in a way she never was.

"… Get up."

My eyes fly open and I dart upright as consciousness struggles to make sense of reality.

It was a dream. It was all just a dream.

My memory comes rushing back to me.

Phoenix storming the wedding. Stabbing Josiah. Saying "I do."

The panic attack, Phoenix ripping my wedding dress off of me, making violent love on the altar…

And then him leaving.

I huddled on the cathedral altar for a while, shivering not with cold but with fear. I didn't dare leave or even budge an inch. Not without knowing what Phoenix intended to do next.

I must've fallen asleep at some point, and Phoenix or his men moved me while I was out.

Now, I'm in a bedroom I don't recognize.

I don't recognize either of the two people standing at my bedside, either. One is a pretty, petite brunette with shy features. The other is a tall man with a blocky chin and pointed nose.

"Easy," says the girl. "Give her a second."

"I have orders," the man barks.

She rolls her eyes. "Men and their orders. Honestly, that boss of yours has you all by the balls."

"Ready to rip them out at a moment's notice," he growls.

"Where's my son?" I choke out, looking at the brunette. "Where's Theo?"

She glances to the side. That's when I notice the black stroller placed by the foot of my bed. It's turned to face me and I can see Theo is sleeping soundly, cocooned in his luxurious little portable bed. He's in clothes I've never seen before and one chubby arm is wrapped around a new stuffed bunny.

My heart steadies a little when I realize that he's obviously been well-cared for. I'm desperate to go scoop him up. But the way the gruff man is eyeing me has me frozen in place for now.

"Who changed him? Is he okay? Has he eaten?" I ask, rattling off questions without waiting for the answers.

"Look at him," the girl says by way of an answer, though her voice is gentle. "He's happy as a clam."

"You need to get dressed," the guard says brusquely. "We're moving out. Leona, get her ready."

The girl—Leona, I suppose—rolls her eyes again. "I'll make sure she's dressed," she says.

"My orders were—"

"I know what your fucking orders are," she snaps. "You've only said it ten thousand times. Wait outside for us."

Her confidence reminds me of Charity, but I'm not looking to make another friend. Not after what happened to the last one.

And certainly not with anyone working for Phoenix.

Leona moves around the bed to a small suitcase in the corner. "Jeans and a t-shirt?" she inquires. "You look like that kinda girl."

"I honestly don't know what kind of girl I am," I murmur. "Not anymore."

She turns to me. Her expression isn't exactly sympathetic, but it's close. "We're all a little lost, honey."

It's something Charity would say. So perfectly on brand for Charity, as a matter of fact, that it makes my heart throb.

I turn my face away to hide the tears in my eyes. "Where are we going?" I ask abruptly.

"I'm not sure I'm at liberty to say."

I laugh bitterly. "Guess the men aren't the only ones that Phoenix has got by the balls, huh?"

Leona grins. "Touché. You know, I really shouldn't play into your hands, but maybe just this one time. Just to prove I'm a rebel. So, to answer your question, we're taking a little jaunt to Mexico." Her smile is infectious.

I stare at her in disbelief. "Mexico?"

"Excellent, your hearing is working well."

"But… why there?"

"I have no earthly idea," she replies with a shrug. "But if you find out, be a pal and let me know."

"How would I find out?"

"You are married to the head honcho, after all."

It's weird hearing her say those words out loud. The ceremony—if you can even call it that—feels like something from a restless dream. Was it real? Did it count? Surely not.

Is it pathetic that I kind of wish it was?

I decide not to dwell as I get up and gather the clothes that Leona has picked out for me. Once I've visited the bathroom and changed, I follow her downstairs where there's a flurry of activity brewing.

A line of huge, armored trucks are parked just outside the mansion. Groups of Sanctuary residents are being herded into each one in single file lines.

"Oh my God... *everyone* is going to Mexico?" I ask.

Leona pushes Theo's stroller down the narrow ramp. "Apparently."

The moment I emerge, I feel everyone's eyes on me. I recognize most of the faces. They're all people I grew up around. Friends and cousins and family members.

At least, that's what they used to be—a lifetime ago. What are they to me now? Enemies? Strangers? Anything? Nothing?

They look at me as if I'm a monster birthed from a nightmare. Like I'm the beast who's unleashed hell into their idyllic lives.

Then I spot my parents. They stand in the center line leading to the third armored truck. No one is chained or cuffed, but they might as well be. The men ushering them into the trucks are all armed and grim. Their faces each bear the latent promise of violence.

I start striding towards my parents, ignoring the looks I'm getting from everyone else. "Mama! Papa!"

I catch a glimpse of my father's fury before he pointedly turns away from me. My mother, on the other hand, pretends like she doesn't even hear me.

My heart hurts, but I continue anyway. Someone behind me calls out my name. I don't know who, but I ignore them all the same.

"Mama," I try again. "Papa, please… look at me."

"What have you done?!" Mama hisses when I'm too close for her to keep overlooking.

"Me? I did nothing! I'm not responsible for any of this!"

"You've destroyed our Sanctuary. You brought evil here." Tears sparkle in my mother's eyes as she turns from me again.

My lip is quivering. "Papa, please believe me—I had nothing to do with any of this. I'm just as much a prisoner as—"

"Enough!" he barks, causing me to jump back in alarm.

My father's the kind of man whose anger burns low and quiet. He doesn't scream. He never yells. But the sound of his voice raised in anger frightens me into silence as I stare at the naked accusation in his eyes.

"You are no longer my daughter," he seethes. "You are nothing to me."

Those words are a knife in the chest. They root themselves into my heart and stay there. Naïve though it may be, I never expected it to hurt so much.

As I pirouette slowly in place, I realize why he shouted. It wasn't solely to hurt me. It was for the benefit of the entire community.

Everyone is shuffling backwards. Looking up, down, left, and right—anywhere but straight at me.

I'm a pariah.

I'm a curse.

I'm dead to all of them.

Fighting tears, I walk back to where Leona is standing. "Come on," she says in a soft voice. It's clear she's seen the whole exchange. "Let's get going."

"Which truck am I being herded into?" I ask bitterly.

"You're the wife of the boss," she says. "You get a proper car."

I cringe as I follow her to the shiny car that pulls up just beyond the line of trucks. Only once I'm inside do my tears come freely and easily.

I don't care who sees them now. I couldn't stop if I tried.

The stroller detaches into a car seat that Leona buckles in the middle of the back seat between us. Somehow, my son has managed to sleep through all the commotion. How lucky he is to be so young and oblivious. I reach out and touch his apple cheek.

"Here," Leona says, offering me a tissue.

"Thanks."

She nods and stares out the window while I cry.

The driver is separated from us by a glass partition, but I can see his surly silhouette. There's another man in the passenger seat.

Neither one is Phoenix. I haven't seen him since he left me on the altar with my center aching from his lovemaking and his seed painted on my thighs.

"Are you hungry?" Leona asks after we've been driving for a while.

"What?"

"Food," she enunciates. "You want any?"

My stomach doesn't register hunger, but I'm aware that I've barely eaten in days. "No, I'm not hungry."

"You should eat anyway," Leona says. "Otherwise, you'll waste away to nothing."

"What would it matter?"

"It might matter to him." She jerks her head towards Theo.

I look at the steady rise and fall of his chest and my heart aches all over again. Glancing up, I see Leona's gaze searching my face. Checking to see how close I am to falling apart completely.

"You noticed, didn't you?" I ask.

She smiles empathetically. "Your parents weren't exactly subtle."

"No," I murmur. "They needed to make a statement."

I wipe away my tears as Leona roots around in a cooler at our feet, pulls out an apple, and takes a bite. She leans back against her seat and crosses her ankle over her knee like a man would. It's a very masculine gesture for someone with such a feminine aura.

"How old are you?" I ask curiously.

"Twenty-eight."

"Oh. I assumed you were younger."

"Most people do. I think it's just my youthful exuberance. Oh, and my flawless complexion. Shoulda been a Cover Girl instead of taking up this gig."

"You work for Phoenix?"

"Actually, up until recently, I worked for his father. But I was reassigned a few weeks ago. Apparently, to play nanny."

I raise my eyebrows. "And you're not happy about that?"

She takes another bite of her apple. "I like action, being in the thick of things," she explains. "Don't get me wrong—Theo's a babe... But this is not the kind of action I had in mind when I was assigned to work for Phoenix Kovalyov." She speaks his name with a reverence that's hard to miss.

"What did you have in mind?"

She shrugs. "Shoot-outs, heists, crazy missions. That kind of thing," she says. "Although, this counts as a crazy mission, I suppose." She gives me a smile. "I'm also a bodyguard, just so you know. For you and for the little angel. My job is to make sure the two of you are safe."

I stiffen. Bad memories resurface. "Oh."

"And in case you're wondering, I know exactly what happened with the last woman who looked after him. You have nothing to worry about. I've pledged my loyalty to the house of Kovalyov and that means something to me."

It's probably stupid of me, but I believe her. She's got weight behind her words. A certain courage that I admire. And I know enough now to know that my son does need protection.

I don't care so much about myself. But Theo?

He deserves the chance at a future.

"Why this life?" I ask suddenly. "You said you wanted to work for Phoenix. Why did you choose this life?"

She shrugs. "My father worked for Don Kovalyov for decades. I always dreamed of doing the same. So when I turned eighteen, I asked for a job. I was turned away and told to come back at twenty-one if I was serious. I don't think either Don Kovalyov or my father expected me to hold the same ambition. But three years later, I proved them both wrong."

"I take it you're a hard woman to say no to."

She smiles triumphantly. "You're right about that. I didn't give them much of a choice."

"And you didn't want to be, I dunno… a doctor or a teacher? Something… normal?"

Leona's grin gets wider. "Normal?" she repeats. "Now, where's the fun in that?"

8
ELYSSA

My head jolts forward with the bump of the vehicle. It forces me awake. I stifle a surprised scream and throw my hand out for something to grab.

"You okay?" Leona asks when I've got my bearings back.

She's cradling Theo, who's awake and clutching her finger tightly. He looks at me and his face splits into a massive, toothless smile.

"My boy," I whisper, reaching for him.

"Just changed him," Leona informs me. "You wanna feed him?"

"Yes, please."

She pops him into the cradle I've made with my arms and pulls out a freshly-made bottle. While Theo drinks, I look out the window. The land we're passing through is oddly foreign.

"Mexico, huh?" I breathe.

"We crossed the border in the night."

"You managed to get through with truckloads full of prisoners?"

"The don has connections," she explains. "And roots."

"Roots?"

Leona just gives me a mysterious wink and doesn't divulge any more information. I sigh and turn my attention back to the landscape. It's desolate out there. No buildings, no vegetation, no sign of life whatsoever.

"Where exactly are we going?"

"Beats me," Leona says. "First time for me, too."

I have no idea whether to believe her or not.

Once I've burped Theo, I sit him up on my lap and drink in his newborn scent. It's changing already, moving from infant to baby. Soon, he'll be a toddler. I wonder where on this planet we'll be when he starts to walk, when he says his first word, when he becomes a man. I wonder what's going to happen to both of us.

The car starts slowing a little and I crane my neck to see why. There's a gated compound rising up in the distance. Standing proudly in the middle of nowhere, its austere walls make me shiver with foreboding.

The gates open just before we drive through. It reminds me of the Sanctuary in the sense that it feels like a contained community, separated from the rest of the world.

The estate is sprawling. A handful of buildings dot the area. All look gleaming new. Bunkers, warehouses, everything sparse and utilitarian.

Except for the structure at the far edge. That is lavishness incarnate. It drips with luxury and fine craftsmanship. I'm guessing those are the don's quarters.

We grind to a halt. My car door is whipped open and one of Phoenix's guards is already waiting for me with a stern expression. "Out," he orders. He holds out a hand to help me down to the dry earth.

I get out with Theo in my clutch and shield my eyes from the sun arrowing down at us. I glance around, but I don't see Phoenix anywhere.

"I'll take him now," Leona says, removing Theo from my arms.

"Why can't he stay with me?"

"You're to be shown to your room now."

I narrow my eyes. "You mean my jail cell?"

"If you want to call it that. It'll be a hell of a lot nicer than the bunkers where the rest of this lot are going," Leona says as she jerks a thumb at the trucks queuing up behind us.

"Bunkers?"

"Don't worry—there are actual beds, running water, the whole nine yards," she assures me. "But it's more, shall we say, spartan than your accommodations will be."

"Perks of being forced into marriage," I ask bitterly.

She just grins at me. "At least you get something out of the bargain."

She proceeds to walk away from me, taking my son with her. I make an automatic step to follow, but the guard who opened my door blocks me.

"Excuse me, ma'am. You'll have to follow me."

I look into his deep-set brown eyes and try and find some humanity in them. If it's there, I certainly can't pick it out.

"I want my son."

"It wasn't a question."

He grabs my wrist, but I yank it away furiously. "Don't touch me."

He backs away and eyes me, considering whether I'm worth the hassle. In the end, he just gives me a small nod and gestures for me to walk ahead of him.

I weigh disobeying. Running away, throwing dirt in his face, kicking this smug prick right between the legs. But I know that none of those things are truly options. I may not have literal chains around my wrists, but I feel their weight nonetheless.

So I trudge along the way he points. We approach the don's quarters. The façade is adobe so smooth it looks like a cloud. Huge swaths of glass drink in the light until the whole place glows like a diamond.

The front door pivots inward and sucks us in with the promise of air conditioning. It must cost a fortune to cool this place, based on the triple-height ceilings and endless open floor plan. I have a feeling that money was no object.

The furniture is as minimalist as the rest of the compound, but it screams money. Fine leather couches, gilded portraits, handwoven rugs lying here and there on the stone floors. Everything luxe and ultra-modern.

The guard leads me to the second floor. I'm shown into a beautiful room with wraparound windows overlooking the garden. My jaw almost drops at the sight. The whole spread is unbelievably green. An oasis in this sandy wasteland. Birds chirp and butterflies flit from bush to bush.

It's beautiful—but I resent the beauty.

Because it's a silent insult. A taunt. Phoenix is using this grand house to force me into a life I didn't choose and then expecting me to be grateful for it.

I turn around to realize the guard who led me here is already backing out of the room. "Hey, wait—!"

He does not wait.

The door shuts on me. A second later, I hear the click of the lock. Scowling, I pace around the room. It matches the rest of the place.

Exquisite.

Immaculate.

And utterly soulless.

This home is a trap, a threat, a promise of violence. I refuse to let it intimidate me.

The bathroom is brimming with luxury products—face washes and creams and lotions, straighteners and mousse, makeup and hundreds of different brushes. The bed is made up with Egyptian cotton sheets with a six-figure thread count. And even though I shouldn't be surprised by it, I can't help letting out a tiny little gasp when I step into the walk-in closet and find it stocked with row after row of clothing—all exactly in my sizes.

I finger the fine fabrics of the dresses. Run my finger along the edge of the shoes. Touch the necklaces, the earrings, the watches.

It all glistens like gold. But I know the truth—it's fool's gold. The truth behind these nice things is rotten to the core.

On a whim, I go back to the front door and start banging. "Hey, is someone there?"

A gruff voice answers immediately. A guard posted at my door, like I expected. "Is there something you need, ma'am?"

"I want my son."

"I'm afraid that's not possible."

"Why not?"

"Boss's orders."

I slam my palms against the door as hard as I can and it bites back. I rub off the sting and try again. "Well, then I want to speak to the boss."

"That's not possible, either," the calm, detached voice replies.

I close my eyes. It's been a long time since I was so tempted to swear. "I need to speak to him," I repeat. "Now."

No answer.

"Matvei then?" I ask.

No answer.

"Goddammit!" I yell in frustration. I have to admit—it feels good coming off my lips.

"If you require food or drink," the voice says, "I can get what you need. Anything else will have to wait."

"Screw you!" I yell. "I need to speak to Phoenix!"

He falls into silence. I bang my fists against the door until my fists swell, but he doesn't answer again. When it's clear he's done talking to me, I retreat back into the bathroom, feeling the swell of failure.

I have no idea what I'm doing here. No idea what my purpose is anymore. I'm doing my best not to think about the bigger picture. Because if I focus on anything other than myself and my son, I'm going to go insane.

It's just too much. Astra Tyrannis. Black swans. Father Josiah. My parents. Phoenix Kovalyov and a wedding I didn't ask for and the look in his eyes when he walked away from me, when he left me behind on that altar marked as his in a way I never, ever dreamed he would do…

There can't be this much hatred and evil and untruth in the world. There just can't be.

I retreat to the bathroom, fill the huge tub with hot water, and watch the steam rise all around me. I discard my clothes, now stained with the grime and sweat of travel, and slip into the tub. The hot water scalds my skin, but I close my eyes and welcome the comforting pain. It distracts me from the thoughts racing through my head.

Relax, I tell myself. *It'll be okay. Don't think about Theo or your parents. Don't think about your first or your second husbands. Don't think about Charity's dead body or—*

I open my eyes. This might be a hopeless endeavor.

My head swarms with images of young women being forced to sell their bodies. Black swans with blood dripping off the tops of their heads. The handsome stranger who has imprisoned me in a gilded cage.

I want to speak to my parents, to ask what they knew and what they know, but they'd only rebuff me. They made that much clear earlier.

Tears leak from my eyes. I just lie there and let them come. I'm powerless to stop them.

"Charity," I whisper. "If only you were here…"

If Charity had been alive, she would never have let me go back to the commune. She would have insisted on going somewhere far away. Leaving all this chaos behind.

If only I could channel even an ounce of her strength, maybe I'd be able to stand up to Phoenix. Maybe I'd be able to confront my parents. Maybe I'd be able to recall the memories I'm too traumatized to remember.

I soak until my skin has turned pruny and the water's turned cold before I get out of the tub. I wipe myself dry and slip on the silky silver robe hanging from a hook next to the sink.

I shudder as I loop the cord loosely around my waist. Not because it feels bad—but because the material is too soft, too comfortable. It's like everything else happening around me: a lie that would be so easy to nestle myself inside of.

I stare at the luxury that I'm surrounded by and I resent all of it.

Am I supposed to be grateful?

Am I supposed to be happy?

A part of me actually wishes I were in one of those bunkers with the rest of the villagers. At least that wouldn't feel like a lie.

My head jerks to the side when I think I hear a cry in the far distance. "Theo?" I whisper.

Of course, no one hears me. No one answers.

I meander aimlessly around the room. Through the windows, I can see the gardens, illuminated by floodlights now that the sun has set. Shadows move in pairs around the perimeter—Phoenix's guards keeping watch, I'm sure. The moonlight occasionally reflects off of the heavy weaponry in their hands.

I hate that my eyes search for Phoenix. That I long to see his form amongst the patrols.

I wish I can say that what he's done—what I've watched him do both to me and others with my own two eyes—extinguished my feelings entirely.

But I'm done lying to myself.

I do have feelings for Phoenix. They're complicated and acute and there's no denying them anymore. That doesn't mean I have to be a slave to them, though. I don't have to be a doormat or a dutiful wife or an obedient daughter.

I don't have to be *anything*. Not unless I want to be.

My eyes fall to the beautiful crystal ornament sitting by the table in front of the window. I pick it up and toss it from one hand to the other.

What are you feeling, Elyssa? Charity asks.

I don't look up. I know Charity's not really there, but I hear her voice in my head all the same. It's comforting. Like she's still with me.

"I'm feeling… helpless," I admit out loud.

And?

"And angry. Really angry."

What have I always told you?

"Whatever I'm feeling, it's okay to let it out."

Bingo. And what do you want to do right now?

I look down at the object in my hand. The answer rises to my lips like I've known it all along. "I want to destroy this beautiful crystal ornament. I want to wreck this perfect room. I want to ruin this glamorous lie."

Atta girl. So then what are you waiting for?

I turn around and fling the crystal ornament right at the door.

It shatters into a rainbow of glass shards. I feel the thrill of adrenaline shoot through my body.

That felt amazing. Better than amazing.

Satisfied? Charity's voice chuckles.

"Not even close," I laugh maniacally, picking up another bauble that I can break.

I hurl it at the door in the same spot as the first.

And the second crash makes me feel like I can breathe again.

"More," I whisper under my breath. "I want more."

Filled with a powerful kind of satisfaction, I start trashing the room. Throwing chairs, ripping curtains, breaking anything that can be broken. I tear portraits off the wall and smash them over my knee. I upend the couch. I take wine glasses from the kitchen cabinets and *boom-boom-boom,* lob them into the chandeliers above. It's raining glass and chaos. I'm laughing like a maniac.

And I feel alive.

When the door bursts open, I don't spare the guard a second glance. "Stop!" he orders. "Have you lost your mind?"

Not a chance, bozo! She's finally fucking found it!

I smile as I grab the letter opener lying on the dressing table and proceed to stab the pillows with it. Downy feathers burst into the air, mingling with the shards of glass still cascading down from the ceiling above.

He charges towards me. "Let me go!" I scream as a pair of massive arms encircle me and hike me up into the air. The guard's grip tugs at the silky, sheer fabric of my bathrobe, undoing the knot. I feel my breasts bounce loose and the cold rush of air between my bare thighs.

I'm pedaling my feet in empty space as hard as I can, thrashing and resisting. Not that it does much good. The man is bigger and stronger than me by a long shot.

But I won't go easily. I won't go quietly.

Not anymore.

Not ever again.

I'm still fighting and the guard is still struggling to pin me in place—until we both hear a sound at the door. A deep, raspy clear of the throat.

In unison, we freeze. We turn. And we see the imposing silhouette framed against the entryway.

His eyes are dark with displeasure as he takes in the damage I've caused. And then they flit down to my exposed nude body and the guard's hands on me. At that, the anger in his irises boils over.

"Enough," he hisses. "She's mine."

9

PHOENIX

I've never seen Elyssa so out of control.

Her eyes are wild, her body tense and ready to strike. The room I'd had prepared specially for her is a shamble of ruins, a victim of her hidden temper.

And yet none of this incites my anger. In fact, I'm mildly amused to see her let loose like this. It's a welcome change from the shy, reclusive wallflower who always seemed to be swallowing her true feelings.

There's real anger there. Hot and sexy. It reminds me of my own.

Her silk robe has come loose, revealing one perfect breast, a long sliver of leg, a tiny nestle of blond hair where her thighs graze together. My cock stiffens at once.

"Ivan," I command, "release her."

He does as I say immediately.

All that does is allow the robe to come apart completely.

I catch another glimpse of her naked pussy and the hard nubs of her nipples before she yanks the robe around her again and ties it tight across her stomach.

Ivan's head is down, but I notice him glance out of the corner of his eye at her as she does up her garment. A lash of fury rises up in my chest at the thought of his hands on Elyssa's skin.

"Now get the fuck out."

He starts to hurry past me, eyes still on the floor. But before he can make it out the door, I pounce on him. Seizing the front of his shirt, I spin and slam him against the wall. He's a few inches shorter than me, but at least fifty pounds heavier. It doesn't make a difference. He might as well be a scared little child in the face of my wrath.

I shove my face in his. "If I ever catch you with your hands on my wife again, I will fucking end you. Understood?"

Fear snakes across his eyes for a moment before he nods. "Yes, don."

"Good. Get out of my sight."

I shove him away. He runs like his life depends on it. Smart man.

That's when I turn my attention to the woman standing across from me, her hands propped resolutely on either side of her hips.

She's done a hasty job of tying up her robe so it still slacks at the center, allowing me a generous view of her cleavage.

My eyes dip down to drink in the sight. She doesn't miss it. Her hands flinch instinctively towards the tie, but she squelches the urge and glares at me. Her cheeks are flushed, though I'm not sure if it's from the mess she's just made or the fact that I'm making no secret of eye-fucking her.

"Found my room, did you?" she snaps.

I raise my eyebrows. The tone is new, too. Usually, even her anger has been muted. But I can sense a change. Things on the surface are cracking, letting in the real stuff underneath. The truth is coming to light.

I've waited a long time for this.

"I had other business I needed to attend to."

"Oh, I'm sure. Why didn't you tell me that you were bringing me to Mexico?"

I shrug. "It was need-to-know information. You didn't need to know."

"I beg to differ."

Her chin juts out slightly. The effect is adorable. She's bristling with anger, but all I can think about is pinning her down and fucking that brattiness out of her.

I slap away the unwanted thought. I have to stop looking at her like that. She's my wife in title only. It was an act of submission, a declaration of my intention. It didn't mean anything personal.

I'd already crossed the line by fucking her the day we got married. I won't make that mistake twice.

"You can differ with me all you want," I say. "It won't change a fucking thing."

She still flinches slightly when I swear. So some things remain the same.

"What are you smiling about?" she demands.

"Nothing to concern yourself with."

"What *am* I to concern myself with then?" she asks. "Because clearly, I have no real purpose here."

"Your purpose is to play the part of my wife."

"That's not a purpose," she hisses. "That's a jail sentence."

I chuckle darkly. "Is that right?"

"You didn't ask me," she says. "You're no different than him." Her eyes flash amber.

I bound forward to close the distance between us and, with one hand on her throat and the other on her hip, I pin her against the floor-to-ceiling windows.

The robe is thin and I can feel the contours of her body against my own. Her nipples are definitely hard. I position myself right between her legs. My cock is a weapon ready to be unleashed.

"We've played this game before, little lamb," I hiss in her ear. "You don't want to go making comparisons you'll end up regretting."

Her eyes glisten as she stares up at me. The fight in her is fucking intoxicating. I've never been more turned on.

"What do you want with me?" she asks.

My answer is immediate: "Everything."

She trembles against me and I feel her body go slack. Like she's given up. But when I look into her eyes, the same vibrant intensity blazes strong.

I'm picking my battles, that light says. *You'd better be careful when picking yours.*

I feel my cock twitch with anticipation.

"You've already taken everything from me," she whispers. "I have no one and nothing left. You've made me an outcast among my friends, my family. You've taken my son. Charity is gone…" Her voice trembles.

"You think you're the only one who's lost things?" I seethe. "You've never held your wife's dead, mutilated body in your hands. You've never breathed in the scent of your son's blanket and forced yourself to accept that he's never, ever coming back. Don't talk to me about loss, little lamb. You don't know the first fucking thing about it."

She breathes heavy, her breasts rising and falling with the motion. Her eyes gleam in the darkness.

"There's only one thing I want from you now," I snarl.

"And what's that?"

"The truth."

She plants two hands on my chest and shoves as hard as she can. It does nothing. "Get off me," she lashes out angrily.

I laugh and shake my head. "No."

She tries to push me again, but this time, I grab both wrists and pin them to the window on either side of her face.

She stares at me with wide eyes that betray more than just anger.

"Do you really want me to get off you?" I ask.

She narrows her eyes. "You know what I really want?"

"Enlighten me."

"My son."

"I will decide when you see him."

"You can't do this. He's my child."

"And you're my wife," I growl.

"I'm not your wife; I'm your prisoner. There's a difference."

"Not to me."

"Well, that certainly says a lot about you," she snaps. "Is this how you treated your first wife?"

I can tell she's not thinking about the words when she says them. The moment they're off her tongue, she goes pale. Embarrassment and regret writhe in her eyes.

In response, I press myself against her body, digging her into the wall and causing her to cry out. Her pulse is racing. I can feel it under my fingers.

"You don't know a fucking thing about Aurora," I sneer. "Do you hear me?"

She's stuttering, "I… I… I'm sorry… I didn't mean…"

"You have no fucking clue. No fucking clue what I'm trying to do here. What I'm trying to unravel."

"Then tell me!" she yells in my face. "Tell me and I'll know."

"Tell you?" I scoff. "You're a child."

She veers back at the insult. But instead of the hurt and withdrawal I normally expect from her, I get anger instead.

This new Elyssa has endless fire.

"Is that why you wanted to marry me?" she demands. "Is that why you get hard every time you're around me? Because I'm just a helpless little girl?"

On the last word, she pushes her hips into my erection to drive home her point.

"I may not be as worldly or as knowledgeable or as high and freaking mighty as you are," she snaps. "But that doesn't make me a child."

"No? Then why can't you answer any of my questions?"

She has a hard time meeting my eye. But it's not secrecy that's holding her tongue. It's embarrassment.

"Because I can't remember," she whispers.

"Speak up."

"I can't remember, okay?" she shouts. "I know it sounds like an excuse, but I don't remember a whole block of time. It's like my life just… didn't exist."

"What the fuck are you talking about?"

"Little details, I can pick out," she explains with evident frustration. "But nothing big. Nothing significant. Whatever happened to me… it scared me so bad I threw my memory away rather than live with the weight of it. It… it broke me, Phoenix. I'm broken."

I look at her for a long time. A shadow passes across her eyes, but she doesn't say a word. It's as though I've caught her in a lie and she's trying to dig her way out of it.

"What did you do?" I whisper.

She blinks in confusion. "Huh?"

"What was your part in all of this?"

I swear, for the tiniest moment, I see her shudder. Like she's just barely come to terms with forming that question in her own head. With wondering if the past she can't remember contains something bad that happened *to* her—or something bad that happened *because* of her.

"Let me go," she says at last, trying to push her body against mine.

I like the feel of her too much to comply. "No."

She tries to thrash around and break free, but she has no chance of succeeding. I let her fight for a moment solely because it amuses me. Then I take control again.

Whipping her around, I press her front up against the window. The knot in her robe comes undone so it's her bare skin against the glass.

I lean in and run my nose along the soft skin at the nape of her neck. She smells like a fucking rose. All I want to do is bury my face between her silky thighs and eat her out like she's my last meal.

My cock strains against the crotch of my pants, but I can't succumb to that urge right now.

"Get your hands off me! I hate you!"

I laugh. "Oh, little lamb, I doubt that."

"I hate you," she snarls again, cheek smashed against the reflection.

"Is that so? Well, then make me believe it."

She jerks her head back hard. It cracks against my nose. I feel the rush of pain, followed quickly by the rush of blood.

Then, to Elyssa's surprise, I laugh. "If I were to slip my fingers between your thighs, what would I find there? Proof of your hate?"

She stiffens. "You wouldn't."

"You're my wife."

"That word doesn't mean anything to you. I'm just another pawn in your game."

"It's not a fucking game," I growl. "This is war."

"And I'm one of the casualties?"

"That remains to be seen."

At that, I release her. She gasps at the sudden chasm between us and slumps down to a huddled puddle at the foot of the window, shaking uncontrollably.

I allow my gaze to linger for a few seconds on her exposed cleavage before I walk over to the mahogany wardrobe on the opposite wall.

The whole time, I can feel her eyes on my back, but I ignore them and open the wardrobe doors. I rifle through the selection of dresses I'd had brought here for her.

I pick out the sleek red dress with the thin straps and open back, then lay it out on the bed in front of her.

"What are you doing?" she asks in a low, hollow croak.

"We're having dinner tonight," I inform her. "You'll be wearing this."

She stares at me in disbelief. "Are you serious?"

"Very."

"I'm not wearing that and I'm not having dinner with you."

"What makes you think you have a choice?"

She shakes her head. "I don't get it. Why go through this whole song and dance? I'm your prisoner, so why bother with wining and dining me?"

"Because I want answers from you that I still haven't gotten." It comes out clipped and cold, harsh enough for her to flinch at my tone, just like I intended.

It's an excuse—not that she knows that. And while there is some truth to it, it's not the whole reason. The whole reason is far more complicated to pick apart.

"I don't remember anything," she says. "I've already told you that."

"If you're so sure, then what are you afraid of?"

That stumps her. She looks down for a moment, her eyes unfocusing.

"If you want to see your son, you will learn to fall in line and do what you're told."

Her face falls. "I can't believe that I ever had fe—" She stops short, just shy of the last word. Her hazel brown eyes dim with self-consciousness.

"What was that?" I inquire innocently.

"Nothing," she mumbles quickly. "Nothing."

I consider pressing further. But the scarlet blush on her cheeks is satisfying enough—for now.

"You have an hour to get ready for dinner," I say. "Someone will be around to escort you to the dining room."

"So that's all you want?" Elyssa calls out after me as I turn and head for the exit. "You want my memories? You want information you think I can give you?"

I pause and spin on the spot to eye her warily. "Yes."

"And there was nothing else you're interested in?" she says. I'm vaguely aware of her hands straying up towards the hem of her robe.

"No."

"Are you sure?"

Carefully, slowly—so fucking slowly—she lifts the robe from her shoulders and lets it cascade down her arms to puddle at her feet. She's standing square in a beam of moonlight and it hits her skin, turning it into a glowing mirage. The swell of her breasts, the flat plane of her stomach, the glistening slit of her pussy…

Fuck.

"Well, then, make me believe it," she croons, throwing my own words back in my face.

I realize how much more difficult this is going to be now. Armed with her beauty, she was already dangerous. Add confidence and fight to the mix, and she's downright deadly.

Now that she's found her voice…

Now that she's using it…

This is going to be a fucking war.

10

ELYSSA

Well, what are you going to do?

I take a deep breath and fall back against the bed, taking care to avoid the dress that's still sprawled out across the sheets.

"I don't know…"

Gotta say, I'm proud of you. That move with the robe—fucking genius. Chef's kiss perfection.

"It didn't feel like me. It felt like—"

Me? Is that what you're gonna say? What's wrong with that?

"Nothing—except that I'm not you."

A person can evolve.

I smile and sit up. The room is empty, of course. No one in here but me. But Charity's voice is still clear as day in my head.

"Is this what it feels like to be haunted?"

I'm more like your fairy godmother. Anyhoo, stop thinking so damn much. It's always been one of your most annoying traits.

"I miss you."

If you're gonna get all sentimental on me, I'm leaving.

"Like you have a better place to be."

Cheeky. Gotta say, I'm loving the new and improved you. You're gonna give that arrogant hottie a run for his money.

"I'm no match for him, Charity."

You're more *than a match for him.*

"You don't understand. I... I... still have feelings for him. Despite—well, despite everything."

Yeah, duh. I get that.

"What is that supposed to mean?"

He's everything you didn't have growing up. A strong man, one who's powerful and confident and knows what he's doing, what he wants, how to get it. A protector, not a manipulator. Not to mention he's sexy as sin. I mean... you're only human.

"He's keeping me from Theo. I should hate him."

Don't you?

"A part of me does."

And the rest of you?

"The rest of me longs for the man who taught me to swim."

He's still in there somewhere.

"How do you know?"

Because you *believe it. That's how.*

I take a deep breath and try to expel Charity's voice from inside my head. I'm not sure if it's doing more harm than good. But I'm realizing more and more how much I'm relying on the conversations.

Although, can you really even call them conversations if they're happening inside your head? I'm basically just talking to myself.

Overthinking again, are we?

I grin, despite myself. "I would never."

If coping mechanisms are what you need to deal with my death, use them. It won't always be so painful. Things heal in time.

"Yes, it will," I whisper. "It'll always hurt."

You have to survive in the meantime, Elyssa. For Theo's sake.

I glance towards the red dress spread out next to me. I reach out and run my hands over the fine silk.

"It's so beautiful," I murmur.

You want to wear it.

"Is that bad?" I hang my head in shame.

Hell no! You're gonna look hot as fuck. Wear it. Mr. Dark and Stormy won't know what hit him.

"He's never going to lose focus."

I blush at the memory of his cock pressed against my inner thigh. I want him so badly that my pussy throbs with impatient desire.

Remember what I taught you. When you're horny... fuck!

"Please stop."

You don't need to be ashamed of your desires. That's something 'they' taught you. And it's pretty clear that everything they taught you is wrong.

"It's not the desire that I'm fighting," I reply. "It's the man."

Fighting while you're fucking can be a lot of fun.

"Oh God," I mutter, torn between a sigh and a giggle.

I get to my feet and start pacing. Every few seconds, I eye the dress, longing to put it on. I've never worn anything so luxurious in my life. And, silly and superficial as it might be, I want to now.

"I'm playing right into his hands," I remark. "Doing exactly what he wants me to do—how's that supposed to help me?"

No, you're doing exactly what you want to do. It just so happens to be what he wants, too. Don't let that confuse you.

I step up to the red dress like I'm facing a firing squad. Picking it up gingerly, I hold it up against my naked body.

I don't have to know much to see that this is the kind of dress that doesn't allow for a bra or proper underwear. So be it. Swallowing down my anxiety, I slip into the dress.

I leave the back unzipped as I step in front of the gilded, full-length mirror. My reflection takes my breath away.

The fabric flows over my curves, hugging my torso before billowing out over my hips. Just the feel of it is exquisite. Like being wrapped in a silk cloud.

But I'm not wholly prepared to see what it does to the rest of me.

I swear that my eyes are brighter. My lips fuller. My hair thicker. I look like someone else entirely. Someone taller, sexier, and far more confident than I've ever been.

My shoulders are bare, with only the thin straps of the dress to hold it up. The V neckline is deep and reveals a generous amount of cleavage, and the material is so filmy that the peaks of my nipples are on display, too.

Don't even think about taking it off. It's perfect on you.

"It's too much."

That's exactly why it's perfect. You want him to eat his heart out at the sight of you. Now, go find a killer pair of heels before I do something drastic.

I pad over to the walk-in closet barefoot. One of the light switches illuminates a section of shelving dozens of layers tall. Each pair of shoes waits in its own little sconce. Calling out to me. I scan over them all, looking for the right one.

But there's one set that my eyes come back to again and again.

They're sleek, black, and absurdly tall—a four-inch heel at least.

Ooh, yes, girl! You know which ones to pick.

"You're a bad influence."

That's why you love me.

I grab them anyway. Sinking down onto the plush footstool, I strap them around my ankles. Once they're on, I go to the bathroom.

The endless racks of makeup are waiting for me. I go shuffling through, seeing what else is here. But I'm not expecting what I find when I open the top drawer: a diamond necklace with a matching bracelet and studded earrings.

"You've gotta be kidding me," I breathe out.

I can practically hear Charity cackling. *This man doesn't know what he's in for!*

I reach out for it, but I hesitate halfway. My hand hovers over the glistening jewels. They look like pure water frozen into shape. A million little miniature versions of me look back from the cut surfaces.

Well, what are you waiting for?!

With trembling fingers, I put the diamonds on.

For a second, I think it'll be too much. But the moment the set is on me, I realize that it's not too much at all.

It's perfect.

Like this is all just another part of the plan.

Trying to suppress my shudder, I make quick work of my makeup and hair. Just a light layer of foundation, exactly the way that Charity taught me. Then a little eyeshadow, eyeliner and some lipstick in a caramel rouge color that complements my skin tone. I brush a comb through my tangled blond locks and rise back to my feet.

Look at you, babe. You can take him. Don't let him intimidate you.

I stare at the mirror and nod. "I can do this."

Hell yeah, you can. Go get yours!

"Not what I meant."

Details.

The smile drops from my face when a knock reverberates through the suite. I take a deep breath and step out of the bedroom just as the door opens.

The guard waiting for me on the other side isn't the one who interrupted my temper tantrum earlier. This one is shy, reserved, hesitant to even look at me the wrong way.

Something tells me good ol' Ivan is not going to be guarding me again any time soon.

Phoenix was more pissed off about homeboy putting his hands on you than he was about you trashing his room! Oh my, this is too good.

"That's not good at all," I mutter under my breath.

Wrong. We can use it. Every man has a weakness and it's usually between his legs.

Without a word, the new guard ushers me out of the room. I trail in his wake through the house. We take a different route than the way I arrived, so I get to see new sights along the way.

The place seems endless. Every hallway turns and reveals another floor, another atrium, another dozen rooms. The mirrors and tinted windows combine with the thousands of lights to make me feel like I'm floating through space filled with stars. In spite of the absurd elegance and the wealth that can pay for this kind of design, the overall effect is almost… understated. Cool without being cold, in the strangest way.

The longer we walk, the more anxious I get. One of these doors has Phoenix Kovalyov waiting on the other side. The only way I'll get my son back in my arms is to play his game.

I need to be ready.

Calm down. You're overthinking again.

"Will you stop?" I hiss.

"What?" the guard balks, freezing in his tracks and looking at me over his shoulder.

"Nothing," I mumble, even as I hear Charity snicker mischievously.

You're not a child. You're not a little girl. You're a jaw-dropping, badass superwoman. Just take a freaking look in the mirror.

The guard opens a pair of double doors to reveal a huge, circular room. On the far side of it, yet another pair of French doors is already opened up. An open, empty veranda beckons beyond. The smell of salt and brine hits my nostrils.

The ocean.

I start walking a little faster. The guard remains behind me at the first set of doors. I leave him there as I step out from underneath the ceiling into the arms of the sea breeze.

It's more beautiful than I could ever have imagined. An infinite field of roiling, white-capped waves. The sound kisses my ears. The salt air licks my face. Every breath feels like the first one I've ever taken.

Then the doors click behind me.

I turn and see Phoenix standing there. It's just him and me out here. No guards.

"You're exquisite," he murmurs.

My skin prickles immediately from head to toe. *Pathetic*, I think. One little compliment and I'm putty already? No, I refuse to be that easy. *Breathe. Focus.*

Phoenix is pretty exquisite himself. Dark suit pants beneath a pure white shirt, open at the throat with the sleeves rolled up to reveal tanned, tattooed forearms ripping with veins. The sea breeze stirs his hair. His eyes glisten, never once wavering from mine.

He gives me a smile—dazzling, every bit as white as his shirt—and suddenly, I'm forgetting everything I told myself on the way here.

"Take a seat."

It's a bad idea to start the evening off taking orders without question. But between the dress I'm wearing, Phoenix's intoxicating smirk, Charity's voice in my head, the whiplash transitions from a wedding to a stabbing to whatever this is, and above all, my clawing desire to hold my son in my arms again, I have a feeling that I need to sit down immediately or else I'm going to promptly collapse.

So when Phoenix draws a seat out from beneath a table covered in flawless white cloth, I sink into it and don't argue.

"I've never seen the sea before," I admit—more to myself than to him.

"Never?"

I turn to him as he takes his seat opposite me. "I lived in an enclosed commune in the desert my entire life," I remind him.

"Well, it suits you."

"What does?"

"The ocean," he explains. "The wind in your hair. The moon in your eyes. Most of all, that dress. It suits you like you were born for it."

I blush and look down at my hands in my lap.

He's polite. Charming, even. But there's something about his manner that makes me wary. He's studying me. Hunting for flaws, vulnerabilities. He said he'd do whatever it takes to find out what's trapped in my head.

Just how far is he willing to go?

"What is the point of all this?" I ask, gesturing at the finery that surrounds us, my expensive dress, the silver cloches waiting on the table between us.

"The point?" he asks innocently. "We just got married. A honeymoon is in order, don't you think?"

I can't quite understand the bitterness in his voice. The barely concealed animosity that he slips between each word, bearing it like knife.

Why does it sound like he's angry at me?

"So," he starts, "what was life like growing up in the cult?"

I flinch at his hard tone, at the barely concealed accusation he's lobbing at me. "Subtle."

"I never claimed to be."

"Is this is your way of coaxing memories out of me?"

"I'm starting off nice. Just remember that."

"So you're threatening me, then. Not coaxing."

"I'm warning you," he clarifies.

I look around, feeling my appetite drain instantly. "I want to see my son."

Phoenix unfolds a napkin and lays it over his lap. "You will see him when I decide the time is right."

I stare at him, searching for the humanity I know is there. From the first moment I'd set eyes on Phoenix, I'd seen him only as a protector. He saved me twice.

This new version of him… I have no idea what to make of. There's a kind Phoenix and a cruel Phoenix. Which version is the lie?

"Why?"

"In the hopes that it will encourage you to remember certain things about the past you claim to have forgotten."

I suck in my breath. "Do you think I'm lying about it?"

He sits back and regards me with a thoughtful expression. "Undecided, as of yet."

I shake my head. "I swear to you, if I thought that the Sanctuary had anything to do with an organization like Astra Tyrannis, I… I…"

"What?" he demands. "Tell me, Elyssa: what would you have done?"

"Something," I finish lamely. "I would have done something."

"Everyone thinks they're a hero until the time comes for action."

I wince. It's as good as a slap in the face. I want to scream, to protest, to defend myself—but how can I? How can I say I didn't do anything when I don't even know what I did? What my family and friends might've done?

There's no telling what kind of sins are lurking in the black chasm of my memory.

"You told me that Josiah raped you," Phoenix says bluntly.

If the first thing was a slap in the face, this is a knife in the gut.

I rear back. "Excuse me?"

"Would you prefer a different word?"

"I…" I stiffen. He's accusing me of being weak. Of wilting from the reality of what I suffered through. "No. He did. It's the truth."

"And yet you went back to the Sanctuary of your own free will," he points out. "You agreed to marry the man you claim raped you."

My eyes sting with tears. "I had no choice…" I whisper.

"What was that?"

"I had no choice," I repeat, raising my voice and looking him directly in the eye. "Nor was I thinking clearly. I was alone with a baby to care for. Charity—my best friend, the closest thing to a sister I ever had—I'd just seen her dead body sprawled out across the floor with you standing over her holding a gun. I was heartbroken. When you kicked me out of the house, I got in the car and started driving. But then I realized that the duffel bag was gone. All the money was in there. I had nothing. So I looked at my son and made a decision. I chose to go back to the one place I knew would take me. And yes, I even agreed to marry Josiah. But… I didn't know how else I was going to survive. If it was just a matter of my future, it would have been easy. But I had my son to think of. Surely you can understand that."

He listens to me with a muted gaze. I can't tell what he's thinking.

But when he doesn't say anything for so long that I'm starting to writhe with anxiety in my seat, I break the pregnant silence.

"I know it looks suspicious that I went back. But I was feeling like… like maybe…"

I choke over my own words and flail around helplessly looking for a lifeline. There's none.

Steady on, girl. You don't have to keep defending yourself. You had your reasons. And they were the right ones.

"Yes?"

I take a deep breath. "I don't have to keep defending myself to you," I say, echoing Charity's words.

"Oh, I think you do," he says grimly. "And if you ever want to see your son again… you will."

11

ELYSSA

Can it be that, not too long ago, he was teaching me to float? Guiding me through the water with sure hands, with loving hands?

I can still spy glimpses of that man hidden behind the steel exterior of the don who now sits opposite me.

At least, I think I can. But it's hard to see past the fiery aura sometimes. He's both glorious and terrifying. Like staring into the sun.

"Why should I have to defend myself to you?" I shoot back. "You've already made up your mind about me."

"Is that what you think?"

"How am I supposed to think any different?" I finger the folds of my dress. "Even this dress is meant to make a point, isn't it? You can keep me from my son. Lock me in a room. Cut me off from my parents. Dress me up the way you want. Because you're the one in control. And I'm just a little doll for you to toss around."

"Is that your assessment?"

"What's yours?"

"That you've been a pawn in Astra Tyrannis's game all these years. That Josiah, that arrogant fucking wannabe Dalai Lama, is the puppeteer working on behalf of the powers that be."

"That doesn't make any sense. How would Josiah have helped—"

"By supplying them with women and children," Phoenix replies, cutting me off. "Breeding stock for those sick motherfuckers to sell like cattle at auction."

I open my mouth but snap it shut almost immediately.

That can't be true. That doesn't make sense.

No.

No.

No.

"Do you recall any young women leaving the community?" he presses through my haze of denial.

"I…" My heart is beating fast in my chest. Do I remember? Maybe. But what I remember most of all was how normal it always seemed.

Girls disappeared. Overnight, in the blink of an eye. One day, they were next to you at meals, at ceremonies, at sermons. The next, they were gone—and no one ever said a word. If you asked, you were told they'd been sent to where they were always meant to be. No follow-up questions permitted.

Funny how you can swallow down evil for so long that it starts to taste like anything else.

"Yes," I whisper. "I remember."

He nods, satisfied. "And you never questioned where they went?"

"It was… normal," I explain in a quivering voice. "They went… where they were supposed to go."

"And what about children?" he asks. "Were they 'supposed to go' somewhere?"

I rack my brain and try to remember. "I… I can't remember…"

"You can't?" he snarls. "Or you don't want to?"

I blink away the burgeoning tears and try to remember that I need to maintain strength in his presence. "Maybe both," I reply honestly.

"Tough. I'm not in the mood for games."

"That's the problem," I sob. "You see this as a game. But it's not to me. This is my life. It's my son's life. Why would I risk everything by lying to you?"

"It wouldn't be the first stupid decision you've made."

He has me there.

Stop it. You're letting your astounding lack of self-worth win. Fight back like I know you can. You're more than a doormat, Lys.

"You're right about that. I've made a lot of stupid decisions. One of which was trusting you."

Phoenix's eyes narrow resolutely. "Ironic."

"I hid things because I was trying to keep my son safe," I snap. "In my position, what would you have done?"

He doesn't answer. I take it as a win.

"Exactly! Because you've never been in my position. No, you've always had wealth and power and status. But not all of us are the children of powerful people. Not all our parents have armies ready to be deployed the moment we're in trouble. Hell, some of us wouldn't even get help even if that were true."

Phoenix's hand clenches the steak knife resting on the table. "You think my life has been easy?" he hisses, his tone dangerously low. "You think that just because I have money, that I don't have problems? That I don't have pain?"

I think about his dead wife. His dead son.

My heart aches for him. Truly, it does. But he's denying me the ability to give him the comfort I so desperately want to offer him.

"I understand that you—"

"You don't know a thing about me," he interrupts.

"And that's my fault?" I ask. "You're the one who keeps pushing me away."

"I don't need a fucking shrink."

"Then how about a friend?" I ask. "Or are you too proud for that?"

"I have a friend."

"Matvei works for you."

"Immaterial."

"Is it?" I ask. "Because I'm not sure I'd like playing second fiddle to my friend all the time. I'm not sure I'd like taking orders from a friend."

He tenses slightly. It's barely noticeable, but I'm paying attention now. I've stumbled across a truth I was never meant to know. Some fissure between the two men.

"We're not talking about me."

"We never really are, are we?"

"Stop." He waves a dismissive hand. "You're deflecting."

"We're always talking about me," I press. "But a conversation is a two-way street. A relationship is a two-way street. You have to give to get."

"Not in my world."

"Then it's not a conversation," I point out. "It's an interrogation."

His eyes narrow into furious slits. "Just be thankful your interrogation comes with a fancy meal and not a prison cell."

The moment he finishes speaking, the veranda doors are pulled open and two waiters emerge pushing a pair of trolleys. They approach the table, then work quickly and silently to unload the food for us.

It makes my eyes nearly pop out of my head.

A tower of lobster thermidor, dripping butter onto the rack of oysters on the half-shell laid out on ice beneath it.

Pan-seared scallops in a creamy mint sauce.

Lobster fettucine with paper-thin slices of truffle shaved on top.

Everything looks just as good as it smells. Phoenix accepts a bottle of wine from one of the servers and pours out two glasses. Then he nods and the two men slink off without a word.

He offers me a glass and I take it reluctantly.

"What would you like to start with?" he asks, gesturing at the dishes.

I'm still cagey after the argument ended so abruptly. "Whatever you want. You're in charge, aren't you, tough guy?"

He nods slowly. "Then I suggest starting with the oysters," he says. "You look like you need a good meal."

"What's that supposed to mean?"

"You've lost weight."

Do I detect a hint of worry in his tone? Surely not. That's just a mirage. A trick of the ear. The don doling oysters onto my plate doesn't care about my weight loss.

"I haven't been hungry lately," I mutter.

"Why is that?" He seems keenly interested, which is bizarre in its own right.

"Oh, gee, I don't know," I reply, not bothering to pare back the sarcasm. "Maybe it had something to do with the fact that I was marrying a man that I…"

"Hate?"

"Don't trust," I correct. "Which is ironic, considering that it ended up happening anyway. Just not the untrustworthy man I had in mind."

The comment doesn't seem to affect him at all. "If you cooperate, you have nothing to worry about with me."

"Cooperate?" I scoff. "That implies I have a choice. I can't remember certain parts of my past. There's nothing I can do to change that."

"You claimed not to remember the night you came to Las Vegas, either," Phoenix points out. "And you remembered that… eventually."

"That was different. You scared the memory out of me."

He smiles in the same bloodless way a shark would. "Is that what you need to motivate you? Fear?"

I feel my body stiffen. My thought jumps to one thing immediately: Theo. "Please don't hurt my son."

His eyes go wide for the briefest of moments. Like he never intended for me to interpret his threat that way. Like he's horrified that I think he'd ever lay a finger on Theo. But just like the concern I thought I heard in his voice, the expression is gone immediately. The ice-cold masks drops back into place.

"Eat," he commands.

I do as he says, but only because it's better than talking. For several long minutes, I sit there silently, tasting as much as I can. Only once I've satisfied my hunger do I look up.

Phoenix is watching me, a thin smile playing around the edges of his lips.

I blush furiously as I wipe my mouth on the pure white napkin one of the servers draped on my lap.

"Good?" he asks.

"Very," I reply. So much for keeping it cool.

"More wine?"

"No, thank you."

"Scared of what you might say after a glass or two?"

I narrow my eyes at him. "I can't say anything if I don't remember. We've been over this before. I'm starting to get a headache from going in circles so many times with you."

He doesn't say a word. But he does keep sipping his wine while he watches me.

"What happens next?" I blurt. "What's your plan?"

He tilts his head and looks at me in a new light. I'm sure he's about to tell me that it's none of my concern. But then, to my surprise, he sets his wine glass down and folds his hands in front of him.

"I'm going to start questioning your fellow sheep," he says. "We'll begin searching for linkages to what we already know. See what else there is to learn."

I swallow past a sudden lump in my throat. "When you say you're going to question them… what does that mean exactly?"

He raises his eyebrows. "Exactly that. Question them."

"And if they don't answer…?"

He shrugs. "Then there will be consequences."

"You're going to torture them?" I ask, immediately horrified. I may be disconnected from these people, but that doesn't mean I don't care what happens to them.

They may not have spoken up for me when I needed help. But I won't be so cruel as to return the favor.

"I'll do what I have to do."

"Phoenix," I say urgently, leaning in towards the table. His eyes go cold, as though he's anticipating my next words. "Please don't do this."

"Everything has already been set in motion, Elyssa. I'm not changing it even if I could."

"You're the boss," I protest. "You can change it at any time."

"These people that you think you love, you think you know? They are guilty of horrendous crimes. They've helped bad men do bad things. I'm going to make sure they pay for those sins. But first, I'm getting answers."

"What if they're innocent?" I ask.

He twists his lips. "They're not."

"What if they didn't know what they were doing then?"

"Ignorance is not an excuse."

"I can't lose them," I whisper through budding tears. "Not after I've already lost so much."

Phoenix's face is an impassive mask of cold cruelty. "Some things are worth losing."

"How would you know?" I ask. "You have the whole world in the palm of your hand."

"Except the things that are most important to me."

"Is that why you married me?" I blurt before I can stop myself. "To try and replace what you lost?"

He stops short, surprised. "Is that what you think?"

"In part. You wanna know what I really think?"

Careful, Lys. Don't push him too far. This might be a bad—

"I think that you want me to be Aurora. And you're furious that I'm not. And that's why you hate me. That's why you want to punish me. You think it'll bring her back in some insanely messed-up way. Or get vengeance for her to punish me for being someone I can never be. But I'm not your wife, Phoenix, remember? Not truly. I'm not anything to you. Aurora's gone and she's not coming back. I can't be her for you."

"I'm aware of that."

His words cut to the core of me, but I keep talking, because that distracts me from the ache in my heart.

"Your obsession with the people who took your family from you is making you lose your humanity."

"What makes you think I had any to begin with?"

"I've seen it," I say fervently. "I've seen it when you were holding Theo. When you were teaching me. When you were… inside me. It's in there and it wants out. You're just trying to keep it caged because you don't know any other way to live."

Something flashes across his eyes. "This conversation is over."

"You have feelings for me! For your son! You just don't want to admit it. Because you're holding onto ghosts that no longer exist."

"Stop talking about her!" he roars.

"I'm sorry you lost your wife, Phoenix. I'm devastated you lost your son. But you can't blame me for their loss. You can't take your anger out on me because you feel guilty for wanting to move on."

The spark in his eyes grows and grows and grows. Then suddenly, there's a blur of motion.

And the table is no longer in front of me.

I'm sitting there, looking at empty space as Phoenix leaps to his feet and catapults the table across the stone-paved veranda. Food and dishes crash and shatter.

Phoenix towers above, staring down at me, his gaze wild and filled with contempt.

I've woken the beast. There's nothing separating us anymore.

And yet somehow, I'm not afraid.

"What do you want from me?" Phoenix growls as he leans forward, plants his huge hands on the armrests of my seat, and thrusts his face into mine. "Huh? What the fuck do you want, Elyssa?" His voice breaks with pent-up fury.

"I want you to admit that there is something between us," I whisper. "I want you to admit that you feel guilty because of it."

"That's fucking bullshit."

"You're in denial."

"This is business," he growls. "This is war."

I shake my head. "It's not." The accusation comes out shaky and uncertain on my lips. But now that it's out there, I know for sure that I'm right.

Even if he doesn't yet.

"Okay. Fine. You want the truth?" Phoenix growls.

"Yes."

"There is something between us. And that something is sex. Do I want your body, your tits, your pussy? Yes. I want it all. And you want my cock. That's all this fucking is. Sex… that's all it ever was."

I shake my head and fight back tears. "No. No, that's not it. The first night we met, what happened between us… Sex isn't always just sex."

That was a Charity saying. *Sex isn't always just sex.* Depending on her mood, the punchline changed. *Sex can be power. Sex can be control. Sex can be a secret, a promise, condemnation or redemption.*

What she never said is what I want to say now: *Sex can be love. Sex can be hope.*

I open my mouth to voice those words. But before I can, Phoenix snarls wordlessly. He seizes my wrists in his grasp and drags me over to the edge of the veranda. Then he swings me around so that I'm facing him and pushes me backwards against the balcony.

I scream, but immediately, his fingers are around my throat.

"Go ahead and scream, little lamb. But no one's coming to save you," he hisses in my face. "You want to know how much you mean to me? Why don't I throw you over this fucking railing and show you?"

I tremble, unmoored by the rage displayed in his flawless face. He's so beautiful, even in anger.

"Please, Phoenix…"

"You wanted the truth, Elyssa. This is the fucking truth. You are nothing to me."

A tear slips from the corner of my eye. "Fine," I whisper. "You want to throw me off the balcony. Then do it. What are you waiting for?"

I don't miss the flash of surprise that darts across his eyes. His hand is painful around my throat, but I ignore it. He needs to rail at the world, and at the moment, I'm the only stand-in.

So I take his pain and make it my own.

"Or maybe you just want to kill me with your bare hands?" I ask. "That's fine, too. Go ahead. Just get it over with."

His eyes dim, but the rage simmers still. "I would," he replies, "if I didn't need you alive. But since you seem to need a fucking explanation, here it is: you and me are lies and deception and fucking sex. Not a goddamn thing more."

He releases my throat and his hand glides down my body. He fists the skirt of my dress and lifts it up.

A few seconds later, I feel his fingers against my bare skin, riding his way up between my legs. I've never felt so exposed.

I'm still bent backwards over the balcony, but he gives me no opportunity to change position as he slips his fingers inside me.

"Ahh…!" I cry out.

"See?" he growls, in my ear. "You're fucking wet. Because you know what I'm saying is true."

I cry out again as he starts finger-fucking me. "Oh God…"

"Don't call for him," Phoenix whispers. "He can't help you now. You're trapped here with the devil."

I cling to his wrist with both hands, trying to peel away his hand from my throat and failing miserably. The hum of pleasure between my legs is building and building—even when I'm trying desperately to clamp down on it. To make it stop. To prove that he's a liar, that he's wrong about this, that there's more here than two bodies craving each other.

But I can't.

I just can't.

"You used me for protection. You manipulated your way into my home."

His fingers circle my walls and I tighten around them involuntarily. My breath is coming in gasping spurts now.

"You used me again by claiming your child was mine."

He's brutal with me, sending alternating waves of pain and pleasure skirting through my spine until all I can do is latch onto him and pray that I'll survive his fire.

"You're trying to manipulate me again now. With lies and accusations."

I can feel my wetness slick against his fingers. The smell of sex competes with the smell of salt in the air.

"But this—your wet thighs, your aching pussy? Your body wants me. Isn't that right, Elyssa?"

I cry out despite myself.

"This. Is. All. We. Are," he growls, his lips pressed against my neck.

He bites down hard. I scream.

"We are sex. Meaningless, violent, cold, hard sex. Nothing more."

I can feel the orgasm claw its way to the surface and I chase the high of it. I need a release; I'm desperate for it.

"You want me to make you come?"

I can only stare back at him, my eyes hazy with lust…

And nod.

"Tell me," he croons. "Use your words."

I nod again frantically. "Yes."

He works his fingers even deeper inside me. "I want to hear you fucking say it. All of it."

"Make me come," I gasp. "Please…"

His eyes blaze for a moment. The peak of our fight. Sex and lust and anger all whirling together in an intoxicating mix, pushing me higher and higher and—

And then suddenly, he tears himself away from me.

"No."

I feel the emptiness, inside and out.

I collapse against the balcony railing as the orgasm fades away without ever truly cresting. Phoenix just stands there and stares at me coldly.

"Fix yourself up," he says, his tone black as midnight.

Then he turns and walks away.

"Guard!" he yells as he goes. "Get her the fuck away from me."

Only then do my tears finally come loose.

12

PHOENIX

Matvei finds me in my office. "Phoenix?" he says cautiously.

I turn from the window. "I hate this fucking room."

"You're the one that designed it."

"Years ago. But I've barely used it. Not enough to realize how flawed it is."

Matvei looks around with a frown. "What are the flaws?"

"The windows," I grunt. "There's going to be a lot of fucking light come morning."

He rolls his eyes. "Does every office space you own have to be depressing as fuck?"

"Yes."

He pulls the door shut and walks in. But he doesn't take a seat and neither do I. The air prickles with unspoken tension.

"Well?" I ask. "Give me your report."

"All of our prisoners have been confined to their cells in the bunker. There are armed guards stationed both inside and out."

"And the man of the hour?" I ask. "Where is he?"

"In the basement cell here," Matvei answers. "As per your orders, don."

I ignore the touch of resentment in his voice. "How are his wounds?"

"Healing. I've had him checked twice today. He needs more time to recuperate, though. The journey here really tired him out."

I scoff. "What a fucking pussy."

"You might be underestimating him, brother. He hasn't said a word in over twenty-four hours. Not even when the stitches ripped out and he started bleeding through his bandages."

"But he's alive?"

"Yes."

"Then I don't really care about the rest."

"My point is that it might not be so easy to get answers out of him."

"I'm not playing nice guy anymore," I snap. "He'll tell me what I want to know."

"Or else?"

"Or else I'll bury him like I plan to bury the men he works for."

Matvei's eyes grow distant. I don't like the look on his face, but I know that asking questions is just going to lead to answers I don't want to hear.

"How did the dinner with Elyssa go?" he asks, pivoting hard.

"It was fine."

"Jesus, that bad?"

I grind my teeth together. "I can handle her."

"Oh yeah, totally. You have my full vote of confidence in that department."

"I detect a note of sarcasm."

He holds up his hands in false innocence. "I would never." Then he drops them at his sides and his voice downshifts. "What happened?"

I contemplate telling him. But the truth is, I'm not sure I know what happened, either. One minute, I was poised, composed, fully in control. And then, in the blink of an eye, I had her bent back over the balcony railing with one hand around her throat and the other in her pussy.

"Nothing happened."

"Your mood suggests otherwise."

"Do you always have to be so damn nosy?" I snap. "This is none of your business."

"I am the fucking underboss of this little organization," he growls back. "And it used to be that this kind of thing was exactly my business."

"She's my wife now. That makes her my business and mine alone."

"Is that right?" Matvei presses. "She's your wife now, is she? Funny, I thought your marriage was meant to be a façade. A mind game."

"She can be both."

"I think the two things are directly antithetical to one another."

"If you're gearing up for a lecture, then at least pour me a fucking drink."

He grabs my shoulders hard in his hands. "Phoenix, I'll only ask you this once: do I need to be worried?"

I roll my eyes and swat his hands away. "What are you, my fucking mother? Even she hasn't suffocated me this much."

"Because she's not around to see how badly you're crashing."

"Crashing?" I growl, my eyes bugging out of the sockets.

"Yeah, that's right. Crashing. You're spinning out of control. You're letting your obsession with Astra Tyrannis overrule your common fucking sense."

"In what way?"

"In that you used to have some and now you have none."

I narrow my eyes at him. "I'm not losing anything. I know what I'm doing. You just need to trust me."

"I would trust you if you were honest with me," Matvei spits back. "Tell me the full truth and I might support you, instead of having to question what the fuck you're doing all the time."

"You want to know what happened?" I seethe. "I had her meet me for dinner on the veranda. We talked, ate, and then it… devolved from there. I held her over the edge, threatened to kill her, and when she called my bluff, I finger-fucked her until she was begging to come. Then I stopped just shy of her orgasm and left her crying on the edge of the balcony. That's what happened. Do you have any follow-up questions, *brother?*"

Silence ensues. Matvei looks horrified. "Jesus Christ, Phoenix."

"She's fighting back this time."

"I don't blame her. You wanted her to take your shit lying down?"

"Do I need to remind you that you're the one who wanted me to get rid of her?" I point out. "You're the one who believed she was a spy."

"Yes, and I thought you'd deal with her as a spy. But you decided to go and marry her. That changes things."

"Not necessarily."

"I see," Matvei says. "So you're toying with her."

I whirl around to face him. "What the fuck is your problem lately?" I demand. "You've been nothing but confrontational with me."

"Because you refuse to be upfront with me!"

"I wonder why," I drawl sarcastically. "I don't care to be questioned."

"That's exactly the goddamn problem."

I narrow my eyes at him. Matvei Tereshkova is my second. My underboss. The man I trust most in the world, as good as blood. But I can feel the chasm that's opened up between us. It's huge, gaping, and it doesn't look to be shrinking down anytime soon.

Bridges in my world are burning. God only knows if they'll ever be rebuilt.

Good thing I don't give a fuck anymore.

"I'm going to talk to Josiah," I snarl finally. "If you'd like to do your job, you're welcome to join me. If not, stay the fuck out of my way."

We stare at each other wordlessly. Chests heaving with barely restrained anger and adrenaline. We've fought before, Matvei and me.

But this… this is different.

In the end, he sighs and his shoulders slump forward. I take that as a sign of victory and stalk out of the office without saying anything.

Matvei follows me wordlessly down to the basement cell. It's a little colder as we descend. "Have a guard posted outside the door when I'm done with him," I order Matvei. Then, without waiting for his response, I yank open the door and stride inside.

Josiah is slumped in the corner, lying on his thin mattress in a fetal position. His face is drained of color, but his bandages are fresh.

Matvei drags in a chair for me, then backs away and lingers in the corner, observing. I set the stool down in front of Josiah's mattress.

"Josiah," I rasp. "Wake up. Time for you and I to chat."

He flinches at the sound of my voice, but his eyes dart open immediately. Wearily, he pulls himself upright and rests his back against the wall.

"Getting settled in nicely?" I ask.

He seems to sigh, but I don't see his shoulders rise or fall. There's a strange expression on his face. It's oddly vacant. Like he's looking at me, but not really seeing me.

"I'm here to continue that conversation we started earlier," I continue.

"I have nothing left to say."

"Do I have to remind you what will happen if you refuse to answer my questions?"

"I was weak before," he says with the kind of manic devoutness that only lunatics and cult leaders have. "I was taken unaware. I should have been stronger."

"Meaning you regret outing your bosses?"

He looks down and I see his jaw set with resoluteness. His silence is an answer.

"How did you get involved with Astra Tyrannis?"

"They came to me," he says shortly. "The powers that be heard of my calling and revealed their face to their prophet."

"And asked you to help them procure women and children for the meat market?"

His eyes flare up to mine, his expression twisting into disgust. "No, of course not! That's not what Astra Tyrannis is about."

I bark out a laugh. "You're kidding me, right?"

"Astra Tyrannis is run by powerful men," Josiah says. "I'm aware of that. But they try to help people."

"So the answer is yes—you're definitely fucking kidding me."

"They've helped the commune over the years. They've shaped the Sanctuary into the holy space it was always meant to be."

"How selfless of them," I declare, glancing back over my shoulder to shoot Matvei a look. "Tell me, how have they helped?"

"Money, of course. It is a foul thing, but no man can exist in this world without it."

"So they give you money. And what do you do in return?"

"Nothing! They ask for nothing in return. The powers that be are selfless and magnanimous."

I rock back on two legs of the stool and run a hand through my hair. "Do you really expect me to believe that?"

"They're our benefactors. They mean us no harm."

"What about all the women who've gone missing from the Sanctuary over the years?" I ask. "Explain that to me."

I'm distantly aware of motion in the corner. Matvei shakes his head and leaves the room, leaving Josiah staring after him like he's worried about ghosts hiding in the shadows.

His eyes eventually flicker back to mine. "There are no missing women. They made choices. They left of their own accord or they were cast out for their crimes."

"Which were...?"

"Adultery, violence, disobedience. There are many ways to displease our creators. We have a code we follow. Those who cannot live up to it have no place in our Sanctuary."

His answers come quick and easy. He's confident in a way he wasn't before.

But I don't believe a word that's coming from his mouth.

Matvei re-enters the room and hands me the file that my men have been compiling ever since I found the tattoo on Anna's corpse.

"Do you know what I have here?" I ask Josiah. "Any idea what this is?"

He shrugs but says nothing.

"Names," I tell him, leaning forward. "So many fucking names. Shall I read some?"

He shrugs again. I notice a bead of sweat gathering at his temple despite the chill in the room.

"Selah Samuelsson. Carys Overstreet. Clementina Elmore. Asriel Godfrey."

Josiah flinches at each one. He tries to hide it, but I see. I see fucking everything.

"You know these names, Father Josiah. Don't you?"

"Of course. Wayward or not, they are my flock; I am their shepherd."

I laugh. "That makes you a pretty shitty fucking shepherd. Because they're all dead. Just like every other woman in this folder. Dozens and dozens and dozens of them."

Unbelievably, the bastard has the balls to shrug again. "The outside world is a cruel place. That is why we built the Sanctuary—to shelter ourselves from its evils."

I feel sick to my goddamn stomach. "They were practically children," I seethe. I glance back down at the list and start reading. "Eighteen years old. Seventeen. Seventeen. Seventeen."

"The Sanctuary is an oasis," he says. "One drop of poison can destroy such a thing."

"They were innocent fucking girls!" I roar in Josiah's face. "You threw them out to the sharks."

His lower lip stiffens and he draws himself up as high as he can, given his injuries. "I would never do anything to harm my people."

"No? Then what would you call raping Elyssa? Is that 'protecting' her?"

He lifts his gaze to mine. Denial bubbles in his irises like venom. "I did no such thing."

"She didn't want your cock inside her," I hiss. "You shoved it in anyway. Should we consult a dictionary on the definition of the term, Father?"

"I had already taken her under my wing."

"What the fuck does that mean?"

"It means she was under my protection. Marked for me. She was as good as my wife."

"You're a delusional fucking psychopath. You forced yourself on her."

"And you didn't?"

His question hangs in the damp air for an uncomfortable moment.

"The fuck did you just say to me?" I breathe eventually.

"You claim I forced myself on her," he says, jutting his chin out at me. "Didn't you do the same when you forced her to marry you?"

This fucking bastard. I'm an inch away from strangling the life out of him. But I have to restrain my anger for now. He knows more than he's telling.

Easy, Phoenix, I tell myself. *Focus. Stay on track.*

"Are you the only one with direct contact to Astra Tyrannis?"

"Yes. The powers that be speak to the world through me, their prophet."

"Who do you meet with?"

"A man with no face."

"The fuck does that mean?"

Instead of answering, Josiah bends his head and starts mumbling words I can't quite catch.

Matvei moves forward. "You're losing him," he mutters to me.

"Like hell I am." I reach out and snare Josiah by the front of his shirt. Rising to my feet, I drag him up and shake him like a ragdoll.

But he looks right past me. Eyes pinwheeling. Lips moving rapidly in some silent mantra or prayer.

"What do you know about Aurora and Yuri?" I demand.

He keeps mumbling. A stream of shit I don't understand and don't want to understand.

"Answer the fucking question!"

More mumbles.

Furious, I hurl him against the wall with all my might. He cries out as he knocks his head against the stones. When he slides down into a whimpering puddle, I see a trail of blood left behind.

It only inflames me.

"Answer me, motherfucker!" I yell as I pounce on him where he's sprawled on the mattress.

I start punching him. He doesn't defend himself in the slightest. His nose breaks underneath my fist. Other things crunch and bleed. I don't stop. I don't breathe.

I just want to destroy.

I'm seconds away from completely ruining his face when an arm grabs my own, preventing me from landing another blow.

"Phoenix!" Matvei's voice lashes out. "Enough!" He hauls me up to my feet.

Beneath me, Josiah is a mess. His eyes are closed and to be honest, I'm not sure if he's unconscious or dead at this point. I'm not even sure I care.

I storm right out of his cell. Matvei is hot on my heels.

"Phoenix," he says softly. I know by his tone I'm not going to like what's coming.

"What?" I snap, not stopping.

"You've lost your way," he says. "That was all the proof I needed."

"You're wrong. I've never been more focused."

"Jesus Christ—you don't even see it, do you?" he says, running his hand over his dark hair. "You have been my brother and my closest friend all these years. But I'm not sure I can continue down this road with you, Phoenix."

At that, I stop and spin in place to face him. My brow furrows. "What are you saying?"

"I'm saying that I'm giving you a week to think about everything. If, by then, your plan of action hasn't changed, if you're not willing to listen to advice and think before you act… then I'm going to have to walk away."

"You're giving me an ultimatum?" I ask incredulously. "You can't be serious."

"It's a choice, Phoenix," Matvei sighs. "I'm tired of having no voice here. I can't sit idly by while you set the world on fire. And if that's going to continue, I might as well move on."

"So you're abandoning the cause."

"You won't listen to reason. You won't temper your emotions. And I'm not willing to watch it destroy you."

I stare at him for a long moment. He doesn't blink or break away. He's proud, certain, and haunted, just like I am. Like looking into a mirror.

"Fine," I snap bitterly. "You want to leave? Then fucking go. You don't have to wait for the end of the week. Door's open anytime you like."

Matvei nods slowly and somberly. As if he expected this all along, but he went through the pain of it anyway. For whose sake, I'm not sure.

Then he turns and heads towards the staircase.

I linger for a long time in the dark hallway, wondering if losing your way feels like madness. Because, if it does… maybe Matvei isn't so far off the mark.

13

ELYSSA
THE NEXT MORNING

Sighing with frustration, I put the book aside. I'm still on the first page of *Sense and Sensibility*. I've read the same paragraph five times over and still retained nothing.

I've been locked up in my room since the horrific dinner with Phoenix last night. Two expressionless guards escorted me back in rather forcefully. And when I was deposited into the room, I realized that the mess I'd created had been cleaned up. The room was back to pristine condition. Like I'd never even been here before.

It did nothing to soothe my nerves.

I've spent the last several hours trying to make sense of what just happened. Dinner had started out reasonably well. And then something had shifted. Phoenix has always been unpredictable. His moods shift like the wind. But I made the mistake of getting comfortable around him. Comfortable enough to show emotion, to get angry and fight back.

Not to mention your intense sexual attraction to him.

"Oh, God. Not now, Char…"

What? You can't deny it.

"It's more than just sex. I don't care what he says. It's more than just sex."

I've been reliving the fight over and over again in my head. The way he had grabbed me. The way he had dragged me to the balcony's edge and threatened to kill me. There was a moment I even believed he would.

Not true. He wouldn't have hurt you.

"You're defending him now, are you?"

No, you are.

"Can you be quiet for two seconds?"

Sure. Make me. I'm not really here, babe.

I sigh in frustration and run my hands over my face. Then I swing my legs off the bed and get to my feet. I'm desperate to see Theo, but after last night, I'm not sure I ever will. I just have to breathe through it. I know he's safe, wherever he is—for all his faults, Phoenix would never hurt an innocent child. But the mere fact that he's not here with me is enough to have me teetering on the edge of another panic attack.

Stop being a negative Nancy. You'll see Theo.

"When?"

Keep the faith.

I stare out the window, searching for any sign of my son. Of Phoenix. Of anything at all, really.

I hate that I still seek him out. I hate that seeing him still gives me some measure of comfort.

You're falling for him, that's why.

"He's a monster."

But he's your *monster. The first man you clung to. The first man you put your faith in. He saved you that first night when you came to Las Vegas.*

"He's not the same man he was then."

Grief can do strange things to a person. I mean, look at you... you're talking to a ghost that doesn't exist.

"I'm talking to myself," I whisper.

Sometimes, survival means compromising the rules of reality. You do whatever you have to do to get by.

"Okay, sensei…"

I imagine Charity's chuckle and my heart squeezes with the pain of her absence. I might not have felt so lonely if she'd been here with me in the flesh.

Through the haze of thought, I hear footsteps approaching my room. I turn around just as the door opens…

And Leona walks in with Theo in her arms.

I can't help screaming. "Theo!" I cry, rushing forward and lifting him from Leona's arms. "Oh, thank God!"

Is it possible he's grown in the few days since I last saw him? I hold him close, dropping kisses everywhere. On his cheeks, his forehead, his little button nose. I inhale his scent, wondering if it's changed or if I have.

"My boy," I breathe. "My sweet boy."

He gurgles up at me and I realize that I don't even need to support his head anymore. He can do it all by himself. When did that even happen?

Leona takes a seat on the chaise lounge seat by the window and kicks her feet up.

"He's been fussy the whole morning," she tells me. "This is the first time he's settled down."

I shoot her a glare. "I wonder why," I reply. "Being separated from your mother can't be easy for a baby."

She raises her hands as though I'm holding a gun at her head. "Hey, I don't make the rules."

"No, you follow them. Like everyone else in this place."

She doesn't seem at all put off by my anger. In fact, she almost seems amused by it. "I gotta earn a living, don't I?"

"Ever heard of waitressing?"

"The tips here are better," she replies. "So's the eye candy."

I roll my eyes. She does remind me a lot of Charity.

Except I was prettier. And had much better fashion sense.

I can't argue with that. Leona is wearing baggy jeans that look exceptionally comfortable and an oversized shirt with stains on the front.

"The eye candy?" I scoff. "If any of the guards in this place smile, their faces might crack."

Leona laughs. "I was referring to the boss man," she says. "If he weren't so scary, I might have made a move."

The jealousy I feel is instant. And I barely know what to do with it. I'm not experienced enough to know how to hide or control it. And I certainly don't have the presence of mind to pretend as though I don't care and just ignore the comment completely.

So I guess I shouldn't be surprised when I blurt, "Has it escaped your notice that he's married?"

She raises her eyebrows, but the smile stays plastered onto her face. "It's not a real marriage, though, is it?" she asks. "I mean, you've been locked in this room for eons and he's been moping around the house looking all hot and broody."

My fingers tighten around Theo. Leona notices.

"I'm sorry. I didn't mean to offend," she says. "I didn't realize there was something real between the two of you. You said yourself it was all a scam."

The thought of her relaying this conversation back to Phoenix makes me cringe inwardly. "There's nothing between us," I say repeating the words that he used on me not too long ago. "But it's just…"

"Yeah?" she persists. She's definitely enjoying herself.

"It's the principle of the thing," I reply, grasping for words. "You don't go after a married man."

She shrugs. "I don't like to play by the rules," she says. "I don't think he does, either."

I frown. Is she trying to goad me into a fight? It becomes more and more apparent from her smile that she's trying to seek out trouble.

"Having fun with all this?" I demand, turning to the window.

She laughs. "Oh, tons, believe me. I've spent most of my time lately hanging with a chubby little guy who doesn't say much in return. This is the longest adult conversation I've had in a while."

"So you decide to mess with me?"

She shrugs. "I'm just kidding around."

"Were you?"

She winks at me. "There's no denying that the boss is drop dead gorgeous. And he's got the whole alpha male, dominant streak that gets me going. But you don't have to worry about me encroaching on your man—"

"He's not my man," I say hurriedly. Fully aware that I'm contradicting myself ten times over in this conversation.

"Mhmm. Sure thing."

"I'm serious."

She rolls her eyes. "I see the way you look at him," she says. "It's not exactly subtle, you know."

My cheeks flame with embarrassment. If she noticed, how many other people had done the same?

"Why should you be ashamed of wanting him?" she continues. "Men never apologize for getting hard over some random girl who walks past them."

I sit down opposite her and adjust Theo on my lap. "Theo looks good. Happy."

"Are you changing the subject?"

"Absolutely."

She laughs. "You have the evening with him. Then I'm taking him back to our wing of the house."

"All I get is a few hours?"

"'Fraid so."

"That's not fair."

"I'm the wrong person to tell."

"You could speak to him for me."

"You trust me with your husband?"

"Stop it!" I glare at her.

She throws another chuckle my way. "Listen—I like you, Elyssa. You seem like a decent human being. But let's be clear here: we're not friends. And I'm not in the business of doing favors for anyone. I know it might not seem like it, but I take orders. And I follow them without question. So no, I will not speak to Phoenix on your behalf. You're gonna have to walk through that particular minefield on your own."

I sigh. "Well, then… thanks for nothing."

She just grins at me, unruffled and impossible to stay mad at. "He might need a bottle soon. I'll go get one."

Leona disappears through the door, but I'm willing to bet that she's just trying to give me a little alone time with my son.

I try to hate her, but it's genuinely hard. She's charming even when she's being irritating.

So I focus on my son instead. I walk him around the room. I tell him stories and when I've exhausted the space available to me, I set him down on the soft white carpet in the middle of the room.

He gurgles up at me and tries to turn onto his stomach. There are a few times he almost succeeds, but then he falls onto his back once more. I don't really care. I clap and cheer as though he's just won the Olympics.

Half an hour later, when Leona returns with a warm bottle, she joins us on the carpet as I collect Theo in my arms and offer him the bottle teat.

I'm pretty sure this isn't a biased opinion, but he really is a beautiful baby. I can't imagine him not being Phoenix's.

But then again, I've been wrong a lot lately.

Always so hard on yourself.

I glance at Leona, who's lying down on her back with her eyes trained on the ceiling, lost in her own world. When Theo's finished with his bottle, she gets to her feet and holds out her hands.

"What?"

"Oh, you know what," she says grimly. "I gotta take him and go."

"And if I say no?"

"Then I'll have to get the guards in here."

"You can't keep us separated like this."

"I'm just the messenger, hon. You have a problem with your situation? Talk to your husband."

Husband… the word still feels strange. It doesn't belong to me. I don't have one of those. I can't. I shouldn't.

Leona pries Theo from my reluctant arms and heads for the door, whistling all the while.

I stare after them, already feeling the weight of emptiness. I want to cry, but the tears won't come. I've spent them all already.

Tears are a waste of time anyway.

"It's all I have."

Stop playing the victim. You've got air in your lungs, don't you?

I'm not in the mood to bicker with a ghost right now. I get in bed and pull a pillow over my head, then just lay there in the darkness, waiting for the helplessness in my chest to subside.

It never really does.

I'm carried off to sleep feeling restless and unnerved. Charity's not in my dreams, though I search for her. I can sense Phoenix's presence, but I never see him, either. I suppose he's the monster inside me. And it's his weight that I feel pressing down on me, demanding attention, demanding answers.

Answers I don't have.

"Elyssa."

I gasp awake, my eyes flying open to see the face of the one monster I can't seem to hide from.

Phoenix is looming over my bed, drenched in midnight shadows. He doesn't apologize or explain his presence. He just straightens slightly and turns to the side.

"Get dressed," he says in a quiet rasp. "We're going for a walk."

"A… a walk?" I ask, in confusion, as I sit up. "What time is it?"

"Late."

He heads for the door without another word. I'm left sitting in bed, wondering if I'm still dreaming.

Trying to grapple with reality, I push away the last vestiges of drowsiness and swap out my sweats for a dress. I hurry into the bathroom to wash my face and run a brush through my teeth.

When I slip into the dimly lit hallway outside of my suite, he's leaning against the wall, waiting for me. There's no one else around. My guards are gone.

I expect to see impatience on his face, but all I see is a faraway look of contemplation.

"Phoenix?"

He meets my eyes. "Come."

His manner is unsettling. If he had been angry or accusatory, I might have felt slightly better. At least I would know where I stand.

But this—solemn, silent—makes no sense. Is he leading me to my death? The errant thought flickers across my paranoid subconscious. Once it's taken root, it's almost impossible to remove.

He leads me out of the house and towards the gardens at the rear of the house. Everything is dark, silent, and still. I've seen it from my suite window, I can't help admiring how pretty it all is now that I'm walking through the paths myself.

He picks his way with sure feet down the central path. I follow, mind still racing with questions. We reach a gate. He unlocks it and ushers me through onto the beach.

I might have been excited if Phoenix didn't feel so distant. So stormy. Something has changed since the last time we were together.

The sound of the ocean is louder and more aggressive than I would have thought. The rolling waves in the distance are black like oil. Overhead, the clouds form rheumy grey patterns in the sky. But as they move on, I catch glimpses of a crescent moon in the gaps.

My feet sink into the soft sand. Phoenix is walking quickly. I have to hurry to keep up.

It strikes me out of nowhere that following him might not be the wisest choice. And still, I can't stop.

"Where are you taking me?" I ask.

"You'll see."

Sighing, I push my windswept hair back, trying to get it out of my face. I can't help glancing over at Phoenix as we stride down the beach side by side.

His profile is perfect. The strong jaw, the straight nose, the slight shine of his dark irises. He's the most beautiful man I've ever seen.

And the most haunted.

A few hundred yards away in the darkness, I start to notice something. Broken shapes rising up from the earth like jagged teeth.

As we get closer, I realize that it's a building. Or at least, it used to be. Now, it's a charred disaster. Nature and fire have reclaimed whatever this place once was.

Phoenix stops suddenly and turns towards the ruins. I might be high on the strangeness of the moment, but I actually think it looks beautiful. In a sad, ominous kind of way. Not unlike Phoenix himself.

"This is what I wanted to show you."

I stare at him, not understanding. "A ruined house?"

"This compound used to belong to my grandfather, Joaquin Moreno."

I frown. "Moreno… You're Mexican? I thought you were Russian."

"Half-Mexican." He smiles darkly. "I favor my father's side."

I look back over at the blackened ruins. "What happened here?"

"It's a long story," he sighs. "One that'll take too long to retell. The important part is that my father is the one that destroyed this place. No one survived the attack… except my mother. He came, burned the place down, killed every living soul, and took her."

Just a few words and already the hair at the back of my neck is standing on end. "He… took her?"

Phoenix nods slowly. "My grandfather ran one of the largest cartels in Mexico. But he was blinded by all the wrong things. Ambition can strangle a man if he's not too careful."

"That's… a lot. I'm not sure I understand your point."

He sighs. "My grandfather chose the underworld over his family. He died for it. I did the same… and my family died for it."

My hand twitches towards him, but I stop myself before I touch him. We're on the precipice of something here. Something big. Something important.

"I know I've become obsessed with Astra Tyrannis. But I lost everything to them. Everything. Even now, I know I need to take a step back, but I can't. I can't let them get away with it. I can't let it go. I'm in too deep now."

"Why are you telling me all this?" I whisper.

"Because I want you to understand," he replies. "Why I can't let myself love you. Even though I want to."

How quickly everything can shift. In a matter of seconds, hope can be born.

"Phoenix…"

"You were right before," he says, cutting me off as though he's scared he won't be able to continue if he's interrupted. "There is something between us. Something more than sex. But I don't want it, Elyssa. I can't afford another weakness that Astra Tyrannis can exploit. I know how that will end."

"You don't," I insist. "You don't know. You'll protect me. And Theo."

"That's what I thought about Aurora and Yuri. I was wrong."

I can see the guilt in his eyes, the weight of his failure. He has never forgiven himself. Even now, all these years later, it runs in his veins like poison.

"I refuse to believe that."

He smiles. "You're still young…"

I shake my head angrily. "No. Stop treating me like a child. Stop treating me like I don't know any better. Stop acting like I don't have a say in this."

He sighs. "You don't."

I grit my teeth and let the anger crash over me. "You're wrong. Let me show you how much."

With that, I launch myself at him. As wise as he thinks himself to be, he doesn't see that coming.

My lips crash down on his and a second later, his arms engulf my body, lifting my feet off the ground. His scent mingles with the ocean salts and the ashy ruins and it all fills my nose, as intoxicating as a drug.

I can feel him. I can smell him. I can touch him. I can love him.

And for the first time in a while…

The voices in my head go quiet.

14

PHOENIX

Her lips seal over mine. She clings to me with more power than I knew she had—and I don't have the strength to push her off.

So I do what I swore I'd never do again.

I kiss her ravenously. I kiss her with every intent that this will be our last.

But even as I make the promise in my head, my will wavers, unsure if I'll follow through. Because she throws everything I've ever believed into question. She makes me feel as though giving up the chase is a viable option.

And I can't allow her to make me abandon my mission. The only thing that matters now is destroying Astra Tyrannis. Killing the people who stole my life away from me.

If I don't succeed in doing that, then she will be in danger for the rest of her life. So will Theo. I will have to relive the nightmare I lived through with Aurora and Yuri. And I'm not sure if I'll survive that pain a second time.

But for now—for this moment, if nothing else—none of that matters. Her lips are too comforting. Too fucking irresistible.

I lose myself in the moment as the wind laps around our bodies. I press my erection into her and she moans into my mouth.

My hand slides down her back. I try and memorize the curve of her spine, the way she's twisted her body into mine. If I never touch her again, I at least want to have the memory to comfort me.

It would take so little effort to part the fabric that separates us and enter her. To claim her again like I want to do every waking second.

She wants me. Every part of her body shivers for me.

But she doesn't know the risks. She doesn't understand this world.

She's bartering away her life without pausing to think of the consequences. She may think she wants me now. But will she still feel the same way in a year? In three? In five? When enemies are knocking down our walls and our children are in danger?

She might say yes to all of that.

But she doesn't even know the meaning of the word.

I allow my tongue to explore her for a moment before I pull away, tearing myself apart from her and setting her down on her feet again.

She still clings to me, but I push her away gently. "No."

She shakes her head. "What are you so scared of, Phoenix?"

"The past repeating itself," I reply. "You don't know what you're asking of me."

"There has to be more to life than revenge," she whispers, her eyes widening with hope and passion. "There has to be."

"Not for me," I tell her. "Not anymore."

Her eyes glisten with unshed tears. The wind laps at her face causing her hair to flutter off over her shoulders. She looks like a daydream come to life.

"Phoenix—" She reaches towards me, but I back away further. Her arm is left suspended between us. It falters slightly before finally dropping to her side.

"You don't understand," I say softly, gazing off in the direction of the ocean. It's easier than looking at those huge, amber eyes, filled with hurt. "I still remember the exact moment when I saw Aurora's body. It was obvious that she suffered before they snuffed her out. But the suffering didn't leave imprints on her body. It was her face. The expression on it…"

I notice that Elyssa's tears are falling fast now. But I keep going regardless.

She needs to know.

She needs to understand.

"When people die, everyone looks at their faces and they can say, 'He looks peaceful now,' or 'She's finally at rest'. You want to know that their suffering is at end. But when I looked at my dead wife's face, I didn't see peace. I saw pain and suffering and fear. And then Yuri… I never saw my son's body. I was denied even the opportunity to bury him. I raged and cursed about that for weeks, months after the fact. But in selfish moments, I'm thankful I didn't have to see what his face would've looked like. I'm not sure I would have survived it."

"You can survive anything," Elyssa says softly.

"You can't possibly believe that."

"I do."

I turn to look at her warily. "Why?"

She shrugs heavily, another tear dropping down onto her clothes. "Because I recognized something in you the night we met. It's the whole reason I gravitated to a stranger I should have been terrified of. Deep down, I knew I could trust you. You haven't lost your humanity, Phoenix. No matter how much you try to convince me otherwise, I refuse to believe it. But I do think you *want* to lose it. I think you believe that, if you lose that part of you that makes you human, you won't feel the pain anymore. The guilt."

I hear my blood rushing in my ears. Or maybe it's the roar of the ocean. I'm not sure. Nothing feels real anymore.

"But you deserve to move on," she adds.

I shake my head, rejecting the words immediately. "No. There will be no moving on for me."

"Please, Phoenix... Please don't push me away."

"I shouldn't have done this," I say before I can stop myself. "This was a mistake."

She goes still. "What are you saying?"

"I should never have married you. It was the wrong decision. But it can be fixed. Dissolved."

"Dissolved?" she repeats.

"I can undo it," I tell her. "And I can release you from your ties to me. To this whole situation. If you want to leave, Elyssa... I won't stop you."

She stares at me uncertainly. I want to shut up and accept what she's giving me. The absolution I've spent five long years craving and rejecting in equal measure.

But I can't. I don't know any other way to exist.

So I keep talking.

I keep pushing.

I keep saying "no" to a future that isn't dripping with pain.

"I'll give you money," I say hoarsely. "Enough money to start a new life somewhere far away. Away from all of this. I can buy you a new name, a new identity, a house, a car. Everything you need."

"Phoenix, you're not—"

"Think about it."

I start walking away down the beach. She just stands there, staring after me.

"You're leaving me here?" she calls into the breeze.

"You have a decision to make."

I know she's not following. I know she won't follow.

As much as I want to, I refuse to look back. If the choice I've given her is to hold any meaning, I can't keep reeling her back in.

∼

When I get back to the house, I go straight to the basement cell to speak to Josiah again.

I've been doing a lot of soul-searching in the last day since my argument with Matvei. I'm not so far gone that I don't see the truth in his warnings.

But my mind is made up. I've come too far to turn back now.

I will not abandon my attempt to destroy Astra Tyrannis and leave thousands of innocent souls at their mercy. My son and wife must be avenged. So too must all those faceless women and children whose lives were stolen and fed to the mill.

The task gives me purpose. Without it, I'd crumble.

I walk into Josiah's cell feeling more in control than I have in months. The rage is still there, but it's tempered now. Tamed.

Josiah snaps upright when I enter, fear pooling in his eyes. I pull up a chair and sit down opposite him.

"Don't worry," I tell him in a cool voice. "I just want to talk."

He looks down cautiously. "Okay."

"Viktor Ozol," I say. "Does that name mean anything to you?"

He shakes his head immediately. I pull out the switchblade knife I keep stowed away in my left boot. Flipping it open, I run it along my finger.

"On another night," I muse, "I'd wave this in your face and threaten you. I'd tell you which finger I'm going to cut off, which vein I'm going to slice open if you don't talk to me."

He blanches and swallows.

"But I'm not going to do that tonight, Josiah," I finish grimly. I flick the knife closed and stow it away again. "Tonight, I'm just going to ask you questions. And you're going to answer me. You're going to answer each and every one of those questions as fully and completely as you can."

My voice is steel itself. Cold. Unyielding. Josiah can feel the difference. I'm not an untamed fire anymore.

I am Don Phoenix Kovalyov and I am here to get what I want.

"Nod if you understand."

He nods.

"Good," I croon. "That's very good. Now, I'll ask again. Does the name Viktor Ozol mean anything to you?"

"He's... one of the powers that be."

"And you've had contact with him?"

"Sometimes," Josiah replies, trembling slightly. He hugs his body close, his eyes darting around the room as though searching for an escape hatch he will never find. "He usually sends emissaries in his place. But... sometimes I speak to him."

"And he gives you money?"

"Yes."

"In exchange for?"

"For... help."

"What kind of help?"

"Rehabilitation."

I raise my eyebrows. "Rehabilitation?"

"Some of our young women need some extra help to be put on the right path," he says. "Mr. Ozol makes sure they get the help they need."

"So you give innocent young girls to a man like him. A man you barely know."

"It's not like that," Josiah protests. "The women are treated well. The place they're taken to is a special place. A healing place. A holy place. They're safe and happy there."

"How do you know?"

"Because I've seen it with my own eyes. If you don't believe me, ask Elyssa."

I stop short, my blood running cold. I can see it on his face: He was lying the last time we spoke.

He's not lying anymore.

"Ask… Elyssa?"

"She knows. She's seen it. She helped rehabilitate the women. She helped take care of their children…" He trails off, watching the expression on my face. "She didn't tell you?"

I can't remember. I'd tell you if I could…

I feel my throat constrict. But I'm not sure what I'm feeling. Is she playing me? Is she just a skilled actor, like Anna was? Or is she just as much a victim as all the women who fall prey to Astra Tyrannis's dealings?

What is hiding in her broken brain?

I can't say. And it's driving me fucking crazy.

"How long?"

"What?"

"How long was Elyssa doing this work?

"A year? Two?" Josiah guesses. "Maybe more. I can't remember. But if you ask her, she'll tell you. It's not a—it's not what you say it is. It's a place where women can start over."

I get to my feet and move towards the door. I've had enough.

"Wait!"

I turn back slowly. Josiah's leaning forward, his eyes wide with hope. "I… I gave you what you wanted. I answered all your questions. Does that mean you'll let me live?"

"For now."

Relief floods across the man's face. He's aged decades in the last week since I arrived at his precious little Sanctuary. Not so long ago, he had the appearance of someone respectable. Now, he looks like hell warmed over.

"Thank you," he whispers.

I shake my head coldly. "Don't thank me just yet."

The relief dies slightly on his face.

"Answer me this," I say. "Why?"

"Why what?" he asks in confusion.

"What is the point of all this?" I demand. "Removing women to this other location, taking their children. What was the point?"

"To cure them, of course," he says as if it's obvious.

"Of what?"

"Sin," he replies.

Again, the irony, the hypocrisy of his statement seems completely lost on him. He's as brain-washed as the people that follow him. A cult through and through.

"And what about *your* sins?" I press. "How will you atone for them?"

"The powers that be are my judges. They will reward or punish me as they see fit. Men like you…"

I laugh. "What about 'men like me,' Father Josiah?"

"Men like you wouldn't understand," he finishes. "Men like you don't see the true purpose of our existence."

"Which is what, exactly?"

"To reform the world in their image."

I shudder. If he thinks Viktor Ozol is reforming the world in God's image, he'd better think again.

"I won't kill you, Josiah," I tell him softly. "But I'm not setting you free either. You reap what you sow."

"I've answered all your questions," he says desperately. "I've done everything you asked of me!"

"You did. But you haven't atoned for your sins. This cell is going to be your home from now on. Death is coming for you, Josiah. You want out? Pray to your gods for a miracle."

I slam the door shut on him and head back upstairs. I wonder what I'll find up there. I gave Elyssa the choice of leaving. What if she's already gone? What if she took the answers I need with her, locked away in her blacked-out memory?

Elyssa knows. She was there...

What the fuck does that mean?

I'm about to find out.

―

I left her down by my grandfather's ruined empire more than half an hour ago. She could be anywhere by now.

But it doesn't take me long at all to find her near where we parted.

The moon is out from behind the clouds now, illuminating her hair into threads of gold. My heart throbs painfully at the sight. Within minutes, we come face to face. Her expression is soft with thought, but she smiles when she sees me.

"I'm not going anywhere, Phoenix," she says fiercely before I can speak. "This is where I want to be. I know the risks and I choose to stay anyway. I choose you."

I stare at her.

Her expression falters. Clearly, this is not the reaction she's expecting. "Phoenix?" She reaches out and takes my hand.

My arm twitches and I'm suspended—as always—between wanting to pull her towards me and wanting to push her away.

"I'm going to ask you one more time, Elyssa," I say softly. "What aren't you telling me?"

15

ELYSSA

His fingers slip out of my grasp. I'm not sure if I've let him go or if it's the other way around.

"We're back to this again?" I ask, the last of my lingering hope draining away into the darkness.

His eyes are cold, but I see the conflict raging there. "You don't get to be angry," he tells me. "You don't get to feel betrayed."

I look away from him so he can't see my angry tears. "And you don't get to tell me how to feel."

"I'll stop telling when you start telling the whole truth."

His eyes sear through me. Trying to rip me apart piece by piece. Trying to uncover my secrets.

I wish I could tell him, *Look all you want. I can't even find them myself.*

"I spoke to Josiah," he rumbles. I can't help flinching. Bad move. Phoenix notices. "Scared about what he might've said about you?"

I nod and shiver. "Yes," I say in as even a voice as I can muster. "But not in the way you think."

"No? Tell me more."

"What's the point?" I ask angrily. "You won't believe me. You don't trust me."

"The point is that you don't get another option, little lamb."

His eyes are hot coals in their sockets. Despite the chill in the air, a bead of sweat trickles down the nape of my neck.

"I don't even know what I might have done," I whisper so quietly I can barely hear myself. "If I made mistakes—well, I didn't know that that's what they were. I just did what I was taught. You have to believe me."

It's getting impossible to keep the quavering out of my voice. Fighting like this? It isn't natural to me. It hurts on a soul-deep level. I've never had to do it myself.

There was no fighting on the Sanctuary. It was heaven on earth, we were told. What could there possibly be to fight about?

And then, after I ran, I had Charity. She fought my battles for me. I had relied on her too much. Maybe I'd even taken advantage of it.

Now you're just being silly, she croons in my ear.

"You're not really here," I whisper.

"What?" Phoenix says, reminding me that I'm not alone on this beach.

I raise my eyes to him, terrified of seeing the expression in his gaze, knowing I can't avoid it. "Phoenix…" I whisper. "I don't know what I've done." My voice breaks with trauma. I say it again: "I don't know what I've done."

This is all too much. The world is starting to blacken and swirl around the edges. My knees buckle and I sway back. Before I can crash into the sand, Phoenix's arms flash out and grab me.

When he pulls me forward, I slam into his hard chest but I don't fight his touch. It's the only thing that's keeping me sane right now.

His fingers curl around my jaw and coaxes my face up to meet his own. His eyes are still cold, his expression still conflicted.

I don't know how to make that go away. But God, I would if I could.

"It's in there somewhere," he says, tightening his grip on my jaw. "Think. Remember. Tell me what you know."

I taste blood. I put a hand on his chest and shove away from him. "I can't give you what you want."

"Can't?" he asks. "Or won't?"

"Why are you so sure I'm one of the bad guys?"

He scoffs. "You've given me every reason to believe it."

"What are your instincts telling you? What is your heart telling you?"

"My instincts?" he repeats in disbelief. I can tell he's not sure whether to laugh or get angry.

"Yes," I plead desperately. "Look at me. Look at me and tell me what you see when you look at me."

He does exactly that. I want to look away, but this is too important to break the moment. I have to stand in the furnace of his gaze and suffer—for him. For myself. For Charity. For my son.

And as I brave the pain of seeing the father of my son stare at me like I'm the one responsible for tearing his world to pieces, I feel it in my chest: hope.

A tiny blossom of hope. Like the first spring flower pushing up through the frozen winter ground.

Say it's okay, I beg Phoenix silently. *Say you forgive whatever I might've done. Say you'll help me fix it.*

Oh God, say anything.

Say anything.

Say anything.

"I see a broken liar," he replies at last.

And just like that, the flower dies.

I turn around and start running in the direction I'd just come from. I don't hear anything apart from my own heavy breaths and my frantic heartbeat, but I know he's following me. Hot on my trail, furious and all-powerful.

A second later, he grabs my arm and spins me back around. "You can't outrun your past."

I shove him, even though I know it's useless. "I can try."

He shakes his head. "It's not possible. I've tried to do the same. It always ends up catching back up to you."

"So what do I do then?"

"Stay," he replies. "And face it."

"I'm not strong enough."

It's probably just my imagination, but I feel his eyes soften. His hand lands on my jaw again, but this time, it's so gentle, so soft, that I barely feel it.

"Most people are stronger than they think," he says.

Is there hope in that sentence? Is there absolution? Maybe. Just maybe.

But I'm scared to take it. Scared that taking it will mean it'll inevitably just hurt more when I lose the lifeline he's throwing me.

I relied on Charity. I can't allow myself to rely on someone else who might leave me one day.

"I'm not most people. I grew up in… in… in a *cult*," I say, wrenching the harsh word from my soul. "I believed the lies they fed me and thanked them for it. I only left because I was scared of the way they would look at me. The way you're looking at me right now…"

"How am I looking at you?"

"Like… like you don't know what I'm capable of," I stammer. "Like you don't know if you can trust me. Like you wish you had never known me."

"Is that what you see on my face?"

"Yes."

"Then you're letting your fears rule you."

"Fear is all I have left."

"Push it away now. It's useless."

"I don't know how."

He stares at me for a moment, his fingers still caressing my jaw. Then he says, "I'll show you."

And before I can process his words, his lips fall against mine. There's tenderness there, some anger, and a whole lot of frustration. I feel the passion and the tension that's been building between us steadily over the past several weeks.

His fingers tighten around my neck, but for once, I'm not scared about being hurt.

Some kinds of pain can heal.

I press my body against his, grappling with the collar of his shirt, desperate to cast it aside. He seems to know what I'm thinking, because a second later, he pulls it off and throws it down on the sand.

Then his hands land on my dress, and he starts tearing it apart like a savage. Buttons pop, clasps come undone, fabric rips, and the sea breeze kisses my bared skin.

When we fall back against the soft, fine sand, I feel his hard length against my thigh. His fingers push aside the fabric of my panties and he explores the folds of my flesh.

I'm wet, trembling, and desperate to feel him inside me. My head is in tatters, utterly confused as to how we could land here after the number of detours we'd taken.

It doesn't matter, Charity whispers in my mind. *Fuck when you're horny. Make love when you need to feel less alone.*

His lips leave a trail of heat down my neck before landing on my breasts. I gasp with want as he rips my bra off and tosses it aside.

Then his lips fall over my nipple and my eyes close in rapture. I grip the back of his head as he sucks me into his mouth, unleashing a shiver that travels all the way down my spine before settling at my toes.

Before I can recover from the feeling, he pushes his cock inside me.

My eyes flash open and I catch a glimpse of the endless midnight sky hanging over us. The stars wink at me, and I shudder at the tentative happiness that's sneaking into my heart.

Happiness is dangerous. Mostly because it can never last. Particularly not here. Not in this place. Not with this man.

But I can't stop it.

Because I am weak, maybe.

Or maybe because I'm just sick of being so scared all the time.

So I part my legs further and invite him in. *Push it away now,* Phoenix told me. *Your fear is useless.* He slams into me—once, twice, again and again. Pleasure floods my senses and crowds out every other emotion that threatens to break the moment.

His body feels gigantic over mine, but I long for the heat of him. The strength of his hips, driving against mine.

I realize a second later that I'm moaning. I have no control over myself. He has me untethered. It almost feels like I'm flying. Like I've thrown off the fear as if it was useless ballast and I'm soaring up and up and up.

But when the orgasm looms on the horizon, the fear resurfaces immediately.

Phoenix notices. He doesn't stop thrusting. But he takes my cheeks in one massive hand, presses his forehead against mine, and whispers in that hair-raising voice of his, "Stop, little lamb. Stop thinking."

I can feel myself at that crossroads. Fear and overthinking lie in the one direction. I'm not exactly sure what the other path holds. Hope? Bravery? A future? I can't be sure until I walk it.

For right now, I want to fly.

So I close my eyes and throw myself off the cliff of the moment.

Seconds later, I come harder than I've ever come in my life. He does, too. We ride the waves out together, clinging to one another as if we're the last two souls alive.

His breath heats my neck as he sinks into me. I'm not sure how long we lie there. When he finally gets to his feet, I sit up in the sand.

Phoenix dresses quickly. Once he's ready, he turns to me and offers me his hand. I stare at him in disbelief. Wondering if all the hope I deluded myself into seeing was nothing more than a mirage in the desert.

But that hand is there. That hand is real.

"Come on," he says impatiently.

"Where are we going?" I ask.

"Home," he replies. "We're going home."

I know he doesn't mean it the way it sounds. But I hold on to the words anyway.

Home and hope are funny things.

16

ELYSSA

I wake up to the sound of a baby crying.

"Theo?" I cry, darting upright in a bed so comfortable that it takes actual effort to pry my eyes open. The sheets enveloping my body fall away to reveal my nakedness.

I feel sore all over, but especially between my legs. It's a comforting ache, though. Not unpleasant.

The echo of a crying baby still rings in my ears as I try to get my bearings. Then I feel a hand graze my back and I twitch with shock as I crane my neck to the man lying next to me in bed.

Phoenix's eyes are hazy with sleep. "Elyssa?" he mumbles. "Everything okay?"

His hand is still on my back, running up and down my spine. His touch is warm, but the tension doesn't leave my bones.

I spent the night with him.

In his room.

In his bed.

And not because he made me do it. I chose this.

He had led me upstairs after we returned from the beach last night and stopped at the landing. "My room is that way," he'd said. "But I can take you to yours instead. If that's what you want."

I shook my head at once. "Take me with you."

He didn't answer. Just nodded once and turned in the darkness. I followed.

We'd showered together in silence with the lights off, just peals of steam rising through the shadows and the harsh slap of our hips meeting as he took me against the slick tile wall.

Once we rinsed the sand from our bodies, he'd carried me to his bed and gone down on me until I came so hard my calves cramped.

My legs tingle at the memory. I feel the blush creeping up my cheeks. The shame I learned as a young girl still hasn't left me, even as Phoenix has taught me all the things our bodies are capable of.

"Elyssa?"

His voice snaps me back to the present. "I'm fine," I replies. "I just... I keep hearing Theo."

"Theo?"

"He's crying for me. Don't you hear that?" I ask, my head snapping to the side as I hear another distant cry.

Phoenix sits up straight. "I don't hear anything."

"You don't hear that? A baby crying?"

"No."

I frown. "I think Theo needs me."

"Theo's fine."

"How do you know?" I ask impatiently.

He doesn't seem turned off by my tone. Instead, he reaches out and picks up his phone from the bedside table next to him. "Because if there was a problem, Leona would have told me."

"And has she?"

He glances at his phone and starts reading out loud for my benefit. "1:25 A.M.: I changed his diaper and gave him a bottle. Little tyke hates sleep. 5:47 A.M.: Woke up again demanding more milk. I made eight ounces, but he only drank five. Tiny bastard. 6:53 A.M.: If I never change another diaper in my life, it'll still be too soon. I'm going to look fifty by the time I'm forty at this rate. You're not paying me enough."

I can't help smiling. "Those are... colorful reports."

"She should have been a poet."

He delivers the line with such seriousness that I actually burst out laughing. A second later, he cracks a smile. He doesn't exactly look comfortable doing it, but he does look beautiful.

"They'll both be sleeping now. She texts me the moment they wake up every morning."

I'm surprised at the extent of the tabs he's keeping on both Leona and Theo. But I can't deny it puts me more at ease.

Somewhat.

"Why are you keeping me from him?" I ask boldly.

I know I'm risking the fragile truce we've called. I also know that it can break at any moment. But I have to take the chance.

Phoenix doesn't really respond, apart from sitting up more against the headboard. He looks relaxed, but I can see the tension rippling in his broad shoulders.

"I was trying to make a point," he rumbles.

I sigh. "You were trying to show me that you were in control. That you had all the power and I had none."

He doesn't deny it.

"He's my son, Phoenix," I whisper. "The most important thing in the world to me. He was the thing that kept me going on my worst days, in my darkest moments."

He nods, but doesn't offer up his thoughts. Despite the intimacy of our current placement, I can feel the distance seeping back in between us. His automatic reaction: retreat behind anger, behind coldness, behind the stone wall of indifference. And I'm desperate not to let that happen. Not again. Not anymore.

I reach out and put my hand on his chest. His eyes flit to mine.

"I know I haven't given you many reasons to trust me," I say. "I know that finding out about Anna was a shock. I don't blame you for being cautious. But I'm not lying to you, Phoenix."

He watches me carefully. Waiting. Listening.

So I continue. "My memory is patchy. It's a form of self-preservation, I think. I'm terrified of what I can't remember, so terrified that it just won't come to me. But that doesn't mean I don't want to remember. If I helped those... those *motherfuckers* in any way... it wasn't with my knowledge or my consent. You have to believe me."

The corner of his mouth turns up in the tiniest smirk when he hears me curse. But his eyes are as steely as ever.

I need him to understand. And more than anything, I want him to believe me.

"I do believe you," he says finally.

As much as I'd hoped, I'm not prepared for that response. "You... you do?" I gape at him, unsure if I've misheard. It feels like so much of our relationship has been built on mistrust.

Take that away, and what do we have? *A future?*

"I probably shouldn't ask," I admit. "But what changed?"

"Maybe nothing," he says with a shrug. "I just decided to trust you. Time will tell if that's foolish or not."

I tighten my grip on his arm and he pulls me a little closer into his embrace.

"I'm sorry I've kept you from Theo," he says softly. "That changes now."

"You'll let me see him more often?"

"As much as you want," he says. "It was wrong of me to separate the two of you. But I was…"

"Angry."

"Yes," he says, with a nod. "I'm used to running things with an iron fist. I don't have the delicacy it takes to handle parenthood."

His words are laced with guilt. I know exactly who he's thinking of when he makes that admission.

"Hey," I say, leaning into his chest and settling into the crook of his arm. "You need to stop blaming yourself, you know."

"Do I?"

"Is that why you don't really look at Theo? Or hold him or spend time with him?"

I'm not trying to make him feel worse, but I can tell that's exactly what I've gone and done. His eyes go cold again. His touch retreats.

"Phoenix, I'm sorry—I didn't mean—"

"It's okay," he says abruptly, cutting me off. "It's a fair question."

"You don't need to answer it," I insist. "I shouldn't have—"

"You may have a point," he interrupts. "But then again, we don't really know if Theo is in fact mine."

I cringe back, irrationally hurt by his words. He has every right to wonder. Every reason to want to know.

"We can get a paternity test," I point out, swallowing the hurt.

Phoenix looks away from me. "We could. But then we'd know."

Then we'd know.

I look down at our intertwined hands. The truth is so fickle, so fragile. How can it be so powerful at the same time?

We're living in the gray space right now of "not sure." And as long as we're here, there's still hope for a happy ending.

But if we step out of that… the world becomes black and white. Things take on harsh edges. And the truth overrides everything.

It's a double-edged sword. Can I live with myself if it cuts me wide open?

"I don't know what to do, Phoenix," I admit.

He looks at me expressionlessly. "We'll figure it out."

I give him a tentative smile, taking the comfort without question.

He leans in a little and I meet him halfway.

Our lips meet and I feel my body tingle with anticipation. The tension and worry that clung to me only moments ago seems to dissipate instantly. I can still hear echoes of crying babies, but I decide that it was just a dream.

The panic in my head is imagined. Or… is it a memory trying to resurface?

I jerk away from Phoenix's lips suddenly, my heart thudding hard against my chest.

"Elyssa?"

"Sorry," I mumble. "I just…"

"He's safe with Leona," Phoenix assures me, misinterpreting my reaction. "You don't have to worry. I know it's a hard ask given what happened with Anna. But—"

"I'm fine," I insist hurriedly. "I just… It's nothing."

"If it's bothering you, it's not nothing."

I take a deep breath and clutch his hands in an attempt to keep myself from losing my grip on reality. I'm still trying to arrange my thoughts when his lips come down over mine. There's nothing gentle about this kiss. It's demanding. Aggressive.

And it's exactly what I need to distract me from the disconcerting sounds in my head. The irrational panic that's threatening to ruin the perfect little slice of heaven we've carved out in this room.

He pushes me back against the bed and rips the sheet from around my body, leaving me exposed beneath him.

His hands run down the side of my body and pulls up my ass so he can cup a cheek as he kisses me. When his fingers slip inside my wet folds, I'm already breathless.

The worry has once again receded, and it's easier to ignore the nagging at the back of my mind. When I melt beneath him, it's easy to pretend that everything in the world is in its rightful place.

I'm expecting him to enter me the way he always does. My legs part accordingly.

But instead, Phoenix flips me around with one huge paw, practically knocking the wind out of me, before he grabs my hips and pulls me onto all fours.

His hands graze my ass as he stares down at my back.

I can feel his eyes. I can feel the length of his cock rubbing between my ass cheeks.

Trembling, I fist handfuls of the sheets beneath my fingers. I'm more aware, more present this morning—and that just makes me more nervous.

Last night, I was riding the high of too many emotions. It was easy to channel that abundance of feeling into sex. But in the light of dawn, with my emotions tempered and pulled thin, I'm conscious of myself in a way I wasn't last night.

"Relax, Elyssa," he whispers. "Stop thinking."

A second later, he pushes into me from behind. I close my eyes as a soft gasp leaves my lips.

The man makes my head spin and my eyes water.

It's not emotion—it's delirium.

I've never felt quite so full as when he's inside me. I lose my sense of self-consciousness in that wild and unadulterated moment. I just give myself over to him with complete devotion, complete submission, complete sacrifice.

And my body rewards me by clenching so tight in an orgasm that I wonder if I'm going to shatter. He pounds me all the way through it, each thrust pushing me higher and higher up on that wave.

I fall from him, twitching and gasping. Every sensation melts together in one hazy blur. Once my breathing has calmed, I turn my face towards him, hair falling over my eyes.

With one corner of his mouth turned up, he pushes the hair away.

"You okay?" he asks.

I blush instantly and he smiles. He's teasing me. Actually teasing me. And it feels good.

I sidle in closer to him and he wraps his arm around me. I notice him lean in a little as though he's about to kiss my forehead. But he stops short of doing so.

Baby steps, I tell myself. *Be patient.*

But now that the high of desire has been sated, the worry and panic start to creep back in again.

We may be married. But that's nothing more than a paper shield. One that can be cast aside the moment that I make a misstep.

Or, even worse… the moment I finally recall the missteps of my past.

"You're thinking again," he points out, forcing me back into the moment. "How about we go for a walk on the beach?"

I smile. "Really?"

"Yes," he says, swinging his legs out of the bed. "We can take Theo with us."

My face brightens instantly. "We can?"

He chuckles. "Yes. Why don't you go shower and I'll send Leona a text?"

I practically vault out of bed and into the bathroom. Closing the door behind me, I crank the shower to its hottest setting and brush my teeth while steam rises to the ceiling. When I get in, I sigh deeply as the hot water hits my sore skin, ironing out my muscles like a massage.

Be careful.

I still instantly. The buoyancy I'd been riding only seconds ago withers on the vine.

"I am being careful."

You're starting to imagine a future with him already.

"No, c'mon, that's not true."

You realize you're lying to yourself right now, right?

I take a deep breath. "Things are changing between us. He believes me."

And what happens when you get your memory back? You know it's coming. Slowly, but it's coming. You can't hide from it forever.

"Stop," I whisper, making the water even hotter.

Pain ripples across my body. I welcome it.

Lys, you—

"Stop!"

I'll worry about all of that later.

For now, I'll think about Phoenix. I'll think about Theo. I'll think about this ivory slice of Pacific beach, where the palm fronds blow in the ocean breeze and everything is right and good and perfect.

17

PHOENIX
THE NEXT DAY

He's a big kid. A happy one, too.

Or maybe that's just because he's cocooned in his mother's arms at the moment.

Can't really blame the tyke. His mother's arms are fucking addictive. I've fucked her at least four times in the last twenty-four hours and I'm still hungry for her.

Every time the neckline of her dress shifts to reveal the swell of one of her breasts, I have to fight the hard-on that's been threatening since we finally left the bedroom.

Theo tries to grab her nose and she giggles and kisses his little palm instead. The two of them murmur nonsense back and forth to each other. I'm content to watch. To hang back and enjoy the radiance of her happiness. Of his. Of theirs—a family the whole world wants desperately to tear apart.

"You cheeky boy. You're the cutest little baby in the whole wide world. Yes, you are. Yes, you are!" she coos at him. He giggles as she blows raspberries on his stomach.

Then he turns his dark brown eyes on me and the laugh fades at once.

In that gaze, for one bizarre moment… I see myself. As good as looking at my own reflection.

It hurts. Well, not quite hurts. But an intensely physical pang all over my body. A head-to-toe clench like being electrocuted.

And I turn away instantly.

"Do you have to go to work today?" Elyssa asks tentatively.

"I decided to take a day off," I explain. "I thought I'd spend the day with you and Theo."

Her eyes go wide with surprise and barely concealed happiness. "That's… wonderful," she says at last.

"Maybe more than a day off," I add. "Maybe something like… a break."

At that, she stops in her tracks. Theo tugs at her hair, but she barely even notices. "A break?" she asks.

I nod slowly. This whole thing has been formulating in my mind, but it's the first time I've said any of it out loud. After the fight with Matvei, the fight with Elyssa… something shifted in me. Like a log in a campfire crumbling and letting cool, fresh air into the heart of the flames.

"But what about the bunkers? You have a lot of people in there."

"I haven't made definitive plans yet," I admit. "But at some point, they'll be moved back to the valley."

"You're just going to dump them back where you took them?"

"Not quite. I plan to rehabilitate all of them," I tell her. "And Josiah will not be the leader anymore."

Elyssa frowns. "What will he be?"

"My prisoner. Until I decide what to do with him."

"You're not going to release him?"

"No. The man's too dangerous. And he might still be valuable," I explain. "In any case, I'm not abandoning my goal to take down Astra Tyrannis. I'm merely taking a step back so that I can give myself some objectivity. Once I've got my head on straight, I will go after them. And I will destroy them once and for all."

She looks shocked, but I notice the fear creeping into her eyes. "And what about my parents?"

"They will be returned to the commune, same as everyone else," I answer. "And they will be rehabilitated, same as everyone else."

She nods slowly as though she's trying to process everything. "Can I ask something?"

"Yes."

"What made you change your mind?"

You did, I almost say. But instead, I growl, "I didn't change my mind. I just changed my plan."

She frowns, but doesn't press me to elaborate. We continue walking down the beach and after a few minutes, the mansion comes back into view.

"Phoenix?"

"Yes?"

"Do you want to hold him?"

I glance at her with more shock than the question deserves. She gives me a nervous smile.

"I don't think that's a good idea," I mutter eventually.

Her lips screw up in a stubborn expression that looks an awful lot like what I remember of Charity. "Just try," she replies. Then, without dallying anymore, she thrusts him into my arms.

Surprised, I cradle him carefully. Elyssa gnaws on her lower lip as she watches us. I slide my gaze down to lock eyes with the boy. He looks up at me suspiciously for a moment.

She reaches out to stroke his thigh and gives him a reassuring smile. "Don't worry, my little angel," she coos gently. "You're safe with him."

His bottom lip goes wobbly for a moment, but he doesn't actually cry. He looks back and forth between the two of us, right on the precipice of bursting into tears.

And then, just as suddenly, he eases up. The lip stops shaking. The chubby smile returns.

"See? You're a natural." Elyssa smiles triumphantly.

Clearing my throat, I deposit him back in Elyssa's arms before she can protest. I don't want to admit it, but holding him is painful.

It's just a reminder of everything I lost. Everything I could still lose.

I can feel her watching me as I turn and stalk up towards the estate, but I ignore her gaze. I don't need any more guilt. I have a lifetime's worth already.

When we get to the back gates, Leona is standing on the deck, waiting for us.

"It's almost time for Theo's nap," she calls over as we approach.

"I can put him to sleep," Elyssa offers.

"Oh, no need," Leona replies quickly. "It's my job."

I chuckle. "I thought babysitting wasn't really your thing, Leona," I point out. "You sure griped about it when I assigned you the job."

"Hey, I don't have a man in my life, okay?" she says defensively. "I got attached to this little guy."

Elyssa smiles. "I don't blame you."

I notice how Elyssa's arms tighten around Theo when Leona draws close, but she bites down on her lower lip and hands him over without a fight. Jealousy sparks at the corner of her eyes as Leona swoops Theo up and disappears into the house.

Without thinking, I put my arm around her. She gives a little jerk of surprise before looking up at me. I don't offer an explanation apart from a small smile.

"It's hard letting him go," she confesses in a soft voice. "And I know it's ungracious, but I just don't want to be… forgotten."

"You're his mother, Elyssa," I remind her quietly. "No one can take your place."

"He's not even six months old yet," she points out. "Anyone can be his mother at this point."

I frown. "And you think I'd let that happen?"

She bites her lip. A little harder this time. "We don't know what the future holds," she says with uncertainty.

I understand what she means.

The paternity test.

Her memory loss.

The dark shadows of the past that follow each of us.

There are so many factors that remain unclear. She's looking up at me with hope in her eyes, though. The kind of hope that makes me feel certain for the first time in as long as I can remember that everything will be okay in the end. I want to tell her that. She needs to hear it.

"Elyssa—"

But the rest of my words are swallowed up in an explosion so loud that it makes my ears ring for several seconds.

A blast of hot air and stinging bits of debris ripples past us.

When my ears stop ringing, I'm aware of the hysterical cry of the baby from inside the house. Elyssa is two steps ahead of me, already rushing towards Leona and Theo.

More shapes are moving, too. My men frantically scrambling to respond to whatever the fuck just happened. Panic etched across their faces.

I catch up to Elyssa, Leona, and Theo.

"Boss, what do we do?" Leona asks. She looks calm. I know that the concern in her eyes is for Theo alone. She's not a woman who shies away from battle. It's one of the reasons I hand-picked her to take care of Theo—she does not fuck around.

Elyssa plucks Theo out of Leona's arms and cradles him close. "Come on," I tell both of them, surveying the grounds for the best avenues of escape. I can see smoke whirling up over the rooftop from the blast site on the other side of the house.

"Leona, find a safe place to take cover and stay with Elyssa and Theo," I order. "And if anyone you don't recognize comes within ten feet of you… fucking shoot them."

"Got it," she says. "Don't worry. They'll be safe with me."

I give her a nod and turn my back on them before running straight into the blistering smoke engulfing the mansion.

I almost run into Konstantin as I burst in through one of the back entrances. The wall has come down on one side and I spy at least two bodies beneath the rubble.

"What the fuck?" I growl.

"Boss!" Konstantin barks. "We've been breached."

"Yeah, no shit. Where are the others?"

"We've got two contingents on either side of the house trying to hold them back. They've come with a small army, though."

"Who?" I ask. "Who has come?"

"The Yakuza," Konstantin explains grimly. "Eiko's here. He's the one who led his men in after the explosion."

Eiko fucking Sakamoto. I should have killed the motherfucker when he'd been within reach.

I curse myself as Konstantin and I maneuver through the rubble. "You got an extra weapon on you?" I ask.

He unholsters a gun from the belt around his waist and throws it to me. I turn off the safety and hold it up as we round the corner.

I pass another body. One of the maids. "Jesus," I growl as I sink to one knee and check her pulse with my gun still at the ready.

"Well?"

"Dead," I sigh. "Those motherfuckers."

"Where's your wife? And the boy?" Konstantin asks.

A shiver of déjà vu surges through my body. I suppress it and get back to my feet. "With Leona out back. I told them to take cover until we could contain the situation."

"He probably wants them," Konstantin muses.

But as we turn the corner, my eyes land on the open door to the basement cellar—and I know immediately what he's really here for.

"Not Elyssa," I reply, shaking my head. "He came for fucking Josiah."

"The crazy pastor?"

"He knows secrets that Astra Tyrannis doesn't want spilled."

I know I should probably wait for more men, but I'm incensed at the arrogance of the attack. Wrath drives me forwards. I'm almost at the open door when a Yakuza solider bursts through the opening and collides into me.

We both land on our backs. But we recover fast, and before he can attack, I twist around on the floor and slice across his throat. The man flops on the floor like a dying fish as he bleeds out.

But before I can regather my bearings, more Yakuza come storming in. Bullets hurtle through the air towards us and we have just enough time to duck to the sides before any of them find their mark.

Behind the swirling guards in riot gear, I see a familiar, bloodied face.

Josiah.

And behind him…

Eiko Sakamoto brings up the rear. He's completely surrounded and well-protected. Just before the men make their exit, Eiko turns his head to the side and catches sight of me peering out from my vantage point.

He throws me a quick smirk. Then the lot of them disappear.

"Fuck!" I roar, unable to contain my frustration.

"Boss?"

"Get a team on those fuckers now!" I yell. "And you! Get out back and find Leona and Elyssa. Get them somewhere safe."

Konstantin moves towards the back, while I head off in the direction that Eiko and his men have just taken.

And that's when I hear it: a scream.

No—*her* scream.

I snap around at the same moment that Konstantin looks to me for confirmation. "Go!"

He jumps over a pile of broken glass and rushes through to the back gardens while I follow. I overtake him in seconds, but the sinking feeling in my chest refuses to budge.

All I can think is…

Not again.

Not again.

I round a thrust of flowering bushes and that's when I catch sight of them. I see Leona raise her gun. But there are too many men and they're surrounded.

She shoots anyway. They return fire.

Only one of them hits their target.

Leona collapses in on herself with a surprised wheeze and falls to the grass. Her hands clutch at her belly. Blood pools between her interlaced fingers.

I raise my gun, but freeze when one of the Yakuza reaches out to ensnare Elyssa. She's screaming and clinging to Theo. I want to shoot, to get the bastard's hands off of my woman, but it's a tangled mess of limbs and I can't be sure I'll hit him and not her.

They're too close.

All too fucking close.

Konstantin is battling the same dilemma. More of my men converge around the loose circle of Yakuza. Realizing that they're about to be outnumbered, one of the soldiers makes a move.

He plucks the baby out of Elyssa's grappling arms and shoves her stumbling backwards.

"If anyone shoots…" the masked soldier threatens. "If anyone so much as moves in our direction or attempts to follow us, I will kill the child."

Then he presses the gun to Theo's temple as the baby cries desperately.

"No!" Elyssa screams in a blood-curdling, heartbreaking wail. "God, please, no…! My baby… just give him back to me… please!"

She's beside herself, her hands clawing out towards her son even as her legs buckle under the terror of losing him.

I have no choice but to stand and watch.

I watch them take the baby.

I've known pain in my life. The kind of biting pain that leaves you with its memory even years after you've healed. But in the wake of Elyssa's cries, I realize I've known nothing of real agony.

Because it's there…

It's all right there in her face.

18

ELYSSA

"No! No! No! Get the fuck off of me!"

My screams fall on deaf ears.

I slam my fist forward and manage to make contact with one of the guard's faces. It doesn't accomplish much. I'm pretty sure I've done more damage to my hand than I have done to his face.

"Restrain her," someone orders.

I know it's not Phoenix. He disappeared minutes after my son was taken. I remember screaming at his back. What I said to him, I don't exactly remember.

Horrible things, probably. Unfair things. But right now, I don't want to take any of them back.

Right now, what I want to do is throw more punches and swear and fight and do whatever I need to do to get my son returned to me.

"Don't touch me. Don't fucking touch me!"

But two different sets of arms lash out in unison and pin my limbs in place. Cuffs snap onto my wrists and I can feel something twist around my ankles as they're forced together.

Then I'm hoisted onto someone's shoulder and carried back into the smoking wreckage of the house.

The smoke makes things seem worse than they are, though. Aside from the rubble at the site of the explosion and the pockmarked scars where bullets chipped away at the floor and walls, most things are relatively intact.

Whichever faceless guard is holding me pants under his breath as he hauls me up the staircase. I close my eyes and try to swallow back the screams building in my throat.

When he sets me back down, I'm shocked to find that I'm back in my old room.

I shake my head, angry tears blurring my vision as my restraints are removed. The men who followed us here are giving me a wide berth, probably anticipating that I'll try to attack one of them.

But I suddenly feel exhausted. Drained. My muscles are lead and my eyelids weigh a thousand pounds and if I never move again, it'll still be too soon.

The men retreat warily. A second after the door closes, I hear the lock turn. And just like that, I'm all alone once again.

I'm still right here, Charity whispers.

"No, you're not," I whisper to the empty room. "You're not here. I'm just speaking to myself. I've lost everyone."

You'll get Theo back.

"Stop!" I scream. I'm tired of the voice in my head, tired of seeking comfort in ghosts and dreams.

I want my son back.

I would trade the future I wished for this morning if it meant that Theo could grow as tall as Phoenix. I would trade my life. My happiness. My entire world, if it just meant my son could live to become a man.

More tears threaten to erupt. I shut the blinds, climb into bed, and bury my face in the pillows.

I want peace and quiet, but even in the relative silence, I know I won't get it. My pain is loud. It sweeps over me like a siren's wail. And all I can do is lie there and suffer.

An hour passes. Even when my limbs grow achy, I don't move. Refusing to change position. Refusing to chase comfort. If my son is in pain, why shouldn't I be in pain, too?

It's only when I hear the lock turn again that I lift my head.

Phoenix steps inside and shuts the door behind him. He pauses at the foot of the bed. I wait for him to speak, but he doesn't.

"Are you going to get my son back?" I demand.

He nods. "That's the plan."

I scowl. "You and your plans. They're not doing much good, are they?"

It's a low blow. Cruel and unnecessary. But Phoenix doesn't take the bait. He just stands there, hands clasped behind his back, surveying me somberly.

"Where were you this whole time?" I ask when he still doesn't speak.

"I was trying to settle things," he says. "I just finished a meeting with my lieutenants."

"A meeting?" I repeat incredulously. "A *meeting*?"

"Yes. A meeting."

"You should have followed them," I snap. "You could have gotten Theo back before he was taken off the compound."

His jaw tightens.

"He would have been killed if we'd tried to follow them," Phoenix points out. "I wasn't willing to risk it."

"He's a baby," I say, struggling for breath. "He was terrified. He's not going to know what's going on. He needs me. He needs his mother."

"Elyssa…"

"He's not with anyone he knows. Not even Leona—" I stop short when I blurt out her name.

One moment, Leona had been standing in front of Theo and me in the gardens like a warrior princess. Hair flowing in the wind, gun raised, pure violence in her every motion.

The next moment, she had crumpled to the ground like a bird shot from the sky.

"Leona…?" I whisper again. It's a question this time.

"Dead," Phoenix says. He doesn't soften the brutal edge of his words or ease me into the revelation. He looks tired. But there's something simmering just beneath his carefully orchestrated expression.

"W… what?"

"The bullet punctured her heart. She bled out within minutes."

I look down, lip wobbling. She died for me. For Theo.

"You don't have to feel guilty," Phoenix tells me gruffly. "She knew the risks of this kind of life. She signed up for it."

"Does that mean *I* should have expected this?" I ask. "I should have expected that being here, being around you, meant losing my son?"

I know I shouldn't say the words even as I say them. But I can't seem to stop myself.

My pain is greedy. It demands space. It demands fuel. It demands room to spread and fester and consume as much as it can.

"You're upset," Phoenix says, his jaw twitching with the effort of staying calm.

"Upset?" I repeat furiously. "Is that what I seem like to you? *Upset?* Am I throwing a temper tantrum, Phoenix?"

"I meant—"

"How many times do I have to tell you not to talk to me as though I'm a child?" I glare at him. "Not to talk to me as though I'm an idiot?"

"I'm going to go after them, you know," Phoenix says with steely-eyed determination. "I'm going to track down the bastards who have Theo. I'm going to get him back. And then… then I'm going to kill every single man who had anything to do with this."

I can hear the promise in his voice. I see the danger in his eyes.

He means every word.

And the thought of him succeeding terrifies me every bit as much as the thought of him failing.

"Phoenix," I beg, "you just said yourself that my son's life hangs in the balance. What if the risk—"

"Everything is a risk, Elyssa."

"It doesn't have to be. Ask for a meeting with Sakamoto. Offer him a deal. Money, territory, whatever he wants. Just get my son back— without any violence. I don't want him caught in the crosshairs of another fight."

"They don't want anything I have to offer," he says. "There was no attempt to get anyone but Theo and Josiah. Which means Eiko and Astra Tyrannis have no interest in the others. They got what they came for."

"They came for my son?"

"They came for *my* son," he corrects. "Anna would have informed them of Theo's parentage. Men like Eiko, like Viktor Ozol... they'd want to inflict as much pain as they could. This is their way."

"I don't care who they are or what they're doing!" I cry out. "I just want my son back."

"And the way to do that is to trust me."

"Do you know where they're headed?" I ask.

"No," he says. "But I'll find out."

"I'm coming with you when you do."

His eyes narrow just the tiniest bit. "Elyssa."

"Don't. Don't say my name like that."

"Like what?"

"Like you expect me to know better," I reply. "I'm coming with you. End of discussion."

"It's too dangerous."

"Which means it'll be doubly dangerous for Theo," I retort. "I don't care what you say. I'm going."

"And if you die?" he demands. "What point will it serve if we get Theo back only to lose you?"

"You think I care about myself?" I scoff. "I don't. The only thing I want is for my baby to be somewhere safe." I choke on my last few words and turn around as tears blur my vision. "Oh God. Oh God..."

Phoenix moves towards me and rests a hand on my shoulder. "Elyssa..."

"Before, when we were at the beach..." I whisper. "When I saw Leona with him, I felt so jealous. I kept thinking that I should be the one with him, taking care of him. And now? Now, I don't care about that at all. I don't care who raises him just so long as he gets to grow up to be a man and live a long, full life. A happy life. A free life."

Once again, Phoenix says nothing. He offers no comfort. No reassurance. The silence feels ominous.

"We will get him back, won't we?" I ask, turning to him and searching his face for a promise.

"I will try."

"'Try' isn't not good enough."

He shakes his head and walks away from me so abruptly that I almost tip forward. When he reaches the end of the room, he veers around and I recoil at the stark and terrifying expression on his face.

"Don't you think I fucking know that?" he seethes at me. "But I won't give you false hope and I won't pretend as though Astra Tyrannis is an enemy that can be fought easily. I've made that mistake once before. I lost a wife and a son because of my arrogance. Because of my pride. You want me to swear to you that I'll get Theo back? Well, I won't do it. But that doesn't mean I'm not going to try like fucking hell to do everything in my power to make it happen."

His fists are clenched, his body taut with stress. With grief that's burrowed its way deep into his bones.

"Theo's your son, you know," I whisper. "I don't need a paternity test to be certain of that."

New anger flashes across Phoenix's eyes. He looks positively murderous as he crosses the space between us to stand in front of me like a demi-god wreathed in fire.

"You think I'll try harder to save him if I believe he's mine?" he demands. "Is that it?"

"I… I…"

"Well, you're wrong about that," he growls, before I can formulate a response. "I'd try just as hard to save him even if he wasn't."

"You would?"

"Yes."

"Why?"

"Because he's *your* son."

Long seconds of silence follows his admission. I feel as though I'm choking.

Then the sob breaks out from my throat, through my lips. I move towards him at the same time he moves towards me.

His hands land on either side of my face, pulling me in against him. Our lips smash together and I feel the heat of our shared turmoil crash against one another.

I don't notice him taking off my clothes.

I don't notice when he takes his off, either.

All I know is that I practically blink and we're naked and clawing at each other desperately, hungrily. Two drowning people each treating the other like the last breath of air they'll ever have.

He backs me up against the bed and then pushes me down against the mattress. It catches me easily and before I can catch my breath, Phoenix falls over me, his body covering mine.

He bites, sucks, teases, tempts. Pain and pleasure intermingle until I lose all sense of where I am. The desperation stays, though. I know it's too much to ask that I be spared that. But in this case, I don't want to forget.

Phoenix rams into me without warning. I'm not expecting the aggressiveness of his entry, but I revel in it. My thighs tighten around his hips as he starts slamming into me, each thrust coming faster than the next.

When I grip his shoulders, he pulls me off him and pins my hands back against the bed on either side of my face.

"Stay right there," he orders. "Don't fucking move."

I try to obey but I can't help twitching as the orgasm heats up in me and sweat beads between us. The moment it crashes down on me, I feel him release, too.

It's over almost as soon as it started. Phoenix rolls off of me, but he stays at my side, one hand grazing my hip, eyes fixed on the ceiling above us.

After a long while, I turn my head to the side and stare at his profile. It's perfection itself—but the torture of his past is etched across every feature.

For a second, I'm able to put my anger aside. I'm able to suspend all the blame I want to throw at him.

Instead, I remember the night we met. The way he had put himself in front of me. The way he had given me a chance at freedom.

He is more than just the harsh mafia don that he appeared to be back then.

He is a man, still trying to figure out a way to live with never-ending sorrow.

I can relate.

There are so many things I want to tell him. Things I'm not sure if I even believe myself, but things that he needs to hear if we're to survive this chaos.

It's going to be alright.

Your family's deaths are not your fault.

I love you.

I love you.

I love you.

But for now, I let the moment draw out in silence. Because I'm afraid it's all we may be given.

"I need him to be okay, Phoenix," I say, breaking the quiet. "I need to know he's going to be alright."

He doesn't look at me when he answers. "I will do everything humanly possible to ensure that."

My hand is lying right next to his on the bed. I resist the urge to reach for him. To cling to him in the same desperate way I've done since the moment I ran into that awful nightclub a year ago.

"How have you managed all this time?" I ask, cursing myself for not having asked sooner. "How have you survived?"

I know he'll know what I'm asking. *What will I do if I lose my son?* But he leaves my question floating in the void for a few moments.

"Sometimes," he rasps, "even I don't know."

I nod, a tear slipping free from my left eye. "When Charity died, it felt like a piece of me went with her."

He still doesn't look at me. "I only remember certain feelings in the days that followed. The hopelessness. The loss. I don't remember much of anything else. It was my mind's way of protecting me. Still is."

It was my mind's way of protecting me. The words echo in my head and they seem to get louder with each repetition.

What is my mind protecting me from?

"Phoenix?" I ask as my thoughts grow heavy. "I feel so weak."

"You're drained," he replies. "It's the shock. You need to sleep. You need to rest."

I want to jerk upright just to prove him wrong, but my body betrays me. I'm so tired that even outrage is difficult to muster.

"I'll rest after my son is safe," I mutter through clumsy lips.

He sighs. And at last, he turns to me. His dark eyes are hooded. And so beautiful. So beautiful I want to cry. I think I am crying.

"You're dead on your feet," he whispers in a husky rasp. "You'll be useless to everyone if you come with me like this."

He's right. I need my strength if I'm to join him. "An hour. Only an hour of sleep, okay?"

"Rest."

As if he said the magic word, I fall asleep. I drop at once into a dream. In it, I hear the sounds of a crying child. And this time, I'm a hundred percent certain it's my baby.

Theo? I cry out. *Theo, where are you?*

I can't see him. What I can see is a line of women. Faceless and dressed in flowing gowns, they all clutch their own babies. All of whom are crying out in a many-voiced wail.

"How can I help?" I want to ask them. "How can I save you?"

But I have no voice. No one hears me say a word.

∼

I wake up with a scream trapped in my throat and pain encircling my wrists and ankles. Phoenix is standing at the side of the bed, fully clothed again. He looks down at me with a steely-eyed apology.

"I wish there was another way," he murmured.

"Wha…?"

I glance down at my wrists and ankles—and realize the source of the pain.

I'm bound to the four posts of the bed. There's enough slack for me to move a few feet in either direction. But one thing is clear: I'm not going far.

My eyes go wide as they snap back to him. "Don't do this, Phoenix!"

"I'm sorry, Elyssa," he says with a pained sigh. "But I can't take you with me. And I need to make sure you can't follow."

"You promised me!"

"I lied."

19

PHOENIX

I'm in the armory when Matvei finds me. It's the first time I've seen him in days. I keep my back to him as I select weapons. I've chosen far more than I can actually carry, but I need to keep moving. I need to keep my hands busy.

"You gonna stand there silent or you gonna say something?" I grunt after a few moments pass without a word from either of us.

"The teams are almost ready," Matvei says at last.

"Good."

"There's some panic in the bunkers," he continues. "The prisoners heard the explosion and the fight that followed."

"What do they know?"

"Nothing specific," Matvei replies. "I gave the men guarding them explicit instructions not to answer any questions."

I turn around and nod. "They're to be transported back to the compound and released to their homes."

His face lifts immediately. "Really?"

"Yes," I say. "But not right now. Not before I've finished my job here."

Matvei's expression falls back into discontent. "You're really going through with it?"

I glare at him. "Are you going to start again?"

"I'm giving you my opinion," he says. "I am entitled to one, you know."

I clench my jaw tight. "You do realize that they didn't just steal a fucking knickknack, right? They took a child. *My* fucking child. Again."

"The attack came out of nowhere. You couldn't have—"

"Don't," I snap. "I don't want the goddamn justifications. How did they even manage to catch us so off-guard?"

"How do you think?" Matvei asks defensively. "This isn't exactly their first rodeo, brother."

I wave my hand at the estate around us. "We have alarms everywhere. Security systems that cost me millions every year and enough ex-special ops security guards to form a fucking army. So I ask again… how the hell did this happen?"

"I can't answer that right now, Phoenix," Matvei sighs. "All I know is that Astra Tyrannis has just made a point: Fuck with them, and they'll fuck us right back."

"So what are you suggesting?" I snap. "Turn a blind eye? Bury my head in the sand until they forget about me?"

"That's not what I'm saying at all."

"Really? Because it seems like every time the stakes get high, you're right there to convince me to stop fighting."

Matvei stops short. I know I've hit below the belt. But my nerves are frayed thin and I'm riding the adrenaline spiked by anger.

"They should have forgotten about Anna and recruited you instead," I add acidly. "You're certainly working hard for the cause."

Matvei's eyes go wide.

There's one brief instant where I could take back the words. Where I could retreat from the brink of the all-out brawl that's been brewing between us for months now.

But I don't.

"You trying to pick a fight so that you don't have to hear me out," Matvei says somberly, forcing himself back into calm. "It's a defense mechanism."

"Pick a fight?" I scoff with condescension. "What are we, a couple of teenagers in a pissing contest?"

"Apparently."

I turn back to my weapons. "I'm gearing up for a real fight, Matvei. I don't need to pick one with you."

"You don't even want to hear my opinion?"

"Not if it doesn't match mine."

"When did you become such an arrogant son of a bitch?" he lashes out.

"Always been one," I say without hesitation. "You're the one who's changed."

"Is that right?" he retorts sarcastically.

"You used to jump into the fray. You were always ready for battle. You fucking loved it."

"And I still do. When we're prepared for it," he replies. "But I'm not a fan of fucking suicide missions."

I tense up. There's truth in his words, but I'm too determined to listen. I know what his counsel will be: *Do the research. Collect intel. Wait before we make our move.*

The only problem is that I can't afford to wait any longer. Theo doesn't have that kind of time. Neither does Elyssa. The woman is chained to her bed right now, furious and inconsolable.

"I have to do this, Matvei."

He takes a deep breath, but the anger remains even after he's exhaled. "I know you feel responsible, Phoenix. I saw them carry that baby out with them. I can't imagine what it must have been like for you. For her. But this is not the way to get him back. All this will do is get you captured right alongside the child."

"And what if they kill him while I'm sitting back, working on a plan? What then?"

"They took him for a reason. And it wasn't to kill him. If it had been, then they'd have finished the job on the spot."

"He was their ticket off the compound," I point out.

"But they sought him out the moment they infiltrated the place," Matvei points out. "They wanted Josiah, but they came here for Theo, too. They're not going to hurt the boy."

His words make sense, but I can't rely on logic. Not when my instincts are screaming at me to get moving.

I heard myself the moment they grabbed the screaming baby and made off with him. The only thing running through my head had been, *My son…*

Fuck a paternity test. I know what I feel in my gut. In my heart.

That boy is mine.

"I can't take that chance," I say. "I can't just sit around here for days knowing they have him. Every second he's with the Yakuza or Astra Tyrannis is one second too fucking long."

"I'm not a parent," Matvei says, trying hard to find some common ground, some sense of agreement amidst all the tension. "I can't imagine what you're going through right now. But I have an idea. I saw what happened when you lost Yuri."

"Then you understand why I can't take your advice."

"On the contrary, I think that's *exactly* why you should take my advice," Matvei retorts. "I don't want you to lose another son, Phoenix. If you go in guns blazing, without a real plan or any significant intel, then Theo is as good as gone. And it'll be your fault."

He winces when he sees my eyes cloud with dark rage.

"Fuck, that came out wrong," he says. "What I mean is—"

"A great many things have come out wrong between us, wouldn't you say, *brother*?" I snarl. "Maybe it's time to acknowledge the end of a chapter. Maybe you should go."

He recoils. "You don't mean that."

"Look me in the eyes and tell me I don't."

His gaze finds mine. And it sees what I feel: hot, churning anger.

"I'm not scared of you, Phoenix. I never have been. It's the reason you used to value my opinion."

"Before you became a coward."

Matvei's hands clench into fists. I wonder for a moment if he's going to use them. A part of me hopes he does, because my own fists are tight and coursing with adrenaline. I could use the fight. I've spent far too much fucking time in my head lately. I need to act. To move. To stop thinking for one goddamn second.

But if Matvei wants to go down that road, then he'll have to throw the first punch.

The moment stretches out. Reaches its breaking point…

And then he exhales.

His fingers unwind. "Call me what you want," he says. "Level your insults at me. I'm strong enough to take it. But I will not leave. I want to be clear, though: it's not you I'm staying for. It's for that girl. For that baby. You need me to keep them safe, even if you don't see that."

This whole thing is fucked. We should be brothers in this. We should be preparing for battle together, striding out side by side, ready to take on our enemies as a single unit.

Instead, we stand at opposite ends, separated by fury and pride and arrogance.

How long has this void been forming? Months? Weeks?

Or longer? From the very beginning?

Maybe two men like us were never meant to be allies.

Maybe I've always been meant to be a lone wolf.

I take a breath. "Fine," I growl. "Stay. But don't bother getting ready with the rest of my men. You can go and guard the prisoners."

It's an obvious insult. He doesn't so much as blink.

"If you want to stay, you will follow orders," I tell him harshly. "Go."

Matvei lingers only a moment. Then he turns to leave. I watch as his shadow dissolves into the hallway and his footsteps fade into silence.

I gather my weapons, but I stay in the room a little longer to check and re-check them. I can feel myself start to unravel at the edges.

I look up, knowing Elyssa is still raging upstairs, trying to fight her restraints. I hate that it's come to this. History circling over itself around and around like buzzards over a rotting carcass in the desert.

I'm going to break that fucking cycle. It won't repeat itself. One way or another, this ends soon.

It's time to fight.

20

ELYSSA

I'm shaking the chains and screaming at the top of my lungs. My cries reverberate throughout the room. No one hears, or if they do, they don't care.

Whoa, he really unleashed the beast, huh?

"Shut up," I snap to Charity.

Hey, hey, that was a compliment. It's good to see you let loose. I like the badass Elyssa. Did you have to wait 'til I died to transform?

I shake my head to try and dislodge Charity's voice, but it doesn't always work.

You miss me. Let yourself miss me.

"They have my son, Charity. They have Theo."

You're thinking yourself into a panic.

She's probably right. I take a deep breath, but the panic doesn't dissipate. Invisible fingers stay latched around my throat. Every time I think of Theo, they tighten.

After several minutes of thrashing and screaming, my throat is hoarse. But I refuse to let him silence me. I'm about to start screaming again—when I hear the lock click and the door opens.

I jerk up in bed, expecting Phoenix.

Instead, Matvei walks in.

His usually calm features are contorted in obvious concern. He looks at me strangely, taking in my restraints with obvious distaste.

"Matvei," I breathe, though his name comes out in barely a whisper. "Have they left yet? Where's Phoenix?"

"Preparing."

"He can't do it like this," I say desperately. "He's putting Theo at risk. Not to mention himself. A brazen attack will put everyone in danger."

Matvei steps up to the edge of the bed. His expression is, as always, unreadable. But there's an odd tone to his aura. Something haunted. Unsettled.

"I agree," he murmurs.

My eyes go wide. "You do?"

"Yes," he says. "I tried to talk him out of it."

My heart drops. "But?"

"But Phoenix and I aren't exactly seeing eye-to-eye lately. I'm not even supposed to accompany them on the attack."

I frown. "What? What will you be doing then?"

"Staying behind," Matvei tells me. "To guard the prisoners."

Guard the prisoners? Even I know that's a menial job, especially for someone of Matvei's stature. Which means something has gone really wrong.

"So you don't want him attacking them either?" I ask tentatively.

"Not like this, no. It's reckless. He needs time to prepare. This isn't some fledgling enemy cartel on the rise. This is Astra fucking Tyrannis. And they've obviously been keeping tabs on the Kovalyov Bratva for a while."

I try and move forward, but I'm held back by my restraints. My wrists have deep welts by now. But the pain is negligible in the face of the panic that's sitting on my chest at the moment.

"Matvei, you have to talk to him. Make him see sense. He's putting my son's life in danger."

"He's not listening to me anymore."

"You have to try harder."

"I have been trying," he says, huffing in frustration. "For weeks, I've been trying to get through to him. He's too…"

"Too what?" I demand.

"Too dredged down in the past," Matvei explains. "He's so determined not to make the same mistakes that I fear that's exactly what he'll end up doing."

"Matvei," I plead, "a mistake in this case will mean my son's life."

"I know that, Elyssa. But he is the don. No one can tell Phoenix what to do."

I stare around the room as though the answers are hidden in there somewhere. I feel torn. Like my insides are fighting each other.

Is that what it is to love a man you're furious with, terrified of, awed by?

"Let me go," I say suddenly.

"What?" Matvei asks, his head snapping to mine.

"Please," I say imploringly. "Let me out of these restraints. Let me…"

"Let you do what?"

"Let me speak to my parents," I blurt out.

He frowns, considering my request. "What about?"

"About everything," I say. "I haven't had an honest conversation with them about all this. About what they know. I need to know if they were involved in some way. Maybe they have an idea of where Theo was taken."

Matvei looks at me intently. Then he nods. "Fine."

He moves forward and pulls out a Swiss army knife from the waistband of his trousers. I watch as he cuts away at my restraints and sets me loose.

I rub my sore wrists the moment I'm free. "Thank you."

"I'll accompany you to the bunkers," Matvei says.

I don't bother arguing. Instead, I jump out of the bed, steadying my shaky legs before we head out of my room together. We get through the house without running into anybody but a few stray maids, who are clearly still shaken by the attack.

Much of the house's first floor has received significant damage from the explosion and the ensuing attack. It'll have to be properly renovated after all this is over.

I step over the remaining rubble as we move through the first floor towards the exit. I squint when we step outside. The Mexican sun is piercing and bright.

The bunkers are just a few minutes from the main house, but somehow, the walk seems to stretch out forever. I'm sweating by the time we arrive.

Only a pair of youngish looking guards man the entrance. When they see me, they get ready to ask questions. When they see Matvei come up behind me, they get right back in place.

"After you," Matvei murmurs, holding the door open.

The bunker I enter is just as cold on the inside as it looks on the outside. The door opens out into a broad corridor with cement floors and artificial lighting. Any and all natural light is completely cut out. There are no windows, no sense whatsoever that it's a hot day on the Pacific coast just outside.

Two rows of doors run down either side of the broad corridor. Each door has a little opening at the top like a prisoner's cell.

"Where are my parents?" I ask.

"The cell in the far right," he says. "Come on."

He leads me to the right door and unbolts it before gesturing me inside.

"The door will lock behind you," he tells me before I walk in. "Just knock twice when you're done."

I nod gratefully and step inside. I'm expecting complete darkness, but I realize there's a small light bulb in the corner that illuminates the depressing space.

It's bigger than I expected. Two low beds pushed to either side of the walls, separated by a bedside table bearing the scraps of a meal and two glasses of water.

There's a tray of bread sitting on it. With a bottle of water and two glasses.

Papa is lying flat on his bed. Mama is curled up in a ball. Both of them jump when they catch sight of me walking through their door.

"Mama. Papa," I say softly.

"How dare you come here?" Mama hisses at me.

I had expected this reaction, but it doesn't stop me from being hurt. Still, my intentions don't change.

I'm here for information. Whatever I can get.

"I need to speak to you both."

"I'm not speaking to you," Mama says firmly, turning away from me like a petulant child.

Papa swings his feet off the bed and stares at me. He looks calmer—marginally.

"What did you come here to speak about?" he asks.

Mama casts him a glare, but he's not looking at her.

"I want to know what you know," I say. "About Astra Tyrannis."

Both of them frown. No sparks of recognition in their eyes. It might be naïve, but I feel like I can trust their disbelief.

"I've never heard the name before," Papa says.

"Mama?"

She shakes her head without looking at me.

"What about Josiah?" I ask. "What do you know about him?"

"Other than he would have been a wonderful husband?" Mama says bitingly. "Nothing you don't already know."

I narrow my eyes at her, sick of watching her victimize herself while she refused to acknowledge what he did to me.

"Josiah is a rapist, Mama," I say strongly. "Is that who you wanted me married to?"

"And what are you married to now?" Mama counters. "A beast of a man who abducts people from their homes and locks them away like rats."

"Is that any different from what you've been involved in?" I say.

Her cheek twitches. "What is that supposed to mean?"

"There's proof that Josiah has been working with Astra Tyrannis for decades now," I tell them. "And Astra Tyrannis is a notorious organization that makes their money on human trafficking."

Mama's eyes go wide—but Papa looks unsurprised.

"I'll ask again: Did you know?" I ask, focusing my attention on him.

He sighs. "I wasn't lying before. I've never heard that name. But…" He stops short.

"Tell me, Papa."

"I knew that Josiah was tied to some powerful men," he admits at last. "How else could he so often bail our little project out of debt and ruin time and time again? He was connected, well-connected. That much I was aware of."

"But you didn't ask questions."

"I couldn't," Papa replied. "Josiah looked after us."

"By selling women and children into modern-day slavery!"

"That's not true," Mama says desperately, looking between me and Papa. "It can't be true. Solomon?"

"I don't know what's true and what's not anymore," he replies weakly.

I want to sit down, but I don't want to get anywhere near my parents.

"They've taken my son," I say into the silence. "Astra Tyrannis attacked earlier and took Theo."

Mama looks at me with wide eyes. "That was the sound we heard?"

"Yes." I can barely look at her. "They have my baby."

"Your husband didn't protect him?" Mama snaps.

I hold my anger at bay. "Papa, you may not have asked questions, but you knew something was happening. You knew Josiah was involved in something."

"Yes."

"Do you know anything that might help me locate my son?"

"No." His answer is immediate, and it makes my blood boil.

"You won't even try—"

"I don't know anything about this business," Papa says, cutting me off. "... But Raj might."

"Raj?" I ask. "Brother Raj?"

"He helped Josiah recover after you left. Acted as interim leader in the meantime."

I frown. "And everyone just accepted that?"

"Josiah gave his blessing. Said it came down from the powers that be."

"Of course," I reply with disdain. "No one would ever dare to question Josiah."

"He looked after us," Mama jumps in.

"He took advantage of you," I snap, glaring at her. "He brainwashed you and then he built the Sanctuary so that he could feed humans to Astra Tyrannis."

"I don't believe that."

"You wouldn't," I reply coldly. "You'll only believe what Josiah tells you to believe."

I'm done with this. I'm almost too angry to speak and all I've learned is that my parents aren't who I thought they were—they're worse. Cowards on their best days. Monsters on their worst.

I turn to the door and knock twice. It pulls open at once with a dull creak. I walk out without looking back at my parents.

The moment the door shuts, I exhale loudly, tears slipping down my cheeks.

"Are you okay?" Matvei asks.

"I… I don't know," I admit. "I think I need to sit down."

"Let me find you a chair."

I wave him away and sink to the floor, leaning back against the wall for support.

"Did they have any information for you?"

"Not really," I admit. "All they told me was—"

"Matvei!"

I shriek as the roar reverberates through the entire bunker. Darting to my feet, I see Phoenix's silhouette in the open door to the bunker.

He walks forward, his eyes black with anger as he glances at me.

"What the fuck is going on here?"

21

PHOENIX

Matvei looks resigned to a fight, but I can tell he's not really in the mood anymore.

Yeah, well, too fucking bad.

Elyssa steps in front of me suddenly, blocking my path to Matvei. She's pale, but her eyes harden with resolve. She puts a hand on my chest. Unable to stop myself, I look down at her.

"Don't blame him. I'm the one who convinced him to bring me here."

I snort. "He should never have been convinced," I say. "But it seems he's not so good at taking my orders."

"Because your orders are off the mark, Phoenix."

I grit my teeth and try to brush past Elyssa, but she holds firm to my chest and I can't bring myself to shove her aside.

"You motherfucker. I told you once already. You don't want to be here, then go. But if you're staying, you better fucking follow my orders. I am your don!"

My words echo through the bunker. I'm sure the prisoners can hear me, but I don't care. He's crossed a line.

"She just wanted to talk to her parents," Matvei responds—as though that qualifies as a defense.

"She was tied to the fucking bed," I reply. "If I'd wanted her free, I'd have let her go myself."

"Stop it!" Elyssa interrupts. "Stop talking about me as though I'm not here."

I grab hold of her wrist and drag her deeper into the bunker. She doesn't protest. Nor does she ask where I'm taking her.

I open the last door on the left and throw her in the empty cell. Then I walk in after her and shut the door on both of us.

When I turn to face her, I notice her jaw is set and her body is tight with tension. Looks like she's not backing down, either.

"Why talk to your parents now?" I demand.

"Because I wanted to see if they know something that might help me get Theo back."

"Your parents don't know a fucking thing. They're mindless sheep who'll do whatever the fuck Josiah wants them to."

I'm right and she knows it, but she looks defensive anyway.

"Maybe you're right," she acknowledges. "But that doesn't mean they haven't noticed things. They lived in that place their whole lives. And Josiah has been in charge that entire time. My parents weren't privy to his private dealings. They don't know details. They don't have names—"

"Then they're fucking useless, aren't they?"

She looks livid. But I'm glad I'm pissing her off. It's riling me up further... in more ways than one.

"You're an arrogant prick," she shoots at me. "Are you so damn proud that you won't even consider that there might be another way at this than the plan you've thought up?"

"Sounds like you've been talking to Matvei," I drawl angrily.

"I *have* been talking to Matvei," she snaps. "As a matter of fact, it's been a breath of fresh air talking to someone who's actually willing to listen."

I try and act like I don't give a shit. Even though my nerves prick with molten jealousy.

"Matvei doesn't have anything to lose here," I tell her. "He can afford to be cautious."

"Listen to yourself. We all have to be cautious. You don't have a plan."

"I do."

"Then what is it?" she says, calling my bluff. "'*Burst in there and open fire*'? That's not a plan. It's a death wish."

"Has everyone forgotten that I'm the fucking don here?"

She strides right up and pokes me in the chest with one finger. "Accepting help doesn't make you weak," she informs me icily. "Listening to advice doesn't make you less capable."

I gaze down at her, impassive and unimpressed. "Don't flatter yourself that you know this world, Elyssa. Fucking a don doesn't make you one."

She rears back like I've struck her. But she's making me fucking crazy and I don't have the capacity to think before I speak right now.

"You are a cold-hearted fool," she hisses. "Most days, I'm sorry I ever met you."

I grab her wrist and push her up against the wall, my hips flush against hers. I'm hard and this position will ensure she knows it, but I'm riding too many emotions right now to care.

"Be sorry all you want. There's no changing the fact that you're mine now, Elyssa. Like it or not, I am your husband. I will do what it takes to keep you safe. You and Theo alike."

"Except Theo's not safe. The enemy has him."

"And I'll get him back."

She shakes her head. "Not this way, you won't."

"And what's your fucking plan?" I grit. "Stand in front of their gates and beg for a conversation? They'll shoot us before you can get the first pathetic 'Please' out."

She shakes her head like that'll undermine the truth of what I've just said. She desperately needs to believe in another way, an alternative that won't result in Theo's death.

"You need to find out more… about where they are. How much security they have. What their plans are," she mumbles.

"What the fuck do you think I've been trying to do?" I ask through gritted teeth.

When I shift position, my hard cock digs into her thigh. A tiny little gasp escapes her lips and that only serves to make me harder. In a moment of insanity, I imagine those plump lips wrapped around my cock. I struggle to push away the inappropriate thought.

But it lingers. It always fucking lingers.

"I've had dozens of my men scouting around for more information. All of them have come up blank."

"Because you haven't given them enough time," she argues. "You can't just go in there guns blazing."

She pushes back against my body—which doesn't help me tame my erection in the slightest.

And that's when I realize…

She knows exactly what she's doing.

"You're playing a dangerous game here, Elyssa."

She doesn't even bother denying it. "I'll play any game I need to in order to get my son back."

I rip her hands off mine and pin both wrists against the wall on either side of her face. Her breasts are pressed up against me, and I can feel her nipples through the thin fabric of her blouse.

"Is that right?"

She doesn't falter. The fire in her eyes glows hot. "That's right."

"What happened to the innocent little girl I found in that nightclub?"

"She's gone," Elyssa says.

"She grew up, huh?"

"No. She woke up," Elyssa snaps back. "You married me, Phoenix. Maybe you plan on casting me aside when I've served my purpose, but for right now, I am your wife. And if you expect me to play the part, then you'll have to try and compromise. This is my son. I deserve a say in how to save him."

I clench my jaw, sick of being questioned and second-guessed at every turn. I lean in. I'm so close that my nose grazes the side of her neck.

She cranes her face away from me. Her breath is coming in fast and I know she's affected by my proximity.

She can deny it all she wants—but the flame between us is burning as hot as ever.

"Okay, little lamb," I say softly. "You want to play at war? Then tell me what you would do now in my place."

I'm so close to her that I can't see her eyes, but I can feel every inch of her. The steadiness of her breaths, the hard nubs of her nipples. The way her fingers tremble just a little against my hands.

"I…"

"Well?" I ask when her answer doesn't come readily. "Tell me."

"I'd… I'd interrogate some of the prisoners," she says shakily. "I'd try and get whatever information I can from them."

"Is that right?" he asks.

"Raj."

I stop short and pull back so that I can look at her face. "What?"

"Raj," she gulps. "That's the name my father gave me. He said that Raj knows things. He was basically in charge until Josiah recovered."

I release her in surprise. I didn't expect a real answer. This is… significant.

"He was assigned to take over Josiah's duties until he got better," Elyssa continues. I'm shocked to hear the guilt that still taints her voice when she speaks of that night.

"Assigned by whom?"

She bites her lip. I know what she's going to say before she even says it. "The powers that be."

"Jesus," I say, pushing off the wall and pacing around the cell. "So that means Astra Tyrannis picked this person. This Raj."

Elyssa's eyes go wide. "Do you think…?"

I don't hesitate. I turn to the door and pull it open violently before turning to Elyssa.

"You want me to do things your way?" I ask. "Come on then. We're doing it your way."

I don't give her a chance to second guess. I leave the cell and she's forced to follow behind me.

Matvei is still standing down at the mouth of the hallway. He looks up as we approach, but I ignore him completely and keep walking until I reach the man guarding the bunker.

"Where are the prisoner logs?" I demand.

He rushes to get me the book.

"Search for someone named Raj," I order. "Quickly."

He runs through the list of names while I stand there, breathing down his neck. Elyssa slinks forward, blinking against the sunlight filtering in through the open door.

It takes several more minutes, but he finally locates the name on the log. "Here, sir," he says. "Bunker two. Cell thirteen."

I nod and make my way to bunker two, one building over. I'm already ten feet away when I realize that Elyssa isn't behind me. I turn to find her still standing by the first bunker's door.

"Well, come on," I say harshly.

She raises her eyebrows. "You want me to come with you for the interrogation?"

"You want to make decisions?" I say. "Then you have to be there to see your decisions unfold. That's what it means to be in charge."

She looks momentarily terrified—and then her face sets with determination.

She has to run to keep up with me, but I don't slow down for her benefit.

The guard at bunker two swings the door open for me when he sees me coming. I breeze past him and go straight for the cell that this Raj motherfucker is apparently in. I find it, unbolt the lock, and stride inside.

The man sitting in the far corner of the cell is thin and short. A diminutive man with features that can only be described as pretty. His dark gaze lands on me with perfect serenity, as though he's not surprised at all by my abrupt arrival.

Of all the prisoners I've laid eyes on, he looks by far the most at ease.

"Raj, I presume," I say, just as Elyssa steps into the room behind me.

He gives me a calm smile. "I was wondering how long it would take."

22

ELYSSA

Raj's dark eyes land on me. His faint smile never fades. "And you brought sweet little Elyssa," he murmurs. His voice contains an undercurrent that I don't like one bit.

I despise the way he's looking at me. Like I amuse him.

"You work for Astra Tyrannis, don't you?" I blurt out, before Phoenix can say anything. He raises his eyebrows and glances at Phoenix.

"I didn't realize she was going to be my interrogator," he chuckles. "I must admit, it's a genius tactic. Though it might have been more effective if you'd sent her in alone. Preferably in a see-through dress."

Phoenix's body goes rigid immediately. "I'd be careful if I were you," he warns in a feral growl.

"But you're not me, are you?" Raj replies. "This is nothing new to me, young master."

"You've never been a prisoner of the Kovalyov Bratva before."

"You're all the same," he snorts. "I don't expect different."

"You will answer my questions."

Raj checks his nails as though he's just completed a manicure. "I don't think so."

Phoenix turns to me, his eyes blazing. I shudder despite myself. "Okay, Elyssa—you wanted things done your way right?" he asks. "Well, this is how we get information out of stubborn men who should know better."

He turns around and grabs hold of Raj by the collar of his discolored shirt. Heaving him high, he brings him smashing down face-first on the concrete floor with a sickening thud. I suppress a scream.

For a moment, I wonder if he's dead. Then there's motion. When Raj lifts his head, I spy blood on the floor and half of a chipped-off tooth. I feel a moment of pity for him as he struggles to right himself.

He's half of Phoenix's size and height. A child in comparison. It hardly seems fair, but I hold my tongue, refusing to intervene.

Phoenix is right: I asked for this.

But the moment Phoenix grabs Raj by the hair at the back of his head, I know I don't have the stomach for it.

I hate Astra Tyrannis. I hate what they do and what they stand for. And now I have a personal reason to hate them, too. But seeing another human being tossed around like a ragdoll feels… wrong. It feels like I shouldn't be here.

As Phoenix throws a punch at Raj's stomach, I look away, cringing against the sound of Raj's muted groans.

"Speak," Phoenix growls.

"You won't get anything from me," spits Raj.

Phoenix butts his head against Raj's. The small man crumples to the ground with another yelp.

He's much more resilient than I would have thought, though. Even when his eyes roll back in his head, the stubborn expression on his face doesn't change.

"Strip."

I freeze, but Phoenix is glaring at Raj with a deadly expression on his face.

"You heard me," he says when Raj doesn't move. "Strip. Now."

I move forward, but refrain from reaching out to Phoenix. "What are you doing?" I whisper to him. We're crowded into the little space, however, and my whisper feels like a shout.

"Yes, Phoenix," Raj chimes in in a condescending tone. "What are you doing?"

"Calling your bluff," Phoenix says. "Now, remove your clothes. I won't ask again."

Raj stands facing the both of us. For a moment, I think he's going to defy Phoenix's order. Then he shrugs and starts removing his clothes.

I back out towards the door, but Phoenix holds out a hand. "Stay," he barks at me. "If you want things done your way, you will stay and watch them play out."

I stop short.

Raj discards his shirt and then his pants. He's scrawny and bony, a twig of a man. He's wearing small grey boxers that sit low on his hips. He doesn't hesitate as he pulls off his boxers and throws them to the side.

I'm trembling with nerves now, wondering how far Phoenix will take this in my presence. I'm close to begging him to stop.

"There," Phoenix says.

I don't know what Phoenix is talking about because I refuse to look. I doubt Raj would care if I did, but for my own sake, I refrain.

"What do you mean?" Raj asks innocently.

"The tattoo," Phoenix replies. "The one at your hip."

Unable to stop myself, my eyes flash to Raj. I see the tiny little black swan inked into his skin.

It's an exact replica of the paperweight that I had used to attack Josiah the night of the rape.

My blood run colds as we're faced with the irrefutable proof. Tension is rolling off Phoenix in waves and making me nervous. Something is going to happen.

And it's not going to be good.

The second the thought flits through my consciousness, Phoenix reaches for a thin blade that he's tucked away beneath his clothes.

Even from where I stand, a few feet away, I can tell it's sharp. Razor sharp.

"Guards!" he calls.

Almost instantly, two men enter the room.

I'm squashed in the corner, feeling claustrophobia overtake me. But there's no way out. I'm trapped here, for better or worse.

"Tie him up," Phoenix orders his soldiers.

I didn't even realize there was a hook on the ceiling until one of the guards reaches up and pulls it down. A thick rope is tied to the hook and then brought down towards Raj's hands. His wrists are forced together and then he's hoisted up by the rope that's connected to the hook hanging from the ceiling.

Then the guards step out of the room, leaving Raj dangling by his wrists like a freshly caught fish. I desperately wish I could go with them. My stomach is churning with bile.

Phoenix steps forward playing with the knife between his fingers. "This is my favorite knife," he tells Raj. "Do you know why?"

"I have a feeling you're quite eager to inform me," the man spits.

I'm not sure whether that's fear I sense in his voice or if I'm just projecting. I try to keep my eyes averted, but at this point, I can't. It's like a train crash you can't turn away from.

"I suppose you're right," Phoenix agrees. "Human flesh... well, that's like cutting through butter. Tell me, Raj, have you ever been sliced like butter?"

Raj's jaw tightens. "Do what you will. I will not speak."

Phoenix shrugs. "Then be prepared for pain."

The scream is caught in my throat as Phoenix raises his knife and slices across the skin just above Raj's groin.

I clench my eyes shut. Then, Phoenix's voice rings out in my head: *If you want things done your way, you will stay and watch them play out.*

Slowly, agonizingly, I open my eyes.

A flap of bloodied skin hangs at Raj's waist. The same patch of skin that was tattooed. The swan flutters with Raj's writhing and screaming.

Nausea rises up to my throat, but I manage to bite it back just barely.

"Don't whine, Raj," Phoenix says coldly. "You could have prevented this."

He reaches for Raj's shirt on the floor and wipes the blade of his knife on it.

"Are you ready to talk to me?"

"Fuck you, motherfucker!"

I cringe at the words. Not because of Raj's language—that particular quirk of innocence is long behind me now—but because I know what will happen if he continues to defy Phoenix.

"I've flayed men with this blade alone," Phoenix tells Raj. "The skin comes off smoothly. Clean. So clean that you don't even notice—at first. The pain comes seconds after I've sliced through. Humans need skin. Without it, you're one raw nerve. Even a gentle breeze is pure agony. And the pain never ends."

Raj is shivering badly now. It's amazing how quickly the sweat has coated his entire body.

I feel my body start to shake, too. This is horrible. Worse than anything I could have imagined.

And I just want it to stop.

"Tell me who you've spoken with," Phoenix hisses. "Give me names."

Raj screams in response and raises his eyes to the ceiling as though he has no idea how to process the pain he's in.

"It'll only get worse the more skin I take," Phoenix promises him. "Don't make this worse for yourself."

Screaming unintelligibly, Raj shakes his head violently, swinging on his hook as he struggles to deal with the pain. The chains creak. The walls echo with his wails.

"Alright then," Phoenix says with a resigned sigh. "Let's move on to the arms."

I cry out, "No!"

Raj doesn't even look like he's heard me. But Phoenix's head snaps to me instantly.

"Phoenix," I whisper, shaking my head hopelessly. "Please... enough of this."

His eyes glint as brightly as his blade does. He sheaths it, grabs my arm, and hauls me out of the room. He doesn't close the door, but he pulls me to the side and presses me up against the wall.

"In case you forgot, you asked for this," he growls, his face just inches from mine.

"I... I... told you we needed more information..."

"And how do you think men like me get information from men like him?" Phoenix demands. "You think we sit around in prayer circles singing kumbaya? You think we make pinky promises and blow flying kisses to one another?"

I cringe against his harsh eyes. "I... I..."

"You have no clue what it takes to survive in this fucking world," he continues furiously. "You don't understand the strength it takes, or the sacrifice. You think it's a matter of walking into the Astra Tyrannis compound and bartering for Theo? They'll sooner kill him than trade him."

Tears threaten to fly loose, but I'm too lost in the intensity of his eyes. "Please, Phoenix," I gasp. "There has to be another way. Please."

His hand comes up and wraps around my throat. I'm surprised by how gentle he is.

"Please what?"

"I... this is... too much..."

"This is the lead you gave me," he points out. "The path you wanted me to take. We can't waste time, which means we need to get information fast."

"I know. I know that. I just..."

"How else do you propose we get information from him?" Phoenix presses.

"You torture a man enough and he'll tell you what you want to hear."

"Except this man has real information," Phoenix points out. "I can see it in his eyes."

I can, too. But I don't say so.

"I just… I can't watch it happen," I tremble out at last.

Phoenix scoffs. "Just like Matvei," he growls. "You criticize and command, but you don't have the fucking stomach to do what needs to be done."

Then he rips away from me and leaves me pressed against the wall. He disappears into Raj's cell. The door clangs shut.

I sink to the floor and bury my face in my hands. While I'm there, I pray.

But I don't know what for.

We're all doomed to hell already.

23

ELYSSA

"Elyssa?"

I look up to see Matvei standing over me. He looks pained. As though he's losing control of his world and he doesn't like the feeling.

I can relate.

"Come on," he says, offering me his hand. "I'll walk you back to your room."

I take his hand and he helps me up to my feet. We're halfway out of the bunker when I hear a bloodcurdling scream. It's distorted by the layers of concrete, by steel bars, by the thudding of my pulse in my ears.

But I know it's Raj who's screaming.

And I know it's Phoenix who's causing the pain.

I cringe and start walking faster. When we get back upstairs to my room, I go straight to the bed and sit down before my legs can give way beneath me.

"Is it always like that?" I whisper.

Matvei pauses by the door, looking as though he wishes he had left before I spoke up. "Interrogations?" he asks. "Usually."

"And how often do you get information from the men you torture?"

"Ninety percent of the time," he says.

"And the information is good?"

"Ninety percent of the time."

I sigh. "I know I asked for this…"

"But you're feeling guilty."

"How could I not?" I say. "He's a human being. When you cut him, he bleeds. Just like the rest of us."

"But unlike the rest of us," Matvei points out, "he's committed crimes that he needs to be held accountable for."

"I know."

"It's a hard thing to watch. No matter how horrible you know they are," Matvei continues. "But you get used to it."

"I don't want to get used to it," I say immediately. "Never, ever, ever."

"Even if it means getting your son back?"

I look down at my trembling fingertips. I'm torn between the person I am and the person I need to be.

Trapped by the present.

Caged by the past.

"I wish I remembered more," I whisper—as much to myself as to Matvei.

"Memory is a tricky thing," he tells me. "Don't strain yourself. It'll come."

"That scares me just as much."

He nods as though he understands completely. His mouth opens and shuts like he can't decide whether or not to say the next piece.

"After Aurora and Yuri's deaths, it was the memories that nearly destroyed Phoenix," Matvei tells me. "He kept remembering things he had forgotten. Each new discovery seemed to chip away at his soul."

I stare at Matvei, trying to read his expression. But he keeps his cards close to the chest, just like his don.

"What changed?"

Matvei shakes his head. "Sometimes, even I don't know. Maybe he ran out of soul to get chipped away."

He laughs like it was a joke, but even I can sense the morsel of truth beneath it.

Then he raises his eyes to mine, and I see it: pain. True pain.

Not for himself—but for his friend.

"It was going to kill him, Elyssa," he says solemnly. "Or he was going to kill himself. That is… until he met you."

His words catch me off guard. I reject them out of hand. "That's not it. I'm just an accident. I ran into the wrong room at the wrong time."

"And made an impression," Matvei corrects. "He won't admit it, but he's terrified of losing you."

"He doesn't even believe Theo is his."

"Do *you* believe that?" Matvei shoots at me.

I recoil, but it's a fair question. I have no right to feel insulted. So I swallow down my hurt. "My gut says he is."

"But you don't know for certain."

"No," I sigh. "No, I don't."

"Then give Phoenix some leeway. He has a right to ask."

"I know that!" I snap, ready to tear my hair out with frustration. "But I didn't ask for any of this, either, in case anyone forgot. I didn't ask to be raped. I didn't ask to meet Phoenix the same night I left behind everyone I've ever known."

"No one asks for their life, Elyssa," Matvei counsels. "We get what we're given. And it's up to us to make the most of it."

I let that sink in for a moment. Wondering if I had made the most of what I'd been given. Somehow, it doesn't feel that way.

"If Raj gives him information, do you think he'll attack today?" I ask.

"He might attack today regardless."

"But you disagree with that?"

"It's been made abundantly clear that my opinion is irrelevant."

"But it's right."

Matvei laughs hollowly. "Of course it is. Phoenix is just too mired down in the past to see that. Maybe you can get him to see things your way."

"If he hasn't listened to you, what makes you think he'll listen to me?"

"He's in love with you," Matvei says simply.

The words coming out of his lips feel strange. And I'm immediately desperate to believe him, but terrified of falling into a trap I won't be able to extricate myself from.

"Try and get some rest, Elyssa," Matvei says. "You look tired." Then he walks out of my room and shuts the door.

But the lock never clicks. It'd be easy to dismiss that as an accident, an oversight. But something tells me that it's a little gift from Matvei. It doesn't go unnoticed.

I fall back against my bed and stare up at the ceiling. It's flawless, arching mahogany. But all I can see is my son's face.

Looking down at me and crying in an endless, silent wail.

∼

I'm not sure how much time passes before the door opens again. I quickly blot at the tears still drying on my cheeks and sit up, expecting Matvei.

Instead: "Phoenix?"

He's changed clothes, no doubt because his previous outfit was too bloody to stay in. Now, he's wearing a white t-shirt and dark trousers. He looks effortlessly breathtaking.

How can something so violent be so beautiful?

"What happened?" I ask. He hasn't said anything since he entered. He's so still, so silent, that I wonder if he's real at all. If he's a statue or a ghost or a figment of my imagination.

Then, finally, he speaks. "He's still refusing to talk. Despite my… persuading."

"Does that mean he's still alive?"

"Of course he is," Phoenix grumbles. "I won't let him die until he's given me what I want."

"Does that mean you won't attack until he does?"

The question is an invitation for yet another fight, but I can't help it. My son's life hangs in the balance. And where I have to fight, I will.

"I've considered it from all angles," he says cautiously. "And it seems unwise to move before Raj tells me what he knows."

Relief floods through me. Followed almost instantly by the dread of knowing that it means Theo will be in the hands of enemies for a little while longer. There's no winning here. Either Phoenix impulsively sets off a war that might claim my son's life, or we all sit around and wait for a miracle.

He walks forward as though he's not sure if he should or not. With each step, Matvei's words ring louder and louder in my ears.

He's in love with you.

He's in love with you.

He's in love with you.

Except that when he's standing in front of me, like right now, it's hard to believe that he feels anything for me but irritation at best and hatred at worst.

I've thrown a spanner into the works. One thing he's wanted for nearly half a decade—destroy the men who destroyed his family—and I've sent it spiraling off the tracks. And beyond that, the secrets he needs to unravel the labyrinth that is Astra Tyrannis are locked somewhere in my head. I can't uncover them no matter how hard I try.

So no, Matvei is wrong—Phoenix doesn't love me. He can't.

I can't even love myself.

I push off the bed and walk over to where Phoenix has stopped in the center of the room. He doesn't move away from me, but he doesn't exactly look thrilled by the proximity, either.

We're hanging in this chasm of love and loss and violence. Neither of us daring to look down, for fear of seeing nothing but shadows and jagged rocks beneath our feet.

I notice a small fleck of blood on the side of his wrist that he's missed. I reach out and rub it away instinctively.

"What did you feel?" he asks suddenly. "When you watched him scream?"

I tense, taken aback by the question. "Pity," I say in the end. "I felt pity."

"Pity? Or sympathy?"

"What's the difference?"

"Everything," Phoenix rasps.

I frown. "Does it matter? Either. Both."

His eyes go cold. "Wrong answer."

I sigh. "You came here to fight, didn't you?"

He growls low in his throat. "I came here to make sure you understood the gravity of the situation. If you want to make certain decisions, then you have to face the consequences. Not that this is even a consequence."

"No?" I ask harshly. "What would you call it then?"

"Progress," he replies. "This is the work. This is the fucking job."

"What will you do if he does start talking?" I ask.

"Make sure he doesn't stop talking until he's bled out every last drop of truth," Phoenix answers grimly. "Then I'll bleed out the rest of him." His voice is frigid. Artic. Not an ounce of compassion anywhere to be found.

Maybe he wasn't lying, back in the cathedral what feels like a lifetime ago. Maybe he really doesn't have any humanity left to give.

"So there's no hope for him," I say tonelessly. "Even after he gives you what you want."

"He chose his fate."

"Why?" I plead. "Why do this?"

"Because he's still the enemy and the enemy can't be trusted."

"Do you trust anyone, Phoenix?" I blurt out.

His eyes narrow infinitesimally. "Not as far as I can help it. But some people still manage to steal your trust when you're least expecting it."

"You make it sound like a commodity."

"It is," he says. "The most valuable commodity there is."

Without even realizing it, we've somehow managed to move even closer to one another. His chest is practically touching mine. The heat coming off him is blistering with electricity.

I desperately want him to touch me—not my head; my head wants him a million miles away—but my stupid, fickle heart wants him so bad it physically aches.

But he doesn't. He just exists. And that's a torture in its own right.

"Let me make one thing clear," he says. "You seem to think there's some convincing me. That we have a give and take. A rapport. You're wrong about that. I am the don, and what I say goes. Is that clear?"

I resist the urge to laugh in his face, but only barely. "Is your ego so fragile that you can't take one word of criticism?"

His jaw tightens. "You're a naïve brat from a godforsaken desert cult. You know nothing of this life or this world. What makes you think you're qualified to tell me what to do, little lamb?"

He's angry and lashing out because of that. I know I shouldn't push him over the deep end. Especially when he seems so close to it already.

But I can't help myself.

"Matvei agrees with me," I counter. "Is he a naïve brat, too?"

His first response is a glare so deadly that I actually contemplate getting into bed and burying my head underneath a pillow.

"Matvei is no longer a part of this Bratva," Phoenix hisses. "Not in any way that matters."

"He cares about you, you know," I say. "He loves you."

"We are no longer on the same path."

"Is that because you pushed him off it?"

"Jesus!" Phoenix roars, ripping away from me and stalking towards the windows like a Greek god of wrath. "What the fuck do you want from me, Elyssa?"

I look down, wondering about that answer myself. "I don't know," I whisper. "I wish I did."

It's the truest thing I've ever said.

He doesn't look at me when he speaks again. Just continues staring out the window, hands clasped behind his back, cutting a brutal silhouette in the low light. "I'm going to do the best I can to get Theo back. In the meantime, you are to follow my orders to the letter."

"I'm your wife, not your employee," I remind him saucily.

That does the trick. Over the edge he goes.

He whips around and comes at me like a hurricane. When he grabs my arm, I try and fail not to cry out. His eyes bore into mine as he leans in. His irises glow luminescent.

"You are whatever I need you to be," he growls right in my face. "Understood?" When I don't answer, he twists my arm painfully and pulls me even closer into his body. "I asked if you fucking understood me."

Fear is the only thing that makes me nod my head. Fear of what a man like him might do when he has lost everything he's ever cared for.

The moment I acknowledge him, he releases me and storms out of the room. His scent lingers in his wake, as do the marks of his fingerprints on my forearm.

He's in love with you, Matvei said.

Is that love?

Because if it is, I certainly don't recognize it.

24

PHOENIX

Why is it that every time I'm with her, I transform into someone I barely recognize?

Actually, that's not quite it. Not quite the problem.

The real problem is that I'm starting to recognize that part of myself a little too well.

I want desperately to maintain some sense of calm and composure. But then she goes and challenges me without realizing what's at stake.

Her life.

Her son's life.

Our son's life.

I feel the walls closing in. My breath gets short like someone's trying to choke me from the inside and the edges of my vision blur and blacken. My feet carry me out of the room before that can happen. I'm barely aware of it. I just stare blankly at the ground as I put one foot in front of the other.

It's only when I hear the crunch of sand under my soles that I realize I've ended up back on the beach. In the periphery of my vision, I see the ghost of a small boy building sandcastles by the shore.

It's not real. He's not there. But my God, I could swear he is.

He would have been five years old now. Would have come up to my knees, at least. Might his hair color have changed? Or his eyes? Aurora always claimed they'd get darker with time.

Memories and failures hit me like a thousand arrows, each one a physical prick of pain in my abdomen. Everything I've lost weighs on my shoulders. The gravity of trauma. Unyielding and cruel.

I find myself reaching for my cell and dialing in a number I haven't called in months now. He answers almost immediately.

"Hello, son."

Artem Kovalyov's voice is the voice of a don if ever I heard one.

"Father," I murmur respectfully as I stare out into the gray horizon.

"What an honor to hear from my boy," he says sarcastically. "Usually, I only get to speak to you when you call your mother."

I can't help smirking. "Making me feel guilty already. That's a new record."

"You can forgive an old man for missing his son."

His words catch me by surprise. He's never been one for sentimentality. Especially not with me. The older I've gotten, the more we've both receded into ourselves. The gulf between us grew. At some point, I'm not sure when, it became impossible to cross.

Or so I thought.

"Something's going on, isn't it?"

"Yes."

"Would you like to tell me about it?"

"I can handle it." I bristle as I say it. Even though I know it's a stupid thing to assert.

"I know you can," he replies without missing a beat. "I just thought you might need a sounding board. Trapped in your head is a lonely place to be, Phoenix."

The ocean looks particularly beautiful today. Mysterious, holding secrets just beneath the surface of every emerald wave. I kick off my shoes and walk in a little deeper so that the water can touch my feet.

"There's a woman," I say. "Elyssa. She's become… important to me."

"I gathered."

Again, I can't help bristling. But it's an automatic reaction, the behavior of an immature boy who doesn't want his daddy's advice.

I'm not a boy anymore. I'm a man. A don. I can face the truth without flinching.

"She has a child. My child. And he's been taken. By Astra Tyrannis."

There's a second of ponderous silence. Then: "If you need me—"

I appreciate that more than he knows. "Thank you, but extra manpower won't help. It's… tricky. I was going to attack today, but I've decided to hold off until I have more information."

"I can have my team dig up what they can," he offers.

"If you wouldn't mind."

"Of course not."

"Papa," I say, falling back on the title I used as a young boy, "don't tell Mama about any of this."

"I won't. Of course not."

"I'll get him back."

"I know that."

"I have to," I say. "I... I don't think I can survive losing another child."

"You can survive anything," Papa says with conviction. "You are a Kovalyov, and we can handle the worst this world has to offer. But you won't have to. You're sure the child is yours?"

I stop short at that one. For a second, I consider telling him the truth. But then I realize something. The kind of answer that's so obvious it slices right through the tangled knot of your problems.

The truth is what we make it. The truth is what we choose to believe.

"Yes," I reply, matching my father's conviction. "The child is mine."

"Then you do what must be done. If you need anything..."

"I'll let you know," I finish.

"Oh, and Phoenix?"

"Yes?"

"Congratulations," he says. "Having a child was the single greatest accomplishment of my life."

I take a deep breath. "Goodnight, Father."

I hang up and stare out at the horizon. I feel lighter than I did a few minutes ago. That weight isn't as crushing.

But I'm far from better. Not everything is so easily resolved. Why does it feel so fucking lonely when she's not with me?

I turn in the direction of the house and spot her step out onto the deck. She's changed into a simple white summer dress. But fuck, she looks angelic in it. Her hair flutters freely around her shoulders and even free of makeup, she's an absolute vision.

A vision with dark circles underneath her eyes and hollowed-in cheeks. Her neck and arms are too gaunt, too thin. Like the pain is eating away at her ounce by ounce by ounce.

She hesitates for a second as she gazes at me. We're too far away for proper facial expressions. But when I hold out my hand and beckon, she slips off her shoes and emerges onto the sand.

I watch her as she walks. Every part of me hurts so fucking bad—but goddamn, she makes it better.

"Phoenix," she murmurs when she's close enough to be heard over the crashing waves.

That's all. Just my name. I don't know what the fuck it means. But at the moment, it doesn't seem to matter.

All that matters is this. Her. Me. Us.

"Are you okay?" I ask, breaking the heavy silence.

"No," she replies quietly. "I'm not. Which is why I didn't want to be alone. I… I don't know what I'll do without him. I don't know how you survived it. And it feels like sitting still is a betrayal somehow. Like I should be doing more. I just wish…"

"Yes?" I ask, when she stops short.

She shakes her head heavily. "I just wish things had turned out differently."

"Differently how?"

She shrugs. Her shoulders look feeble, especially in the sheer fabric of her dress. "I don't know. Differently enough that Charity would still be alive and Theo would never have been in danger."

"There's no point in thinking about alternatives to what has happened, Elyssa. It'll tear you apart. Break you. Trust me—I know."

"Sometimes, I think that if I worry enough, I'll develop the ability to go back in time and change everything," Elyssa admits with an anxious chuckle.

I almost smile. "What would you change first?"

"I used to think I would change that night," she suggests in a soft voice. "But lately, I'm not so sure."

That surprises me. "You wouldn't change the rape?" I ask. "The fire? The gunfight?"

"No," she says, avoiding my eyes. "I wouldn't."

"Why the fuck not?"

She sighs. "Because if it hadn't been for that night. I wouldn't have met you. And if I hadn't met you, I wouldn't have Theo."

Well, fuck. What the hell am I supposed to say to that?

"For the record, I believe he's my son," I admit.

She raises her amber eyes up to mine. They're so full of love and trust. I called her a naïve brat earlier, but that wasn't fair. It's not naïveté I see in Elyssa.

It's hope.

It's purity.

It's salvation.

"I know," she says simply.

She smiles so beautifully that I can't stop myself from looking at her. I wish I had the words to tell her what this moment means to me. But I don't. And, without that, I wish I could reach out to touch her and show her what it means to me.

But I can't.

Because everything I touch dies.

And there's no fucking chance I'd survive the pain of losing her.

"Walk with me," I rasp.

She nods and slips her hand into mine. We meander down the beach, not saying a word. Just breathing together and listening to the sound of the waves kissing the shore.

But when the skyline of the old ruins comes into sight, Elyssa stops and turns towards them. "Why hasn't it been cleared away?" she asks.

"My mother gave it to me years ago," I explain. "She said it was a part of her past she no longer wanted. I didn't understand that back then. Maybe I do now; I'm not sure. I intended to rebuild it—to do it my way. But… I never got around to it, I guess. Life happened. Death happened."

Elyssa looks back at the ruin. "I want to look closer."

I raise an eyebrow. "It's not exactly good viewing. It's a bloodstained, burned-out wreck. Lots of people died in there."

"I can handle it," she snaps.

I suppress a grin. "If you say so. Come on then. Watch your step."

We put our backs to the water and weave through the dunes until the remnant husks of ashen buildings rise up around us. I keep a tight grip on Elyssa's hand in case she stumbles.

She notices me wrinkling my nose. "What's wrong? What do you smell?"

"The stink of death," I murmur. "It never goes away."

25

PHOENIX

"Does it feel weird?" Elyssa asks, stepping over rubble. "Being here?"

"Yes and no." She raises her eyebrows and I chuckle. "That's not helpful, is it?"

Her eyes sparkle brightly underneath the muted moonlight. As she walks ahead of me, it's hard not to miss the fact that her dress is translucent. I can see the perfect curve of her hips and the graceful lines of her long, lean legs as she picks her way through the devastation.

"Not particularly, no," she says. "Care to elaborate?"

"All this happened before I was born," I explain. "I've only ever seen it like this. So in a way, my attachment is to the ruins."

She smiles, but it's a forlorn smile. The kind of smile that only comes from someone who knows what it's like to lose everything. "I suppose I can relate. Everything I've ever loved was broken."

As we enter what remains of the main body of the house, the moonlight never truly fades because the ceiling has been blown apart on one end and caved in on the other. The remaining beams form a jagged trellis over our heads. Bats flit from crevice to crevice.

Elyssa hops up onto a precarious wooden log jutting out from a mound of rubble. She turns and curtsies like a debutante, then giggles. It's a sound this place hasn't heard in a long, long time. Hell, it's a sound *I* haven't heard in a long time, either.

Even still, I move forward protectively, ready to catch her in case she loses her balance.

"Don't stop talking," she encourages. "I like listening to you."

I shrug and let my hands fall by my sides, though I don't stray far from her. "My parents brought me here when I was a little boy. Showed me around, told me what happened."

"That's morbid. Especially for a little kid."

"Not in so many details," I assure her. "Just enough so that I understood where I came from."

"And where do you come from?"

"A long lineage of mafia royalty," I reply solemnly. "Don after don after don. I was destined to be what I am from the day I was born."

"Did you ever want anything else?" she asks curiously.

"Meaning?"

"Did you ever want to be anything other than... well, than what you are?"

I consider that a moment. "No," I say. "Not really."

She nods. Expected me to say that, I'm sure. But I can't help wondering if she'd allowed herself to hope—even if just for a fraction of a second—that I'd say something else instead.

"But there couldn't have been any other life for me," I continue. "You can't just stop this and become a doctor or a lawyer or a fucking accountant."

"I can't exactly see you sitting in a cubicle all day," she laughs. "You'd burn the place to the ground."

As she rises up on her tiptoes, the fallen beam groans under her weight and she wavers to the side a bit. She doesn't look like she's losing control, but I reach out and scoop her up in my arms anyway. Just an automatic reaction, unthinking: *Protect her.*

Her hands loop around my neck and I stare down at her, marveling at how beautiful she is. Her high cheekbones. The golden hair. Those liquid eyes, like honey frozen in time.

But there's no avoiding the sadness etched across every feature on her face. It clings to her stubbornly, refusing to let go. A veil she cannot rip away no matter how hard she tries. No matter how hard I try.

"You're not going to lose him," I whisper to her softly, fiercely.

She tenses, caught in the act. "How did you know I was thinking about Theo?"

"Because I've been where you are now. In fact, I'm reliving it all over again. There's no way to stop thinking about it."

She stares at me, her eyes thick with unshed tears. "Sometimes, it feels like I'm going insane."

I nod. "Sounds about right."

"Is there any way to make it stop?"

"I tried alcohol," I admit. "A lot of it. And it does numb you—for a time. But then you realize you've just piled onto your problems."

She sighs. "It's not that I want to forget. I just want to keep my thoughts clear enough so that I can actually be of use."

"You're a mother. Worrying is second nature."

"Does that imply that fathers don't worry as much?"

"Not at all. They just work harder to hide it."

She takes a deep breath and looks up towards the sky. I take the moment to examine the arch of her neck. I desperately want to press my lips to her nape and drink in her scent. It's the only thing that will calm me down at the moment.

But whatever is still there between us—if in fact there's still something there at all—is still too fragile and strange for that. I don't want to crush it the way I crush everything else in my world.

This will have to be enough for now.

Slowly, she brings her face back down to earth. But her eyes settle on me. "What do we do, Phoenix?"

"Our best," I say. "That's all any of us can ever do."

A diamond tear drips down her cheek. She shivers against me. And with that tear, I realize how much she's holding in.

"Hey," I whisper. "You're strong enough to get through this."

"If you're talking about my son's possible death, then you're wrong."

She shakes her head and wriggles out of my arms. Turning away, she strides towards the yawning hole where a window once was. The breeze catches the edge of her dress, playing with it to reveal a slice of pale ankle in the moonlight.

"I'm sorry. I know that's not what you meant," she says flatly, keeping her back to me. She wraps her arms around her body and hugs herself. "I'm just... I feel so lost."

I come up behind her, as close as I can get without actually hugging her myself. She tenses slightly, but she doesn't turn around.

"I don't even know why I tried to stop you today," she admits. "Don't hate me for saying so."

"I don't hate you."

Elyssa glances back at me over her shoulder. "I just… I kept thinking about what a spontaneous attack might mean. What if they'd killed Theo in retaliation or to save their own skin? What if you had been injured or worse in the fight? If you go in there without preparing… if I end up losing both of you…"

The tremor in her words shows how hard all of this is to say. How much effort it's costing her.

I twist her around to face me. "You're scared of losing me?"

She hesitates for a second, but it's self-consciousness that's got her tongue. She nods after a moment.

"What happened to hating my guts?"

She smiles, but there's more sadness in it than humor. "Sometimes, love and hate aren't so far apart."

Immediately after, her cheeks flush with color and all I can think is…

I need to kiss this woman.

But I don't want her to think I'm taking advantage of her vulnerability. Nor do I want her recoiling from me. So I suppress every instinct in my body, wondering if maybe that's the opposite of what she needs from me.

"Elyssa?"

"Hm?"

"I know it's hard. But you need to get some sleep tonight. Tomorrow, we'll discuss the plan. I swear."

Another lone tear trickles down her cheek. "My baby has been taken by a human trafficking ring, Phoenix," she says. "I don't think I'll sleep until he's in my arms again."

"What can I do to put your mind at ease?" I press. "Tell me what you need and I'll give it to you."

She stares at me for a long time before I realize she's trembling all over. I grab her face in both my hands and force her to meet my eyes.

"Listen. Don't you fucking give up yet. Do you hear me?"

She nods—or attempts to, anyway—but it falls short of true belief. She needs to turn her mind off. There's only one sure fire way I know to achieve that. The same thing that brought our worlds crashing together in the first place.

So I give into my desires and grab her without warning. Two hands on her hips, hoisting her up and setting her on the windowsill.

I catch her gasp in my tongue and swallow it like fine wine. For a second, I think she might haul back and slap me.

But she doesn't. Instead, the tension in her body gives rise to a new kind of heat. The kind of fire that demands an equal response.

Dust mushrooms around us as I step forward and press her to the crumbling stone. My hands tug at her flimsy white dress. It's suddenly offensive to me. Like, how dare this fabric stand between us?

I want her naked and trembling.

I want her completely at my mercy.

I want to reduce her down to an animal, so I can silence the never-ending cacophony in her head.

She won't be able to think about anything else.

One moment of peace. That's the promise I can give.

I tear the dress off her with fistfuls of fabric in each hand. Her panties give up the same way, with barely a fight.

I pull back to drink in the sight of her. Pale, surrounded by torn cloth, naked and beautiful like starlight and so desperate for me to touch her that it looks like she's burning up from the inside out.

Her eyes, though, are still wild. Still tormented.

Still too much thinking.

I jam two of my fingers into her mouth, forcing them deep before pulling them out again. I repeat the process until they're slick with her saliva. She gasps but complies each time. Then I reach down and coax my fingers into her.

Her thighs are clenched tight, but they part for me gradually. My thumb strokes across her needy little clit as I pull her off the ledge and into my embrace. I cover her body with mine. Hot pressure against hot pressure.

And the sound of Elyssa's moans mingles with the distant, crashing ocean.

Her head falls back. Throat exposed, eyes closed, face washed in moonlight. Maybe desperation isn't the right thing to be fueling this moment.

But it's all we've got.

So I'll use it.

Once she's dripping wet and trembling, I withdraw my fingers and unbuckle my pants. She looks at me hungrily, but I can still see the shadow of pain in her eyes.

I shove my pants down and step out of them. My cock springs forward like a spear. I'm erect and already glistening with pre-come because of her.

Hesitantly but hungrily, she reaches out and wraps her hand around my shaft. She starts to stroke. Slowly—painfully, agonizingly slowly.

"Fuck, little lamb…" I groan. I start to reach for her because if I don't taste her right now I'm going to fucking die.

But before I can take back the reins, she drops her head low and licks the drop of pre-cum right off my tip.

I choke and splutter. She looks up at me, but she doesn't release my cock from her grasp.

"I want to take you in my mouth," she whispers like she's in a fever dream.

"You don't have to."

She frowns. "I know that," she says. "I want to."

Then, without waiting for my answer, she sinks to her knees and slips the head of my cock between her sweet lips.

It's a miracle I don't explode in the first fucking second. She stays at my head, lapping her tongue over and under, before licking around my shaft. My vision blurs and distorts. I have to reach out to plant my palm against the wall behind Elyssa so I don't fall over.

She slurps and strokes at me with both hands. It's uncertain, it's inexperienced, and yet it's the most pleasurable experience of my life.

Standing on the destroyed grounds of my past.

Surrendering to my future.

She pulls back suddenly, sending a rush of cold air around my cock. I'm grateful for it, if only because it keeps me from erupting in her mouth.

"Was that… good?" she asks nervously.

"It was fucking amazing," I tell her, near breathless.

She looks down at my cock and examines it tenderly. Then, without warning, she slips me back into her mouth. This time, she swallows me to the base.

"Jesus!" I growl.

I have to cling to the broken walls on either side of me while she starts bobbing her head in and out, taking me deeper and deeper, until I'm hitting the back of her throat.

I feel like I'm vibrating as each endless second ticks past and the pleasure builds. I'm the one who stops her. I won't be able to hold myself back any longer if I don't.

I use the back of my arm to sweep away the remaining debris along the ledge. Then I grab her hips, spin her around to face away from me, and bend her over it.

Her breathing gets heavier and heavier as she realizes what's coming. And when I push inside of her, she cries out.

There's not an ounce of self-consciousness in that cry. No room to think. No room to worry.

She can only feel.

I don't have the self-control to go slow, so I drive hard into her, making each thrust more powerful than the last. Her legs tremble as she grapples with my force.

But I know that she's about to come when I feel her insides start to convulse rapidly around my cock.

"Oh God," she whimpers. "Oh God!"

I'm holding her hips so tightly that I can see the imprints of my fingers when I move them. I slap her ass every few seconds and she clenches up hard every time as I increase my speed and fuck her with the ruthlessness she needs. The ruthlessness we *both* need.

She explodes on my cock seconds later, but I still keep pumping into her. I don't have any goddamn clue how I'm lasting this long. I'm grateful for it, though. A minute later, she comes on my cock all over again.

Whimpering the same as before, a sound that sets my hair on end and sends shivers radiating all the way through me.

Only then do I allow myself to release.

It feels like my entire fucking soul comes out with the orgasm. She's never been tighter. Never been wetter. Never been hotter.

My thrusts slow. I can feel the wetness dripping down my cock as I give a few more shallow pumps before pulling out.

When she straightens, the line of the rock ledge is pressed into her stomach. She doesn't seem to mind, though. Because when she looks at me with misty eyes, thick with desire, I know I've succeeded.

For one blissful moment, she wasn't thinking.

26

ELYSSA
SOMETIME LATER

I wake up in the dark with a pain in my abdomen and a frown on my lips. It takes a second to orient myself to my surroundings.

His musky smell is what triggers my memory. Sweat, sand, whiskey, cologne. I sit up, looking around for him, but it's just me in here. The bed is empty.

His bed. *His* room. I'm surrounded by Phoenix's things, but the room lacks a personal touch. It might as well be a hotel suite.

I touch the other side of the mattress. There's an indent where he was, but it's gone cold. He must've left a while ago. And at that realization, a jarring thought flashes across my mind like a lightning bolt: *He's begun.*

I just know it, deep in my bones. He launched the attack. He went after Theo without a plan, without preparation, without caution.

Panic grips my chest as I leap out of bed, ignoring my complaining body. I stumble towards the window and thrust the curtains aside. Sunlight blares in, harsh and unrelenting. It takes a few long moments for my eyes to adjust.

When I look out over the courtyard that precedes the bunkers, I see a bunch of men milling around. But not frantically. They seem relaxed, unconcerned.

The panic squeezing my ribcage eases up. I was wrong; he hasn't left for battle yet.

That's something, I guess. But it's not everything. Because there's still the lingering doubt: what if I pushed him onto the wrong course of action? What if Phoenix was right and I was wrong, Matvei was wrong, everyone else was wrong?

What if, by waiting, we missed the only chance we'll ever get to save my son?

So many diverging thoughts rattle around in my brain. I can't seem to hold any of them together long enough to make sense of a single one.

I need to get out of my head. I decide to get dressed and go find him.

I rinse quickly in the shower, but when I reach for the white dress I was wearing last night, I realize it's torn into tatters. I end up rifling through Phoenix's drawers in search of something I can borrow.

I pick out a pair of navy-blue boxers with an elastic waistband and slip into them. I'm pulling out a fresh white t-shirt—when I come across an old leather wallet tucked away in the folds. It plunks to the floor and splays open.

A picture of a young woman stares back at me from the photo sleeve inside.

I sink to my knees slowly, never breaking eye contact. The woman is pretty. She's got a wry smile, bright green eyes, a dimple in her cheek. Her dark hair is effortlessly wavy.

"Aurora," I whisper. It's her. I know it.

My eyes slide down the photograph, to the bundle of blankets in her arms. A baby, swaddled but alert.

"Yuri." He looks around the same age as Theo is now.

My heart constricts as I stare down at the two of them. They're framed by greenery, wherever and whenever this was taken. Yuri smolders like his father, gruff despite his young age. But Aurora is glowing with happiness.

"I'm sorry," I whisper to them, though I'm not quite sure what I'm saying sorry for.

Reverently, I put the wallet back where I found it, lay the t-shirt back on top, and move onto another drawer. I pick out a black t-shirt from there and shrug it on over the boxer shorts.

I'm still working my arms through the sleeves as I scurry out the door, so I'm not looking where I'm going…

And I promptly run into a wall of human.

"Oof!"

My hair has fallen over my eyes, so I can't see who it is. But I don't have to see to know. I'd recognize his scent anywhere.

"Good morning to you, too," I grumble when Phoenix says nothing. I comb the bangs out of my face.

Phoenix's eyes trail up and down the length of my body. I can only stand there, twisting the hem of the t-shirt in my hands like a kid caught out in an act of rebellion.

"You look comfortable," he says with a small smirk.

I roll my eyes. "I couldn't wear my dress. Someone I know ripped it to pieces."

His smirk only gets more pronounced. "You're lucky there's any fabric left."

That elicits a blush I couldn't hold back if my life depended on it. He reaches out and runs the back of his hand across my cheek.

I try not to let the gesture go to my head. We're suspended together. Caught in a fragment of a moment, dangling over the edge. So we're just comforting each other through it. That's all this is. It doesn't necessarily mean we have a definitive future. Even if there's love somewhere between us, who knows if it will last? Everything hinges on the next few days.

But I can still feel the ghost of his touch, long after he's withdrawn it.

"I was just heading back to my room," I say.

"Why?"

"Uh…" I say, looking down at my clothes. "Because I need to change."

"You look perfect like this."

"These are your clothes," I point out with a laugh. "And I'm drowning in them."

He shrugs. "I think it suits you." Then he walks past me and grabs my arm as he goes.

"Hey! Where are we going?" I balk as he tows me along.

"I have a meeting set up with my lieutenants," he explains. "I assumed you'd want to be there."

"Phoenix, I can't go like this!"

"Why not?"

"Because I'm not dressed."

"That t-shirt practically comes down to your knees."

"Yes, but everyone will know it's yours." I realize how childish I sound the second the words leave my lips.

Phoenix must agree, because he scoffs, "You're my wife, Elyssa. They already know we're fucking."

I cringe, freeze, and yank my arm away from him.

He turns to look at me. "Now what?"

"Can you not say it like that?"

He stares at me with detached amusement. "The part about us fucking?"

I bristle again. "Yes."

"It's just a word."

"A vulgar one," I tell him. "A nasty word. A word that people use when they… when it doesn't mean anything to them. When they don't mean anything to each other."

It's an honest explanation. And yet the moment I say it, I regret it.

Phoenix's eyebrow arches high on his forehead.

"Never mind," I blurt quickly. "Forget I said anything. Call it whatever you want to. Let's go."

I don't wait for him to answer. I just stride past him so I don't have to see those dark eyes raking over me again and again.

Out of nowhere comes Charity's voice again: *So insecure.*

"Not you again," I mutter.

"Did you say something?" Phoenix asks, falling into step with me.

"No! Nothing," I say quickly. I pick up the pace.

This time, Phoenix doesn't follow. "Elyssa?"

"What?" I ask, glancing back over my shoulder.

"It's this way."

He points towards another broad corridor, one that was untouched by the attack—though the Bratva's construction crews have swooped down so quickly to fix the damaged areas that it won't be long until all evidence of the Yakuza ambush is wiped away.

I shake my head and take a deep breath before walking through the door that Phoenix is holding open for me.

He's not smiling anymore. His eyes have gone flat with darkness, which only makes my nerves rise.

It does help that it's not the boardroom full of sneering mafiosos I expected. There are only three other men standing around waiting for us. I'm surprised not to see Matvei amongst them. I consider asking Phoenix where he is, but then I think better of it.

All the men stay standing while Phoenix walks to the head of the table. No one moves or speaks. The windows are thrown open and the light streams in, but it still feels dark, somehow. Ominous.

"Elyssa."

"Huh?" I jerk, turning to him.

"Sit." He points out the chair at his right hand.

Swallowing back the anxiety rising in my belly, I sink to the seat. When I sit, Phoenix sits, and when Phoenix sits, everyone else follows suit. There's a weird tingle in the air. Like we're all playing by a set of rules I'm not familiar with.

Though not a single man seems surprised by my presence.

"So," he starts, "I've decided to delay our attack. We need a plan. We need information. I want to hear what we know. Konstantin?"

Konstantin has a sharkish glint to his eyes and a lithe grace in his fingers. He strikes me as someone who's seen things, who's done things. A Bratva man through and through.

"I've had two teams pursuing a pair of leads," he says. "We have tails on all known Astra Tyrannis compounds."

"And?"

"Nothing," Konstantin sighs. "No movement. No sign of Astra Tyrannis agents or the Yakuza. Silent as the grave, to be honest."

"Doesn't mean they're not there," another man speaks up.

Phoenix eyes flicker over to him and then back to Konstantin. "Continue."

"They're covering their tracks, boss," Konstantin continues. "They know we're looking for them."

"They know we're looking for them in places we're aware of," Phoenix points out. "What we need to do is find the places they're trying to keep secret."

"But how do we do that?" one of the men asks. "They're secret."

I can tell that Phoenix is trying very hard not to roll his eyes. "Yes, thank you, Ilya, for your enlightening observation. What I'm saying is—"

"It seems to me our best source of information is right here," I blurt out before I lose my courage.

All of the men look at me. Not with shock or irritation, like I might've expected. But calm acceptance. Like I belong here.

I wish I knew how to describe the feeling that stirs up in me.

"Explain," Phoenix orders.

"Raj," I say. "It's obvious he knows something. We need to convince him to talk."

"We tried—"

"You tortured him," I interrupt. "You didn't try to convince him. There's a difference."

A flicker of annoyance flits across Phoenix's face. Maybe I made a mistake. Maybe he brought me here to be an ornament, not a contributor, and by speaking up, I've broken some rule I didn't know existed.

But he's the one who invited me into this meeting. If he didn't want my honest opinions, then he shouldn't have asked me at all.

You tell him, girl, Charity croons in my head.

"You don't know how things are done here," Phoenix says softly.

His expression brooks no argument, but I'm suddenly aware that of everyone in this room, I'm the only one who can get away with arguing with him.

"Just because it's how things are done doesn't mean it's how things should be done," I snap back.

He raises his eyebrows, and I wonder when his patience will start to give way. And what it will mean for me when it does.

I can't worry about that, though. My son's life hangs in the balance, and I refuse to cow back and be a doormat. Even though a part of me really wants to fall back into that comfort zone. Into the safe sanctuary of submitting to the world around me.

Stop it. You're stronger than that. You just never believed you were.

"Phoenix, listen to me," I insist. "Torturing the man for information is not the right way to get him to talk. He'll end up telling you what you want to hear, as opposed to the truth. And we don't have time to make detours. Not while… not while they have my son."

He's listening intently. So is everyone else. I've never been in this position before, the center of attention at a moment when everything hangs by a thread.

It's terrifying—and incredibly empowering.

"This is not a therapy session, Elyssa," Phoenix says harshly. "And we don't have that kind of time."

"But—"

"I agreed to let you be a part of this," he cuts in. "But there are conditions. You have the right to speak. But I am still the don. And I make the final decisions."

"What's the point in taking my opinions on board if you just do what you were going to do in the first place?" I retort.

For the first time, the men in the room are starting to stir uncomfortably. They're not used to seeing anyone talk to their boss like this.

Well, tough shit. You reap what you sow.

"Would you rather wait outside?" he threatens.

"That's not what I'm saying and you know it."

He looks at me and broods for what feels like an eternity. One finger strokes at his stubbled jaw. His eyes see right through me.

The air bristles. My skin crawls.

And then Phoenix stands up abruptly. All his men get to their feet a second later. I stay defiantly seated and stare up at all of them, wondering what the hell I'm supposed to do now. If standing my ground is the right thing. If *anything* I'm doing is the right thing.

"So be it," Phoenix concedes unexpectedly. I can hardly believe what I'm hearing. "Raj is our best source of information. Ilya, how's he doing?"

"We patched him up and had the doctor in to see him," Ilya answers at once. "He's had a good night of sleep. He isn't dead yet, that's for sure."

"Good. Then it's time for another chat with our dear friend Raj. Elyssa, are you coming?" Phoenix asks.

I desperately want to turn him down and beg off being there. But it's the look in his eyes that convinces me otherwise. That condescending expression that's convinced I won't be able to stomach doing what it takes to save my son.

He's wrong.

"I know he's wrong, Char," I whisper back. "I fucking know."

To Phoenix, I call out, "Of course I'm coming."

He cocks his head to the side. "You're sure?"

"Very, very sure."

I brush past him and head out of the room. But I make a left instead of a right and walk fast down the corridor.

"Where are you going?" he calls after me. "The bunkers are this way."

"I know," I say without slowing down. "But if I'm going to be doing this, I'll do it in my clothes. Not yours."

27

PHOENIX
BUNKER TWO, CELL THIRTEEN

We pause outside the cell. "You're sure you're ready for this?" I ask.

Elyssa bites her lip, then straightens up to her full height and nods. "I'm ready."

"Okay," I say. "I'll be watching."

I leave her in the hallway as I step into the control room. A screen displays footage from the cell, and when I slip on the headset, I can hear the audio feed as well.

Raj looks like hell warmed over. Pale and gaunt with blood loss and hunger. But the steely determination in his eyes doesn't bode well for our mission here.

Elyssa is still standing in the hallway where I left her, breathing softly. Then, as if making up her mind, she steps inside the cell.

"Raj," she says, a little shakily.

"I don't want to fucking talk to you, whore."

She doesn't rear back like I expect her to. She just takes it all in stride. Nodding, she sinks into the chair my men set up for her. Perched on the edge, she looks into Raj's eyes with something that resembles compassion, if I'm not mistaken.

Part of me wants this to fail. She is so pure that she thinks the whole world works how she does. Thinks how she does. Feels how she does.

She hasn't seen of the darkness to understand just how wrong she is.

"Can I tell you something, Raj?" she probes gently.

My ears perk up. Raj's do, too, though he tries to hide his interest.

"I worry sometimes that I'm broken. I spent my whole life in the Sanctuary, and I can barely remember any of it. It's almost like... Don't laugh at this, but it's almost like I was born again the night I left. I know that must sound silly. It sounds silly to me, too."

He swings slowly from his cuffs. Not answering, but not looking away, either.

"Whole chunks of time are just gone. Years and years, hidden away in my head behind stone walls of trauma and fear. But you know something, Raj? I think... I think I'm starting to remember some things."

Now, he's definitely paying attention. So am I. There's an energy in the air that I'm not sure if I like or not. Raw and pulsing. Dangerous.

She brushes a stray lock of hair behind her ear. It's a casual, automatic gesture, but something about it makes my chest constrict painfully.

"Can I tell you something else?" she continues. "Lately, I've been hearing crying children. All the time. Whenever I'm alone in a room or on the beach or in the shower, I hear them. I even have dreams about them. I used to think it was my son crying for me. But now I realize that it's not him I'm hearing at all. Who is it, Raj? Whose children am I hearing?"

"How the fuck am I supposed to know?" he growls.

"That's the thing," Elyssa says softly. "I think you *do* know. I think you know a lot more than you're letting on."

"I had nothing to do with your runt being taken, if that's what you're asking."

She flinches at that one. I nearly leave my seat to charge into the room and beat some respect into this son of a bitch. But then I notice her hand. She doesn't lift it past her shoulder, but the gesture is clear. *Don't interfere.*

As annoyed as I am right now, there's also something intensely sexy about watching her take charge. She's soft-spoken and gentle, but there's determination there. A steely strength that I never noticed before, though I don't know how I could've missed it.

"Maybe not. But the people you work for, the people who sent you to the Sanctuary in the first place… The powers that be? They did. They have my little boy."

"Can't help you."

To my surprise and his, Elyssa suddenly lunges forward to her knees. She grabs a fistful of Raj's bloodied white pants in each hand as she looks up at him and says, "Yes, Raj, you can. You know things. Because I'm not the first one this has happened to, am I? I'm not the first mother separated from her baby."

He stiffens. For a long moment, we're all suspended in time, wondering if he's going to crack. If the truth will finally emerge.

He grits his teeth. I can practically hear them grinding together.

"Children need their mothers," Elyssa presses in a tear-stained whisper. "I know… I used to work at an orphan—"

She breaks off suddenly. Her hands fall slack, her eyes go wide, her face drains of color. I almost stand up and go to her, but I stop myself.

Someone cracked, indeed.

But it wasn't Raj.

Elyssa slumps back against the legs of the chair. Her eyes pinwheel, wild and unfocused.

"What did you remember, little lamb?" I whisper to myself in the empty control room.

Her voice pings through the headset, but it's so low that I almost miss it. I crank up the volume and hunch over to listen close.

"…There's a place near the Sanctuary," she murmurs. "In the valley. A place…"

I frown and lean in. This is new information to me.

But apparently, not to Raj.

The man is tenser than I've ever seen him. He looks as though he's going to throw up right on Elyssa's head.

Her gaze tracks upward. From the puddle of blood beneath his feet, to the stained hem of his pants, all the way up to his swollen, hardened face.

"Do you know it?" she asks.

"No." He gives himself away by answering too quickly. This is the opening we needed. I'm about to charge in there and cut the rest of the truth out of him.

But Elyssa isn't finished yet.

"I think… I think *I* know it," Elyssa says.

She's still looking pale and unsteady. As though she's seen a ghost. Every few seconds, she keeps shaking her head.

"There's a place… It's called…"

Her words mesh together and I can't make them out.

She stumbles upright and turns around so that her back is to Raj. She's got her arms wrapped around her torso to quell the tremors and her lips move silently, numbly.

That's enough for me. I rip the headphones off and charge back down the corridor. I burst through the door. "Elyssa!"

She whips around.

But not towards me. It's Raj she faces.

"How could you do it?" she demands. Her voice is shot through with fire and ice. "I didn't know what I was doing. But you did. You do. You knew."

"Elyssa, you—" I reach out for her but she slaps me away without looking.

"I thought I needed information from you," she says. "But I don't. Not really. I needed to unlock all the things I'd forgotten."

He glares at her, still trying to cling to his venom and his training. But I can see his will start to crumble.

"You and Josiah… You were supplying them with children. With young girls, too. You were cogs in the wheel of some awful machine. A meat grinder for the innocent."

The steely control I saw earlier is gone. She's coming unraveled now. Her voice breaks, her hair flies as she trembles with rage and sorrow in equal measure.

For the first time since I met her, her emotions are in control.

"Were you around to watch?" she cries. "Were you there to see them being separated? You monster! You—"

"Don't act so innocent," Raj interjects. "You were there. So why don't you tell me?"

She gapes at him for a moment. First, I see the denial flash across her eyes. Then I see the horror. The horror of the other memories that are only now tunneling their way to the surface.

She backs away from him slowly. "Oh God," she breathes. "Oh God…"

"You stand there and judge me," Raj continues. He rattles his chains. "But you were the one who lived in the Garden. You worked there. Got your own hands dirty."

Numbness washes over me. I know it's true, because the understanding is written all over Elyssa's face.

The truth is always uglier than we think it will be.

She stumbles back out of the room. I rush out after her.

"Close the door and get the fuck out of here," I instruct the two men who are standing guard outside the cell. "Now!"

They do as I say and leave quickly. The whole time, I keep my eyes on Elyssa.

She's pacing back and forth like an angry lioness. Her face is ashen.

"Elyssa," I say when we're alone. "Elyssa, you—"

She stops short when she hears her name. Her eyes land on me and tears slip down her cheeks.

"Oh, Phoenix," she says helplessly. "What have I done?"

She retreats into a concrete corner and stops only when her back hits the wall. Then she slides down as though she can no longer hold herself up anymore.

I walk over to her and squat down so that I'm at eye level with her.

"Take a deep breath," I instruct her. "And then… tell me what you remember."

28

ELYSSA

The memories feel like wisps of lace blowing in the wind. I try and reach for them, but they're elusive. They slide out of my metaphorical hands, slapping my face as they go past, leaving me with barely-grasped snippets of my adolescence.

An adolescence I spent working at the Garden.

The Garden.

It's been knocking at the door of my mind for weeks now. It started with the crying babies. It continued with devastating dreams.

Now, here it is: the truth.

Part of the truth, at least.

And all of my guilt.

"Tell me what you remember," Phoenix says to me.

I shake my head. "You'll hate me."

"What's the alternative?" he asks. "You can't hide the truth. Not for long. Not from yourself."

He's right about that. It's the one absolute that I feel like I've been blind to this entire time.

I raise my eyes and try to blink away my tears. I don't want to make myself the victim in this. Because I'm not. I may have once believed what I was doing was right, good—even noble.

But that was my crime.

I was ignorant. Willfully ignorant. I refused to think for myself. Instead, I believed what they fed me and I bought into the meat grinder they'd set up in the guise of a sanctuary from the world.

"Elyssa," Phoenix presses, "it's time to talk."

I take a deep breath, just like he'd suggested. It doesn't help much. "The Garden," I manage to choke out.

"What is that? Some Astra Tyrannis hideout?"

I flinch when he invokes their name. "Not exactly. Although, at this point, I suppose they're the same thing."

"What is it?"

"We—I—believed it was a place for rehabilitation," I try to explain, glancing at him from underneath my eyelashes. "It was a place where broken people could heal. And it was a great honor to be allowed to serve there. To volunteer your service and help the people who couldn't or wouldn't see the light."

"And you volunteered," he infers.

"Yes. I started when I was fifteen, I think. Or maybe sixteen. I can't quite remember. It all blends together."

"And what was it like?"

"It was... beautiful," I admit, trying to bring forth more memories than the meager few I've managed to unearth. "So green. A compound with little homes, shelters, healing spaces, surrounded by so many gardens."

"And what did you do while you were there?"

"I looked after... the children."

Faces flash past my mind's eye. The faces of children. Blue eyes, brown eyes, green eyes. Blond and brunette and red-headed as the setting sun.

I can't remember a single one of their names. I hate myself for it.

"Why you? Why not their mothers, their parents?"

"Their mothers were... dead," I say haltingly. "Or they'd abandoned them. Or they were... unsuitable. That's what they told us. Then they told us not to ask anymore."

I'm echoing words I was told. Regurgitating the lies that were shoved down my own throat. But even as I say them, they ring hollow.

"I... I'm sorry..." I say in barely a whisper.

"What are you sorry for?" he asks bluntly.

"For being part of it," I say. "For so many things really. But that, mostly. There was so much wrong and I never once questioned it. Any of it."

"Why not?"

"The children were happy. They were looked after. I thought I was taking care of them until they found happy, stable homes to go to. That was the party line and whenever something strange happened, I just ignored it. Because in my head, Josiah and the powers that be would never guide us wrong. They looked after us. They loved us."

I feel sick to my stomach. I have to close my eyes and ride out the nausea so I don't vomit right onto Phoenix's lap.

He doesn't say anything. He stares off towards Raj's cell, his eyes flitting this way and that, never landing long enough to give me an indication of what he's thinking.

When I can no longer stand the silence, I speak up. "I only just remembered all this, Phoenix," I tell him. "I was thinking of Theo and panicking and suddenly, it hit me. Not all of it. But parts. Enough."

His eyes flicker to my face and then back to the cell door.

"You... you do believe me, don't you?"

My voice shivers as I ask the question, but I don't want to avoid asking it.

He doesn't look at me for a long time. Fresh tears pool in my eyes. I'm beginning to realize the expression on his face, and it's worse than I could have ever imagined.

I wipe away my tears and try to hold my sorrow in. I deserve his disappointment. I'm disappointed in myself. So why shouldn't he be?

"I know it sounds like a lie," I say. "I know it's hard to believe. I know—"

"Stop, Elyssa," Phoenix says abruptly.

I cease talking instantly, waiting for the storm in his eyes to break. When he looks at me, I have to suppress the shiver in my spine.

"I believe you."

"You do?"

He nods.

"Oh." I'm not prepared for this.

He changes position and sits down next to me. Our shoulders touch and I turn to the side, staring at him with obvious disbelief.

I don't know what's going on in his head. I decide not to press him. It's enough for now to have those three crucial words—*I believe you.* They feel like the first sip of water after days in the desert.

"What do we do now?" I ask, before the silence can suffocate me any longer.

"We get back in there and get some tactical information out of Raj," Phoenix says with renewed determination. "I'm willing to bet that it's not easy to get in and out of this so-called Garden."

"Raj will know how," I whisper softly.

"Exactly. Raj will know how. And he'll tell us, one way or another."

"And then what?"

Phoenix's eyes are onyx black. "Then we go to the Garden and uproot the whole fucking thing until I find my son."

29

PHOENIX
ONE DAY LATER

I haven't spoken to her in hours. Not since we hit the road, just the two of us, like we're on some sort of perverse road trip.

I have a team already stationed ahead of us, near the Sanctuary. But they're not going to be involved in the break-in. We can't afford that risk. The plan is to be surreptitious about it. Sneak in, find Theo, and get the fuck out.

Then we'll be free to burn the place to the ground without worrying that he'll be caught in the crossfire.

It was a good plan—right up until the minute Elyssa insisted on coming.

"You need me," she had argued. "I know these people, their customs, the way they think. If something happens, maybe I can help throw them off our scent."

My first thought was, *Hell no.*

My second thought was, *Goddammit—she's right.*

Hence the silence.

She's glancing at me now. Then she turns away with a shake of her head.

"What?" I demand when she does it for the tenth time in an hour.

She snorts. "Stop pouting."

"I'm not sure you realize what you're getting yourself into."

"I'm not sure *you* do."

"You're overthinking."

"And you're not thinking enough," she snaps. She settles back against the seat, eyes closed, arms crossed.

There's a new strength in her voice. A pride in her posture. Some confidence in her that's impossible to deny. I can't deny that it's powerfully attractive.

But I don't want her clinging to false hope. Sure, chances are high that Theo is at the Garden, based on all the intel we've managed to gather from our interrogation of Raj and the tracking of my teams across the area.

But it's only an educated guess. Not a certainty. A million other possibilities exist and none of them can be ruled out yet.

Even if, in Elyssa's mind, there's only one.

Experience tells me it's never that simple.

"We're here," I announce a few minutes later.

She opens her eyes and peers out the windshield as we come to a stop.

It doesn't seem like much. Another outcropping of red rock in the desert. But this is where Raj said the place was. And sure enough, when I look close through the binoculars, I see tire tracks in the dirt. They lead up to a subtle gate in the cliffside.

I park the car behind a huge boulder on the lip of a distant dune and get out. Elyssa rushes to my side. At first, she's looking out at the Garden.

"There it is," she says. "You know, I expected to feel something. To remember something."

"It'll come," I assure her. "It'll definitely come."

I only say that because part of me thinks she's on the verge of collapse and she's just barely holding it together. If Theo is lost, I'm afraid she'll crumble completely.

Her eyes flit down to the edge of the rocky edifice we're standing on. "Wait a sec. We're still at least a mile away. Why are we parked?"

"Because my car is recognizable, the guard at the gate has a big fucking gun, and I don't need any more holes in my body," I drawl. "We go in on foot."

I hand her the binoculars so she can see for herself. She takes a look through, then turns to me with a furrowed brow. "Okay. So now what?"

I point down. "We climb."

Her eyes bulge out of her head when she peers over the windswept edge of the rock structure. "Are you out of your mind?" she yelps. "It's like five hundred feet down!"

"Better get started then," I say grimly. "You wanted to come on this little adventure? Well, little lamb, the adventure has begun."

∼

We touch down twenty minutes later. I flex my hands and forearms. The scar in my bicep where Anna shot me is pinging with pain, but I ignore it. I'll suffer when I'm dead.

Elyssa is sweaty, trembling, and pale. "You good?" I ask her.

She swallows, stiffens her lip, and nods. "Fine. Stop asking. Let's go."

I turn, stifling a smile. I like her like this. Fiery. Out of her shell. A fucking warrior princess, unafraid of battle.

I take her hand in mine and we start the long trek towards the gate. Neither of us says a word for the whole walk. The pressure of our intertwined fingers is all the reassurance we need.

When we reach the final dune separating us from the guard's eyeline, I pause. "You ready?"

"I told you to stop asking me that," she snaps. Then she softens into a soft smile. "But yeah. I'm ready."

I nod. Then I seize her by the upper arm and drag her forward like an unruly child around the edge of the dune.

As soon as the guard sees us, he leaps off his seat. He aims the rifle right at us.

"Who the hell are you?" he yells. "Stop right there! Don't come any closer."

I raise my free hand and jerk a thumb back in the direction we came from. "Here with a delivery. Fuckin' car broke down a couple miles back, if you can believe that shit. But the boss told me this one was important, so we hoofed it."

"What's the passphrase?" he demands. He's still got the weapon trained in our faces. I'm getting really sick of people pointing guns at me. It's taking everything I have not to unleash on this bastard right now.

But we can't afford to raise alarms. Not yet. So the show must go on.

"*In Tyrannis Speramus*," I say, reciting the words Raj told me to say.

The guard widens his eyes. "Blessed are the powers that be," he replies cautiously, completing the ritualized exchange. He lets the gun swing down by his side. "What little filly have you got here?"

"I wasn't told her name," I answer. I give Elyssa a rough shake. She yelps and cowers away from me as though she's terrified.

"She's a pretty one," the guard observes, licking his lips. "I'm surprised she wasn't snapped up immediately."

"Yeah, well, I don't ask questions," I say. "I just follow orders. Anyway, I gotta get going. You gonna let me through?"

"No," he grunts. "We're on lockdown. I'll take the girl in myself."

I feel Elyssa tense beside me immediately. This is not part of the plan. I'm not willing to wing it either.

"My orders were to drop her off personally."

"Which you have done," he points out.

"New protocol," I lie. "Direct handoffs only."

The guard frowns at that. *Fuck*—I went too far.

Time for Plan B.

I reach for my gun at the same time he reaches for his. But the poor bastard never had a chance. He doesn't even manage to get his weapon leveled at me before he dies.

I've got a silencer screwed on, so the gunshot barely sounds out. The surly guard drops to the sandy ground, blood gushing from the hole in his skull.

"Oh God," Elyssa says, turning from the sight and retching.

"Let's go," I order. "You can puke later."

"I'm fine," she says. She wipes her mouth and spits in the dirt.

We haul the gate open and slip through the crack. I'm struck immediately by how different this is from the world around it. Outside the gate is barren, sun-roasted desert. Hardly a damn thing lives or breathes.

But inside this rock-walled compound, we're surrounded by lush greenery. The sound of lapping water and laughing children sounds from somewhere far in the distance.

The name makes sense now: *The Garden*. Like Eden. Pure and beautiful.

It'd be an easy place to fall in love with if you didn't know the kind of rot that lingers at its core.

Suddenly, we hear the slam of boots on gravel. Elyssa's eyes lock onto mine.

"Soldiers," we both say at once.

I grab her and duck into a little alcove in the rock.

Once we're hidden, I peer out. Four uniformed guards march through the area, heads on a swivel. One of the guards stops and looks around. Then he picks up his walkie-talkie and punches the button.

"No sign of a breach here," he barks. "But we're checking the perimeter now."

"Fuck," I growl.

"They're going to find his body," Elyssa hisses.

I pull her down the corridor behind us in search of somewhere better to hide. A pair of doors waits at the end, but when I try the handles, both are locked.

"What are we going to do?"

I hold my finger up to my lips. Then I remove my jacket and wrap it around my hand. Using it as a buffer, I shove my fist through the big glass window in the door. It shatters. I knock out the rest of the shards, then reach through and open the door from the inside.

We both slip in and shut it behind us. I stand to the side and peer out through the broken glass, waiting to see if we'll be discovered. When the noise of the soldiers moves past us and fades away, I relax a little.

"Alright, now we can—"

Except she's not by my side like I'd expected. She's in the far corner of the dark room.

"Elyssa?" I call after her softly.

"Phoenix!" she whisper-shouts back. "I think someone's in here."

I jump forward, ready to fight whoever it is, when I realize that Elyssa's not talking about a possible enemy hiding in the corner.

She's talking about the young woman cowering in the cell set up in the far corner of the room.

Elyssa slides to her knees in front of the wrought iron bars. "Hey," she croons. "What's your name?"

The young woman's eyes are wide with fear as she takes in the two of us. She doesn't speak, but her eyes linger. She's young—no more than sixteen—with dark rings under her eyes and bedraggled auburn hair.

"We can help you," Elyssa adds. "But you have to trust me."

"Trust?" the woman laughs scornfully. "Trust is what led me here in the first place."

"My name is Elyssa. And this is P—"

"Elyssa!" I interrupt sharply. I grab her arm and yank her back up onto her feet. "What the hell do you think you're doing?"

"Trying to figure out what's happened to her," she retorts. "What does it look like?"

"She's not our problem at the moment. We need to be searching for Theo."

"And how do you propose we do that without some help? She's obviously been here a while. She might be able to help us."

"That wasn't the plan."

"It wasn't *your* plan. There are more ways to do things than just the Phoenix way."

If the situation weren't so serious, I might have laughed.

While we've been arguing, the woman has gotten to her feet. She's standing in front of the bars now, looking between the two of us.

"You're not from here," she remarks in an awed voice.

"No," Elyssa says, "we're not. We're here to look for someone. My son, actually."

The woman's eyes go wide. She looks normal enough, as far as those things go. She might even be pretty. But it's hard to tell with all the mottled bruises covering her face.

"You're here to rescue your son?" she asks. "God help you…"

"What's your name?" Elyssa tries again.

"Violet," the woman murmurs.

"Why are you in jail, Violet?" I cut in. "How'd you get here?"

"I was brought to the Garden weeks ago. To… to serve the powers that be. But I… I broke the rules," she explains. "I did something they told me not to."

"Which was?" I ask impatiently, glancing back towards the broken window. It'll definitely give us away if one of those soldiers decide to make a detour down this hallway. We need to move quickly.

"There's a building here that's off-limits," she replies. "It's filled with records. Records of the women and children who've passed through here. I went looking."

"You broke in?" Elyssa gapes at her. "Why?"

"My sister came to work here before I did," Violet explains. "That's what they told us, at least. She never came home. I just wanted to find her…"

"Do you know what they're going to do with you?" Elyssa asks.

"They told me they're waiting for my bruises to heal," Violet replies. "Then they'll transfer me to a place where I can be healed, where they can fix my brain and take my pain away."

Elyssa frowns. "What place is that?"

"Wild Night Blossom," Violet whispers reverently, like it's some holy place.

Elyssa eyes latch onto mine immediately. *Wild Night Blossom.* The nightclub where we met. Ozol's den.

Not a holy place in the slightest.

Fuck.

"Have… have you heard of it?" Violet asks, taking note of our expressions.

"Yes," Elyssa mumbles. "And it's not a place you want to go."

Violet's eyes seem to shiver. Only then do I realize she's close to tears.

"Oh, Violet," Elyssa says sympathetically, reaching between the bars to put her hand on the young woman's shoulder.

"Time's up. We have to get going," I tell Elyssa urgently. "We didn't prepare for so many guards."

I walk to the door of the cell and aim my gun at the lock. I shoot twice, then kick the door open.

"Come on," I tell Violet. "If you want to get out of here, you'll have to help us."

"How?"

"Take us to the records building."

She pales instantly. "We'll definitely get caught."

"No, we won't," I say. "I'll make sure of that."

"But—"

Elyssa grabs a hold of Violet's hand, effectively cutting her off. "Please, Violet," she begs. "We need your help. And your only way out of this compound is with us. Please."

Taking a deep breath, Violet nods. "Okay."

"Good," I say curtly as we head back towards the door. "I'll get down first and make sure the coast is clear."

I let us out the door as silently as possible. Violet is glancing around nervously like a frightened doe. When I look at her, she points a trembling finger to the far side of the compound.

"Over there," she says.

I take the lead, bumping into Elyssa as I move past her. We creep down the hallways carved into the rock. Birds flit from tree to tree overhead. And no matter how far we go, that sound of children laughing never gets any closer. I'm starting to wonder if I'm imagining it entirely.

Strangely, we don't see a soul until we come across an unmarked iron door. I look back at Violet and she nods.

I try the handle. It's open.

Even more strange.

Every sense is pinging on high alarm. Something about this is very fucking wrong. But what choice do we have? The place is too big to search without getting caught. First, we see what we can find in here.

Confirm Theo is on the premises. And buy ourselves time to think of what comes second.

So I step inside the room. It's cool and dark in here. Chilled by air-conditioning and lit only by red lamps set in neat rows along the ceiling.

"Where's Violet?" I ask when only Elyssa comes up next to me as I keep tip-toeing down the long aisles.

"She's standing guard by the door. She was too spooked to come in."

I shrug and turn my attention back to the room. We're surrounded by row after row of filing cabinets. My skin crawls at the thought of how much information must be contained in here. How many innocent souls with their torture documented for posterity.

At the very far end of the central aisle, one of the drawers is still cracked open. My gut tingles when I see it.

Yanking the drawer all the way open, I start rifling through the files stacked inside. Each one is exactly what I suspected—dossiers on women and children that've passed through this godforsaken place. Photos. Names. Birth records.

I feel like vomiting and killing someone at the same fucking time.

My wife might be in a file somewhere in here. My son, too.

"Elyssa!" Violet's face appears at the mouth of the aisle. She looks completely drained of color. "They're coming. They're headed straight here."

"*Blyat*," I curse. I grab three thick files at random, then take off running back towards the entrance.

We burst out at a full sprint. I have my gun in one hand and the files in the other.

"What happened to sneaking back out?" Elyssa hisses.

"That time has passed. Now, we run."

"We're going back the way we came?" Elyssa asks, sounding incredulous.

"You got a better plan?"

She doesn't reply to that one. Just quickens her pace. We catch sight of the gates ahead and everything looks quiet. Calm.

So, obviously, I don't trust it.

That's when I look over my shoulder and see them pouring out from a different hallway—at least half a dozen guards with their weapons at the ready.

I don't waste any time. I raise my hand and start shooting.

"Elyssa, get Violet out of here!" I roar.

"What about you?" she gasps.

"Just fucking run," I growl. "This is not the day I die."

30

ELYSSA

We burst through the front gates as gunshots fire off behind us. Violet trips and lands in the sand, kicking up a cloud of dust. I grab her and pull her up onto her feet.

"Don't stop," I tell her urgently. "And don't look back."

We run the way Phoenix and I came, until my breath is like a dagger in my chest and my feet are as raw and bloody as they were the night I ran from the Sanctuary. Violet stays with me the whole time, even when it looks like she's on the verge of passing out.

Fear can make a person do crazy things.

I follow my own advice and I don't look back. It's what Phoenix would want, even though I hate it with every fiber of my being. I'm stricken with fear, but I have no choice but to keep going. We reach the foot of the cliff and start climbing at once.

"Eyes up," I tell Violet. "Forget the ground even exists."

When we finally make it to the jeep, I open the door and gesture for Violet to get inside. Then I stare at the front of the vehicle, wondering if I should get in the driver's seat or not.

"Are we waiting for him?" Violet asks as I stare out at the hills below.

I can still hear gunshots.

"Please, God…" I whisper.

"Elyssa?"

"Quiet," I snap. "Sorry. Sorry, Violet. I just need to think…"

I think about getting in the driver's seat and just driving off. It's what he'd tell me to do, I'm sure. But like I told him earlier, there are more ways to do things than just the Phoenix way.

And in fact, it's long past time that I started doing things the Elyssa way.

I climb into the front seat and twist the keys that he left in the ignition. The engine roars to life. My hand is on the gear shifter, but I'm hesitating. I'm lingering.

What are you doing? Charity yelps in my head. *Pedal to the metal, girl! Let's get moving!*

"We can't leave him," I whisper back to her.

"What?" Violet says, blinking in confusion.

"Nothing," I say. I shake my head to clear the cobwebs out. "I just…"

Suddenly, there's an angry rapping on the window. I scream as I twist around to see…

A bloody, dust-stained Phoenix.

"You're in my seat," he drawls.

I burst through the door and into his arms. He smells like sweat and blood, but I don't care. "You're alive," I whisper into his neck. "Thank God, you're alive."

"I thought I told you to get the hell away from here," Phoenix growls.

"Apparently, I don't follow instructions very well."

He holds me at arms' length and at last, a smile breaks across his face. "No," he agrees, "you do not."

Within seconds, we're speeding through the rough terrain. Phoenix presses the jeep to its limits. He doesn't slow until twenty minutes later.

The fear takes a little while to die down. But when it does, it's replaced with the swell of disappointment. I'm glad we'd managed to get out of there alive. But the plan had been to locate Theo—and we hadn't even come close.

So the question is… what do we do now?

Phoenix doesn't seem to be in the mood to talk. He keeps two hands on the wheel and an angry scowl on his face as we cross into the city limits.

Violet keeps looking back over her shoulder every few minutes. I recognize the signs of shock and trauma in her. She's jumpy and pale. Sweat beads up along her brow and her eyes keep darting around as though she's worried someone is following her.

I twist around and reach for her hand. "Violet," I say gently. "I know this is a lot. But we are going to help you."

"How?" she asks.

"I… I don't know yet," I reply honestly. "But we'll figure something out."

"They'll come after me."

"We'll make sure they don't," Phoenix says firmly. "They won't be able to find you once I'm done."

"And… my sister?" she asks hesitantly.

Phoenix exchanges a dark glance with me. *You tell her,* his eyes seem to be saying.

"Listen, Violet," I tell her. "I can't make any promises. We can try to locate your sister if you give us her information. But the chances are—assuming she got out—that she's changed her name, covered her tracks. She probably lives a completely different life now."

"I still want to find her."

"I know you do," I soothe. "Of course you do. I just want you to have a realistic outlook of what's possible."

Violet slumps in the back seat and looks out the window. I hope she'll sleep—God knows she needs it—but her eyes stay open until we get to Phoenix's mansion.

It's clear Violet is not prepared for the beauty and grandeur of the mansion as the jeep pulls up the private driveway.

"This is where you live?" she wheezes.

"This is... Phoenix's home," I say. I may be his wife, but I don't feel right claiming the mansion as mine just yet.

He helps us both out of the car and into the house. When we enter the main foyer, Phoenix turns to Violet. "You must be hungry," he says. "I've had the chef make something for you to eat. Come on."

The dining table is laden with comfort food. Casseroles, lasagnas, sandwiches.

"Eat something," Phoenix tells me, though he makes no attempt to eat himself.

I force myself to nibble on a piece of bread as Violet loads her plate with the casserole. We all sink down into seats and sit in silence for a while.

"Violet," Phoenix asks, when her plate is half-empty. "Can you tell us how you got to the Garden?"

I give him a frown. "Is this really the time?"

"We don't have the luxury of taking things slow," he reminds me. "They know there's been a breach."

"But you got the files," I remind him.

"Only a few," he admits. "And I plan to pour over those in a minute. But first, Violet, we need you to tell us anything of importance."

"I… I'm not important," she says, looking down at her plate. "I don't think I'll have anything to tell you."

"Let's start with your story," he says.

She looks at him out of the corner of her eye. I see the fear there and I recognize it. The same fear I had when I first saw Phoenix.

But I also see the other thing I felt: trust. An inexplicable sense that he's not quite what he appears to be.

She voices that exact thought. "You're one of the good guys, aren't you?" Violet stammers.

I step in before Phoenix can reply. "He is, Violet," I tell her. "I know he looks big and scary. But he's not like the men who did that to your face. He's trying to stop those men."

She nods and takes another bite of food. Then, swallowing hard, she starts to talk. "We first came to the Sanctuary a year ago. Me, Mama, my sister Caroline. Daddy was a mean drunk, so we left him when Mama heard about this place. They told her it was a safe place for… for women like us. Scared and alone." She raises her eyes up to meet mine and adds, "I guess we were stupid enough to believe them."

I reach out to stroke the back of her hand. "I believed them, too," I assure her. "You're not alone. Keep going."

"So we moved to the Sanctuary. It was good at first. We got clothes and food and a place to stay. And they taught us all kinds of stuff.

How to think, how girls are supposed to act. It seemed nice. Weird, but nice. And I guess I was stupid enough to believe all that, too."

Phoenix's fist tightens on the edge of the table. I can see the anger coursing through him.

"Then, after a couple months, one of the important men came to our little house. Ra... Rag..."

"Raj," I finish for her.

She nods. "Yeah, that's it. Raj. He came and he told us that my sister had been selected for a special task. A job at the Garden, where she could serve the community. I didn't want her to go, but he didn't really give us the choice, you know?"

A tear glimmers at the corner of her eye and then falls to the tabletop. I feel nauseous and achy. Like my body is taking on Violet's pain for her. Helping her shoulder the burden that's crushing her.

"I shouldn't have let her go," she says, voice cracking. "I shoulda fought harder. But I... I trusted them, you know? He seemed so... certain. About his 'mission,' he called it. He said Caroline was a special girl and when I got old enough, I'd be special, too."

"Then what happened?" I press.

"She disappeared. Six months passed and she was supposed to come home, but she never did. Mama didn't care anymore. She just prayed with the women's circles and did her chores and that was that. She's had a hard life, so I don't blame her for just wanting to feel safe somewhere. But I wasn't feeling safe anymore. I was having nightmares, the kind that feel realer than life. I kept seeing my sister in some horrible place, screaming for me to come help her. So I went looking for Raj."

She sobs, then straightens up and wipes her nose. "I told him I wanted to go where my sister had gone. To the Garden. And he smiled in this way that, like—I probably shoulda known it wasn't a nice smile. But I just missed Caroline so much and those nightmares wouldn't stop, so I had to go looking for her. And he told me he'd get me a job there. The next morning, I went. They wouldn't even let me say bye to Mama. Just put me in the back of a truck and drove me from the Sanctuary to the Garden. And then… and then…"

That's when she loses the thread of the story completely and dissolves into tears. I just stroke her back and murmur comforting words as best as I can. Even though I want to cry right along with her. I hurt with her, for her.

She deserves better.

We all do.

"She's gone, isn't she?" Violet whimpers.

"We can't know anything for sure," I tell her. "Don't lose hope."

"They said they were going to send me somewhere to take my pain away. The Wild Night Blossom. You said you knew what that was? Someone told me maybe Caroline went there."

Staring at her face, I realize how young she is. I couldn't tell at first past the bruises, but with her crying like this, I can tell. She's a child. My heart cracks even further.

"Wild Night Blossom is a sex club," I explain to her as gently as I can. "It's not a good place."

Her eyes bulge. She slumps back in her chair. She looks positively shattered. "So that means my sister…"

"I'm sorry, Violet," I tell her. "I'm so sorry."

A maid comes into the room and knocks politely. "The guest room is made up, sir," she tells Phoenix.

He nods and turns to Violet. "Go sleep," he orders, though his voice is more tender than usual. "Sleep as long as you need. You don't have to decide anything right now. You're safe here."

Violet sniffles and nods. "Thank you," she whispers.

"Marie will take you up to your room."

Violet gives him another shy nod. Then she leaves with the maid.

The moment she's gone, I stand up. "I should have told her," I blurt. "I should have told her I was there once."

"What purpose would it have served?" Phoenix sighs. "Knowing your past doesn't change hers. She needs to trust us right now. And if you tell her, you'll break it."

He's right. But the guilt lingers at the bottom of my stomach.

I shake my head. "I was complicit. I helped. I…"

It's getting harder to breathe, harder to think beyond my panic, my sense of shame. It feels like I'm being buried by the weight of my own emotions.

"Elyssa, calm down."

"Calm down?" I gasp. "Calm down? I've participated in the destruction of so many lives. I don't even know. I can't even count. It's—"

I break off, trembling. Phoenix stands suddenly. His chair scrapes backwards and then he strides around the table and plucks me out of my seat.

"Come with me."

He guides me through the house, up the stairs. We walk into his office and that rich smell of leather and cologne fills my nostrils. It's soothing in a way I desperately need.

He closes the door behind us and steers me towards the massive wall filled with information and pictures of everyone he knows who's connected with Astra Tyrannis.

"Look," he instructs me.

I shake my head.

"Elyssa," he says firmly. "Look."

I raise my eyes to the photographs pinned on the wall.

"*Those* are the people responsible," he tells me. "*Those* are the people we're going to hold accountable. You? You were just a victim of your environment."

"It sounds like an excuse."

"It's not," Phoenix says. "I know it feels like we failed today. I know you're out of your mind with worry for Theo. But I got some files out of there. And that's more than we had before."

He sounds so certain. I want to believe him. But my own sins are staring me in the face, refusing to be cowed.

"Maybe… maybe this is divine retribution," I whisper.

"What do you mean?"

I raise my eyes to his. "God is punishing me for what I've done. That's why he's taken my son away. That's why he took my baby."

31

PHOENIX

Her whiskey-colored eyes seem even larger with all those tears glistening in them. I want to wipe them away, but I stay my hand. She doesn't need my comfort right now.

She needs to be heard.

"I don't believe in God, Elyssa," I tell her. "Or 'the powers that be' or any of that bullshit. I believe in us. We make choices and we must deal with the consequences of those choices. It's that simple and that complicated at the same time."

She shakes her head. "I didn't even think—"

"Because you weren't taught to think," I say. "You weren't taught to have opinions or to question authority. You were taught to listen. To obey."

Something about those words triggers a violent reaction. Her eyes bulge. She claps her hands to her stomach and keels over as though she's trying to keep her organs from spewing out.

She's mumbling something on the ground. I kneel next to her. "Elyssa?"

"We had this prayer… They taught it to us as children," she says softly. Her eyes are gazing—not ahead, but into the past. "I used to say it to myself every night before I went to bed. Before every meal. In church every Sunday."

A tear runs down her cheek as she begins to recite it in a mechanical voice that doesn't sound like her own.

"To serve is to find peace. To obey is to find happiness. To listen is to find truth."

When she finishes, the silence crashes down on us like a tidal wave. It's brainwashing, pure and simple. It's manipulation. It's cruelty.

And it makes me so fucking angry that I have to restrain myself from punching a hole in the window.

"I used to think it was so beautiful," she admits, the shame thick in her voice.

"That was what you were meant to think."

"That's my excuse?" she asks. "That I was brainwashed?"

"It's the truth."

She turns her face away from me. She looks broken.

No—she looks like she's breaking apart, one piece at a time. Crushed by the sins she committed when she was too young and too indoctrinated to know any better.

"Listen to me," I say, reaching out for her.

But she recoils from my touch as though she doesn't think she deserves the comfort. "Please, no…"

"Stop," I say. "You have to fucking stop this."

"Stop what?"

"There's no time for this, Elyssa. You can fight your inner demons another fucking day. Right now, I need you in my corner."

She shakes her head robotically. "I can't fight. You don't want me in the fight."

I grab her face and force her to make eye contact with me. "You can't fight? Bullshit. Fucking bullshit. You realize that those were real guns pointed at us back in the Garden, right? Those big bangs weren't just for show. You stayed calm during all of it. You kept Violet calm. You kept her safe."

"Did it seem that way to you?" she asks. "Because that's not how I felt."

"Elyssa, you're strong. Stronger even than I thought."

"They still have my son," she points out. "What good does all that bravery do if they still have the only thing that matters? And now, they know we tried to rescue him. They'll move him. We'll never find him again. I can't lose him, Phoenix. He's all I have."

"He's not all you have," I assure her. "You have me, too."

She laughs bitterly. "You don't mean that."

"I wouldn't have said it if I didn't mean it."

She shakes her head. "You deserve better."

"Stop—"

"It's true. You deserve better than—"

I silence her with a kiss so sudden and so fierce that I feel her gasp release in my mouth. She goes stiff and her hands patter lifelessly against my chest.

Until she recovers a second later and pushes me off. "What are you doing?"

"Trying to stop you from giving up," I growl. "This is not the fucking end, Elyssa. We will get Theo back."

"You can't know that."

"I do know it," I say, grabbing her by the arms and pulling her back against my body. "Kiss me again and tell me I'm not very fucking certain."

Our lips crash together. Bodies melt into each other. Breath mingles, panting and desperate. We back into one of the walls, upending something that clatters to the ground.

Let it break.

Let everything break.

This is what matters.

I tear at her clothes while she tears at mine. We attack one another like rabid animals at a feeding frenzy. When I pull back, her paleness has given way to color. Her cheeks are flushed pink and her lips look swollen.

"You've been a fucking dream since the moment I met you," I rasp.

Then I shove her backwards. She falls against the thin console table, looking slightly shocked at my sudden display of aggression. I don't stop there. I yank her shirt over her head and rip her pants and panties down her legs and hurl all of it over my shoulder.

She's lying back now, her chest rising and falling frantically. Her breasts are beautifully round, nipples piqued and ready. Her slim thighs tremble on either side of me. I run my hands up and down those beautiful legs. Fingers tap-dancing on her skin.

I drink her in, thinking of all the ways I'd like to devour her. To break her just to hear the sounds she'd make—and then put her back together again, one soft kiss at a time.

I caress her cheek for a moment before slipping two fingers into her mouth. She keeps her eyes on me as she sucks slowly.

I use my free hand to explore her pussy. I caress her lips, teasing out her desire until I can feel her moistness start to leak out. Then I pull my wet fingers from between her lips and slip them inside her. She moans low, her eyes fluttering as I start fingering her gently.

I'm desperate to fuck her. My erection is throbbing painfully, greedily. But I know that taking my time will pay off. The slow burn will just build the anticipation until we explode like supernovas.

I curl my fingers inside her, watching every little movement she makes. Savoring it like something I'll never get to witness again.

She groans. Her eyes open. They lock on mine just as I find her clit and run slow circles over it with my thumb.

"Ah…" she moans. "Phoenix…"

The sound of my name on her lips is so fucking erotic that I nearly burst right then and there. But I curb my instincts and focus on giving her the release she needs.

Slowly, I retreat from her pussy and raise my soaking wet fingers to my lips. Without ever looking away from her, I lick them clean.

She trembles as she watches. Her mouth moves, but no words come out. Just a groan that says, *Please don't make me wait any longer.*

But I will.

I'll make her wait just long enough for it all to be worth it in the end.

Then, still staring into the depths of her soul, I kneel down and run my tongue up and down her slit. She jerks hard, her head almost knocking against the back wall.

I re-position her so that she won't hurt herself, then I hoist both her legs over my shoulders. That leaves her in a position of powerlessness, but then again, that's the point.

I need her to let go.

I need her to surrender.

She twitches upward, trying to straighten herself, but with one gentle push, I have her leaning back again. Then I push my tongue inside her, and she melts into putty in my hands.

"Oh God," she gasps as I lap her up. She's sweetness, honey itself, and the feeling of those thighs clenching around my head is the most delicious sensation I've ever experienced.

I slide back and forth from teasing her lips to licking circles across her throbbing clit. When I suck it into my mouth, she cries out again and arches her back so hard I wonder if it will snap. Her hands knot in my hair as she pulls me into her.

One more lick and then the orgasm hits her like a runaway train. She goes stiff from head to toe, then starts shaking with powerful tremors.

I think I hear her whisper my name as she coasts down from her peak.

I wipe her taste off my mouth and get to my feet. She's still sprawled before me, her limbs splayed out like a gift I've unwrapped and devoured. The fact that she's so unkempt, so disheveled? It only increases my desire. That thin sheen of sweat on her body makes her look like she's glowing. I want to lick each drop of it from her.

She's looking at me like we're caught in a fever dream. Her eyes are unfocused and hazy. Her hair is a wild mess around her head.

"You look fucking magnificent," I tell her.

She shakes her head in disbelief. "W... what have you done to me?" she whispers blearily.

I pull her forward and grip her under the ass before lifting her off the console table. Her legs wrap around my waist as I carry her over to my desk.

The files are still sitting in the middle of the desk top, but I shove them aside and set her down in their place. Her body is limp with release. Liquid.

But it's not over. She has farther yet to go.

Her eyes go wide as she realizes that I'm not finished with her. Then the surprise gives way to hunger as her eyes flit down to my cock.

I push her on her back again, prying her legs apart as I press myself deeper between her thighs.

She props back on her elbows and keeps her eyes on me. I free my cock from my pants, align it with her pussy, and rub her slit with my tip. She's soaking wet, so my cock glides up and down easily.

"Get inside me," she begs.

"You want me to fuck you?" I ask.

I know she doesn't like the word, or the way I've used it. But I want her to see that there's no shame in it. In this. In us.

Fucking can be transformative.

Fucking can be beautiful.

Fucking can be love.

She nods slowly.

I put my fingers to her lips and trace the perfect curve of her mouth. "Say it."

"Fuck me," she whispers.

My cock jumps at her plea. I wince at the unexpected need that's so fucking strong it hurts. Coming from her, this innocent little lamb… it's almost too much.

"Say that again," I tell her.

"Fuck me, Phoenix Kovalyov."

The moment she finishes speaking, I bury myself inside of her.

She cries out and collapses backwards. The desk starts to squeak as I ram hard. This time, I'm not prepared to take it slow. I want to chase my own desire now. With her body laid out before me, it's impossible not to.

I squeeze her breasts as I slam into her. Cups and pens go clattering off the desk. Papers fly everywhere.

Neither of us give a fuck.

Elyssa is lost in the throes of her rising moans, all semblance of self-consciousness gone as I fuck her hard and fast. Her walls contract around my cock and I know she's seconds from her second orgasm.

I clench my jaw and grit my teeth as the tension builds. I don't have much longer left myself.

I dig deep and pull on my last reserves of energy as I fuck her even harder, even faster. She's in danger of spinning right off the desk if I weren't holding her so tightly. The files we stole from the Garden are teetering on the edge. One more thrust and they'll hit the floor along with the rest of my shit.

I don't stop until I've stolen another orgasm from her.

I don't stop until I explode inside her.

I don't stop until I've made her mine again.

The world blacks out when I come. It takes a long time for the light to come back into my eyes. I brace my hands on either side of her on the desk and wait until my breathing returns.

Trembling, she sits up, wincing at her soreness and fatigue. I grab a couple of tissues and wipe myself off. Then I move to the floor to recover the files that we'd upended.

When I bend down to pick them up, I see the contents of one have spilled loose. A paperclipped stack of glossy photos, fanned out on the carpet. All show the faces of young women, none of whom could possibly be out of their teens.

It makes my stomach turn to think of where they might be now. Scattered in the dark corners of the world. Being used by men who don't give a shit. Robbed of hope or love or a chance at a real future.

Elyssa groans as she pushes herself off the desk and limps over to where her clothes are piled on the floor.

I'm about to stuff the photos back in the file folder—when I spy something sickeningly familiar.

I pull out the picture and stare at the young woman staring back at me.

It's Elyssa.

And in her arms is a baby boy. He can't be more than two. In fact, I know for damn sure that's how old he is.

Because I know that boy.

I mourned that boy.

I think of that boy every single fucking day.

When I turn to Elyssa, she's already dressed and looking like she's floating on a cloud of bliss. But her expression curdles the moment she sees my face.

"Phoenix…?" she asks. "What is it?"

All the hope that had gripped me moments ago is gone.

All the love has vanished.

All I can say are four little words: "What have you done?"

32

ELYSSA

"Phoenix?" I ask. "What is it?" My head is still whirring after that violent, passionate sex. I'm having a hard time focusing.

He doesn't answer immediately. He just stares at me as though he doesn't recognize me anymore.

That's what scares me the most.

"What have you done?" he says again in a barely audible whisper.

Oh, so many things, I want to say. *So many things that I regret. That I wish I could take back.*

"What did you find?" I choke out the question, even though I want to run from the answer.

He holds up something. I can tell it's a photograph, but I can't see who's in it. Taking a tentative step forward, I take it in my shaking hands.

I don't look at it right away. My eyes are still fixed on Phoenix's face. On the man I thought I knew. Thought I loved.

The change in him is so stark that it takes my breath away.

I look down.

And I see why.

My blood goes cold with dread as I stare at a younger version of me. My hair was longer back then, and braided back into a thick braid that falls over one shoulder.

What's most striking is the look in my eyes. Dazed, hazy, placid. I hardly recognize myself. This picture is a stranger without a mind of her own. A fool who thought she was serving her purpose, when all she was doing was aiding and abetting crimes that she couldn't even have begun to fathom.

Only when a tear splashes down onto the picture do I realize that I'm crying. Crying for myself, in part. But mostly for the child in the picture. And all the children just outside of it.

I don't want to face Phoenix, but I don't want to be a coward, either. The girl in this picture was a coward, even if she didn't know it. I don't have that choice anymore.

"I… I can't deny what I did. What I helped do," I tell him, my voice breaking as I struggle through it. "All I can say is—"

"The boy," he interrupts gruffly.

I haven't heard that timbre in his voice for months now. I thought we'd moved past it. I thought he loved me, too—maybe.

"What?"

"The boy in this picture," he says, his eyes turning colder than I've ever seen them. "Do you know his name?"

Frowning, I look back down at the photograph. I have to wipe the tears from my eyes before I can take a good look.

He's a dark-haired boy. Vivacious, handsome already. But nothing about him rings a bell in the shadowy recesses of my memory.

"Look at him, Elyssa," he spits. "Fucking look at him."

I do as he says. I stare at the child and try to see what Phoenix wants me to see.

And then it hits me.

I don't remember this boy from my time in the Garden—I remember him from a picture in a wallet that fell out of Phoenix's dresser drawer.

A picture of Aurora and Yuri.

He was younger in that one. About five or six months, just old enough to hold his head up on his own.

This one, he's at least a year and half. Maybe two.

Which means…

I drop to my knees, still clutching the picture between my fingers. I'm shaking now so badly that I can barely think straight. When I look up, Phoenix is staring down at me with his cold, angry eyes.

"That's my son in your arms, Elyssa," he rumbles. "My firstborn son was in the Garden. He was there at the same time you were there."

"I… I don't understand," I stammer. "I thought… Anna said she…"

"Anna obviously fucking lied," he growls. "This is just another game to them. They would have seen my son as a bargaining chip or a power play. They didn't kill him… but they may have since then."

I keep staring down at the picture, hoping that I can remember something that will help us. Nothing comes to light.

"What happened to him, Elyssa?" he continues. "What happened to my son?"

I shake my head. "Phoenix…"

"Fucking answer me!"

I cringe back. I deserve every bit of his fury, but I still don't know if I'm strong enough to survive it. He turns away from me. His back rises and falls with each shuddering breath.

"Phoenix, I'm sorry. I'm so sorry, but I don't know… I don't remember what happened to him."

Phoenix suddenly bellows at the top of his lungs and sweeps everything off of his desk. "Fuck!" he roars. "Fuck, fuck, fuck!"

I scream and stumble backwards. I bury my forehead in my hands. The tears come hot and fast and thick. But the pain doesn't change. The pain remains exactly as it has been since I realized that the black hole in my memory is filled with things I can never, ever undo.

All I can say is that I'm sorry. Even though I know it's a useless, pointless word that holds no true peace. It's a word you use when all is said and done. When there is nothing left to do.

He twists around, his face a black cloud of despair. "You met him, Elyssa! That's my fucking boy in your arms! And you don't even remember?"

I have no defense. No justification. "I know. I know."

I wish I could give him the details he craves. But I have nothing. Only excuses. Only the truth: that I remember my life up until I turned fourteen. Up until I went to the Garden.

And that everything after then is a barely-remembered dream.

"I know how much you're hurting right now…" I say.

"Fuck me," he growls, almost like he's talking to himself. "I thought we had moved past this. I thought we'd finally gotten somewhere…"

It breaks my heart to hear him say those words.

He turns around. My cheeks burn with the heat of his gaze.

"What can I do?" I ask helplessly.

"You've done fucking plenty."

I drop my head. I deserve this, but it hurts nonetheless.

He doesn't say anything else for a long time. He circles around his desk and for one insane moment, I think he might hug me. Might wipe away my tears and tell me it's okay, that we'll work through this together.

That we're a team, like he said.

That I'm brave, like he said.

That he loves me—like I've dreamed he'd one day say.

But he keeps his distance.

Then, without another word, he walks out of the office and leaves me standing in front of the wall that's consumed his life these past five years.

More tears slip from my eyes, but I force myself to stare at the wall. Perhaps I should be up there myself. Enemy number one.

"I'm sorry," I sob to the empty room. "I'm so, so sorry."

33

PHOENIX

I've destroyed most of the room, but I keep going anyway.

It feels good to break shit.

It feels good to destroy.

"Jesus Christ, Phoenix! What the fuck is going on?!"

I turn to the door to find Matvei standing there looking stunned. He's half-shielded by the door, but when I stop flinging things around, he enters the room cautiously.

"Fuck, didn't you just refurbish this room last year?"

I glare at him. "What's your point?"

"Twenty-seven thousand dollars," he says, looking around. "I believe that was your total bill for the renovations."

"Will you shut the fuck up?"

He gives me a tired glance. "Are we still doing this?" he asks. "Yelling at each other instead of just talking? We used to be good at that, you know."

He's right. I take a deep breath and resist the urge to break the last vase standing.

"How did you get here so fast?"

"I've been here for the last two days," he replies.

I blink. "What?"

He shrugs. "After you called off the attack, I decided to come back. I figured you wanted me out of your hair. Thought some space would do us both some good. Room to breathe, you know?"

"Matvei…"

"Don't," he says at once. "It's okay."

The fact that he knows exactly what I was about to say makes me feel even worse for treating him like some lackey over the last few weeks. I doubt he wanted to hear my bastardized attempt at an apology, anyway. We both know I don't know how to say sorry.

"I've been a fucking asshole lately," I say.

Matvei smiles. "Hey, no arguments there."

I smirk. And it actually feels good.

"Anyway, enough of that shit. Are you gonna tell me what happened, or do we have to keep talking about our feelings?"

I give him a recap of our visit to the Garden. I tell him about Violet and our subsequent getaway with the files. By the time I'm done, I'm exhausted. I slump onto the chaise and close my eyes.

"I know you didn't get Theo back," Matvei says after listening carefully. "But you did manage to accomplish something."

"That's not why I'm pissed."

"No?"

Matvei sits down in the other armchair.

"The files," I say. "I found something in them. A picture. A picture of Elyssa, specifically. A picture of Elyssa… holding Yuri."

Each word is agonizing, like they have thorns tearing me open on the way past my lips.

Matvei's jaw drops open in shock. "So maybe she remembers—"

"She doesn't fucking remember," I say bitterly. "She was too young. And you should've seen the look in her eyes—like a drugged cow on its way to the slaughterhouse. But it was definitely her in that picture. And it was definitely Yuri."

"So she worked in the Garden."

"Yes," I say with a heavy nod.

"But you already knew that."

"Somehow, it was different before I knew about Yuri."

"Because it wasn't personal," Matvei points out. "Now, it is."

"Yeah. Maybe. Fuck."

"She doesn't remember anything about him?" Matvei presses. "Where he went? If he's still there?"

"He's definitely not still there," I say.

"How do you know?"

"I just do," I reply stubbornly. "Gut instinct."

Matvei sits there silently for a long time.

I shake my head. "This was a mistake."

"Marrying her?"

"Yes."

"No," he says. "It wasn't."

"How can you say that?" I argue. "After what I just told you?"

"Because I know you, Phoenix. You're angry now, so you're saying shit. And breaking shit," he adds, scanning the room. "But you're in love with her."

I glare at him. "Jesus. I take back the apology."

"It's true," Matvei presses, refusing to back down. "You wanna deny it? Go ahead, deny it. I'm waiting."

"You're getting sentimental in your old age."

He shudders. "God forbid."

I raise my eyebrows and look at Matvei. "What do you think needs to be done?"

It's a question I should have asked a long time ago. He's my best friend and advisor for a reason. Because he knows me. He knows this world.

"You want my honest answer?" he asks.

"Nothing but."

"Our priority now is getting Theo back," Matvei says. "But I'm willing to bet he's going to be closely guarded. They'll want to keep him close. And safe."

"That's what I'm counting on."

"Well, there's no reason to believe that our main players won't all be together."

"Eiko and Ozol?"

"Not sure about Ozol," Matvei says regretfully. "He's a slippery motherfucker. But Eiko and Josiah might be in one place. Along with Theo."

"These are just assumptions, though."

"That's all we have to go on."

"Not quite," I say. "I've got files. Details about the names of women and children who passed through the Garden. We also have Violet."

"Has she given you anything of use?"

"She was going to be sent to Wild Night Blossom."

Matvei leans in a little. "So it's definitely an Astra Tyrannis spot."

"No doubt about it."

"That's a good place to start, then."

"We have to be careful," I tell Matvei. "It's a club. We don't know that anyone of importance will necessarily be there."

"You never know," Matvei muses. "We have to look."

I nod. I rest my arms on my knees and stare at the broken glass that glints off the sofa opposite it. "I'll probably regret this mess another day," I sigh. "But today, it felt fucking good."

"It would have been cheaper to have just taken a bat to a wall, you know."

I shrug. "I've got money."

"That's good, cause you've got no common sense."

I smile. But soon after, the smile slides off my face. "I don't know what to do about her, you know."

"You could try forgiving her," Matvei suggests.

My eyes snap to his. "Are you fucking serious?"

"She wasn't responsible for her actions. She belonged to a fucking cult, Phoenix. It's all she's ever known. And they told her she was volunteering at a fucking orphanage. How was she supposed to see the whole picture?"

"That's quite the fucking excuse."

"It most certainly is," Matvei says with utmost seriousness.

"You're suddenly in her corner?"

"I am," Matvei concedes freely. "Because I've been thinking about your relationship with her for the last several weeks. And I realize three things that changed my mind."

"Which is?"

"The first, she's your wife. The second, she's the mother of your son. The third, you fucking love her. Even though your instinct is to deny it."

I sink deeper into the couch. "Every time I think we've moved past her past, something comes up."

"And it'll probably keep coming up, too," Matvei retorts. "We all have baggage. You know that better than anyone."

"Yeah. Maybe you're right."

"You've spent months with her now," he says. "Do you think she's intentionally capable of hurting anyone?"

"No," I answer without hesitation.

"She's changed. She's evolved. She's not a naïve brain-washed cult member anymore. Give her credit for that."

"I keep seeing that picture," I admit. "He was older than he was when they took him. They didn't kill him right away."

"Don't you see the silver lining in all this, Phoenix?" Matvei says with patience.

"What?"

"Yuri may still be alive."

I scoff at that. But it's nothing more than self-preservation. "I can't put my hopes in that, Matvei."

"Why not?" he says. "Hope is the driving force that keeps us going."

"And if it turns out he's been dead for years?"

"Then you're strong enough to deal with it. You've been dealing with it for five years. But for now, he might be out there. He might be within reach."

"You're playing a dangerous game with me, Matvei."

"Haven't you realized by now, Phoenix? It's all dangerous, my brother."

I get to my feet. Matvei does, too. I stretch my arm out and he clasps it tightly. "I'm sorry, brother," I say to him solemnly. "I got lost somewhere along the way."

"I knew you'd find your way back," he tells me confidently.

"Did you?"

He smiles. "Well, I hoped you would, anyway. A dumbass of your magnitude certainly takes your time getting back on track, though. Now, I've got shit to do. Firstly, we'll get the prisoners moved back to the commune. Then we'll weed out the guilty from the ignorant and do what we need to do."

I nod. "Before you do, though, I want to talk to the ones who knew shit. I'll need a little more information before we go in guns blazing."

"Glad to see I've rubbed off on you."

I roll my eyes. "Don't flatter yourself."

We meet each other's eyes and I give him a nod. Things are still a fucking mess, but to have Matvei at my side again, a small part of my world feels like it's back in its rightful place.

As for Elyssa, I don't know how to move forward. Forgiveness seems like an impossible stretch. But I can't see myself giving her up, either.

Which leaves me with only one option: Wait it out. Give it time.

And hope that somehow, we find our way again.

34

ELYSSA
TWO DAYS LATER

You should speak to your parents.

"What would I say?" I ask my dead friend. "Thanks for making my whole life a lie? Thanks for making me complicit in heinous crimes that I'll always feel responsible for? Thanks for ruining any chance I had to find happiness in the real world?"

You've been holding that in a long time, huh?

I take a deep breath.

I've been alone for the last two days—self-imposed solitude. I've seen Phoenix only once. We made eye contact once for the length of a blink. When he turned away, it felt like a slap in the face.

He's not avoiding you.

"Shut up," I mutter.

Meow. Don't bite my head off.

"You don't have a head remember? You're dead."

Rude. Extremely rude.

"I'm being honest. You're not here, Charity. I need to stop talking to you."

So stop talking to me then.

"Shut up," I mutter again. "Please just… let me think."

I walk to the window and sit down on the cushioned ledge as I look out into the gardens.

I'd spent the first day curled up in a ball on my bed, cursing myself for the horrors I'd committed without my knowledge. The second day was mostly occupied with pacing the perimeter of my room, having imaginary conversations with my parents, and raging at them for being so blind, for raising their daughter to be a foolish, mindless sheep like themselves.

The only interruption to my isolation came when Matvei knocked on my door to tell me that the prisoners had been returned to the Sanctuary.

All except my parents—who had been given quarters in this very house.

"What? Why?" I'd asked, too shocked to formulate anything longer than a one-word question.

"Because they're your parents," he replied. Simple as that.

I'm still trying to make sense of it.

Oh, for Pete's sake, don't be such an airhead. It's because Phoenix ordered it! They're your parents and you're his wife. Of course he wanted to protect them from all the shit everyone in the commune was giving them.

"That can't be it," I whisper softly to the empty room. "Phoenix doesn't think of me that way. As his wife. Not anymore."

He'll forgive you eventually. He just needs time.

"I saw the way he looked at me. It was… Let's just say I know how he feels about me now."

No, you're assuming you know. And I wouldn't assume if I were you.

"It doesn't matter. He deserves better."

Stop it.

"I'm being serious. He may be a Bratva boss. He may have done bad things. But he was doing them to bad people. We're different."

In a hundred different ways. But not in the ways you're implying.

"Can you be quiet now?"

That is all in your control, sweetheart.

I sigh and stare at the beautiful gardens sprawled out before me. I catch sight of a tall man in the distance and my spine stiffens instantly.

I force myself to snuff out the hope when I realize it's not Phoenix. I'd know his stride, his posture, from a thousand yards away. The disappointment stings.

You miss him. There's no crime in that.

"I think I'm going to have to get used to missing him. But is it any wonder…?"

What do you mean?

"Love is a luxury. I was raised to be a good wife. To listen. To obey. Love doesn't factor into that."

Fuck all that nonsense. You're more than just a glorified doormat.

"I have to fix it, Charity. My son is still with them. I handed those monsters so many little children and now they have mine. But I'm going to get him back."

I know you are. And when you get Theo back, you can tell him all about me. His brave and beautiful and extremely attractive Aunt Charity.

A bittersweet tear slips from my eye. "You can count on it."

I get off the window seat and head for the door. Matvei told me which room my parents were in. It's on the floor below mine, the room in the far corner. It's been locked from the outside, so all I need to do is unlock it and walk in.

I do it before I can second-guess myself.

They're clearly not expecting me. Mama is sitting at the desk and Papa is sitting on the armchair by the window. Both of them leap to their feet when I enter.

"Elyssa!" Mama exclaims.

I shut the door behind me, take a deep breath to compose myself, then turn to face them.

Papa starts to say, "I—" But I hold up a hand to cut him off.

"I'm here to say something and I want you both to listen to me," I say firmly. "You can speak after I'm done. But for right now, I need you to just listen."

Both look a little shell-shocked, but neither one says a word. I take the moment to look them over from head to toe. They look clean, well-cared-for. Dressed in fresh clothes. The room is big and nicely furnished as well.

Told you. This has "Phoenix" written all over it.

I wave Charity's voice away. Now is not the time.

"The Sanctuary was and is a cult," I begin. "It's not the holy community you led me to believe. And the things, the values, the customs it teaches? They're not just ridiculous. They're dangerous. They're hypocritical. And you wanna know why? Because the whole thing is a lie."

Papa's brows furrow. "Daughter, you—"

"I'm not finished," I say coolly but calmly. "Under Josiah's leadership, the Sanctuary and the Garden have been aiding and abetting an organization called Astra Tyrannis. This organization traffics in people. They take women and children who need homes and help and they sell them into sex slavery. The poor souls who get trafficked spent their lives being used and abused by powerful men and they're powerless to stop it."

Mama opens her mouth to interrupt again, but to my surprise, Papa reaches out and rests a hand on her shoulder. She falls silent as they both cluster together, looking at me with solemn eyes.

"It's a cult and a front. I'm ashamed you let me be sent to the Garden to participate in it. That place is nothing more than a conveyor belt to ship innocent people off to the darkest futures imaginable. It grinds up their souls and their bodies until there's nothing left."

It all sounds very dramatic. But then again, it is. It's the most dramatic, most painful, most horrific thing I've ever had to confront. Especially coming from the sheltered, protected world I once called home.

Somehow, it feels all the more hypocritical because of that. I was shielded from so much. But the children I looked after weren't.

I think about the night of the rape I suffered. I don't often think of it as such, but I'm done hiding from uncomfortable truths. Even if they reflect badly on me.

I was raised to be wary of sex. To keep my distance from men. Raised to be a "good girl," in every sense of the term.

And then I'd been wrapped up like a present and sent into the home of a man who swore he had my best interests at heart.

He raped me. And when he did, it robbed me of something. It tore the veil from my eyes and showed me that there is no such thing as a sanctuary, no such thing as a safe place, no such thing as protection.

You have to fight for your place in this world. Like Phoenix does. Like I'm going to do from now on.

Because I'm done being blind and ignorant.

I'm done being a sheep.

I'm done being anything but myself.

My parents are both watching me from a distance. Like I'm a madwoman melting down incoherently, disturbing their tranquility and threatening what they think is real and true.

I might have felt guilty for that days ago. But not anymore.

None of us here deserve to sleep soundly at night.

"I want no part of this sick and twisted thing you raised me in. And if the two of you still have some warped sense of loyalty towards it, then I want nothing to do with either one of you. You're my parents and I will always love you. But some lies are too dangerous to live on."

I stop short, breathing heavily as I look between their shocked expressions. Waiting for something, anything. At least a sign that they've heard me. Even if they dismiss everything I've said out of hand, I just need them to hear me.

A whole minute passes in silence. The disappointment has settled steadfastly in my stomach. I turn to leave. Then:

"Elyssa…"

It's so soft that I almost miss it. I turn back around to see that my mother has tears in her eyes.

"Yes, Mama?"

"Is it true?" she asks.

"Which part?"

"The... the... trafficking..." she stammers.

I know she wants to avoid saying the word "sex." No wonder my rape was such a difficult topic for her to discuss.

"It is."

"I... I..."

I look between my parents. "Are you telling me you didn't know?"

"Elyssa, of course we didn't know," Papa says, taking a tentative step towards me. "We knew Josiah had his secrets. But we never thought..."

"It was this bad?"

"Yes."

"You knew he had secrets, though," I point out. "And you still trusted him."

"He looked after us," Mama says pleadingly. "He looked after all of us."

The tear finally slips from Mama's eyes. I want to offer her some comfort. But the void between us is too vast.

And I have my own mission now.

"You both are here because of Phoenix," I tell them, "in case you're wondering why you were separated from the others. He married me, which makes you both his problem now. He may seem like he's on the wrong side, but he's one of the good ones. If you get a chance to thank him, you should. And if you get a chance to beg for his forgiveness... well, I wouldn't hold out for it to be given."

Without another word, I turn around and walk out of their room. I make sure to lock it before I go.

The sun has set while I was in my parent's room. The maids are going through the house, turning on the lights.

"Have you seen Master Phoenix?" I ask one as I walk down the hall.

"Outside, ma'am," the older of the two replies. "In the garden."

I thank her and head outside. It doesn't take too long before I find him in a secluded part of the gardens. He's staring up at the sky, but I'm betting that all his thoughts are earthbound.

"Phoenix," I whisper.

He doesn't turn around. Doesn't even react. It's like I'm not there at all, like I never spoke.

I don't push him. Instead I walk forward until I'm standing at his side. When I look over, I see only his perfect profile.

The elegant nose. The strong jaw. The beautiful lips.

All composed into the quintessential portrait of sorrow.

I feel as though my heart is breaking.

It's okay. You feel what he feels. That's what love is.

"I know you don't want to see or speak to me right now," I mumble to him. "I know I've hurt and disappointed you. I know—"

"You don't know anything," he says, cutting me off.

He turns to me slowly. "I *do* want to speak to you," he says. "And I do want to see you. That's what hurts so much. Because despite everything, I still want you."

That takes me by surprise. And it makes what I have to do next so much harder.

But it doesn't shake my resolve. I've relied too much on Phoenix, on Charity, on everyone one else. It's time to stop hiding behind stronger people and figure out what I'm made of all on my own. And if I fail in the attempt—well, I'm willing to fail.

"I've been busy getting everything organized," he tells me.

"You have a plan."

"Yes."

That makes two of you. You should tell him.

I bite my lip. It feels too big to voice aloud.

Rip the Band-Aid, babe. It's the only way to get it out.

"I want you to know something," I tell him. My heart is beating fast and I'm scared out of my mind. But I have to say this now. I might never get the chance again.

I reach out and take his hand. It's a selfish gesture. I want his touch to reassure me. To ground me. To take the trembling away.

He doesn't shake me off, so I take comfort in that and tighten my grip around his fingers. It feels so good, that I wish for one crazy, desperate moment that we could just stay here like this forever. In the gap between now and everything that happens next.

"Elyssa?"

"I don't think I knew much about love before I left the Sanctuary," I start. "What I felt for my parents seemed more like... obligation, I guess you'd call it. A sense of duty. My love for them was always tied to that. But once I left the commune, I met you and everything changed."

I veer off unsteadily, realizing how sentimental and nauseating I must sound to him. His expression is unreadable, as always.

"What I'm trying to say is, you introduced me to love. Real love. You gave me Theo. You let me into your life. And I want you to know that you changed me for the better."

His fingers curl around my hand. "That's not something I'm accused of very often."

I smile sadly. "I hope one day you'll be able to forgive me."

His eyes grow troubled. I think he's about to say something, but in the end, he doesn't. And in that space, that breath, that silence, there's something close to absolution.

Maybe that's why I lean up to kiss him. Or maybe it's because I know that I might never see him again after tonight ends.

Whatever the reason, the moment my lips sink into his, I know he's been waiting for me to do exactly that.

Usually, he's the one who takes the lead. I've never had the confidence to do anything more than let him.

But tonight is different. *I'm* different.

I can feel myself changing. A year ago—heck, even a month ago—I would have thought it would be terrifying. Now, though, it feels liberating. Empowering. Like a caterpillar bursting out of its cocoon to realize there's a whole, huge world out there, and it finally has the wings to explore it.

I start tugging at his clothes. He murmurs my name, almost like a question—"Elyssa?"—but I ignore it, spurred on by a sudden desperate hunger.

I pull off his shirt and start unbuckling his pants. When we fall back onto the soft grass, I scamper on top of him, hiking my dress up around my thighs and straddling him.

His cock springs free from his zipper. I wrap my hand around it. It's warm and throbbing in my grasp and I can't help letting out an eager moan.

I can't get him inside of me fast enough. I'm already dripping wet, so when I tease the head of his erection against my opening, my body draws him in.

His eyes are unfocused now, his breathing has ramped up, and there's a glimmer of sweat on his inked chest. I run my fingertips along the lines of the angel wing tattoo he told me never to ask about again.

And at the same time, I drop my hips down flush against his and let the man I love fill me completely.

He tries to say my name again—"Elyssa"—but I silence him with a kiss. This isn't a time for talking. I'm too terrified of what I might say if I open my lips again.

Instead, I start riding him with an intensity that I didn't realize I possessed. It feels euphoric to take control, to go at my own pace, to chase pleasure for pleasure's sake.

To fuck when you're horny.

The whole time, Phoenix watches me, his hands tight on my hips. I put my palms on his chest and start bucking against him so hard that I have to arch my back and turn my head up to the stars.

That's how I come—moaning up at the moon.

I lean in after his orgasm spurts up inside me. I kiss his brow and his neck, his hair and his jaw, his lips. As much of him as I can get. I drink in his scent and try to commit his features to memory.

Tell him you love him. Tell him now, before it's too late.

Charity is right. I should.

But the words don't come. Apparently, there are things I'm still not brave enough for.

It's okay, sunshine. You'll get another chance to say them.

She sounds sure. But I know she's wrong.

I've said my piece.

And now, I've said goodbye.

35

PHOENIX

THE NEXT MORNING—PHOENIX'S BEDROOM

When I wake up, she's gone.

I look over to the other side of the bed. I'd laid her down there just a few hours ago. She'd be breathing softly and I was sure she was asleep. I undressed as quietly as I could so as not to wake.

When I turned around, though, I could swear that for one brief instant, I saw her eyes open.

And they were the saddest amber I've ever seen.

But then I blinked and she was asleep again. Or maybe I imagined the whole thing. I'd dismissed it, slid under the covers, and fallen asleep next to her.

Now, I'm wondering if I missed a sign.

I launch myself out of bed and pull on my pants and shirt. Several of my men are patrolling the corridors when I emerge, waiting for their orders to be handed out. But I ignore all of them. I need to find out where she is.

I burst into her room, my eyes scanning every inch of the space even as my body registers her stark absence.

The room is empty. It feels like it's stood empty for a very long time.

Even her scent is gone.

"Elyssa?"

Of course she doesn't answer.

I stride into the adjoining bathroom anyway. There's a tiny splash of water lingering in the shower, which tells me it was used. But when I run a finger through the remaining puddle, it's cold.

She's been gone for hours, at least.

"Fuck," I growl. "Fuck!"

I head back into the room and check for what else is missing. Her clothes are still in the wardrobe. Nothing else seems to be amiss.

I don't believe she's run away. Not without Theo.

Which means she's decided to go after him alone.

Figuring out what made her choose that route is a problem for a different day. Right now, I need to go after her. And there's no fucking time for planning.

I tear out of her room and down the stairs. I catch sight of Konstantin at the entrance and I shout out my orders.

"Get one of the vehicles out," I command. "Something bulletproof. Immediately!"

Konstantin wastes no time in disappearing back out of the door he was just about to enter from. I follow him outside and almost collide with Matvei.

"Jesus," he breathes. "What the fuck is happening?"

"Elyssa is gone."

Matvei frowns. "What do you mean, 'gone'?"

"I mean she's fucking gone. Up and left. Last night, or hours ago, I'm not sure. I was fucking sleeping."

"Calm down," he says in a measured voice. "We'll get her back."

"Get her back?" I growl. "She's probably already with them—those fucking…"

"Phoenix," Matvei says, putting his hand on my shoulder, "you're not in any fit condition to go after her."

"There's no time to be cautious here, Matvei. She's going to put herself directly in their path."

"How do you know she's going to them?"

"Because she knows they have Theo," I tell him. "She thinks this is the only way."

"Why would she do it alone?" Matvei wonders out loud.

I shake my head. "Because she felt she has something to answer for. She's working off the guilt she feels. The guilt I made her feel for her part in all of this."

Matvei looks worried. "But where do you think she's going? Let's say you're right and she's trying to get in contact with them, to trade herself in or barter for a deal or whatever. How would she even go about doing that?"

I stop short and consider this. The answer becomes obvious at once.

"Wild Night Blossom."

Matvei closes his eyes as if the thought of that place alone hurts him. "Fuck."

"She clearly hasn't thought this through, Matvei. She's doing this because of me."

"Stop, *sobrat*. Blaming yourself is not going to bring her back."

I hear the spin of wheels on gravel just as Konstantin rounds the corner in an armored black jeep.

"You're going after her in that?" Matvei asks. "So I take it you're not planning on flying under the radar then."

I ignore that and jump into the front seat the moment Konstantin vacates it. From the driver's seat, I look down at the two of them. "I'll keep you informed. Get the teams ready. I want everyone ready for battle at a moment's notice. Matvei, I'll give you the signal—"

"No," he responds before I've even finished talking. "You can give Konstantin the signal." Then he opens the passenger side door and jumps in next to me. "I'm coming with you."

I clench my jaw. "Are you sure? This is my battle. My mistake. Not yours."

He scoffs. "Elyssa went into the fucking lion's den. Of course we have to go after her. And if you're going, so am I."

"You don't think this is foolish? Reckless? Stupid?"

Matvei smirks. "Oh, it's definitely all of the above. But sometimes, that can't be helped. And anyway, I trust you. What more do we need than that?"

I don't realize how much I need to hear those words until Matvei says them. I clap him on the shoulder. "Thank you, brother."

He laughs, then knocks my hand off. "Don't get all touchy-feely on me. It doesn't suit you."

"Fair enough," I chuckle. "Pure asshole, from here on out."

"Good. Just the way it's supposed to be. Now, are you ready?"

"As I'll ever be," I reply.

Then I tear out of the driveway, zooming out between the gates just as they open for us.

For a few minutes, the only sound is the roar of the engine as I rip past cars on the road. Horns squeal, but I don't give a fuck. And as soon as they see the kind of car I'm driving, they shut right up.

Matvei is oddly silent.

"Tell me what you're thinking," I urge. "The quiet is creeping me the fuck out."

"Oh, nothing, nothing."

"Fuck off, Matvei. Out with it."

He sighs, then shifts around in his seat. "Okay. So why is Elyssa going to confront Astra Tyrannis?"

"To get Theo back," I say. "I thought that was obvious."

"Right. But why do they have him in the first place?"

I ponder that for a second. "Leverage."

Matvei nods sagely. "Exactly. But leverage against whom?"

"I fucking hate guessing games, Matvei. Get to the point."

"Fine," he grumbles. "'What is *'Leverage against you'?'* for five hundred, Alex."

"So…"

"So that doesn't answer this: what if the boy is Josiah's?" he points out. "We never got the paternity test sorted."

"And we're not going to." I don't even realize I've made the decision until the words come spilling out of my mouth.

"Say that again for the slow kids in the back," Matvei says in shock.

"I'm serious," I say, doubling down on the decision. "There's no need for a paternity test. The child isn't Josiah's. He's mine."

"How do you know? Like, biologically?"

I glance at him, making sure to meet his eye. "I don't. But it doesn't matter."

Matvei raises his eyebrows, but his nod is full of understanding. "You're sure?"

"A hundred percent," I say. "Elyssa is my wife. And Theo is my son."

Fuck, that feels so good to say.

He claps his hands as if that settles the matter. "Alright, good. Glad we got that figured out. Next question: Do you think we should call in reinforcements?"

"Meaning my father?"

"Yes."

"He already knows too much."

"He should know more."

"This is my fight."

"Asking for help doesn't make you weak, you know. In fact, I would argue the opposite."

"We don't have time, Matvei," I tell him. "I'm not too proud. But I don't think they'll be here in time to make a difference. This is up to us."

Matvei nods and drops the subject. I keep glancing at the time. It's only been nine minutes since we left the compound, but somehow it still seems like we have forever to go.

The feeling rising in my chest feels like, of all things, déjà vu. I remember that sinking feeling of loss that accompanied the realization that my family was missing. It chipped away at my soul. The helplessness. The uncertainty.

The difference here is that I know who's involved. And it's not too late to stop it.

Which means, if I fail, it's all on me.

When I blink, I see a flash of Aurora's tortured body the way I found it. It was clear she had suffered in her last moments. Her mouth was open in a permanent scream and tear tracks were practically tattooed in her cheeks.

I don't want to relive that moment with Elyssa. I cannot handle another dead body. Another lost wife. Another lost future.

"Stop reliving it," Matvei interrupts. "That's not gonna help you now."

"How do you know what I was thinking about?"

"I know you," he says simply. "And I saw that expression a lot in the days following Aurora's funeral."

"Sometimes, I forget how much you were around for."

"Everything," he says. "I was around for everything."

I glance at him. "I'm glad you're around for this."

He smiles. "I thought we did the sentimental stuff already?"

"Fair enough. Fuck you, then."

Matvei grins at me. "Fuck you, too, brother. Forever and always."

I press the pedal down and hurtle us towards the destination. My resolve is iron. I failed once before.

I am not going to fail again.

36

ELYSSA
WILD NIGHT BLOSSOM

A nightclub in the daytime is a disgusting thing. It's like roadkill. Unclean, unappealing, with everything living taking a wide radius to avoid it.

Wild Night Blossom is just like that.

But it doesn't give away any of its secrets as I stand at the bottom of the steps and look up at it.

This is the third time I've done this. Once, I was a naïve little lamb with bloody feet and a ripped wedding dress. Once, I was a frightened coward who thought retreating into the past was the only way forward.

Now, I'm something else. Something different. Something more.

"Please," I whisper to myself. "Please let me find my son. Please let me get him away from here safe."

You will. You can do this, Elyssa. You're capable of so much more than you know.

For once, I don't try to push Charity out of my head. I need her now more than ever.

The main door is closed. I mount the steps and raise my hand to knock, but I stop short at the last moment. Knocking feels silly. But should I just…?

I reach out, grip the ornate knob, and pull.

It opens.

Like it was always meant to welcome me in.

I step inside, moving slowly and keeping my eyes open. The door swings shut behind me on silent hinges.

There are no windows in the passageway, so the only light comes from dim red lamp sconces mounted on the velvet walls. The wainscoting is black and the mirrors on either side of the corridor make me feel like I've entered an old madam's brothel. They reflect a million different versions of me up and down the space, each one washed in red.

I follow the corridor down. Just before I make the left-hand turn, I think I feel a flutter of movement behind me.

I whip back around. But the only thing there is my own shadow.

Easy, girl. Stay alert, but don't get spooked.

Shuddering in a long breath, I pivot once more and resume my creep. The hallway spits me out into an open, oval room adorned with plush sofas—and more mirrors.

That's the only reason I see him behind me.

His eyes narrowed in concentration as he comes at me from the back. I have time for fear, nothing else.

A second later, I see black.

I wake up with a throbbing headache. I sit up suddenly, but that only ignites more complaints from my body.

"How are you feeling?"

I cringe at the all-too-familiar voice. When I slowly rotate my head, I see him, leaning casually against the back wall like an old friend.

He looks more gaunt than I remember. The scars on his face and arm look more grotesque, too. Paler. Nastier.

"Josiah." His name tastes bitter coming out.

"Did you miss me?"

I don't bother answering. I'm sitting on a thick mattress shoved into a dusty corner. Josiah is closer than I'd like, but the room is small enough that there's not much room to scoot away from him.

"Are we still in the club?" I ask.

"As a matter of fact, we are," he says. "They have all sorts of accommodations here. Unfortunately, you've got the worst room in the building."

"I didn't come for bed and breakfast," I snap at him.

I'm not bound. Definitely not gagged. I can try to run or fight back if I choose. But everything feels so heavy and slow. Just raising my eyes to meet his feels like a Herculean task.

"Something the matter?" Josiah inquires.

"Why do I feel so strange?"

"Do you, my dear?"

He takes a step forward and I back away instantly. I press my back to the rear wall and glare at him with disgust.

"Come now, Elyssa. I thought you and I were close."

"Which just goes to show you how delusional you are."

Josiah just sighs. Now that I know what he is, it's hard to see anything but a monster.

But if I concentrate really hard, I can see why so many were so deceived by the man. His face is carved in straight lines and good intentions. He plays his part to perfection.

Does he believe his own lies, I wonder?

"You have spent too long outside of the warm embrace of the Sanctuary. This is why I've always said that the outside world has a way of corrupting a woman's soul."

"Is that right?" I ask. "Does the Garden count as the outside world?"

"No, of course not. The Garden is a haven for enlightenment and reform. It's a place for new beginnings."

"Are you insane?"

"Elyssa, my frightened doe—"

"No, I'm genuinely asking. You know what they do there, surely?"

"We rehabilitate young women," Josiah replies sternly. "We give them a chance at a better life. Where they can start again and be self-sufficient."

"It's a cattle shed," I hiss. "A clearinghouse for women who are about to be sold into sex slavery."

Josiah's expression crumples into irritation. "Don't be ridiculous."

"I'm not lying. It's the truth. You know it!"

"You've been brainwashed, Elyssa," he tells me. "I can see the delusion in your eyes."

I actually want to laugh. The irony is too much.

"Where is my son?" I snap, unable to continue this conversation any longer. "You must know where he is."

"I do know," he says. "And don't worry—he'll be taken care of."

"What does that mean?" I ask desperately.

"It means that he's not your concern anymore, Elyssa, darling," Josiah continues. He moves closer still. I try to inch away from him, but the weight in my body only seems to be getting heavier.

"What did you give me?" I slur through numb lips.

"Don't worry, dear. It's just a little pill. To calm you, you see? I didn't want you getting hysterical when we talked."

"You drugged me."

"I soothed your mind," he corrects. "You have so much pain that needs healing."

"I… I want to see my son."

"As I said, he's not your concern anymore."

"Did you k-kill him?" I ask. "Is… is he dead?"

Just saying those words is the hardest thing I've ever done.

Josiah looks horrified by the very thought. "Of course not," he says with all apparent sincerity. "As I said, he is being well cared-for. Soon, he will be moved."

"Moved where?"

"Somewhere safe. Where he can start again."

Oh God. Oh God, oh God, oh God.

"I need to see him. Let me see him," I demand, trying to think of something that might get through to the monster standing in front of me.

"I can't do that, I'm afraid."

"He's your son, too!" I lie, clinging to the last thread I have left to pull. "Why would you send him away?"

Josiah's face clouds over slightly. "Because he's not my son."

I freeze. "W… what?"

"I asked permission from the powers that be to get a paternity test done on the child," Josiah explains acidly. "I wanted to know for sure, considering your… escapades. The test was conclusive. The boy's not mine."

I can't pretend I'm not relieved, but there is a bite of fear that tempers that relief. The one thing that might have protected him was being Josiah's child.

Without that shielding him, he's definitely a target. The spawn of their sworn enemy, the Kovalyov Bratva.

A leverage tactic at best. A human sacrifice at worst.

"So that means…"

"Phoenix Kovalyov is the boy's father," Josiah finishes. "Unless, of course, you were … *busier*… than our sources report."

He shakes his head and claps to change the subject. "Anyway, I'm not going to do a thing to the child. He's of no concern to me any longer. Nor should he be to you. We're going to make a fresh start of it, you and I."

I stare at him in shock. "You're joking. A fresh start?"

"Exactly that. I'm going to be reinstated as the leader of the Sanctuary, once the powers that be have taken control of the land back from the Bratva. And once I'm in charge, life will continue as normal. We can pick up where we left off. We can be together as we were always meant to be. I have never stopped being your shepherd, Elyssa."

His eyes spark with devout faith. He truly believes the things he's saying. Even in my drugged state, I know he's a monster.

"Oh my God," I breathe. "You are insane."

He sighs. "I really wish you'd be sensible."

"I'd invite you to take your own advice."

"Any other man would have cast you aside long ago."

I shake my head. "Cast me aside, please. I have no desire to be with you."

"That's grief talking. You're mourning the loss of your son. That's okay. I can be patient. I've known you were going to be my wife for a long time now, Elyssa. Since you were thirteen years old."

My stomach twists with nausea. Thankfully, there's nothing in there to come out.

"Don't you realize how disgusting that is? How perverse?"

"Perverse?" Josiah looks confused now. "I never touched you. I admired you from afar, until you came of age." He looks hurt by the very accusation.

"Until you raped me before our wedding day."

"That wasn't rape."

"And the sky's not blue."

He exhales deeply again, holding his long-suffering expression like I'm the one who's deluded. If I had the energy, I'd claw that look right off his face.

"And you're forgetting something," I add, feeling the slightest twinge of smugness about his one oversight.

"What is that?"

"I'm already married."

He smiles thinly. "I won't have to worry about your so-called husband for much longer. The powers that be will take care of him."

"He won't die," I hear myself say. "You can't kill him."

"He's a man like any other. He bleeds. And if he bleeds, he can die."

"He's more than a man."

He throws back his head and chuckles. "I see you're still under his spell. That's okay. It might take time. But as I said, I can be patient."

He reaches out to stroke my cheek with one clammy hand. It takes all of my strength, but I manage to slap it away weakly.

"No!" I cry out. "Don't you dare touch me!"

A shadow darkens Josiah's face.

"Very well. I've tried to be patient. I've tried to be understanding. You want to do this the hard way? So be it," he seethes. "Guards!"

Two guards burst into the room like they were chomping at the bit for this chance. Both of them look like the Yakuza soldiers who slaughtered Leona. They grab me roughly, one on each arm, and haul me from the room.

I don't even scream. At the moment, I'm just glad to be away from Josiah. I should fight, scream, do something, but my limbs are heavy with the drug and my mind is preoccupied with thoughts of my baby boy, shrouded in darkness I cannot penetrate.

When we start descending down a narrow staircase, I start paying attention to where they're taking me. Even though my body feels paralyzed, my eyes take everything in.

We reach the end of the staircase. I'm faced with a line of caged cells. They look like the kind you would see ferocious animals in.

Except these cages don't hold animals.

They hold young women.

My eyes scan the sorry group of women. Some of them can't be older than ten or eleven. They all look pale and hungry.

I'm shoved into an empty cell at the far end of the corridor. My guards slam the door shut and disappear at once.

I slump against a wall and catch my breath, eyes closed, head hanging low. I can't find a way to think about failure or freedom, about Phoenix or Theo, or anything at all. My mind is just a cloud of blackness.

Until I hear a sound from just outside the cell.

In the shadows clustered at the far corner of the aisle, something emerges. A silhouette. A young boy's silhouette.

He steps forward into the meager light. He's got chains around his hands and legs and a collar around his neck. He's five, maybe six years old, with eyes that look like they've seen enough horrors for a hundred lifetimes.

He's absolutely filthy, and also much calmer than I'd expect. Like he's been locked in here for far too long and knows there's no chance of escape.

"Have some water," he whispers, offering me a dirty bottle with a thin opening.

"Thank you," I whisper.

I'm about to take a sip when I look at the boy's face again. Cold realization starts spreading through me as my eyes are confronted with a truth that my brain isn't capable of handling yet.

"W... what's your name?" I ask shakily.

"Yuri," the boy replies softly. "My name is Yuri."

37

PHOENIX

We're almost at Wild Night Blossom when a call comes in.

Matvei presses the answer button on the dash. After a crackle, Konstantin's voice comes through on the loudspeaker. He sounds rattled.

"Boss... something just arrived for you."

"What kind of something?

"I don't know exactly. There's a little box and a letter. It's addressed to you."

"From?"

"Viktor Ozol."

Matvei and I make eye contact. I veer the car to the side of the road and slam on the brakes.

"Fucking hell," Matvei breathes. "What do we do now?"

"We see what the motherfucker sent," I say. "Konstantin, bring the package and the letter to the eastern safehouse. Drive as fast as you can."

I hang up and swing the jeep in the opposite direction. We rock up to the safehouse in seven minutes. Konstantin will need at least another fifteen to get here.

"Too much time," I mutter to myself. "Too much time to fucking think."

"Phoenix," Matvei cautions, "whatever's in that letter… You need to be able to keep your head."

He's right. But I've told him that plenty in the last few days. Right now, my impatience has its hands on the steering wheel.

"Where the fuck is Konstantin?" I growl, pacing back and forth. "It's been a fucking century."

"It's been two minutes," Matvei reminds me. "Literally. Let's go wait inside, yeah?"

The safehouse is a roomy two-story house in a nondescript suburban neighborhood. High fences, a broad backyard, but nothing that you'd ever look twice at. The Bratva lives in places like this. Simple and efficient. Hidden in plain sight.

"Fine," I snap. I jump out of the car and head up the walk to the front door.

I knock twice. The door swings open.

"Mabel," I say to our resident safehouse keeper.

She's an older woman, pushing sixty and trying hard to fight it. She's dyed her hair jet black and she wears way too much makeup. But she's loyal as hell. And that's my only requirement.

"Master Phoenix!" Mabel says, looking delighted to see me. "What a surprise."

I blow right past her with a wordless grunt.

"Oh dear," she murmurs. "What's happened?"

"Same old shit. Astra Tyrannis trying to fucking destroy my family."

She turns around, looking between Matvei and me with a warm look of concern on her face. "Shall I put on some coffee?"

"Did any of the boys come by here today?" I ask, ignoring her question.

"No, I believe they're all at the main compound. Didn't you put them on alert this morning?"

"That's right," I say. "But the plans have changed. Matvei?"

"I'll sort it out," he says, taking his phone out and walking into an empty room. Mabel is staring at me with concern, and that's the last thing I need right now.

"Don't worry, son," she says gently. "You'll get her back."

I frown. "How do you…?"

"Women have a bad rep, but it's men that are the real gossipers," she remarks with a wink. "All your men know how obsessed you are with your new wife."

"Fucking gossipy little schoolgirls. I don't pay them to talk. I pay them to follow orders."

"And they do. But they have to keep occupied somehow."

"Preferably not with my fucking personal life."

She smiles, not at all fazed by my anger. A moment later, the doorbell rings. I rush to answer it. Konstantin is standing on the other side—with the package in hand.

It's smaller than what I was picturing. The size of a ring box. I snatch it from his hands without a word. Rip it apart. And inside, I find…

A lock of curling blond hair.

Fury surges through my veins. I sense Matvei come up behind me.

"Is that…?"

"Elyssa's hair," I confirm. I'd know it anywhere.

I tear open the letter, hands shaking with rage. *How dare he?* I'm thinking. *How dare he fucking touch her?*

"*Phoenix Kovalyov—We have danced this dance for long enough. It's time we talked face to face. Come to Wild Night Blossom as soon as this letter reaches you. Bring no one. If you don't follow my instructions, the part of your precious little wife I send next will require a much bigger box.*"

The letter flutters from my hand like a fallen leaf. It takes a long time before I stop seeing red.

The only way I'm able to contain my anger is the knowledge that getting Elyssa back is within my power. But only if I stay calm. Only if I act smart.

"Phoenix?" Matvei asks. "What did it say? Was it really from Ozol?"

"Yes," I answer. "Matvei, I need to speak to you privately."

"Uh, yeah, sure. Of course." He turns back into the house. I stride in behind him, dipping into a small drawer on the entryway table as we pass by it to grab something and stick it in my pocket. He doesn't notice, thankfully. He will in just a moment, and he won't like it one bit.

We go down the hallway into one of the spare bedrooms. I shut the door behind us.

"Alright, what's with the secrecy?" he says. "What'd the letter say?"

"Mostly pontificating bullshit." I tuck the object in my pocket into my hand. I'll only get one shot at this. I have to nail it. "But I have to go and get her."

"Of course," Matvei scoffs. "And let me guess: he said, 'Come alone or I'll do something really melodramatic.'"

"Exactly."

"Well, we have teams ready to intervene at a moment's notice," Matvei says. "And I'll come with you, of course."

"You're going to be in a lot of danger if you come with me."

"When have I ever cared about that shit?" he counters.

I smile. "You've always been a true friend. A true brother. Never afraid to ride into battle." I hold out my hand and he clasps it with a matching grin.

That's when I make my move.

The first cuff goes around his wrist.

The second cuff secures him to the thick metal post of the bed.

"I'm sorry, brother," I say sincerely as it dawns on him what I've just done. "But I can't take you with me."

"And this is the solution?!" he roars furiously, pulling at the cuffs.

"Of all my men, you're the one who's least likely to listen. So it was necessary." I start backing out of the room.

"Phoenix, walking into that club alone is suicide." He yanks at the cuffs with his full strength. The bedpost groans, but it doesn't give. He'll have to make that effort a few thousand more times before he's freed. Hopefully, that's enough time for this kamikaze mission of mine.

"He has Elyssa, Matvei," I say grimly. "And he's promised to hurt her if I don't show up alone."

"They always say that! You know they always fucking say that shit!"

"But in his case, he means it. I know he does. This is not a man who's got to where he is by making hollow threats."

"Phoenix, he'll kill you," Matvei says, trying desperately to reason with me before I leave.

But I won't be talked off this ledge. Elyssa's in the hands of that fucking monster and I don't intend to sit around and wait for the right plan to fall into place.

I'm done waiting.

It's time to act.

"Phoenix! PHOENIX!"

I shut the door on him, burying my guilt in the same moment. Mabel and Konstantin are standing on opposite sides of the room, looking wary.

"Do not let him out of those goddamn restraints," I instruct both of them. "Is that understood?"

Konstantin nods, but Mabel looks less sure. "Master Phoenix…"

"That's a fucking order," I snap.

She flinches back and nods.

I head out of the safehouse at a jog. Konstantin follows me outside. "Boss, what are your orders?"

My orders. What the fuck are my orders?

"Give me three hours," I reply. "Then release Matvei. He'll take the lead in my absence."

Truth be told, I have no idea what the fuck is going to happen three hours from now. Who will be alive. Who will be dead.

But it doesn't matter. The whole world has boiled down to this moment.

I stomp on the accelerator and take off through the streets in the direction of Wild Night Blossom. I don't bother with being discreet when I arrive. I run up on the curb and park the jeep there, right in front of the entrance so that it's blocking the door.

Then I jump out of the jeep and slam the door knocker as hard as I can. It opens immediately—and I'm greeted with five guns aimed right in my face. The Yakuza men holding the weapons are grim-faced and stoic.

They step aside, guns still raised, and usher me in. As soon as the door closes behind me, two of the men holster their arms and give me a head-to-toe patdown.

They remove weapons from my hips, my boots, my belt. I let them— even though my fists are clenched, eager to break the skulls of every single one of these motherfuckers.

"This way," one of the guards says when they're done, nudging my back with the butt of his gun.

I start walking, following the two guards in front of me. How easy it would be to take them all down now. I glance around at their expressionless faces as the adrenaline in my body screams to be made use of.

Wait for it...

Wait for it...

NOW.

I duck suddenly and hurl myself backwards into the guards at my rear. I throw my elbow into one soldier's face and then swing him around to use as a human shield.

The gunshot from his comrade gets him instead of me. But not before I've managed to get hold of his weapon. I rip it from its holster and deliver a quick trio of shots into the throats of the others.

That leaves one standing.

Having served his purpose, I toss my dead human shield to the side and stare at the last man left. His face is no longer expressionless. He looks like he's about to shit himself, actually.

I point my gun at him. "Where am I supposed to go?"

"I... I..."

"Answer me now or I'll kill you like the rest of this scum."

"Straight ahead and make a left," he manages to stammer.

"Thank you," I reply politely.

Then I shoot him in the head.

I step over his still-twitching body and make my way down the broad corridor. I take the first left I find and walk into a large, shadowy space that has many doors and many opportunities to hide.

I can't see anyone, but I know I'm not alone.

Just as I suspected, a handful of Yakuza goons step out of the shadows at my sides and another rank of them approaches from the distant shadows.

All of them are armed. All of them look perfectly at ease.

The line ahead of me parts for two men. I tense instantly when I see their faces.

Viktor Ozol and Eiko Sakamoto.

"My guards?" Eiko asks sourly.

"Dead," I reply with a smug smirk as I toss the pistol at his feet. "I believe that belongs to one of them."

"All five of them?

"Even if you'd sent ten, the outcome would have been no different."

Eiko narrows his eyes. "You will pay for that."

I roll my eyes. "I'm still waiting to pay for your brother's death. Seems like my bill is getting pretty large."

Ozol turns his shrewd, watchful eyes on me. "Phoenix Kovalyov, you've proved to be much more trouble than I expected."

"You're not the first man who's made the mistake of underestimating me."

"Actually, Phoenix, you'll find that you're the one who's underestimated me," he retorts. "I was surprised to learn that your undoing is a woman. A rather foolish one, at that."

I stiffen. "Where is she?"

"Somewhere in this building."

"I've come to exchange my life for hers," I say.

Ozol raises his eyebrows. "Is that so?"

"You have no real use for her—"

"On the contrary, her body will be extremely useful to me. For as long as she lasts, of course."

I glare at him. "If you touch her, I will murder you. And I'll make sure to draw it out, too."

"You realize you have twenty different guns pointed at you right now?" he asks with mild amusement. "You make one wrong move and you'll be dead before you draw your next breath."

"Are you underestimating me again?" I ask. "And I thought you were a smart man."

He sneers at me, trying to keep the upper hand. "Careful, boy; I hold more cards than you now."

That statement strikes me as odd, but I know how men like Viktor Ozol work. Of course he feels he has a hand to play.

"I want to speak to her."

"I don't think you're in any position to be making demands."

"And yet, here I am, demanding away."

Ozol smiles. "You know, in another life, you would have been the perfect ally."

I spit on the ground in response.

He sighs. "Pity."

His freakishly light eyes scan my face as though trying to wrench my secrets lose. "Let me tell you something, Phoenix: I always win," he remarks. "One way or another, I always come out on top. Now, take him down to one of the basement cells. I want him hurt, but not dead."

"What?!" Eiko exclaims.

Ozol turns towards the Yakuza don, looking visibly annoyed.

"Viktor," Eiko says, his tone respectful but firm, "you promised me that I would be given the right to murder this *yowamushi*. There is a code of honor that must be obeyed. He killed my brother."

"That's right," Ozol says with a nod. "I did promise you that."

I'm the only one who notices more men creeping out of the shadows as Eiko and Viktor bicker.

And by the time they've fired their deadly barrage, I'm the only one left standing who doesn't work for Viktor.

Silence fills the room again as every single member of the Yakuza crumples dead to the ground.

Eiko is sprawled at Ozol's feet, blood sluicing out from a dozen different bullet wounds.

Viktor looks at me and smiles. "Like I said: I always win in the end."

38

ELYSSA

THE CELLS BENEATH WILD NIGHT BLOSSOM

"What did you say your name was?" I ask again.

"Yuri," the boy repeats in a voice that sounds much older than he looks.

"Where are your parents?" I don't know why I'm asking this. It's a sick question. But something tells me there are answers in this little boy's head. Answers to five years' worth of mysteries.

"They didn't want me," he says with the air of a kid repeating what he's been told to say. "So they sent me here. Master Viktor keeps me safe. He protects me."

I shudder inside, horrified at what's been done to this sweet, innocent child. And in looking at Yuri, I see the life that awaits my own son.

My insides are clamoring to come out. I want to scream, to cry, to tear this horrible place down brick by brick with my bare hands.

But I have to be strong.

Not just for Theo—but also for the tiny boy standing in front of me. The first son of the man that I love.

"Yuri, my name is Elyssa," I tell him tenderly. "And I knew... I *know* your father."

The words don't make any impact at all—at first. Then he raises his eyes to mine. They're dark, just like his dad's.

"My... father?"

I nod.

He shuffles on his feet. The chains clank. I cringe looking at the collar around his neck. What kind of monster could do this to an innocent child?

"Yuri, please listen to me. I know you don't know me. I know you don't have any reason to trust me, but..."

He's starting to back away, receding back down the corridor. His chains drag over the concrete floor with a hair-raising scraping noise.

"Yuri, wait! I know your father, and he loves you, and he wants you—"

He blinks as the words die on my lips. I'm not even sure that what I'm saying is registering. His eyes glaze over and he retreats within himself.

"I... I have to go," he mutters. "I have to give the others water. It's my job."

"No!" I cry out, sliding my hand through the gaps between the bars to grab the front of his filthy shirt. "Please, Yuri, just listen to me..."

He doesn't react at all, even when I realize how violently I've snatched him towards me, how crazy I must look, how threatening.

And it's because he's used to this. He's used to being touched without permission. He's used to being mistreated and abused.

The weight of all the unspoken horrors he's spent five years living is almost enough to drown me.

"Yuri, I won't hurt you," I whisper. "Neither will your father. We just want to help."

He shakes his head. "Only Master Viktor can help me."

"Your father loves you so much, Yuri. He's been destroyed since you disappeared. The only reason he didn't search for you is because he thought you were dead."

I see a flame of hope in the boy's eyes, but it extinguishes almost immediately.

"No. My father didn't want me," he intones like something that's been drilled into his head again and again.

He tries to shrug away from me, but I grab his shirt again.

"Yuri, please, I need you to believe me."

"What he needs is for you to let him go."

I turn to the woman who spoke. She's lying in the cell right next to me. She looks about my age, with large blue eyes and a wealth of red hair blurring in a halo around her head. She's beautiful, but the beauty is hidden by a layer of dirt and grime that clings to her skin.

"It ain't gonna do him no good, you giving him false hope. Lying to the poor boy."

"I'm not lying!"

"Who the fuck cares?" she drawls. "Even if it's true, you'll be sold long before his daddy knows a thing. So you could at least leave the poor runt alone and let the rest of us have a drink of water."

I shudder at her callousness and turn back to the boy. "Yuri…"

"Please let me go," he begs, his voice barely above a whisper. "I'll be punished if I don't do my duty."

As a tear slides down my cheek, my hands loosen. He backs away slowly at first, then turns and starts his shuffle down the line of cells, offering each woman a sip of water, same as he did for me. I can't take my eyes off him.

"Is it true?" the redheaded woman asks, sidling a little closer to the bars of my cell.

"What?"

"That his father is some big shot?"

"Yes."

"Does he know the boy is here?"

"No."

"Does he know you're here?"

I meet her gaze for the first time. I know instantly why she's asking me such leading questions. She wants to know if rescue is imminent. She wants to know if she should hope.

"No," I say. "He doesn't."

Her face crumples. "Then how's he supposed to find you, eh? You're just wasting everyone's time. Stupid bitch."

I turn my back on her and wrap my arms around my body. It feels so damn cold all of a sudden. And I feel so tired. If I just close my eyes, maybe I could sleep forever…

Cut that shit right the fuck out. You can't give up now.

"Giving up seems like the best option right now," I whisper. "The only one, really."

Yuri is alive. Do you know what that means?

"It means he's been used and abused for the last four years. It means he's been made the pet of an evil, sadistic sex trafficker who's waiting until the moment he can use him in revenge."

It means Phoenix hasn't lost his son. He hasn't lost either one of his sons yet. And you're the only one who knows that. You have to do something. You have to keep fighting.

"I can't keep fighting. I don't have the strength."

Yes, you do. Remember how all this started? Josiah touched you and you fought back. You were brave enough even back then, and look how far you've come! You're brave enough now. You're more than brave enough.

"I don't know, Char. I just don't know."

Do it for your son. For both of them.

Slowly, I sit up and struggle to my feet.

My body feels strange, but at least I can feel all my limbs again. The drugs Josiah gave me earlier have mostly worn off. I test one leg at a time, flexing my arms, bending side to side to make sure I can move.

"You getting ready to run a marathon or something?" the redhead in the cell next to me asks sarcastically.

I ignore her and head to the front of my cell. When I lean out a little, I can still see Yuri walking down the row of cells, supplying the caged women with water.

Suddenly, a door clangs open. I hear steps thumping on the staircase. A moment later, a pair of wingtip shoes appear on the landing. Followed by a man.

I recognize his face immediately. I saw it a year ago in this very building, and I've seen it in a picture: one skewered to the dead center of the wall in Phoenix's office.

Viktor Ozol.

The other women fall silent. Everyone shrinks into the farthest reaches of their cell, like every inch between themselves and Viktor is vital.

But I stay where I am.

I know instinctively he's come here for me.

He's got two hulking guards at his back. "Elyssa," he says, giving me a smile that's almost charming. "You are even more alluring than I recall. He certainly has good taste."

"You're pure evil. Do you know that?"

He shrugs. "It's all about perception."

"You've enslaved a child," I say. "A child!"

Ozol's eyes flicker over to Yuri, who keeps glancing over at us every few seconds. "He should be thanking me. He's lived a much better life than some other children who've crossed my path."

"What is wrong with you?" I hiss. "Where is your heart? Your humanity?"

"I abandoned my sense of morality a long time ago," he shrugs. "It got me nowhere and only made me weak. Without the constraints of conscience, you can do anything. And I can indeed do anything."

"Phoenix will get you," I say confidently. "Even if everyone else fails, he won't."

Ozol throws back his head and laughs. "It'll interest you to know that Phoenix is upstairs right now, in a cell much like yours."

That takes the wind right out of my sails. I shouldn't give him the satisfaction, but I can't help stammering, "W… what?"

The man's sky blue eyes gleam with satisfaction. He's enjoying himself. "May I come in?" he asks. "Although, I don't know why I bother asking. I own this place inside and out. I go wherever I like." He hums softly to himself as he pulls out a little key and sticks it in the lock of my cell.

I back away immediately as he opens the door and steps into the cell with me. I slap him across the face as hard as I can the second he turns to face me. My hand burns with the contact.

He smiles again. That same sickly, creeping smile that makes my skin crawl.

Then he hits me across the face so hard my world explodes.

I feel myself falling, but he lashes out a hand and snatches me back upright by my hair. Shoving me against the dank concrete wall, he presses his chest into mine and squeezes my cheeks between his clammy fingers.

"So very beautiful," he says, licking his lips. "I wonder what you taste like."

"Where is my son?" I ask, my voice shaky.

"He's here somewhere. All the pieces of my collection, finally under one roof." He chuckles. "Isn't it funny how life turns out? I now have Phoenix Kovalyov's entire life in the palm of my hand. The man himself, both his sons, and his pretty little wife."

"What do you want from me?" I manage to choke out. "You have Phoenix. What good am I? What good is Yuri? What good is Theo?"

"I want the sweet pleasures of your body," Ozol replies. "So I can see what drove young Phoenix so fucking wild. I want your obedience. Your devotion. Your loyalty. And if you don't give me anything I ask, it won't matter anyway, because I'll take what I need from you."

He bends down and runs his nose along my cheek. He smells of smoke and whiskey.

I probably smell of fear.

"Such soft, young skin..." He presses himself up against me. I can feel his foul erection. His hand lands on my breast and I gasp.

I try and jerk away from him, but he's got me skewered against the wall and there's nowhere to go. When I keep struggling, he slugs me in the gut. The breath rushes from my lungs. I see stars.

"I'm a different kind of beast altogether, Elyssa," he warns me. "I keep my promises. If you displease me, you will regret it. Now, are you going to be a good little girl?"

He grabs my jaw again and turns it up to his face.

Don't kiss me. Don't kiss me. Don't kiss me.

If he does, I'm not sure I'll be able to stop myself from throwing up.

He doesn't kiss me. But he does lean down, ensnare my bottom lip between his teeth, and bite down hard enough to draw blood.

I cry out in pain. Laughing, he steps back and looks me up and down with venomous eyes, my blood slicking his chin.

"Would you like to see Phoenix?" he asks me. "He'll love that black eye and bloody lip of yours. It goes quite well with your complexion."

"Fuck you," I snarl. If there were ever a time to start swearing, it's now. "Phoenix will kill you."

He smiles thinly. "Do you get wet for him?" he ponders.

My face twists into a grimace. "You're disgusting. You make me sick."

"Do I?" he asks dangerously. He lunges towards me and presses his palm against my windpipe. "Be careful, little girl. I don't tolerate backtalk from my whores."

I can't draw in enough air to speak, so I spit in his face instead.

"You've got a lot to learn, it seems," he sneers. "I have a feeling I'm going to enjoy teaching you."

"Go ahead. You can't hurt me."

"Oh, you naïve little girl. Everyone has a breaking point," he sighs. He drops his hand from my throat, steps back, and withdraws a handkerchief from his pocket to dab the saliva from his face.

I raise my eyes and notice that Yuri is standing just outside my cell. His eyes are wide with concern as he looks at me. Those sad eyes that have seen far too much for someone so young.

Ozol spies the glance. And when he does, his grin grows a notch wider. "Ah. And there is yours. Simple as could be."

I blanch. "No. No! Don't hurt him."

"No? You don't want to see me do… this?" At the last word, he pounces towards the bars of the cell, grabs Yuri by the shirt, and drags him close enough to clench his throat the same way he was just choking me.

Yuri splutters at once, but he doesn't cry out. His eyes just bulge with fear and confusion.

"Every time you talk back to me, I will hurt Yuri. Every time you disobey me, I will hurt Theo."

Terror like I've never known grips me. I believe him instantly.

"Please stop!" I cry out. "Don't hurt them."

"What was that?" he taunts, raising his voice.

"Please don't hurt them. I'll do anything."

"Anything?" he asks.

I nod.

He smiles, the triumph evident in the sinister glow of his eyes. "That's good to know," he says. "Now, come here."

I do as he says, slinking forward with dread wracking me head to toe.

"I'm going to take you up to see your beloved husband now," he informs me as I step closer. "You are not to utter a single word to him without my explicit permission. Is that understood?"

I nod.

"If you even so much as whisper, I will make you regret it. I will make you watch while these children suffer on your behalf."

"I understand."

His smile grows a notch wider. "Then this looks like the start of a beautiful new relationship," he says. "Now, come."

And I do.

39
PHOENIX
A CELL BENEATH WILD NIGHT BLOSSOM

The biggest cell in the place, all to myself. What a treat. Ozol must think I'm fucking special.

When I hear footsteps, I straighten immediately. But it's not Ozol like I expected.

"Josiah," I growl, moving towards the cell bars. "I should have fucking killed you when I had the chance."

He looks pale. "You should have known better than to mess with the powers that be."

"For fuck's sake, stop talking about them like gods. They're men, Josiah. Nothing more."

He gulps. The Adam's apple in his throat rides up and down. "I... I always suspected they were... were not the saints they claimed to be."

"Understatement of the fucking year."

"But..."

I frown, taking in his ashen face. "But what?"

He shakes his head.

"What just happened?" I press. "Why do you look like you've seen a ghost?"

"I just passed at least a dozen dead bodies."

I nod grimly. "Murder is so much more shocking when you witness it up close, huh?"

"I'm not supposed to be here," he says with a horrified shudder. "I'm just waiting to go back to the Sanctuary. Then life will go on as usual."

"You mean you'll continue selling women and children into sex slavery?"

"That's not what this is. I'm helping to give them a second chance."

"You still believe that?" I demand. "Even after spending time in this place?"

"I'll admit, there are unsavory aspects to this—"

"You are fucking delusional," I snarl. "But I suppose denial is the only way you can justify your part in this."

He cringes at my words, but I don't pause to give him room to think. He doesn't deserve even that tiny mercy.

"Now, where is my wife?"

"Elyssa is being held," he replies guiltily.

"Held?"

He nods uncomfortably. "Until she accepts…"

"Accepts what exactly?"

"Accepts that she is to be *my* wife," Josiah says. He seems to straighten up slightly as he speaks. He's still clinging to hope that the future he prophesized will come to pass. Like I said, fucking delusional. "And that she will be my right hand in the running of the Sanctuary."

So be it. The time for words is done. I need to beat the truth into this bastard's thick skull.

My hand snakes through the cell's bars and I grab hold of Josiah's shirt. Taken completely by surprise, he gasps and screams like a bitch as I yank him against the bars with a hard clang.

"You dumb motherfucker," I spit. "You better start praying to whatever you believe in, because I'm going to fucking kill you."

A light chuckle comes from beyond Josiah.

"I have no objection to that," Ozol says, coming into view from the shadows. "But it'll be more fun if you wait."

Distracted, I release Josiah. Not because of Ozol…

But because of the person standing just behind him.

"Elyssa!"

She's standing just behind his left shoulder. Her shoulders are hunched forward, slumped with defeat. And even though I'm seeing red with rage and the cells are dark, my eyesight is sharp enough to make out the purpling bruises of fingerprints around her neck.

I grab a metal bar in each hand and shake the whole cage, roaring. "You motherfucker!"

"Now, now, Phoenix," Ozol croons in a condescending tone. "You'll need to rein in that beastly temper of yours if you want things to go smoothly."

I ignore him. "Elyssa," I say. "Look at me."

She doesn't. She keeps her head down and her eyes averted.

Something is wrong. He's done something to her. Said something to her. Pushed her over the edge she's been teetering on for a long, long time now.

"I will destroy you," I vow. "I will make you wish you'd never been fucking born."

"Strong words coming from the man behind bars," Ozol laughs.

He ambles forward casually, hands clasped behind his back. Elyssa follows him without a word, like she's entranced. Like she's his shadow. His puppet.

"I have a proposition for you, Phoenix," he says pleasantly. "Would you like to hear it?"

"Elyssa, what's wrong?"

"She's not going to talk to you," Ozol remarks with a self-satisfied quirk of the eyebrows.

"What the fuck does that mean?"

"Exactly that. I've told her not to. So she won't."

Ozol reaches back and grazes Elyssa's cheek with the back of his hand. He tucks a lock of hair back behind her ear and gives her a sickening smile.

I'm not the only one that tenses. Josiah does, too.

Ozol turns back to me pointedly. "She's mine now. She's willing to do as I instruct. The question is… are you?"

My body feels like steel, hardened towards its purpose. If only I wasn't stuck behind bars, I'd kill the motherfucker with my bare hands.

"Elyssa, my dear," Ozol starts with the air of a professor giving a lecture, "do you know why Phoenix came today?"

She doesn't say a word. She doesn't even move.

He just smiles as if she's done exactly as she's supposed to. "It was to save you. To exchange his life for yours. Isn't that noble?"

He gets nothing from Elyssa apart from the tiniest of flinches. Hardly a blink. He might not notice it, but I do.

"Well, perhaps 'noble' is a stretch. But still—even I can see that it's very, shall we say, *romantic*."

His voice curls around the word, turning it into something dirty. Something pathetic.

"You've exposed yourself, Phoenix," he tells me. "You've given me the power to hurt you and your Bratva. But—I'm not an unreasonable man. I like a good trade as much as anyone. You want Elyssa freed?" he asks. "I can make that happen."

I'm not stupid. I can see a trap coming from a mile away. But what choice do I have?

"What are your terms?"

His smile gets wider. "Oh, nothing too unbearable," he says. Reaching behind him with the speed of a viper, he snatches Elyssa and throws her towards the bars of my cage. "Fuck her. Fuck her like you love her. Fuck her like you'll never get to fuck her again."

My blood runs cold. "What the hell did you just say to me?"

He laughs. "Generous, isn't it? Well, what do you say, Phoenix? Fuck her here and now, in front of me and Josiah and my men, and she'll be free as a bird."

"What's the catch?" I demand. "What do you get out of this?"

"The pleasure of watching a drowning man take his last breath of air." Ozol's smile broadens one tooth wider. His teeth are sharp and tiny like a crocodile's. The effect is nauseating. "Clock's ticking, Master Phoenix. Do we have a deal?"

I stare into those hauntingly pale eyes of his.

And I nod. "I accept."

Elyssa's eyes go wide. She looks terrified, but she still doesn't utter a single word.

"Guard," Ozol orders, "open the door."

An unexpected voice pipes up. "S... sir?" Everyone looks towards Josiah where he's standing in the corner.

He looks shrunken. The charisma he used to possess seems to have shriveled up and died the moment Ozol entered the room.

"Sir, you told me... You told me that..."

"Spit it out."

"You said she was to be mine. After you took care of him."

Ozol smiles, but it's twisted. Josiah recoils. "And she will be. But not before I have my fun."

Viktor holds eye contact with the poor bastard until Josiah is squirming in place. When his head falls, Ozol knows he's won.

"Just a few ground rules, Phoenix," Viktor says, turning back to me. "If you try anything, anything at all—she dies."

I look past him at Elyssa's grim expression. "Oh, don't worry about her," he adds. "She already knows the ground rules."

He shoves her through the open cell door without warning. She crashes into me and my arms wrap around her instinctively.

"Elyssa," I whisper, "are you okay?"

She looks up at me, her eyes filmy and desperate.

But she still doesn't say a word.

Ozol laughs and snaps his fingers. All his men start filing into the huge space, bumping Elyssa and me into the center. They form an impenetrable circle around us.

"Now," Ozol says, stepping between his men, "let's begin. Josiah, come here!"

Josiah stumbles forward by his side. He's gone from pale as a ghost to seasick green.

"I want to make sure you have a good view," Ozol explains salaciously.

Then he nods towards me.

"Take off her clothes."

One of the men kicks over the thin, filthy mattress that was pushed against the back wall of the cell. I ignore it, my hands clenching into fists. Elyssa turns to me and nods as though she wants me to follow Ozol's instructions.

"I would suggest you follow my instructions, Mr. Kovalyov," Ozol says. "I'm not a patient man."

There are at least fifteen men staring at Elyssa like she's a piece of meat. When I still hesitate, she starts undressing.

I reach out and stop her before her top is off.

"Learn from your wife, Phoenix," Ozol tells me. "I'm giving you a gift. You might as well enjoy it. You won't see her after today."

"I have your word that you'll set her free?"

Ozol smiles. "Of course," he says, sounding affronted that I've even asked.

I look at Elyssa, who nods again. *Why won't you talk? Say something, for fuck's sake!* I'm bellowing inside.

The only answer is a tear slipping from her eyes.

Fine. Fuck it. We'll do this. Not for Ozol. Not for Josiah. Not for the faceless Yakuza and Astra Tyrannis troops clustered around.

But for us.

Because I love her.

I reach out and pull off her shirt. Her bra comes next. Her jeans. But when I finally get to her panties, I hesitate, hating what I'm being forced to do.

She's mine. Not theirs, but *mine.*

Suddenly, I feel her hand against my cheek. She lifts my face to hers and the expression there is pleading.

She wants me to do this.

She wants me to follow instructions.

She's saying, *If we have to do this… let's make the most of it.*

So we do. I strip out of my clothes, and when I'm standing there as naked as she is, I pull her to me. We sink down to the mattress together.

It takes me a moment longer than usual to get hard, and that's only possible because I block out everyone else and focus only on Elyssa.

She looks tired, pale and terrified. But her beauty shines through despite it.

Is this the last time I'll ever see her? I don't believe it. There's a way out of this. I don't know what it is yet, but I swear on my son's grave that I'll find it.

I can feel Ozol's eyes on my back. He wants me to fuck her. He wants to turn as into animals. He wants to humiliate us.

But that's not up to him. This isn't his moment—it's ours.

So I don't fuck Elyssa. I make love to her.

I lean in and kiss her, long and slow. She kisses me back, clinging to my shoulders like her life depends on it. When I pull back, I see the glint of her tears, but she manages a small smile.

I reach down between her legs and slip my finger inside her. Her muscles clench around me. "Forget them all," I whisper fiercely. "It's just me and you, little lamb. It's just me and you."

I look her in the eye as I finger her. It takes some time for her to open up, but before long, she's wet. Only then do I lay her on her back and slide inside of her.

I move slowly, taking my time, savoring every inch of her. Trying to memorize the curve of her hips. The peak of her nipples. The way her hair splays around her head like a halo and her mouth opens with each subtle moan and all the other million things about her that I love, that I crave, that I need.

The sound of our bodies crashing together feels like triumph. A "fuck you" middle finger to the man who wants to break us.

I lock eyes with Elyssa and never look away. The rest of the world can go to hell. This cell, the men in it, even this disgusting mattress we're on… it all fades away.

And then it's just Elyssa and me. My lost little lamb.

Exactly how we're meant to be.

I'm approaching my peak. She's almost at hers, too. I know those sounds, those sensations—her clenching and clawing at my back, biting down on my shoulder, squeezing her thighs behind me…

When suddenly, I feel a savage pain in my ribs.

It rips me down from the cloud of euphoria we were floating on. Suddenly, I'm right back to cold, hard reality. To a dank cell. An army of bad men.

And pain. A lot of fucking pain.

I look up and see Ozol standing above me. His eyes are wide with manic bloodlust.

Then I hear a scream. Elyssa's scream.

I see blood drenching her lily-white skin. Rage overcomes me. *If he touched her...*

But a second later, I feel relief. Because I realize it's not her blood.

It's mine.

Ozol wrenches the bloody knife out of my side. At the same moment, a dozen hands grab me and tear me off my wife. She cries out, tears streaming down her face, but she still never utters a word.

"Take her away," Ozol orders. "And lock the Russian in again. Oh, and wipe that sour look off your face, Josiah. All is well. The fun has just begun."

40

ELYSSA

I'm crying as I'm carried through the dark halls of Wild Night Blossom. But I don't fight. I just close my eyes and sag limply in the arms of the pair of guards hauling me out of here.

But I endured. I was silent even when it hurt more than anything not to be able to tell Phoenix I loved him. That I'll always love him.

I stayed silent for Theo. For Yuri.

And for them, I'll endure anything. I'll endure everything.

My eyes are still closed when we come to an unexpected stop. "Where did you come from?" the guard holding me asks to someone in the shadows I can't see.

"Just heading up to speak to the boss."

"Well, get out of my way."

"No can do."

I hear a dull grunt. A sick squelch. And then I feel myself falling.

It doesn't matter. Nothing matters. I keep my eyes closed even when I hit the ground. There's another grunt, a sound that sounds like a punch, something I could swear is a muffled gunshot. A thick droplet of something wet hits me in the cheek.

I keep my eyes closed. I don't want to see anyone or anything ever again. I just want to sleep forever.

"Elyssa."

I frown. I know that voice.

"Elyssa, get up. I've got to get you out of here fast."

My eyes fly open, but it takes me three full seconds to register the face I'm staring at. He has a name, right on the tip of my tongue…

"Matvei?"

"We don't have much time. I can hear more guards coming."

I want to pick myself up, but my legs are weak. Everything is weak.

Sighing, Matvei wraps something around me—a jacket, I think—then scoops me up in his arms like a doll. Then he starts to run. Warm air rushes past my face as we hurry through darkened spaces that I can only half-see through my tear-filled eyes. Is it really Matvei, or is this just a dream?

Get a hold of yourself, woman. You're being rescued!

I try and blink my tears away as I look up at his solemn face. "Wait!"

"Shh!" he hisses at me.

"Let me down."

He sighs, stops, and sets me down on my feet. But instead of joining him in the direction we were headed, I turn back the way we came.

He snags my wrist out of the air and reels me back in towards him. "Elyssa, it's this way."

"No," I say, shaking my head furiously. "I have to go back."

"We can't save Phoenix, Elyssa," he says urgently. "Not today. But I can get you out of here."

I keep shaking my head. "I have to go back," I repeat stupidly.

"He's too well-guarded, and I'm the only one who managed to get in here. If we linger any longer, we'll be caught."

"I have to go back for them. Theo. Yuri."

"Yuri?" Matvei's brows knit together. He's looking at me like I've lost it now.

I don't have time to explain, though. I try to disentangle myself from Matvei, but he grabs me roughly and hoists me over his shoulder like a sack of potatoes. I can't do anything except beat my hands against his back as he resumes his sprint out of this hellacious nightclub.

"Matvei, please," I sob. He ignores me.

When we burst out of a rear entrance into the light of day, I have to shut my eyes tight. The sun is so bright it hurts.

But not so bright that I don't notice the five dead Yakuza bodies lying in the alleyway, piled up at the feet of a handful of Bratva soldiers.

"Matvei?" one of the soldiers asks.

"Come on," Matvei answers. "Let's get out of here."

"What about the boss?"

"That's a rescue mission for another day," Matvei grimaces. "Right now, we've got to get out of here. We have minutes before we're discovered."

"Put me down," I say softly.

He does—right into the back of an unmarked van. The soldiers pile in after me hurriedly. Then we're whizzing away from Wild Night

Blossom.

And all I can do is look out at that godforsaken building with a sinking feeling in my chest.

"Matvei, we have to go back."

He sighs. "I would if I could, Elyssa," he says. "But Phoenix tied my hands—literally and figuratively—when he went off in search of you."

"Literally?"

"It's a long story."

"You don't understand," I protest, deciding that I don't need the whole story. "It's not just Phoenix we have to save…"

"They're not going to hurt your son. They still need him."

"Yuri's alive," I blurt out.

The whole van seems to go quiet. Glances are exchanged. The atmosphere prickles with disbelief.

"Who told you that?" Matvei asks at last.

"No one. I saw him with my own eyes," I reveal. "I know you think I might be wrong, but I'm not, Matvei. Ozol has had him this whole time. He makes him wear chains and a collar. It's horrific. We have to do something."

"That motherfucker," Matvei says. I'm relieved to see that he believes me. "That fucking sadistic motherfucker."

"So you see?" I say desperately. "You see why we need to go back?"

Matvei reaches out and puts his hand over mine. "I understand, Elyssa. But we can't go back. Not now."

"But—"

"It's too risky. And they have the upper hand. We need a plan of action. We need to be cautious."

I preached the same to Phoenix not long ago. Now, in a cruel twist of fate, I find myself seeing his side of things.

"What if he hurts the boys?" I ask, more tears rising to my eyes.

"He's kept them alive this long," Matvei assures me. "He's not going to kill them now."

I try and hold on to that hope, but it's feeble and flickering.

When the van stops, I look up in shock. How did we already get to the mansion? It feels so wrong to be coming here when Phoenix and the boys are trapped in that hellhole with the devil himself.

"Go inside," Matvei tells me. "Go to your room and get some rest."

"You think I can rest?" I scoff. "I won't rest until all three of them are back here. Safe. Alive."

Matvei sighs. I can see the worry in his eyes.

"I know," he says with a tired nod. "I know, Elyssa. But we need to make sure that when we go in, we can get them all out."

I bite my lip and turn away from him. "We don't have time to waste, Matvei."

"Trust me."

"The man I trust is locked in a cell in Wild Night Blossom."

He nods solemnly. "Well, the man you trust trusts me," he says. "Maybe you can find a way to do the same."

I look at him. He's still a stranger, but at the moment, he's all I have.

"Okay."

"Thank you," he says sincerely. "Now please, go up and try and rest. You're going to need all the strength you have to get through the next few days."

I nod and make my way into the mansion. It feels cold and empty without my men.

I stumble up the stairs. Each step feels heavier than the last. The plan is to head to my room, but somehow, I end up in Phoenix's instead. It hurts to be in here, but I think it might hurt worse not to be. I climb into his bed and collapse into a fetal position.

I try desperately to hold myself together. But it feels like my limbs are made of sand, and all my pain is running through me like rainwater in the thirsty desert.

I'm here. Safe. Meanwhile, Phoenix is probably bleeding out from his stab wound. Yuri is walking around like an animal with a collar around his neck. And Theo—my poor Theo who can't even speak yet—where is he? What have they done with him?

I start sobbing, because really, that's all I can do. Cry until my body goes stiff with dehydration.

Stop it. You're acting like it's over. It's not.

"Isn't it?"

Don't be a Negative Nancy.

"Did you miss the last few hours? Because last I checked, Phoenix is with that monster. So is Yuri. So is Theo."

You'll get them back.

I just drown out Charity's voice in my head with more sobs. An hour later, I'm vaguely aware of a knock on my door. But I ignore it.

Whoever it is won't be denied, though. It sounds again. Along with my name: "Elyssa, are you in there?"

The door swings open. Matvei steps in. "Are you awake?"

"Have you come to tell me that you have a plan for getting back all three of them?" I ask. "If not, then yes, I'm asleep."

"Sit up and drink some water."

"I don't want to."

"Dying of dehydration isn't going to help get them back, you know."

Sighing, I struggle upright and turn around to glare at him.

"Come on," he says, offering me a tall glass of water. "You can't have lost all your fight."

"I can't lose them."

"Then don't throw in the towel just yet," he tells me. "It's not over. As long as there's air in our lungs, we can still fight."

I nod slowly and take the glass of water. I only want to take a sip so he stops harassing me about it, but it tastes so good that I keep drinking until the glass is drained.

"Feel better?" Matvei asks with a soft chuckle.

"A little." I wipe my lips.

"If we survive this, Elyssa," he sighs, "you're going to have to get used to this life. It's hard. Brutal at times, but it's part of the package."

"It's torture."

"That might be the price of being with Phoenix."

I nod, realizing what he's telling me. He's not asking me to change—not quite. He's asking me to *evolve*.

To become stronger. Braver. More daring.

He gives me an understanding nod as I struggle to process what that means, what it might look like. "So the question is," he continues, "do you want to be with him enough?"

I haven't admitted it out loud, not even to myself. But near-death experiences have a way of forcing honesty out of even the most stubborn of people.

"Yes," I croak. "I do."

He smiles. "Then we'll get him back together."

"Do we even have a plan?"

"The plan is to wait for reinforcements to arrive. And when they do, we're going to prepare for an attack."

"Reinforcements?"

"Phoenix comes from an old Bratva family," Matvei tells me. "His father called me earlier today and I admitted that more men would be helpful. He's sending a contingent over as we speak."

That makes me feel better. "When will they be here?"

"A day or so."

That makes my stomach plummet back down again. "Matvei…"

"I know how you feel about this, Elyssa. But rushing into things is not going to serve us well. This is not some random thug we're talking about. Viktor Ozol is a dangerous man, and he's dangerous because he's smart. He'll have planned ahead. Which means we need to do the same."

What can I do but nod? Matvei is right: I don't know this world. Not yet. But I'm learning as fast as I can. I just have to pray that it's fast enough.

"Okay, Matvei. Okay."

He touches my shoulder gently. Then he turns and walks out of the room, shutting the door behind him.

Atta girl. You had me worried there for a second.

"Yeah," I mumble, "I had myself worried there for a minute, too."

So not giving up then?

"No," I say fiercely. "Not a fucking chance."

41

PHOENIX

TWO DAYS LATER—A CELL BENEATH WILD NIGHT BLOSSOM

The ice-cold slap of water being thrown in my face jerks me awake. I struggle to suck in a breath as the freezing trickle snakes down my spine, drenching my clothes.

What's left of my clothes, that is.

The last two days has been a fog of torture. Brutal beatings. Some recreational waterboarding. And the loudest, fucking godawful heavy metal music ever recorded blaring around the clock to make sure I don't get a wink of sleep.

A weaker man would be long dead. But the bastards that be are determined not to let me off that easy. A doctor comes in and checks on me every few hours. If one of my injuries looks particularly gruesome, he warns the guards to go easy on me. I'm a fucking patchwork ragdoll at this point. I can barely see through one eye and my entire body is wracked with mottled bruises and open wounds, half of which are still fresh and seeping blood.

"If you keep this up, he'll die," I heard the doctor tell Ozol about twelve hours ago.

"If he dies, then you do."

"Then in my professional opinion, I suggest you let him sleep. You have to give his body a chance to recover. Otherwise, he won't last the night."

I wanted to scoff at that. Die? No fucking way. I may look like a dead man—but inside, I'm fighting fit. I'm ready to tear this place apart, brick by brick.

Just as soon as I get the chance.

I just wish my mind weren't so fucking messed up. My soul, my willpower? Those things have never faded. They never will. But the damage to my body is starting to take a toll on my thoughts.

At some point, when I manage to doze off, I dream.

I dream about my past, my crash course in the underworld just before I moved out here to head my own faction of the Kovalyov Bratva. I realize belatedly that this one is less a dream, and more of a memory. I remember my father's words to me just before I left home to apprentice under Uncle Kian, lifetimes ago.

"Being a Bratva Don means sacrifice," he had told me. "It may not seem like it now, but soon, you'll understand."

Is this the moment I'm enlightened? I wonder idly in the present moment. *The picture perfect movie montage where the old man's wisdom saves the day?*

Then my father turns into some bizarre flying beast and takes off into the wind.

Guess not.

∽

Another splash of water to the face. I open my eyes and see Viktor Ozol standing in front of me.

He's holding the hand of a small boy with dark eyes. They're both staring at me. The boy is somber, far more weary than a boy of his age ought to be. Ozol is smiling evilly, as per usual. His eyes gleam as he takes me in, reveling in my sorry state.

I close my eyes again. Just another fucked-up dream. The torture has moved inside my own head, I guess.

The one thing keeping me going is the knowledge that Elyssa is out of this place. She's safe.

I'd heard the uproar just before the beatings started. Ozol never planned on releasing her, it seemed. He was just playing his games. But Matvei, that beautiful motherfucker, had used his wits to get in here and steal her away right after Ozol's power play.

The satisfaction of hearing the monster rage at his men was incomparable. Euphoria on earth.

The third bucket of ice water wakes me up completely. I cough and force my gaze up to face whatever comes next. When my vision clears, Ozol comes into focus again, his eyes narrowed at me with irritation.

I've been strung up by my hands once more, but they've allowed my feet to reach the floor. How fucking kind.

"Good morning, Phoenix," Viktor greets, the very specter of politeness.

"The fuck do you want?"

"Is that anyway to greet your host?"

"Cut the shit," I sigh. "What do you want?"

"What makes you think I want something?"

"Why else am I alive?"

He smiles. It betrays the near madness that lies just beneath his façade of normalcy. "You're alive because I haven't yet decided to end your life yet," he says. "You see? You see how much you owe me?"

I shake my head. "You want something."

"You've got me all wrong," Ozol murmurs, shaking his head. "You assume you have something of worth that I want. But you don't. I'm not doing this to barter or bargain. This is about power, plain and simple. About sending a message."

"Meaning…?"

"Meaning that my idea of entertainment is very different from most. You see, when you're raised in the underworld, when you grow up around rape and murder and everything in between, it takes a lot to keep a man amused."

I stare at the madman in front of me in disgust. But he's not done yet.

"So you start having to invent games. Create your own entertainment."

"This is a game to you?"

"Oh yes, it most certainly is," Ozol nods, as though he's thrilled that I've finally understood him. "The kind of games that only a god understands."

I laugh bitterly. "Now you're a god?"

He raises his eyebrows. "As I said, I decide whether you live or not. And I will decide when you die. Just like I decide the fate of every woman and child that crosses my path. You're in my hands, Master Phoenix."

"But Elyssa is not," I hiss. "She slipped away when you weren't looking. Aren't gods supposed to be all-knowing and all-seeing? When you look at it from my perspective, you're just a regular old run-of-the-mill fuck-up."

His jaw twitches. It's only a tiny crack in his charade, but it's satisfying for me. It shows me the fury surging through him beneath that carefully composed mask.

I drink in his anger. It gives me the fuel I need.

"Oh, don't you worry," he says, recovering fast. "I'll get her back. And when I do, she will suffer for running. I thought I had her broken in. But apparently, I underestimated the bitch."

"I will kill you long before you get the chance to talk about her like that again, motherfucker."

Ozol cocks his head to the side. "I can't decide if you're very brave or very, very stupid." He straightens up. "I must admit you're right, though. I don't have Elyssa. But I do have someone else."

He turns towards the cell door and pulls it open again. Bending out, he ushers forward someone I can't see.

A moment later, I notice a little shadow. And then a dark-haired boy steps in the opening of the door, right next to Ozol. The same boy from my maybe-hallucination earlier.

"Turn to him," Ozol orders. "Let him get a good look at you."

The boy does as he's told.

And I go cold.

Colder than the ice cold water still dripping down my back.

"No. No. No…"

Ozol's smile grows wider and more cruel. "Oh, yes, Phoenix. Yes, yes, yes."

"Yuri?" I croak.

The boy's eyes bulge wide. Then he breaks away and looks down, as though he's terrified to look at me too long.

"Yuri," I breathe. "Yuri, my son…"

Ozol clamps his claw on the back of Yuri's neck and they take a step forward together. "I'm glad you recognize the boy," he says. "After all, it's been so long. Five years, right?"

Viktor loops two fingers casually through the back of the collar fastened around Yuri's neck. As though my firstborn son is no better than a rabid dog.

"You fucking bastard," I snarl. I can barely find the words to express the white-hot rage surging through every inch of me, from my numb fingertips to the ripped-apart soles of my feet.

"Now, now," Ozol croons, "don't frighten the child."

"Remove that collar," I growl. "Get that fucking shit off my boy."

Ozol laughs. "Why? Yuri, you like the collar, don't you?"

To my horror, Yuri nods immediately, an automated response that's no doubt been drummed into him. His eyes are cloudy and distant. The spark in them is just about gone.

"Yuri," I say, desperate for him to look at me. "Yuri, please…"

His cheeks tremble like he wants to look at me but can't.

"I know you're confused," I press. "But—"

"You know the truth already, Yuri," Ozol interrupts immediately. "Your father never wanted you. He discarded you after your mother died, and I saved you. I gave you a second chance at life. And aren't you grateful?"

"Yes, Master Viktor."

"Yuri, whatever he's told you about me, it's not true," I say desperately. "He's a liar. All this time… all this time, I thought you were dead. I thought you were gone. If I'd only known, I would have come for you. I would have—"

"You see, Yuri?" Ozol says, cutting me off. "Didn't I tell you he would say that?"

Yuri nods.

This fucker. This dirty, evil, psychotic motherfucker.

Somehow, seeing Yuri like this… it's worse than anything I could've imagined in my worst nightmares. At least in death, I had imagined him at peace. He was with his mother. He was happy and free of pain.

But this? This is a hell that Ozol has constructed for one reason: to hurt me.

To lord my own boy over me, to make me feel pain in my heart so acute that for the first time since the torture began, I think I am capable of giving up and dying. Because it shouldn't be possible for life to contain this much agony.

"Yuri, my boy…" Ozol croons, even though he never takes his eyes off me. "Go and bring our second little surprise."

Yuri turns and walks out of my cell. The moment he disappears, I explode.

"You motherfucker!" I scream, pulling at my chains, making the whole ceiling shiver with my strength.

It even causes Ozol to look up in mild concern. "If you break the ceiling, it'll only come down on your head."

"As long as I take you with me."

He smiles. "Haven't you realized by now? I'm immortal, Phoenix. I am a god. I am the powers that be."

"What have you done to him?"

"Just what I said: I gave him a second chance."

"I believed he was dead all this time…"

"That was what you were supposed to believe. So that I could orchestrate this little reunion when it suited me most."

His expression is almost gleeful. I've never seen such blatant excitement on anyone's face before. These are the games he plays to entertain himself. Because rape and murder have grown boring after so many years of causing that kind of suffering.

He's no god.

He's the motherfucking devil.

"You should be thanking me," he goes on. "I will turn your little boy into the exact mirror image of me. And one day, he will stand in my place, walk in my shoes. He will make the decisions for Astra Tyrannis. You see? I'm giving him an empire."

"I will kill you long before that happens, *mudak*."

He laughs. "Says the man hanging from the ceiling. It's a shame, really. You could have done so much. If you'd only chosen your friends more carefully."

"I'd rather die than be a part of anything to do with Astra Tyrannis."

"Then you will die indeed. But before you go, I still have games to play."

"Master Viktor?"

I cringe again as Yuri appears. This time, he's holding something carefully. He steps forward and my heart stops for a moment when I see the burden in his arms.

"Theo…"

Ozol throws back his head and laughs. "Isn't it ironic?" he asks. "For all your strength and power, you couldn't even hold on to your own sons. You couldn't keep them safe."

"*Ty budesh' goret' v adu za eto!*" I roar.

"So there we have it. Two Kovalyov boys are in my custody," he says triumphantly. "Two little toys for me to do with as I please."

"I will fucking murder you," I say. "I don't know how and I don't know when, but you will die by my hand. I swear that to you."

"It's good to have dreams," Ozol chuckles. "Hold onto them. But in the meantime, I'll be making plans."

He steers Yuri around and pushes them both out of the door.

"No!" I scream at their retreating backs. "No!"

But the only response is the clang of my cell door as it slams shut. I can only scream and struggle against my restraints like a fucking marionette.

The whole room shakes, but nothing gives way.

Not yet, at least.

But I meant what I swore. When I get out of this cell, Viktor Ozol is going to burn.

42

ELYSSA
PHOENIX'S MANSION

I know I'm dreaming. I know this isn't real.

But as long as Phoenix is in it, I cling to the blurry images, knowing that they'll fade when I wake up.

In the dream, he's lying on top of me, his cock deep inside me, pumping slowly, his eyes locked on mine.

"I will get you back," I tell him.

He doesn't respond—but then again, he's not really there.

Still, I can feel him inside me. He's still fucking me slowly, still looking me in the eye…

When suddenly blood starts to pour out of his mouth.

"No!" I shout. I try to grab him, but then he disappears in a cloud of blood.

I gasp awake for the third time that night, but despite my restless sleep, I feel wide awake. I feel ready. I vault out of bed and get dressed fast. It's still dark, but I don't care. I'll wake Matvei up if I have to.

I head out of my room—or more accurately, Phoenix's room—and head straight for the office.

Matvei is behind the desk, like I expected. It looks like he's slept there. But his eyes are sharp and alert when I walk in.

"You're up early," he comments. "Or late?" He checks his watch. "Fuck, I don't even know what time means anymore."

"I'm done waiting," I say, slamming my hands down on the desk in front of him.

"Elyssa…"

"There's such a thing as being too cautious, you know."

"I have to be," Matvei argues. "Phoenix left me in charge. If I think this through carefully, maybe the odds will work in our favor."

"This is Astra Tyrannis we're talking about," I say. "This is Viktor Ozol. I've had an education on the man while I was his captive. He's pure evil, plain and simple. The only way forward is through."

He sighs and rubs at his bloodshot eyes. "I don't know if it's just the hour, but you're not making sense."

"Reinforcements arrived last night, didn't they?"

He sighs. "Yes."

"You didn't inform me like you promised."

"You needed rest," he says defensively. "I didn't want to—"

"To trouble me?" I ask. "Worry me, upset me? Why do you even care? I am all of those things already. And do you know why? Because my husband is in hell right now. So are his sons. I need to get them back now. All of them."

"Elyssa…"

"I am his wife," I say, raising my voice. "I have a say here, Matvei. I know you've been doing this a lot longer. I know you know what you're doing. But I am his wife. And I should have a right to make some of the decisions."

"This is a pretty big one."

"It's been almost three days."

"Security has tripled around Wild Night Blossom, Elyssa."

"You think they're going to reduce it any time soon?" I scoff. "He knows we're after them! He's anticipating an attack."

"Which is exactly why attacking now seems foolhardy."

"No, it means we have no choice but to meet fire with fire."

"You're starting to sound like Phoenix."

"Well, apparently he's rubbed off on me."

I stare down Matvei until he stands up. He looks dead on his feet. I know he's spent the last few days planning intensely, trying to figure out the best possible way to infiltrate the building and get Phoenix and the boys out. But he's not moving fast enough for me.

"Matvei, I know why you're being cautious. But you didn't see what they're going through. Yuri's five years old and he wears a collar around his neck like some wild animal. Phoenix was stabbed when he was pulled off me. And Theo, my baby... I have no idea what they're even doing to him."

"I know," he mutters. "I fucking know."

"Please, Matvei," I beg. "I'd much rather do this with you than without you."

He nods slowly. "Okay. Fine. Fuck. But we need to figure out how to—"

"We go in with full force," I interrupt, having formulated the plan the moment I'd woken up. "We'll blow up the front of the building if we need to. While their men are dealing with ours, I'll sneak into the back and locate the boys and Phoenix."

Matvei frowns. "That's the dumbest shit I've ever heard. Phoenix really is rubbing off on you."

"It's the only plan that doesn't involve waiting around. I'm not waiting anymore, Matvei. If you don't help me, I'll take my plan to the men. Those who agree with me can join and the rest are free to stay here and listen to your orders."

Matvei raises his eyebrows. "You'd do that?"

"If you make me."

For a second, I think he's going to tear down my plan with logic and reason. But then he smiles.

"What are you smiling about?" I demand.

"Nothing," he murmurs. "Just that…"

"Just that what?"

"Phoenix would be proud."

That silences me for a moment. A giddy surge of pride rushes through me.

"You're the one who inspired me," I admit sheepishly.

"Me?"

"You said that if I want to be a part of Phoenix's life, it means getting used to his world. It means being braver and stronger and more resilient. I've relied on other people my entire life. But that's going to stop, starting now. I'm taking my life into my own hands. And the first thing I'm going to do is get my family back. I'd just rather not do it alone. But I will if I have to."

"Well, luckily, you don't have to," Matvei says. "I will—"

Before he can finish his thought, the phone rings. Matvei's expression changes when he looks at the caller ID.

"What's wrong?" I ask. "Who is it?"

"You'll see," he says, answering the call and putting it on speaker immediately.

Matvei says something in Russian. It sounds formal and respectful and makes me instantly nervous. Then he switches to English.

"You should know that I'm not alone, sir. Elyssa is with me, too."

"Is she?" a deep voice responds. "Well, Elyssa, I wish we could have been introduced under different circumstances. But I suppose this will have to do."

I glance at Matvei. "Who...?"

"I'm Artem Kovalyov," the man says.

Oh my God. Phoenix's father.

"It's, uh... it's good to meet you, sir," I say, stumbling a little.

Is there a protocol for talking to a man like Artem Kovalyov? I'm not sure and I have no idea how to ask with him on the phone. I shoot Matvei a glare, but he's not looking at me.

"Please call me Artem," he chuckles.

I make an immediate mental note to never, ever call him that.

"Matvei," Artem Kovalyov says, his tone shifting considerably, "what news of my son?"

"Nothing yet, sir," Matvei says. "I'm readying the men. We're working on a plan to –"

"We're attacking the club today," I cut in.

I'm shocked at myself, but I can't stop it, either. Now that I've made up my mind, there's no turning back. I wasn't kidding when I told Matvei I would do this on my own if I had to. I'm done sitting around and waiting for men to make all the decisions.

My judgement is as good as the next man's.

At least, I hope it is.

Of course it is! Girls run the world. The future is female. Lady-boss shit. Your turn now, boo.

I can't help a sly grin as I push Charity's voice out of my head and focus on Matvei.

"Matvei and I just discussed it," I continue, trying to keep my voice strong and confident. "We're going in soon. A few hours from now."

"Is that right?" Artem Kovalyov asks.

"Actually—"

"It was my idea," I say, interrupting Matvei again. "And I think it's a good one. The club is on high alert now, I know. But that's going to be true of the next few months, if not longer. We can't afford to wait anymore. Phoenix is injured. The boys… Their scars run much deeper. I don't want them in that place a second longer."

I know my nerves are acting up now, making me speak too often and too much. But I also don't want either man to convince the other that listening to me is a mistake.

There's a moment of silence from the machine on the table.

"Well, I have to say, you're not at all what I expected," Artem Kovalyov remarks. I imagine he's smiling.

"What were you expecting?"

"Less," he replies. I can almost hear the ghost of a chuckle underneath the word. "You sound ready. And I agree. My son and grandsons have been captive for long enough."

I hear some shuffling on the other line and a second later, another voice comes through on the speaker.

"Elyssa?"

It's soft and gentle and very feminine. It's also laced with worry.

"Yes?"

"I'm Esme, Phoenix's mother," she says.

"Oh, Mrs. Kovalyov—"

"Esme, please," she says. "Call me Esme. I would love it if you do."

I'm still nervous, but there's something more relatable about this woman. She puts me at ease instantly, in the same way her husband seems to make me feel like a bug under a microscope.

"Okay. Esme it is."

"Is it true that I have another grandson?"

My heart beats hard against my chest. I haven't been grateful for much in the last few days. But right now, I'm grateful that I can give them a true and definitive answer.

"You do," I say. "His name is Theo. He's an angel."

I can hear her exhale with joy. "That's the best news I've had in years."

"Matvei," Esme says, "you'll bring them all home safe, won't you?"

"I will do my very best, Madam," he says.

"Good. Then best of luck to you both," she says.

"Matvei," Artem adds, "keep me informed."

"Will do, sir."

"And if you need anything else…"

"I'll call."

The line goes dead. I square my shoulders and look Matvei in the eye. "I don't care how big and dangerous and powerful Astra Tyrannis is. I don't care how long they've been around or how far they've spread. There's a time for everything to die and this will be theirs. I'm getting my boys back. All three of them."

Matvei seems to stand a little straighter as he gives me a salute that's only partially teasing. "As you command, Madam," he says, using the same reverential term he had used for Esme.

I don't deserve it.

Not yet.

But I will.

43

ELYSSA

IN A VAN HEADED TOWARDS WILD NIGHT BLOSSOM

"Stop that."

I frown as I look down at my knee. Only now that Matvei has said something do I realize that I've been bouncing it frenetically for at least ten straight minutes.

"Sorry," I mumble. "I can't help it. I'm nervous."

"This was your plan."

"Why do you think I'm nervous?" I snap back at him. "If this fails, it's all on me."

"I wouldn't say that."

"What would you say then?"

"That you did the best you could."

I shake my head. "That doesn't cut it. My best means nothing if it doesn't set them free."

Matvei falls silent. I scan the back of the van we're sitting in. Given the ten other men cramped into the back with us, it's stifling hot. Like the heat itself is choking the oxygen from my lungs.

I try drawing in a big breath to steady my lungs, but it's like inhaling campfire smoke. It does nothing to settle my nerves.

I have a feeling I'm going to have to get used to that.

"Who's coming with me?" I ask.

"Konstantin, Ilya, Grigori, and Vitaly."

I frown. "That's not what we discussed—"

"Jesus, Elyssa. I can't send you in there with only one man," Matvei retorts.

The van rocks to the side as we round a sharp corner. "Why not?" I argue. "I'm more likely to fly under the radar with just one person. Three more is definitely going to draw attention."

"This plan is risky enough."

"It's not risky; it's bold."

"Same difference," Matvei says irritably.

"Once you've blown apart the building's façade, they'll have no choice but to meet you out there in the open. You have enough men to hold them at bay until I can locate Phoenix and the boys. While you're fighting, I can get them to safety."

"And you really think it's going to be as easy as sneaking them out while Ozol's men are fighting us?"

"Why shouldn't it be?" I ask. "They'll need all hands on deck."

"Ozol is too shrewd a man to leave valuable assets unguarded, even in a crisis."

"I'll have one man with me," I point out. "And I'm well-armed."

Matvei rolls his eyes. "But do you know how to use any of those weapons?"

"It's a gun," I say, trying to pass off my nerves as confidence. "You aim and shoot. And as for the knife, you poke the pointy end at the other guy. Have I got that right?"

"Very funny. It's not that simple."

"It never is with you, Matvei," I sigh.

I'm trying to be patient with him. He's thrown his weight behind my plan, after all, and marshalled the entire Kovalyov Bratva—Artem and Esme's contingent included—to go along with it.

Besides, his heart is in the right place. He just wants his friend to be safe.

I can get behind that.

"There's such a thing as overthinking," I add.

"Not where you're concerned."

I waggle my eyebrows. "I'm flattered and everything," I say, trying to make light of the seriousness of the moment. "But I'm taken."

He very nearly smiles. "Who the hell are you these days?" he laughs. "I barely recognize you."

Honestly, some moments, even I'm not sure. But I do like the new me.

Nothing is less scary. Somehow, though, I feel like I can face it all, no matter how scary it gets.

You go girl!

"Shut it."

"Did you say something?" Matvei asks.

"Nothing," I say, my cheeks coloring in embarrassment. I change the subject quickly before he starts to think I'm a raving lunatic. "I just feel like these kinds of missions are always going to be filled with unknown factors."

"Fine," he concedes grudgingly. "One man will accompany you."

I smile triumphantly. "Great."

"But you have to pick."

My smile falls at once. "Oh. Um..."

"Let me come with you, Madam," Konstantin speaks up immediately. "It would be an honor to protect you."

Jesus. Talk about bold declarations. This is a new me and all, yes, but I don't know if I'd call it an "honor to protect me."

I gulp. "Please call me Elyssa. 'Madam' sounds... terrifying."

He smiles. "Is that a yes?"

I nod. "Honor's all mine," I croak.

When the van finally comes to a stop, the men file out one by one, leaving Matvei and me behind.

"You're not going to talk me out of this, are you?" I ask.

"No," he sighs. "I gave up on that this morning."

"Then what is it?"

He hesitates. Then he says, "I've been with Phoenix through thick and thin. I've known the man through his best moments, but when things are going smoothly, it's easy to be around for that. It's the bad times that really make you understand a person. And Phoenix... after he lost Aurora and Yuri, he became a shadow of the man he was. Until he met you."

I try to sit perfectly still. I don't know what to do with the torrent of emotions buzzing through me at Matvei's words. There's so much he's implying that I can't even begin to process it. Not yet, at least. And maybe not for a long, long time.

"What I'm saying is, do not die in there," Matvei concludes. "Because if you do, he will murder me."

I smile and pat the back of his hand. "I'm not planning on dying today. Or anytime soon, for that matter."

"Spoken like Phoenix Kovalyov's wife."

"Time to show Viktor Ozol just who I am."

He nods to me and we get out of the van together.

I'm dressed in black tights, a high-necked black sweater and combat boots. I feel like some sort of spy in an action movie.

Look good, feel good, am I right? Dress for the job you want, not the job you have? I dunno, I'm running out of motivational slogans here. Take your pick.

"When did you turn into a Sex & the City monologue?" I grumble to Charity.

But I can't deny she's right. It makes me feel closer to the part I'm trying to play.

Konstantin moves to my side like a shadow. I check to make sure all the weapons Matvei equipped me with are still in the right places.

"Remember," Matvei says to me, "don't be shy about using that gun. Stay behind the building. When you hear the explosion, that's your cue."

I can feel the emotion rising up inside me—the fear, the anxiety, the endless rushing thoughts—but I squash it all down. I have to stay focused.

Phoenix needs me.

"Matvei," I say, stopping him before he can walk away. "Be careful out there, too, okay?"

He nods and heads off with the bulk of the men.

Konstantin and I head around to the back of the building and watch the side door that leads into the innards of Wild Night Blossom.

I check my watch again and again as the seconds tick past. At three minutes, I brace for the explosion and plug my ears, as per our plan.

But it doesn't come.

"What's wrong?" I ask, glancing at Konstantin.

More minutes whisk away. Nothing goes *boom*.

"Bombs are tricky things," he responds patiently. "Don't worry. If it takes longer than fifteen, I'll go—"

A second later, my ears are ringing with a strange whistling. But I don't immediately notice because I find myself on my back, staring up at the peaks of buildings and a little slice of sky.

Then I see Konstantin's face hanging over mine. He's speaking but I can't hear a thing.

A second later, the whistling fades and I hear his rushed words come pouring in.

"Quickly! The fight will spill out here in moments. We need to be inside before it does."

Marshaling my courage, I grab his hand and he pulls me back to my feet. Then we both run towards the back door. It's locked, but Konstantin shoots at the handle twice and then kicks it open.

Immediately, we're met with two armed guards. But Konstantin has them both dead on the ground instantly with a pair of rapid shots.

We jump over them and rush into the darkened alleys of the club. The ringing has all but cleared now. Just in time for me to hear the sounds of war.

Bullets. Screams. The crunch of exploding concrete.

"When this is all over, you're going to have to teach me to shoot," I tell him. "Your aim is fantastic."

He shoots me a pleased smile. "Damn right. I taught Phoenix everything he knows."

If my lungs weren't about to burst from our sprint through the meandering hallways, I'd have laughed.

We come to a stop at a junction of two corridors. Konstantin looks at me. "Which way?"

I'm not a hundred percent sure, but I go with my instincts and vague, drug-tinged memories of this place. "Straight. I think."

He's alert. He hears the sound of oncoming footsteps before I do.

When he grabs my arm and pulls me back behind the wall, I stumble into him, panic starting to get the better of me.

"More guards?" I mouth.

He nods and holds up four fingers.

He presses a finger up to his lips, and then, without any warning, he darts out of his hiding place and starts shooting. By the time I lift my gun, he's already taken out two men. He turns his focus on the third, but I'm determined to help.

I take a deep breath and aim at the fourth man.

He hasn't even seen me, so it's not exactly fair, but to hell with that. None of these men deserve a fair fight.

I shoot three times. The second bullet ends his life. The third one just adds insult to injury.

But instead of the guilt I'm expecting, I feel pure relief. Maybe even a smidgeon of pride.

Phoenix was right: there's a savage beauty in killing men who deserve to die.

"Nice shot," Konstantin remarks.

"I needed three bullets."

"He's dead, isn't he?"

I glance down at the man as the last of the blood trickles out of the hole in his throat. "Yeah," I say grimly. "I guess so."

We leave them behind and delve deeper. Down hallways, down a staircase, and then we burst into the circular space that precedes Phoenix's cell. I catch a glimpse of his silhouette strung from the ceiling before we're besieged by another half a dozen enemy troops.

Konstantin jumps in front of me and starts shooting. His aim really is brilliant. He moves fast and confidently. But even I can see that he's severely outnumbered. His reflexes can only get him so far.

I start shooting, too, but all of my first few bullets miss the mark by miles. They also alert the men to my presence.

Obviously, I'm the easier target, so two of them turn to me.

In a blind panic, I shoot off one round after the other. I'm not particularly skilled, nor is my aim very accurate. But if you shoot off enough bullets, one of them is bound to meet its mark.

Sure enough, the closer soldier drops to the floor.

He's not dead, but I have a feeling he's on his way there. His friend, on the other hand, is more determined than ever to get to me before I can squeeze off another round.

He bellows and charges forward like a buffalo. I back up instinctively and hit the wall behind me. The unexpected contact jars the gun from my hand. It goes clattering to the ground. I start fumbling for my knife. I don't have much time. I can't get it out of the holster, though, and my hands are shaking and he's almost on me and—

BANG.

A shot rings out. I turn and see Konstantin standing a few yards away, with his smoking gun aimed at the man who was just about to wring the life from my throat.

He saved me.

But at the expense of letting his own guard down.

He knows it, too. Konstantin looks at me with solemn eyes that contain not the tiniest morsel of fear. Just bravery. Just loyalty. He says, "Madam…"

And then the man I shot but didn't kill raises his arm limply from the ground and fires.

I have only enough time to scream.

Konstantin drops to the ground, blood flowing out of the nauseating crater in his temple.

"No!" I cry. "No…"

I don't have time to feel anything. The threat isn't gone yet.

I drop to the ground, pick up my fallen weapon, point it at Konstantin's murderer, and fire. I fire and fire and fire until the *click* of the mechanism tells me the chamber is empty.

He's dead. But even then, he's not dead enough. He'll never be dead enough. Not if I had a million bullets.

I drop the useless gun and stare down at Konstantin's body. Is it even possible that a person can be so full of life one second, and then gone the next?

Of course it can. Look at Charity. Apparently, death in this world takes the brightest flames first.

Those are the stakes. Those are the rules. Those are the consequences of the games the Bratva plays.

No one else has come to attend to the commotion down here. I can hear the vague thumps of the war raging at the main entrance, though. I don't know how long I have left to complete my job. I have to move.

Taking advantage of my isolation, I rush towards Phoenix's cell. I grab another gun from one of the fallen Yakuza guards, mimic Konstantin's entry from earlier, and shoot the lock twice.

When I kick the door, it collapses inwards.

"Phoenix…"

"El… Elyssa," Phoenix murmurs dreamily, taking in my appearance as though he can't quite believe his eyes. "Is it really you?"

"In the flesh," I say. "Come on. We've got to go."

I look up at the rope that has him partially suspended above the ground. I pull out the knife Matvei had given me and start cutting through the stubborn bonds.

It takes my full effort to saw through the thick rope, but eventually, the last thread parts and Phoenix collapses to the ground. He groans, but swats away my offer of a hand up to stand on his own power.

Even beaten, even bloodied, even dragged to death's doorstep, he looks magnificent.

"Who's with you?" he says in the low, rasping voice that makes my blood run hot even now.

A lump forms in my throat. "Konstantin…"

"Good. Where is he…?"

"Dead," I say with a catch in my voice. "I'm sorry. It happened when we were trying to get in here. He saved me."

I grab hold of him, wanting to make sure he's really here, really with me. He looks as solid as ever, despite the fact that his body is riddled with the signs of torture.

"It's okay," Phoenix says, reading the expression on my face. "I'm okay."

I nod and pass him a gun. "Let's go get the boys," I tell him.

He takes it from me and checks the chamber with expert efficiency. He's recovering rapidly now that he's back on his feet. "Do you have any idea where they are?"

"Yuri might be down in the other block of cells," I reply. "That's where I first met him. But Theo… I have no idea."

"That means we need to move fast," Phoenix says, instantly going into alpha mode.

You can kick the life out of the don, it seems.

But you can't kick the don out of the life.

Taking the lead, I navigate us down the dark corridors until we hit the staircase that leads down to the lower cells. The door is wide open. I sprint straight through and down into its depths.

I take the steps two at a time until I emerge into the dimly lit room. The cells are all full, except for the one in the corner that I used to occupy. The women in them leap to their feet when they see who it is. The redhead who'd scoffed at me earlier looks positively dumbfounded.

"Don't worry," I tell all of them. "We'll get you out one way or another."

"How?" the redhead demands. "You don't have the keys."

"I'll find them," I snap. "Where's the little boy? Yuri?"

"The master came down minutes ago and took him."

The hope drains from Phoenix's face. I'm sure I look the same—like I've just seen death itself. Phoenix sags against a moldy stone wall, his eyes unfocused and scarred.

"Phoenix," I say, "we should get you out of here."

"I'm not leaving without those boys," he growls.

I grab a hold of his hand. "Neither am I. But we're running out of time…"

A foul voice emerges from the shadows at the mouth of the staircase. "As it turns out, you've already run out of time."

We both pivot in place to find Ozol stepping out into the cell space. Yuri is standing in front of him and a guard approaches on his left—with Theo bundled in his arms.

"Theo…!"

I take a step forward but Ozol stops me in my tracks by raising a gun to Yuri's head.

"Now, let's all calm down and have a little chat," he says with his signature snaky smile. "Or else you'll have to watch while I shoot the brains out of both your little runts."

44

PHOENIX

I didn't know I could hurt this much and keep moving.

But I can. I have to. For my boys.

Elyssa looks beside herself with worry. Ozol keeps his pistol pressed to the back of Yuri's shaved head. The guard holding Theo stays close at his side.

"Now," Ozol says, "let's talk like civilized people, shall we?"

To my surprise, Elyssa pipes up before I can even formulate a response. "Fuck you," she spits.

I almost laugh. Hearing her curse is still strange and new. But the venom, the fire in her voice? That's here to stay, I think.

Viktor simply grins. "Elyssa, my dear, I must say—this life seems to suit you. More than I would have ever thought. It's a shame your road ends here."

"You're delusional," she snarls viciously. "Your men are dying by the dozens upstairs right now. It's your road that's ending."

He waggles his eyebrows. "That may be true. But I have the only gun that matters. Right here."

As much as I hate to admit it, he's right. We could have every Bratva man in the country here with guns pointed at Viktor's face. And the pistol he has against Yuri's skull would still protect him forever.

"So let's talk business. We have played this game a long time," he says to me. "And I have to admit, I've even enjoyed it at times. But now I'm getting tired. Impatient."

"Because you can sense your own death on the horizon."

He narrows his eyes at me. "Hardly."

"You know what's coming," I say. "And there's no way out of it. So look at me, Victor Ozol. Look at me well, because I am your death."

I want to cross the space between us and murder the motherfucker with my bare hands right now. I'm itching to act. To break him again and again until there's nothing left to break.

He just sighs, though. "So many promises you've made. I'm getting tired of those, too. Now, here's what's going to happen: we're all going to walk out of here together like one big, happy family. You're going to tell your men upstairs to let me pass through—because if you don't, both of your boys will end up as roadkill. Do you understand me? Both of you?"

I'm at a loss for words. I've told this motherfucker that I will kill him. I meant it. But how? How can I do that without losing my sons —again?

Elyssa looks like the same thoughts are running through her head. I reach out and grab her hand in mine. She clings to me, strong but desperate. Hoping for something to happen that will change the calculus here. For one last chance at a future.

And it comes.

But not how I ever expected.

From the staircase we came down, I notice a blur of motion.

And then, of all people, Josiah leaps forward with a rabid yell. For one wild moment, I think he's come to attack us. But it's not Elyssa or me that he's after.

It's Ozol.

Before Viktor can react, Josiah is on him, wailing and screaming and grabbing for Ozol's gun.

"No!" I bellow. If Ozol fires…

I try to lunge towards them. To grab my son away, to knock the gun out of Viktor's hands—anything I can do to protect my boys. But my body is too broken from the days of torture. I make it only one step before my leg collapses beneath me and I fall towards the grimy stone floor.

I can only watch helplessly as Viktor and Josiah struggle back and forth, back and forth…

And then a gunshot goes off.

Elyssa screams. I roar. Josiah and Viktor both emit banshee cries of their own…

And then Josiah slumps to his knees with blood gushing from his stomach.

Elyssa moves before I can. She leaps forward, withdrawing a knife from her belt, and plunges it into Ozol's neck. It catches him by surprise. The gun falls clattering from his hand. It skitters across the floor right into my reach.

I grab it, aim, and fire—and the guard holding Theo grunts as he falls to the ground.

Silence resumes, punctuated only by the drip of blood hitting concrete. I force myself to my feet. Every inch of me is in bleeding, broken agony. But I don't care. This is what matters.

Elyssa has scurried over to Theo and scooped him up in her arms, crying and clutching him close. Yuri is standing still, shell-shocked and immobile.

I want to go to him.

But I need to make sure the devil is dead first.

So I limp over to Ozol. He's still twitching, one hand clapped over the knife in his neck. But those pale eyes are fading to nothingness.

"Rest in hell, motherfucker," I whisper.

Then I turn my back on him forever.

Next to him, Josiah is still sputtering. There's no hope for him to survive the wound. But he redeemed himself at the end—as much as it's possible for a man like him to ever be redeemed.

I may never know what changed his heart. I suppose it doesn't matter. We're all a little good and a little evil. It's what we choose in the ultimate moments that defines who we are. Josiah chose right.

As I watch, he takes one more shuddering breath and then stills. I close his eyelids.

Then, with that business done, I go to Yuri and kneel in front of him with a pained wince. "Yuri, my son…" I murmur.

He looks at me like this is all some dream. Five years of nightmares and this is how it ends? I'd have a hard time believing it, too.

So I tell him the simplest truth possible: "I'm here. We're here. I never stopped searching."

A long silence stretches out. The most painful silence of my life. Is he too broken to be saved? Am I? Is there hope?

And then he says the one word I've been waiting five long years to hear. "Papa?"

I wrap him in my arms and hold my son close. My heart hurts, but by God, it is so full.

Elyssa meets my gaze over Yuri's head. Theo reaches out to touch her chin as she gives me a shaky smile.

I nod. We have a long road to walk towards healing, all of us. But that's okay—we'll do it together.

EPILOGUE: PHOENIX
SIX MONTHS LATER—OUTSIDE OF WILD NIGHT BLOSSOM

I find Matvei skulking in the shadows, smoking a cigarette.

"When did you take up smoking again?" I ask.

"Since you started stressing me out."

I smile. "Touché."

Matvei glances at me out of the corner of his eyes. He's been keeping his distance lately. At first, I hadn't even noticed. I'd been busy dealing with domestic life. I'd gone from a single man with no children, to a married one with two in the span of days. It's been a lot to juggle.

Then, when I had started noticing that he was keeping his distance, I'd just assumed he was trying to give me and my new family some time and privacy. Now, I'm beginning to think it's more than that.

"Is there something you need to tell me?" I ask.

Matvei looks out into the throng of people gathered outside the site. The street has been cleared for the demolition. The only people on site are the ones who wanted to be present to see this fucking black hole of a building go down.

"Can't believe your father came," Matvei says, purposefully ignoring my question and confirming my suspicions.

"I think it's his way of saying I did good," I reply. "Although I'm guessing my mother was the one that pushed him into it."

Matvei smiles. "She dotes on those boys, doesn't she?"

I roll my eyes. "She spoils them rotten, you mean."

Matvei shrugs. "They both deserve it. Especially Yuri."

He does deserve it. He's had a hard time adjusting. Not because he doesn't enjoy being with us, but because a part of him is terrified that the whole arrangement is just temporary.

The first week after the fight at Wild Night Blossom, Elyssa slept with the boys in the room next to mine. He trusted her right off the bat. It's taking him more time to accept me again.

I tried not to take that personally. I'm still trying.

Then again, I can't really blame him.

Elyssa was born to be a mother. She's loving and caring by nature, and her favorite thing in the world is to spend the day in the garden with both boys. That's what he needs—healing. Hope. Happiness.

"He's getting better," I tell Matvei. "We started the counseling sessions last month. They seem to be helping."

"Are they?"

I shrug. "That's what Elyssa tells me."

"She's right," Matvei says. "I dropped in yesterday and I saw Yuri playing in the garden with Cillian and Kian. It was like the old days."

"Nothing will ever be like the old days," I say at once. "But this… this is good."

"I can see that," Matvei replies. "And I'm glad for you, Phoenix. After everything you've been through. You deserve this."

"It's not over, you know," I say. "Ozol might be dead. His goons might be dead. This building will be nothing but dust and ash within the hour. But Astra Tyrannis is still alive and well."

Matvei looks at me with raised eyebrows. "You're not going to stop going after them?"

"Elyssa and I discussed it at length," I admit. "But in the end, we decided we can't just let them get away with the atrocities they commit every day. It wouldn't be right, and we're the only ones with the power to stop them. We saved thirty-three women from that hellhole. Shit, half of them weren't even women—they were little girls, no older than thirteen. We can't just let that kind of shit continue."

Matvei nods. "I knew you'd say that."

"And you don't approve?"

"On the contrary, I completely approve. I just want you to keep your family safe."

"Oh, trust me, I've made all the arrangements. No one is ever going to get near any of them ever again."

"Glad to hear it."

"Now, since we've covered me, let's talk about what's been bothering you lately."

Matvei sighs. "We don't have to. This is a big day for you."

"Matvei..."

He smirks. "I'm dropping by tomorrow for lunch with the whole gang. We can talk after."

I tense. "I'd rather hear it now."

He sighs. "Very well. I wanted to tell you that… I'm leaving."

I'd been expecting this. But it's still a gut punch.

"You're going back home, aren't you?"

Matvei nods. "You've been a great friend, and these last few years, I've needed a break from my life, my obligations. But I've been away long enough. These last few months have made me realize that it's time to grow up. Time to face my demons. Take back what's mine."

"You're really going to do it?" I ask. "Take back your father's Bratva?"

"That's just it," Matvei says. "It's my Bratva now."

I smile. "Well, it's about fucking time."

"So… you're not going to hold it against me?"

"Fuck no," I say, clapping him hard on the back. "In fact, anything I can do to help, just say the word."

Matvei nods gratefully. "I appreciate that, but I'm going to do this on my own. I chose to walk away. So now I have to go back and prove that I'm worthy of stepping back into things."

"Which you will do. I have no doubt."

Matvei smiles. "Thanks, brother."

"When will you leave?"

"The day after tomorrow."

"That fucking soon?"

"Now that I've told you, there's no point in waiting."

"Thanks for waiting for the demolition."

"Are you kidding me?" Matvei snorts. "I wouldn't miss this for the fucking world. To see this shithole club crash to the ground… it's poetic justice."

Epilogue: Phoenix

I nod, pushing myself back to my feet. "I'll drink to that."

Matvei stands with me and we clasp hands.

"You'll keep me posted?" I ask. "Before you leave?"

"Of course."

I nod and head off in search of my wife.

It's been hard to get hold of her these days. Between the boys and planning the new women's shelter that's going to be erected on this site once the rubble has been cleared away, she's been busy. Too busy, in my opinion.

Never thought I'd be jealous of a project. But I can see what the work has done for her.

She hasn't said it quite so explicitly, but I know she sees Charity in all the women she's helped so far. And all the faceless women she's yet to help.

She wants to save the world, one life at a time.

"Looking for someone?"

I turn to my Uncle Kian as he walks over to me. The fact that they're all here means a lot to me. Not that I've said as much, but I know they all know.

"My wife," I reply—mostly because I love saying those words.

"Last I saw her, she was sitting over by the demolition point with your mother."

I turn around and catch a glimpse of them. They're both nursing drinks and laughing about something.

"I think my mom prefers Elyssa to me now," I say.

Kian laughs. "So she has good taste."

"Screw you, too," I chuckle. I clap him on the shoulder. "I'm glad you're here. It's good for family to be together."

He nods in agreement. "I heard Elyssa's going to be running the shelter once it's up and running."

I nod. "It'll take a while to rebuild, especially because of the scale of the structure. She's not one to do things halfway."

"No wonder you two get along."

"I learned from the best," I say, giving him a wink. "Now, if you'll excuse me, I'm going to go kiss my wife."

I head over towards the demolition point. Elyssa turns to me at the last moment. Her eyes brighten instantly. She pushes herself off the stoop she's sitting on and loops her arm around my waist.

I rest my arm over her shoulders and we turn to face my mother.

"I'm surprised to see you here," I tease. "I would have thought you'd want to stay at home with the boys."

"Just wanted to show my support," my mother replies. I can see age start to creep in around her eyes. There's a little grey at her temples, too. A sign that time spares none of us. "But I'm leaving soon."

"Before the demolition?" I ask.

"I've seen enough buildings go down in my time," she says with a barely suppressed shudder. "It's enough to know that this one won't survive the night. Besides, I'd rather go home now and spend some time with my grandkids. I only have a week left with them."

"You can always stay longer," Elyssa says. "In fact, I wish you would."

"Don't tempt a grandmother to stay long past her welcome," she chuckles. She gives us a parting smile and a kiss on the cheek, and then heads off in search of my father.

"What were you two discussing?" I ask Elyssa when we're alone again.

She smiles. "When we're going to give her another grandchild."

I raise my eyebrows. "Seriously?"

Elyssa shrugs. "Would that be so bad?"

"Not at all," I say. "But I've had enough of sharing you for the time being. I want you all to myself once this demolition is done. Heaven knows you'll be busy enough once the shelter's up and running."

"Don't worry," she says, reaching up on her tiptoes to kiss my cheek. "I'll always make room for you and the boys."

"Come on," I tell her, pulling back into the building.

"What are you doing?"

"I'm trying to recreate an old memory," I tell her as I steer her through the deserted pathways of the club.

It looks different now. Without the garish furniture and the lights, without any people, it's just a building. A haunted building. A scarred building. But a building nonetheless.

When I pull her into the bathroom where Theo was conceived, she starts to realize what I'm getting at.

"Phoenix, no! We can't…"

I grab her and pull her against my erection. "Why not?" I growl, pressing my lips to her neck.

"Because… because… God, it's really hard to concentrate when you're doing that."

"Stop thinking then."

"They're waiting for us!"

"Let them wait. We can take all the time we need."

I grab her hips and lift her onto the countertop. She's wearing a thin summer dress and my hands explore her hungrily as I try to contain my own desire.

Our lips come together and we ravage each other's mouths. I know that the memory of our first time is thick in Elyssa's head.

Except the woman she was then has all but disappeared.

She'd been shy and awkward then. She'd let me take the lead. She'd barely said a word.

This time, she's an active participant. She tugs off my clothes and reaches for the buckle of my pants unreservedly.

I bend down and press my tongue to her folds to discover she's already dripping wet. She bucks against my tongue and I eat her out until her body is trembling with a growing orgasm. Reaching up, I cup her breasts in my hands, teasing her nipples between my fingers. Once she's moaning desperately, I stand back up and enter her in one quick thrust.

"Yes, oh God... Phoenix..."

I mean to go slow, but once I'm inside her, that intention goes out the window. I start fucking her furiously.

The only thing either one of us can hear is the hard slap of flesh on flesh.

She comes with a scream that echoes throughout the empty hallways of Wild Night Blossom. and I pump into her a few more times before I release.

I kiss my wife's neck and her beautiful, trembling breasts as she runs her hands up and down my back and we both coast back to earth together.

"That came full circle," she says, trying to comb through her wild hair.

I smile. "No better feeling." Now come on—let's go watch this fucking building crumble."

She gives me a wink and a kiss on the cheek. "After you, sir," she whispers seductively.

I let her go first so I can watch how her ass move in the sundress and marvel that she's mine—all fucking mine.

"After you, Madam."

EXTENDED EPILOGUE

Thanks for reading RIPPED LACE—but don't stop now! Click the link below to get your hands on the exclusive Extended Epilogue to see Phoenix and Elyssa's family a year into the future!

DOWNLOAD THE EXTENDED EPILOGUE TO RIPPED LACE

MAILING LIST

Sign up to my mailing list!
New subscribers receive a FREE steamy bad boy romance novel.

Click the link below to join.
https://sendfox.com/nicolefox

ALSO BY NICOLE FOX

Romanoff Bratva

Immaculate Deception

Immaculate Corruption

Kovalyov Bratva

Gilded Cage

Gilded Tears

Jaded Soul

Jaded Devil

Mazzeo Mafia Duet

Liar's Lullaby (Book 1)

Sinner's Lullaby (Book 2)

Bratva Crime Syndicate

Can be read in any order!

Lies He Told Me

Scars He Gave Me

Sins He Taught Me

Belluci Mafia Trilogy

Corrupted Angel (Book 1)

Corrupted Queen (Book 2)

Corrupted Empire (Book 3)

De Maggio Mafia Duet

Devil in a Suit (Book 1)

Devil at the Altar (Book 2)

Kornilov Bratva Duet

Married to the Don (Book 1)

Til Death Do Us Part (Book 2)

Heirs to the Bratva Empire

Can be read in any order!

Kostya

Maksim

Andrei

Princes of Ravenlake Academy (Bully Romance)

Can be read as standalones!

Cruel Prep

Cruel Academy

Cruel Elite

Tsezar Bratva

Nightfall (Book 1)

Daybreak (Book 2)

Russian Crime Brotherhood

Can be read in any order!

Owned by the Mob Boss

Unprotected with the Mob Boss

Knocked Up by the Mob Boss

Sold to the Mob Boss

Stolen by the Mob Boss

Trapped with the Mob Boss

Volkov Bratva

Broken Vows (Book 1)
Broken Hope (Book 2)
Broken Sins *(standalone)*

Other Standalones
Vin: A Mafia Romance

Box Sets
Bratva Mob Bosses (Russian Crime Brotherhood Books 1-6)
Tsezar Bratva (Tsezar Bratva Duet Books 1-2)
Heirs to the Bratva Empire
The Mafia Dons Collection
The Don's Corruption

Printed in Great Britain
by Amazon